the
Sea
of
Japan

the Sea of Japan

A NOVEL

KEITA NAGANO

SparkPress, a BookSparks imprint
A Division of SparkPoint Studio, LLC

Published by SparkPress, a BookSparks imprint,
A division of SparkPoint Studio, LLC
Phoenix, Arizona, USA, 85007
www.gosparkpress.com

Published 2019
Printed in the United States of America

ISBN: 978-1-68463-012-7 (pbk)
ISBN: 978-1-68463-013-4 (e-bk)
Library of Congress Control Number: 2019936684

Formatting by Katherine Lloyd, The DESK

Dedicated to all Americans in the fifty states,
which I have proudly been to.

Prologue

I was okay with living in a town where work was boring, there was no entertainment, and almost nobody spoke English when I thought I could leave whenever I wanted. When I learned that I couldn't leave on a whim, I decided that I wanted to quit my school teacher's job as soon as possible.

I felt a great pain. I was confined in this place, a fishermen's town in Japan.

On one of our daily Skype phone calls, my best friend Judy asked me what I wanted.

"I want to go back to Boston. I want to quit my job."

"You can't quit your job."

"What do you mean?"

"I understand that living in Japan is 100 times more difficult than you imagined, but I don't think you should return to Boston this soon. You haven't accomplished anything in the month you've been in Japan. If you leave now, this whole thing will have been pointless."

"I didn't know what I wanted, Judy. You knew that. I just wanted to escape from my peers at the school, the freaking Boston school district, Paul, and the temptation of the places where I used to gamble."

Keita Nagano

"Right. It was a good escape. A constructive escape. I thought you could turn yourself around in a new place and find a seed for your new career," Judy said in her usual passionate voice. Since our days as roommates at the University of Delaware, she had been the person who always looked out for me.

"Look. Japan did not mean anything to me when I decided to come here, and it still doesn't mean much to me now. I just followed you," I said. "But I thought I could at least live close to you in this foreign country. I would have never expected that we would have been given such different assignments."

It still stung when I thought about the moment that Judy and I opened our assignment packets and learned where we were going. She had gasped with excitement when she read that she was assigned to the Tokyo governor's office, and my heart had dropped as I read where I was going: Hime. A small town on the opposite side of the country from Tokyo, 250 miles away from the capital to the northwest. Between Hime and Tokyo were mountains that divided Japan like a back bone. It would take more than seven hours to drive over those mountains and reach Judy.

"You should have read the orientation materials. We don't have control over our assignment."

"Can't you understand my pain? Just get me out of here, Judy."

"I'm sorry that you don't like the people there that much."

"People are nice here. But I am a Bostonian, Judy. I don't fit into a town with just 50,000 people. Plus, teaching English to twelve-year-olds who have never spoken English before is the most boring thing in the world."

"You have the freedom to quit. But I know you wouldn't like what would happen if you did."

"What do you mean?"

"JET's staff and your school had prepared to have someone from America for more than twelve months. They had to do a lot

— 2 —

of work to create this position, get your housing, and put together your work visa."

I thought about everything JET did for me. The Japanese government program provided native English people like me with jobs aiding teachers in their classrooms and helping students learn English. They also helped people find positions in local governments. People came from around the world to take part in the program.

Judy continued. "Most importantly, they had arranged for you to teach your students an authentic English academic curriculum. And for that, your job is paid very well. If you simply quit, students who thought they had earned a great opportunity to learn real English will lose a whole academic year. I know you are not going to ruin children's dreams."

"Oh, I am sure they can find a substitute American teacher easily. They constantly have 5,000 people in the program, and Americans make up about half of that."

"But do you think that they'll be able to teach the students as well as you?"

I got her point. Yes, she knew me too well. I don't care about anything but students. It makes my blood boil when I think about students suffering because of problems in the adult world.

The reason why I had a fight against the Boston school district and a cold relationship with teachers in my old school was because I prioritized my students 100 percent and paid zero respect to the school district politics. That stirred the pot, I became hated by many, and I naturally fell into my gambling addiction trap again.

"I can guarantee that your Hime Junior High School will not have another American until next year."

"Come on, Judy, 'I have a pen' or 'This is a dog' is not teaching English at all. It's better to watch a Disney movie or YouTube. Or, buy a Taylor Swift CD. I offered a more creative teaching proposal to my peers, but it was ignored. My resignation will not ruin anything." My voice got weaker as I admitted that.

"Taylor Swift cannot answer students' questions. Your existence at Hime Junior High School is much more valued than you think."

"I doubt that's true."

"Realistically, if you leave now, JET will make your school ineligible for the next five years for a new English teacher. And your future successor will probably not be a professional teacher like you."

I didn't say anything. I sipped a cup of green tea in front of my iPhone. Judy drank sake in front of hers. My tea tasted nicer than any green tea I had had in Boston. Green tea alleviated my emotional pain.

She got me.

I couldn't penalize my students because I was unhappy with my oversight on the JET application.

I should have vetoed Hime before I started.

But I knew I could swap my position with some peer in Japan. All I had to do was recruit just one person out of 5,000.

"Lindsey, come on. You've never been a quitter."

"I'm not as smart as you or Paul. I'm not Harvard Business School material like you two," I said. "I don't know how to find a seed for my future career here in Hime."

"What you want me to say? Isn't it a good time to push yourself a little harder and become a bit more sociable? You haven't tried to make friends. You've been complaining that people in Hime don't speak English. But you're in Japan, and you haven't made any effort to learn Japanese. Isn't that a pity?"

Judy was starting to sound like a mentor. I didn't like it, but I was always grateful to her for telling the truth.

"One more thing, Lindsey. I found where Paul lives."

"What?"

"You want me to kick his ass, or do you want me to persuade him to come down there to have a romantic reunion tea party with you?"

"I don't know—"

"I know it sounds awful to you, but as soon as you contact him, this jerk will try to get back with you. Just in case he doesn't find any other attractive woman like you during his four-year stay in Japan."

"I am not attractive at all—"

"Yes, you are, and don't let me argue on that point. Tall, skinny, and blond. Hello? The problem is you are extremely unsociable, and that makes others bored."

Judy had no problem talking about my looks because she was confident with hers. Judy was rather short, and she had beautiful pure black hair and large breasts that men loved.

"Thanks for being blunt." I shook my head, my long ponytail swinging hard.

Paul ditched me after he finished his MBA to take a job with the gigantic Japanese seafood company Hakodate Marine. As a Harvard graduate, he was looking for a global business job opportunity, and he thought that Hakodate Marine was the perfect match for his desire. According to Paul, Japan had fallen from number one to number seven in the world fishery volume ranking due to their mismanagement and overfishing. Paul wanted to turn the fishery industry of Japan around by helping the conglomerate company. He hoped to use the results to facilitate his move to another global company somewhere else in the world. While he was off in Japan, I thought we could maintain a long-distance romance, but he thought it would not be realistic.

It was a coincidence that both Paul and I had ended up in Japan. I hadn't moved to Japan to be closer to him, and Judy hadn't signed up for the JET program because of him. Judy joined the Harvard MBA program with a specialization in marketing to fulfill her desire to bring her parents' Jewish delicatessen business in Manhattan to the next level. Since Americans were eating less and less deli food, she thought she should cultivate the overseas market. Judy knew she needed a job while she worked on her main goal of revitalizing the deli industry. And when she found JET, she thought it was perfect. She also convinced me to go with her.

"Look, Lindsey. Paul's friends know you're here now, and they'll probably tell him soon. When he finds out, he'll think you came to the country because you were chasing him. In that case, how would you like to appear in front of him? Do you want to show him you're wandering like an isolated American *gaijin*? Or, do you want to show that you're breaking through the cultural barrier and intermingling with the Japanese people around you?"

"Judy, it's not that easy," I said, raising my voice.

"Has anything in your life been easy at the start, except for maybe your card counting when we played Blackjack?"

As Judy laughed on my iPhone screen, I thought of our long-ago glory days. Hopping on a bus to Atlantic City on Friday night, spending our days in casinos, eating the best steak, and drinking the most expensive champagne. I had had an unusual photographic memory ever since my biological parents died in an accident. This skill made my memories of our trip to Atlantic City seem even more joyous.

After we hung up the Skype call, I stared at the reflection of my confused face in the dark iPhone screen.

I was determined to find a replacement for me at the school and get out of Hime.

But after that, I thought, *what do you want for yourself, Lindsey?*

Chapter One

I talked to a JET staff member. She said I could discuss whatever I wanted with my 5,000 peers on the JET membership website forum. She said I could directly contact whoever I thought the position might fit.

I jumped on the forum and made a post asking about a job swap. For a week, I didn't receive any responses. Then, I went into the huge directory and started sending solicitation emails to all potential candidates. I estimated the pool was about 2,000. I sent twenty emails a day.

Two weeks passed, and there was still no response.

My feelings of boredom and isolation continued to grow. In addition to my video streaming of Red Sox games, I became an Amazon Prime member and started watching many movies for free, but my feeling of confinement made me focus on the suffering and nullified the joy.

One morning, I received a phone call from Erica, a woman who also taught English at Hime Junior High School. She was also thirty years old, same as me, Judy, and Paul. She was my only Japanese friend in town, but she had three kids at home and no time to hang out with me.

"Good morning, Lindsey. Sorry to bother you."

"No worries. I woke up a while ago." I didn't mention I woke up early because life here was too boring, especially at night. "What's up?"

"Can you come to school about thirty minutes earlier than usual? Mr. Principal wants to discuss something with us."

She explained that an English teacher who was in charge of senior students had become seriously ill.

"I'm on my way."

I walked out of my tiny apartment. Mornings in this small town were quiet, the air fresh. I rode my new bicycle on the main street in the retail corridor. It reminded me of some of the small towns in Massachusetts, but this town had much more homogenized shops. Many of them were lined up side by side in a long stretch along the main street. At the end of the street, there was nothing but fields.

I rode up the hill, climbing a steep, winding road.

Our school sat on top of the hill, looking down at the entire city of Hime. The Sea of Japan was a crisp blue, and it spread out as far as I could see.

When I got to the school, Mr. Principal was waiting outside for me.

"Good morning, Lindsey san!"

He bowed to me, and I bowed back.

"How are you, Mr. Principal? You are here too early."

"Oh, not at all. How long has it been since you came here?" he said in his slow but accurate English.

"Just seven weeks."

"Time flies, doesn't it?"

"Yes, it does." As I smiled politely, I thought about how the past seven weeks had felt like the slowest time in my life.

On my first day in Hime, he and Erica came to the Hime Station to greet me. It was the first week of April and the first day of the Japanese academic year. Outside the classroom windows, I saw beautiful cherry blossoms, petals falling off the tree as the wind blew. I stared at one petal as it swayed to the right and to the left before rising again and then falling onto the huge sports ground in front of the building.

I thought about that memory as Mr. Principal and I walked through the school, heading toward his office. There was one private office for the principal, and the rest of the teachers each had their desks in a large staff room. He escorted me to his room, and we sat at a small conference table.

"What is your impression about our school so far, Lindsey san?"

"Well, the school building is solid and well maintained. They keep everything so clean and neat. But as soon as I walk inside the building, I feel something is wrong, to be honest with you. Don't get me wrong. The students are happy and hardworking, and all the teachers are kind to me. But it feels like the school is shrinking. This school has more than 100 years of history, yet, I see the building has many unoccupied rooms. Perhaps, only 50 percent of it is being used. No offense, but I feel a bit scared."

"You made a good point. I am scared, too. In the last fifteen years, the city of Hime has shrunk from 2,300 junior high school students to 1,300. It is a sharp decline. The school district is contemplating the merger of some schools. Recently, Hime decided to just have only one high school in the town. Our junior high school may also be forced to merge with the other one," the principal said, half in anger and half in disappointment.

Erica and another English teacher came in. Mr. Principal started the discussion immediately.

"Thanks for coming, everyone. Unfortunately, the English teacher who is ill isn't going to be able to continue on, and we will need to replace her."

The school had three grades from seventh to ninth, and each grade had two classes. One class had about thirty-five students. In total, there were 200 students at the school.

He continued, "The academic year started in April, so it will be difficult for us to make a replacement in May. Normally, any school system in Japan would rely on substitute teachers, but I confirmed with the city official yesterday that there is no substitute teacher in Hime city."

I couldn't believe my ears. Japan spends more budget on public schools per capita than the US. I just didn't understand why we didn't have substitutes.

Erica frowned. She said doubtfully, "How about Toyama city? In the past, we depended on them for substitutes."

"I called them, but they are shorthanded, too. They said they could arrange a biology substitute teacher who is also licensed for English."

"License means little. Experience matters, Mr. Principal. Why we are facing this issue?"

"Toyama city is expanding. That's why they are shorthanded. But we are shrinking. That's why we have a tight budget and could not afford a substitute teacher."

In order to get out of my own suffering, I thought I could give my position to a Japanese teacher who spoke good English as a last resort. But this conversation made me realize that I had no hope for that strategy.

"Why are we shrinking, Mr. Principal?" I said. I just couldn't help saying something.

"The main industry of this city is fishery and fishery-related business. The port is located in the center of the city, facing Toyama Bay. The bay is one of the world's best fish tanks because 500 kinds of sea creatures are living in it. Half of the students' parents in this school are engaged in fishery-related business. The problem is that the fishery volume in Hime has been declining for the last twenty years. That is why people have been moving out."

Hearing about that made me think of my grandfather. My grandpa was the only fisherman I knew, and I used to visit him to escape my parents in my defiant youth.

Erica added, "And fishing is a very complicated business with many complicated regulations and economic factors. It is not easy to revitalize this business. When the fishery shrinks, the city shrinks and the schools shrink."

I remembered that the principal was the son of a fisherman, and Erica's sister had also married a fisherman.

The principal said, "Because of the low volume, fishermen are now starting to catch fish before they bore eggs. The good news is that the fishery association decided to implement the individual quota system, like America or Norway, to prevent overfishing. We will preserve the sea stock with this quota system."

Erica nodded. "And the bad news is that this will lower the fishery volume for the next three years until the stock recovers, and this creates even bigger clouds in our sky."

I realized how small a chance I had of swapping my job. Who would want to relocate to an area with this big risk? If we were to merge with the other school, my position would be eliminated.

Then, Erica and the other teacher began debating how two teachers could take turns to fill in the senior class curriculum. It seemed impossible no matter what they did. So I raised my hand.

"I'll do it."

All of them looked at me with surprised eyes.

"I wanted to have some challenges. I will learn Japanese more rapidly, and I will do my best to make my classes as effective as possible. Unlike my JET peers throughout Japan, I am a licensed Massachusetts teacher."

I was more surprised than anybody here to hear myself say

that, since this position would make it even harder to leave Hime. Still, I thought that this would give me the challenge I needed. It would alleviate my pain.

The principal and the other two English teachers seemed relieved. Even though the English teachers hadn't liked my first creative proposal, they didn't oppose my idea this time. The principal immediately gave me the discretion to make classes more creative and fun as long as I stuck to the curriculum.

After the meeting, I called Judy, and she congratulated my move. I preemptively said, "I still need to find out the way to get out of this town."

I explained that I had already increased my daily quota of direct email solicitations.

Instead of scolding my desire to leave Hime, Judy seemed to think that praising my proactive attitude would make me want to spread more roots in this city.

"When it comes to teaching, you are such a professional and you have my continuous respect."

"I just can't let children be disadvantaged because of the adults' world, my mundane life, or the senior teacher's illness."

When I examined the textbooks for the senior classes, I found that I would be teaching more serious English, longer sentences, and more complicated grammar.

It was a positive surprise that starting from 'This is a pen', in two years, they have come to subjunctive past perfect. By the summer, they would even train in cumulative syntax.

As I began the senior classes, it seemed to work much better than I expected. The senior students reacted to me very seriously and listened to me well. I started feeling more excited when I walked into the classroom in the morning.

I got some relief for my pain, but I still had to get out of the sinking city of Hime. I would keep doing my best for the students, but I had to find seeds for my future. I didn't want to go back to the same teaching job in America when I finished the JET program in a year. I needed to come across *something*, and I knew there was no *something* in this city.

◄ ⅢⅢⅢⅢⅢ ►

An incident happened two days later.

In late afternoon, I was watching my school's baseball practice like usual. It was a good way to kill time after school. As a boy hit a foul ball, I noticed several of our senior students go into the back corner of the building. They were pushing a young boy, around ten years old, and nudging him with their elbows. I had been in a teaching job long enough to know when something wasn't right.

I went over there, trying not to make a sound. Sure enough, I found the students were bullying a fourth grade student. They said something, and when the boy talked back to them, they kicked his legs or punched his stomach.

"Hey, stop it! What are you doing?" I said in Japanese.

Everyone turned to me, surprised. In every school, there is always a spot that teachers' eyes would never reach. That's where kids harass other kids, smoke, or drink. Sometimes, they did things that were even worse. I had been there, done that. In Boston, I couldn't ignore my inner voice, and I directed myself to their hidden spot. I found some students doing wrong, and reprimanded them fairly.

In Boston, I was supposed to report everything to the school compliance office, but I didn't always do that. I confronted the kids, and if they had just committed a light offense, I gave them a warning and didn't report it. Just like a traffic cop sometimes gives a verbal warning without issuing a citation. On the other hand, if I saw some ugly bullying or some other deeply troubling activity, I reported them, and they got kicked out.

Parents in Boston accused me of playing judge and jury when that should have been the school's job, but I didn't care. I had to be reasonable and fair. There were some small offenses that weren't worth reporting, but my school in Boston had zero tolerance, and even a student who committed a small offense would have been kicked out. That's wrong.

The students in front of me had dark eyes, and I instantly felt that they had repeatedly bullied this little boy, who I assumed went to the elementary school next door.

I said, "What are your names? You are seniors, aren't you? Which is your home class?"

They understood me and talked back to me in a wild tone. I had to make a judgement if I should go back to the teachers' room and seek help from peers or if I should confront them myself.

I chose the latter and looked at them carefully. I pulled up my iPhone, started recording what they were saying, and shot pictures of them. Teaching in both good and bad areas of Boston, I had learned that the way students talk back to teachers reflects the level of the control of the school. These kids were not too bad. They just wanted to rebel.

They raised their voices, and I realized that they were testing me. This was the only chance for a teacher to show the proper authority. If the teacher didn't do it right then, it would take them a year to regain their control over the students.

"You kicked and punched that boy. Explain why." I raised my voice, speaking in English this time. I had inherited a healthy set of vocal cords from my grandpa. He still had the loudest voice of all my relatives, and I was the second loudest even though I was the thinnest. I had never lost a shouting match.

They said something louder while shaking their heads, meaning they didn't understand English.

I continued speaking to them in a loud, authoritative voice.

They didn't seem to know what to do. I had already decided to simply let them go. But since I was doing that, I had to show my anger at their actions. Four fifteen-year-olds bullying a ten-year-old boy is not acceptable.

"Get away from here. If you do that again, I will go to the principal's office and kick your asses out," I said, half in Japanese and half in English.

"I have no freaking idea who your parents are or who your uncles or grandfathers are and how many political ties they have got with the school district. But I don't give a damn. I have kicked out the grandson of a Massachusetts senator and the grand-daughter of the attorney general," I said, reviving the distasteful memories. Thinking of those times helped me yell at the boys. "I've been trained well. If you are forced out, you are out. Then you have to ride on a bus or ride a bike to a different school! Got it? This is not acceptable in my school."

I pointed out the exit with my finger. They saw my rage and they dropped all of their rebellious will.

"Do you understand me? By the way, you haven't told me your names, but that doesn't mean that I don't know you. You are Taro Suzuki, Koji Hayashi, Osamu Ishida, and Masa Koda."

Their eyes widened. I knew they thought I wouldn't remember their faces since I had just started the senior English classes two days ago. With my photographic memory, one day was enough for me to match names to faces.

They ran away. I approached the fourth grader and asked if he was all right with my horrible Japanese. The boy nodded. I looked over his face quickly to make sure that nothing swollen or bleeding. Once I saw that he was okay, the boy left.

I exhaled deeply, happy that my Japanese made sense to those boys. As I calmed down, I realized that when I was talking to the boys, I had called the school "my school."

◄ ‖‖‖‖‖‖ ►

As my solo-English class was working fine, I gained a good momentum. My students had a great attitude, and for the first time, I felt deeply respected by them.

One day, when I came back to my apartment, I found a letter from my mom in the mailbox. After my biological parents had died, my dad's brother and his wife had adopted me, and they always treated me like their own daughter. After a few years of living with them, I had started calling them Mom and Dad, which made my aunt cry the first time she heard it.

Mom told me that, unfortunately, the contention between Grandpa and Dad continued. Dad worried about Grandpa getting injured on the ocean, and Grandpa told Dad to leave him alone.

I Skyped Mom.

"Hey, baby. Wow, I can see my daughter in Japan live, full on the screen, anytime I want!"

"We did this before, Mom. So, is Dad still mad at Grandpa?"

"He sure is. See, the local fishery association firmly encourages fishermen to wear lifejackets. But nobody wears them. People have to work on the deck, and they have to be speedy. The lifejacket slows them down. Your dad hates such noncompliance."

My biological father had hated it too.

"I remember Grandpa said, 'It's like working in a McDonald's kitchen with ski gear,' I told Mom. "'It just doesn't work. Nobody gives a shit if you fall. I don't give a shit if I fall. That's the way this men's club works.' He said it's his life."

"I know, honey. But at the same time, if something happens, everyone would blame your dad, letting Grandpa continue fishing. Your aunts would have stopped speaking to him if they learned that Grandpa fell overboard last month."

"It seems like Grandpa is having the best relationship with you, Mom."

"Oh, god. I am doing my best." She rolled her eyes and laughed hard. "How's your teaching going?"

"It's interesting. They're fourteen or fifteen years old, but the language I use is more limited than the fourth graders in Boston. Teaching English to foreign students is a totally different experience."

"Are they serious?"

"Oh, yeah. They are all serious in English, especially when we have an exam coming up. Many students come and visit me at lunchtime or after hours for questions. They know the grammar well. Some students have started speaking very well, and they're excited to try out their English on me."

"The real games are a lot more fun than the spring training."

"Good metaphor, Mom."

I didn't tell my mom about all the other, boring parts of my life.

In the last week, in addition to my daily email solicitations, I reached out to several English teachers in the JET program on the phone. I realized that I had to sell this village to those candidates much more passionately.

"It's May, still chilly. As chilly as Boston, but the sky is clear, and the slight ocean breeze feels nice," I told Mom, making sure to use a positive tone. "The combination of blue sky, blue ocean, and the snow covering the mountains is unbelievably gorgeous."

"Shoot as many pictures as you can for me, sweetheart. Are you eating okay?"

"I started going out to local restaurants, and I've been seeking out local food, mainly seafood. I've been going to one restaurant, Bamboo Sushi, very often. I remember all the sushi I've ever eaten, but this sushi tasted far better than any memories I had. The owner said the freshness of the fish greatly attributes to the taste of sushi. He said he was surprised that I could tell him the name of the fish off the top of my head by just looking at the meat."

We talked about our shared interest, food, for another twenty minutes. For a while, I let go of my complex feeling toward the town and let myself enjoy talking about all the things I liked about Hime. But then, I couldn't help but mention some of that bothered me in Hime.

"The language barrier is big, and it blocks me from getting to know the people in this town, not to mention the cultural difference."

"Don't rush, Lindsey. You sound as if you want to leave Hime." Her gut feelings were always right. "But all fishery villages are like that. I've been to Gloucester, Portsmouth, and Rockport, and they are the same. Even fishermen communities in big cities like Long Beach or New Orleans are the same. It takes time to be accepted in a fishermen community. But once you are accepted, the bond with the locals gets very strong. It's like getting accepted into a closed club."

"Okay, okay, Mom. Don't preach to me over the Pacific Ocean."

Even though Mom made some good points, I was still determined to move out of the city. I just need to find a way to do it without sacrificing the kids' education.

I decided to take some pictures of the sunrise over the ocean for Mom. Mom used to be a commercial vessel salesperson, and my dad was still a vessel engineer. They met at the Commercial Marine Expo. She was a natural born, die-hard sociable saleswoman, and my father was the opposite: a stubborn engineer who liked computers more than human beings.

She loved to see the sunrise or sunset over the ocean, and she took pictures of it wherever she went to shores or beaches. She framed them and used them to decorate her house.

the Sea of Japan

I rode my bike to the Toyama Bay. I had found a great spot on the seashore the other day. There were some big rocks on the beach, near the shoreline, and I climbed up one and sat on top. I could see the beautiful view of tall mountains, called the Tateyama Mountains, where the 1998 winter Olympics were held. It was now a ski resort that many Japanese people went to.

The gorgeous part of this was that Hime sat on the west side of Toyama Bay, which was half-moon shaped. So, looking east, I could see those mountains very clearly beyond the Sea of Japan. It looked like the mountains were floating on the sea. The mountains were also still covered with white-silver snow, reflecting on the ocean.

It was still half-dark and chilly. I brought whiskey to keep me warm while I waited for the sunrise. It worked perfectly. I gently played some smooth jazz from my iPhone and sipped whiskey. Finally, the tip of the sun appeared on the horizon, illuminating the dark sky. The orange light even illuminated the white snow on top of the Tateyama Mountains beyond the dark ocean. It was the most beautiful sunrise I had ever seen.

This was going to be the best scenery picture for Mom. I stood up and got the camera ready. But the rock was slippery, and as I stood, I lost my footing. I fell off the rock, hitting my head hard. I was thrown into the sea.

The last thing I saw before I lost consciousness was the water rising over my head.

◀ ▌▌▌▌▌▌ ▶

I drifted between consciousness and unconsciousness, lost in what I could only describe as footage from my life. I wasn't sure if I could call it a dream since it was so real, and I knew I couldn't end this footage by simply opening up my eyelids.

I was fishing with my grandpa in the ocean near New Bedford,

Massachusetts. His boat smashed into something, and Grandpa forced me to wear a lifejacket. There was only one lifejacket stuffed underneath the captain's chair, and it was dusty and covered in old coffee stains. I refused to wear it, and I shouted that I was young and a good swimmer. I tried to make Grandpa take it, but he yelled until I finally obeyed him. He was as mad as I was, but his voice was louder.

The water poured onto the deck and into the fish tank, engine room, and cabin. As water filled the boat, it started to sink farther and farther into the water. Finally, the boat was totally underneath the water. Before that, Grandpa simply smiled and said, "Do whatever you want to do in your long life, Lindsey. Just don't let anybody define your life."

I opened my eyes and screamed for Grandpa.

When I calmed down, I realized that I was staring up at a white ceiling rather than the brown ceiling in my apartment. Then, I realized that I was in a hospital bed, and when I tried to move, excruciating pain shot through my head, shoulders, and elbows. The pain seemed to go through my entire body.

I screamed for help.

There was a nurse call button hanging on the bed rim. I pushed hard, and a nurse came. She explained everything she knew. I fell from the rock and became unconscious, but a woman saw me fall. She called the Hime fishery association and asked for an ambulance. The fishery association radioed all the fishermen who were out at sea, and the nearest fisherman rushed over and rescued me. At the shore, they put me in an ambulance and took me to the hospital.

The nurse gently scolded me for the substantial level of alcohol in my blood. "You shouldn't get near the water if you have alcohol in your system. Moreover, it was still dark, usually nobody would have been around. You were very lucky."

"I'm sorry."

After the nurse was gone, I heard a knock at the door.

"Come in," I said in hesitant Japanese.

When the door opened, I saw the fourth grader who I had rescued from his junior high school bullies.

"*Konnichi wa*," he said.

I said the same thing.

Then, he said something in English, but I couldn't get it. So I said something in Japanese, but he seemed not to get it. After the bullying incident, I had done some research on the boy. I had thought that the boys bullied him because they thought he was from the neighboring Itokawa prefecture. But it turned out, he was actually from a different neighboring prefecture, Niigata. I heard that the animosity between Itokawa and Toyama ran deep and wide. Even junior high schoolers had biased thoughts against each other. This animosity went back to the samurai era, when Itokawa suppressed Toyama.

We stared at each other for a long moment, and then we laughed. His eyes were round like a teddy bears'.

He gave me something wrapped by a big cloth.

"What is it?" I said, but then I noticed a note attached to the cloth:

My name is Ichiro Yamada. This is my brother, Satoshi. Thank you for saving him from the bully the other day. I wanted to thank you in person, but I apologize that I have failed to do so out of my busy work schedule. I hope this will make you feel better.

It was a big Tupperware. When I unsealed the top, a spicy, rich scent rose up to my nose. I immediately knew what it was.

"Chili! Thank you!"

I shook hands with Satoshi.

Satoshi grinned, looking satisfied.

It was a wonderful soup with lots of grinded meat and red

chili beans. It was perhaps the first real American food I had eaten since I got to Hime.

I felt myself getting stronger as I ate the hearty soup.

After the boy left, I wondered how he knew where to find me. I asked the nurse when she came to my room, and she told me that Satoshi's brother was the fisherman who saved me and gave me an emergency blood transfusion.

"Blood transfusion?"

"Your scar is rather light and shallow. But you were bleeding for a long time and almost to death."

◄ ▌▍▎▏ ►

For two days, I was kept in the hospital, where I was poked and prodded and tested. Finally, the doctors said that I was well enough to get released. After a couple more days of rest at home, I was ready to go back to work. I hoped work would be relaxing, but that wasn't the case.

A few days after I got back to school, the gymnastics teacher came to my desk. His nickname was Kong since he was a former college Sumo wrestling champion. There were four students behind him: Satoshi's bullies.

"Lindsey san," Kong said in a very friendly tone, reminding me of a used car salesman in Boston.

"Good morning. Just Lindsey is fine."

"Okay, Lindsey. Do you know these kids?" He grabbed the neck of the student closest to him. Before I answered, I stood up and took a good look at those four faces. I was trying to see if they had marks from physical reprimands. I saw several red patches on their cheeks. It was obvious—these students had been hit by Kong, probably with open palms. My blood boiled—I had no tolerance for physical violence.

"Yes, I do. I also remember that they didn't have these marks on their cheeks when I last saw them," I said. The teachers around me immediately stopped chatting.

"Wow, you don't have to be so argumentative, Lindsey." He laughed, but it was clearly fake. "Let me explain the situation: I spotted some other students bullying some elementary boys. I beat the crap out of them. But they said it wasn't fair because when their buddies did the same thing, they didn't receive any reprimands. I hate excuses. I hate rotten girly weeping excuses. These are the bullies' buddies. I asked these kids what happened, and they confessed. So, I just gave them a fair share—"

"You can't call it a fair share," I said. "That's not funny."

Kong frowned, but he pushed the bitterness out of his face, and tried hard to laugh again.

"Lindsey, relax. We are a team."

"Teamwork is only effective when the members share the same philosophy."

"You don't understand the way this school works." His fleshy face hardened, and his tiny eyes became even smaller.

I didn't back off. The dark memories of my Boston teaching era came back and poured oil onto my fire.

"Why did you hit them?" I said, raising my voice so it was even louder than Kong's.

"I did the right thing. Kids forget things easily. But with this, they will remember." He raised his open palm, his fingers straight and shaking with anger. It felt like a threat. I stood up taller, tensing my shoulders, ready for a fight.

"Some kids will forget easily, some kids will remember until they die. You can't just generalize it." I grabbed his hand and brought it down. I felt many eyeballs in the room on my hand. Everybody held their breath.

"I have more experience, twice as much as you." He raised his hand again, open palm still shaking.

"That's a crime, isn't it? You hit them. That's called battery." I hit his open palm with my open palm. The sharp sound echoed loudly.

"What are you doing?" Kong said.

"The boys who you hit must have felt ten times as much pain as that. Ouch, huh? You have committed a crime, that's what I mean." I knew I shouldn't say these things in front of the students, but I couldn't stop.

Memories of Boston were truly coming back to me. I now saw the ceiling stains in the staff room, heard the ridiculously loud bell for the start of the class, and smelled the strong sanitization from the janitor's closet. Every corner of my Boston school loomed in front of me.

"Who do you think you are? Things don't work the same here as they do in America. You have to punish kids, otherwise they won't learn. It was not battery. It was an open palm, and it was a weak, healthy tap. If you want to be truly responsible for these kids' futures, you should give them a punishment."

The four students stared at the tips of their shoes. To retain professional respect and authority, teachers shouldn't argue in front of students. But in Boston, my peers didn't wait either. If they got mad, they argued, no matter who was watching.

"I have read the entire teachers' manual, and I didn't see any section saying that."

"Teachers' manual? Fuck the teachers' manual. Nobody cares. This is called common sense."

Some male teachers who had been waiting for the right moment to intervene tried to step in between us, but they were pushed back by Kong's swinging arms.

"Interesting. So in your sumo wrestling world, do you go by the rules or common sense?" I said.

"Stop saying stupid things. It's irrelevant." He stepped closer, his big face looming over me.

"Stop saying nonsense." I stepped in closer. There was only a fist-sized distance between his face and mine. We were like boxers staring at each other in the ring before the fight. Some teachers were speaking, trying to stop us. But we completely ignored them.

"I don't believe that teachers in your old school followed the spectacular teachers' manual. All I've heard is that you guys have more problems than us. Here, some students do smoke or drink, but they don't do drugs or bring guns to the school. We don't even have a school police or security."

"So since you don't have school police, you think you should be the police officer?"

"I'm not saying that at all. You are just being unreasonable and outrageous. See, if you have a loose grip on students out of your cheap humanity, you may be able to feel good about yourself. But the reality is you are simply ignoring the bad ideas growing in the kids' minds."

"Look. I don't shut my mouth when I see violence. A teacher physically reprimanding their students is just sick."

"Whether it is wrong or not depends on—"

"Depends on what? The principal's judgment? Then you and I should go to his room and ask him."

He then yelled some derogatory words I didn't understand. I yelled back at him. His eyes failed to hide his surprise—they revealed that nobody had ever shouted back at him.

Suddenly, the teachers surrounding us stepped aside and made a path. The principal walked through, his face red. He stretched his arms and stepped between Kong and me.

"What are you doing here? Classes have already started.

What? All of you." As the teachers quickly left, the principal stared at Kong, and then me. "I don't want to ever hear about my teachers fighting again. Next time, there will be a punishment. Got it? Now just go to class. Go!"

◀ ▥▥▥▥▶

My argument against Kong seemed to have shocked all the students. Every class I went to, I was treated as a hero. I knew I shouldn't look too proud about what I'd done, since the students would think that yelling at a colleague was okay, so I just ignored their questions and told them to open their textbooks. Then, we went through my creative curriculum.

I personally thought that the Japanese textbook for English was a little too formal and rigid with grammar. I told the students to forget about the rules for a while, and I instructed them to immerse themselves with day-to-day English until they dreamed in English. With the internet, the students had millions of English materials available. They could watch past presidential debates, sports, cooking shows, dramas, or the news.

"Guys, if you pull up any American English video from YouTube, you'll see that the speaker's words are full of grammar issues, errors, and wrong uses of vocabulary. But at least it flows smoothly. You want to click with somebody in your conversation. If you do, you have more joy. And if you have more joy, you'll be able to speak more effectively."

When my students got tired, we took a break from stumbling through English conversations. For fun, I had the students ask me any trivial question about the Red Sox, and I answered every one of them correctly.

After our break, I said, "I want you to connect yourself with anything in America. Whatever you like. That will help you memorize more vocabulary, instead of reading SAT prep books."

the Sea of Japan

It almost never happened in Japanese schools, but I forced them to speak to the person sitting next to them in English and talk about local things they were proud of, such as mountains, fish, rice, flowers, sweets, festivals, or traditional dances. Also, I had them start writing to their favorite American movie stars. One boy wrote to Chris Evans, saying he was a big fan of Captain America, and another girl wrote to Jennifer Lawrence and explained how much she loved the *Hunger Games* franchise.

My effort to find a person who would swap positions with me had brought no success so far. The more conversations I had with them, the more I realized that every person in the JET program had clear goals for their time in Japan and beyond. Everyone saw the clear picture of their career path. I felt more pressure to figure out where I wanted to go next. Otherwise, I would ruin my life.

◀ ▥▥▥ ◀

One early morning, Erica and I were having coffee in her classroom, preparing for the day's lessons.

"I've been getting positive feedback from students about your lessons," she said as she flipped through her planner.

"Thank you, Erica. That means a lot to me."

"I will try to copy what you do," she said, smiling. "Also, you are learning Japanese amazingly quickly. I'm impressed."

"The more I learn Japanese, the more fun I get out of it."

"I know you have read several books. What else do you do?"

"I go to Bamboo Sushi almost every other day, and the owner and his wife have become good teachers. I've also gone out of my way to try and speak to strangers. I use new words every day. People become much friendlier when they know I can communicate in Japanese."

Keita Nagano

From our window, I could see the elementary school building. I thought of Satoshi, the bullied boy. At the hospital, I gave Satoshi a thank you note to take to his brother Ichiro with my phone number and email address. Since then, we had exchanged some emails, and I had asked to meet him in person so I could thank him for fishing me from the sea and giving me his blood.

One day, I finally visited his pier. It was next to the Hime Fishery Association's huge auction market. At the pier, nobody spoke English. Nobody met my eyes. But when I said the name of the boat, people kindly pointed out the direction.

There, I saw a man untangling the fishing rope on his boat.

"Hello," I said loudly to be heard over the breezy air and the rumble of engines.

"How are you, Thatcher san?"

"You still remember my face?"

"You are the only American in this town."

"Yeah, right." I looked up at the clear blue sky and laughed.

"Thank you for your note," Ichiro said. "I have never seen such beautiful cursive in my life."

"Thank you. It's nice when a man compliments a woman on something other than their looks."

He smiled gently, and his face was open and welcoming. He wore blue hard-vinyl fishing gear with water resistant boots. And strangely, he had on a baseball cap with the Kansas City Royals' logo. His thick handwriting had made me think he was a big guy. He was tall, but rather skinny. Yet, as he was hauling the ropes, I saw that his biceps had tight muscles.

"How are you feeling?" Ichiro asked.

"Good. The doctor said the scar will be totally gone in six months."

He smiled. "Do you want to come aboard? I'll move the boat

closer for you." He started pulling the boat's rope so that the boat was much closer to the pier.

"No worries," I said as I jumped over easily.

"Wow."

"I used to do this all the time when I was a little kid. Every summer vacation, I visited a fishing town."

"Oh, yeah? Where?"

"My grandpa's place. A city called New Bedford."

"I know where that is. That's the number one commercial fishery port in America, right?"

"Yes, but the competition is always tough, especially with Alaska. By the way, thank you very much for the chili, it reminded me of the hearty food they serve to fishermen in New Bedford. And . . ." I paused, suddenly feeling shy. "Ichiro san, thank you so much for saving my life."

"You are welcome, Thatcher san. Call me Ichiro. And thank you again for saving my brother."

"You're welcome too. Call me Lindsey. Your English is very good, by the way. Where did you learn it?"

"It's not good at all, but I grew up in a small town called Tokamachi in Niigata prefecture, next to Toyama prefecture. My high school had a teacher just like you, a JET program participant from Kansas City. So I had a big advantage over regular high school students."

When I heard 'a big advantage,' the words stuck in my heart. I was trying to be creative at the school to help my students enjoy learning English, and I felt I was doing a somewhat good job. But I had never felt that I was providing 'a big advantage' to my students.

"I see. I now understand why you are wearing a Royals' baseball cap."

"I guess you are a Red Sox fan with the big 'B' mark on your jacket."

"Sure thing."

We were both quiet for a moment, and I took the opportunity to look around Ichiro's boat. His boat was a bit smaller than my grandpa's. Grandpa's fishing method was called bottom trawling. He trawls a big net almost at the bottom of the bay of New Bedford and catches ground fish, so he equips a big winch to pull the net back.

Ichiro didn't have a winch.

Thinking about Grandpa's boat reminded me of a conversation Erica and I had had about the current contention between Toyama prefecture and Itokawa prefecture's fisheries. This contention was strongest between Hime and its neighboring city, Nanae. Toyama and Itokawa both had their own water jurisdictions in Toyama Bay. Itokawa was lucky enough to have the entrance of the bay in their jurisdiction. Because of that, Itokawa strategically licensed more bottom trawling vessels, and they caught an enormous volume of fish coming into Toyama Bay before they reached Hime's jurisdiction. They were abusing their location advantage, but there was nothing Hime could do about it.

"You operate this boat by yourself?" I asked.

"Yes. I do the hooks and lines method. I used to work for a large ship that traveled around the world. They provided a good wage, but not many people can go on boats for that long, especially if they have a family. And because you can't spend money when you are on the sea, it's a good way to save up. I always wanted to become independent. I saved my money and bought this boat. Some people hire one person to operate the boat too, but I am good with just doing it by myself."

"What do you fish?"

"Well, I catch many kinds of fish, but I target this kind."

He pulled a red fish out of his cooler, about twenty inches long.

"Oh, red snapper? It's a beautiful color."

"It does look like a red snapper, doesn't it? But it's not. It's called a golden eyes snapper."

As he talked, he washed a golden eyes snapper, removed the scale, and cut it into three parts with his knife. Then, he sliced them thinly and made sashimi for us. It was a rather wild cut and wasted a lot of the meat. But it was the freshest sashimi I'd ever eaten. Then, he boiled water on a hot plate with miso and the rest of the body of the snapper. The miso soup with the condensed flavor of the snapper made the best, freshest bouillabaisse I had ever had.

"Wow, this is incredibly delicious. Thank you."

As we ate, we talked more about fisheries.

Ichiro said, "In general, Japanese fisheries are suffering. The fishing volume is declining big time. What is worse is we're catching smaller fish than we used to."

"I heard you've had limitations put on how much you're allowed to catch."

"You know a lot about the fishing industry."

"About half of the teachers at my school are related in some way to the fishery here. I heard that Toyama and Itokawa are trying to implement an Individual Transferable Quota together instead of a total allowable catch. But two independent prefectures' working together is always difficult."

"Impressive."

"Erica mentioned that. Her sister's husband is a fisherman here."

"Oh, that's right. His name is Hideki. He operates a bottom trawling vessel. Sails out a longer distance within Toyama Bay."

"Do you know how the Individual Transferable Quota works?" I asked.

"Basically, every fisherman receives an individual quota for the fishery volume. If you go over, you will be fined. Also, you can transfer the portion of your quota to another fisherman for money."

"With ITQ, everything is going to be just fine? It's just a matter of getting two independent governments to work together?"

"Not quite. ITQ is the best choice, but it's far from perfect. The quota has to come from the total cap, but the right cap is such a moving target to pursue. Nobody is 100 percent sure about the real stock volume. The realization comes in too late sometimes. For example, 25 percent of all canned tuna consumed in the main land of the US is produced in American Samoa. And almost 100 percent of the tuna produced in Hawaii is consumed on the main land. Yet, Samoa and Hawaii have imposed historically low quotas this year, so many fishermen are out of a job."

"It sounds very harsh."

"Still, ITQ is probably the only answer, and it's good that prefectural governments are going to implement it to nurture the fish. I'm just saying that people are afraid of change, and there's going to be a huge negative financial impact on all fishermen here, just like what happened to Samoa or Hawaii."

"I know what you mean. You have to wait until the child fish becomes an adult to bore the baby fish. That time lag makes fishermen suffer. My grandpa always used to tell me that."

"Right. Take Alaskan red king crab for example. In two regions in Alaska, they now see an increasing abundance. The stock is coming back to where it used to be. Or, there's Monterey, California, which used to be a huge sardine producer in the early twentieth century. By 1950, their fishing industry had collapsed due to extreme overfishing."

"I read a book about that, *Cannery Row* by John Steinbeck."

"That's exactly where it was. The Cannery Row was forced

to close in the 1970s, but they implemented one of the toughest marine conservation regulations in the nation. And their stock has improved dramatically. They went from catching 25,000 pounds of fish in 1993 to 3.4 million pounds in 2000. Our fishing town is in danger, just like Cannery Row. But if we do it right and endure the suffering, maybe we will be able to see the light at the end of the tunnel in three to five years."

I wanted to ask how he felt about Itokawa's unethical tactic of putting more trawling vessels at the entrance of Toyama Bay to raise this year's fishery volume so that the quota next year would be favored toward Itokawans. But before I could ask, the fishery association paged Ichiro.

"I have to go, my receipt is ready for me to pick up."

"What's that?" I asked.

"In Hime, fishermen just catch the fish. Then, we ask the fishery association to sell our fish at the live auction. Once the auction is finished, we go back to the association, and they give us a receipt showing how much our fish sold for."

"I see. I'll let you go. Let's talk more. I've been trying to mostly speak Japanese these days, but speaking English with you gives me a nice break."

"I enjoyed the conversation, too. Let's do another seafood lunch on my boat again. See you soon, Lindsey."

"See you, Ichiro."

Ichiro stood, but then he hesitated. "Ah, one more thing—"

"What?"

"Please don't quit Hime Junior High School."

I stared at him, too surprised to speak. "Who told you I am quitting?"

"This is a very small town. I hear all the rumors. Both the students and teachers like you very much."

I thought about pretending like I had never thought about

quitting. But it was clear that Ichiro knew the truth, and there was no point hiding it.

I stared at Ichiro for a moment, speechless, and then I simply nodded.

Ichiro grinned, and I couldn't help but notice the adorable dimple on his right cheek.

A few days later, my argument with Kong led to an unexpected event.

The parents of the four students Kong reprimanded came to our school and sought an explanation from Kong.

I asked Erica, who had been in the teachers' shared office when the parents came in, what happened.

"Well, I think that the students had believed what Kong was doing was lawful and complied with the teachers' rules. When you told Kong that what he did was illegal, those students realized that what he did was wrong, and they told their parents."

"I have done research, and unlike the United States, I did not anticipate any big legal issues here," I said. "But then, I realized every time parents came to the school, every teacher became nervous."

"I saw the same thing. Our ultimate boss is the school board, and the board is working for the city hall. The city hall's customers are general citizens."

"I feel like I've opened up Pandora's Box by yelling at Kong."

"Don't feel guilty, Lindsey. You did the right thing. At least, you have my support."

A few days later, Kong and I got called in by the principal after he had a sudden visit from the school board staff. Kong and I arrived at the office at the same time, and we waited silently in front of the principal's closed door. When he opened the door, his face was red in anger.

"Come in," he said, his voice tense and angry, like he was telling criminals to get into their jail cell.

Kong and I sat down on the plastic chairs in front of the principal's desk. The principal quickly began reprimanding us. Kong was told off for using physical contact. Once he was done with Kong, he reminded me that we were a team, and yelling at a peer in front of students wasn't acceptable. Several teachers had testified that I created a hostile environment.

Hostile environment?

I decided to go to the port and talk to Ichiro, thinking he could tell me more about the politics of the town, so I could understand why I was being accused of creating a hostile environment. But, if I was being honest with myself, I was also just looking for an excuse to spend more time with Ichiro.

When I got to the port, Ichiro was hosing down his boat's deck. In fishing ports, no matter where you go, people are always hosing water all over the place for sanitation.

I explained what happened in the principal's office to Ichiro, and then I told him what happened afterward. "Kong and I didn't apologize to each other. When we left the office, I got tired of Kong's Yankees' fan look, and I yelled at him and we had another fight. I wish I was better at controlling my anger, but it's so hard to back down from a fight."

It was just like what happened while I was in Boston, but I didn't tell Ichiro that.

He stopped hosing for a moment and looked me straight in the eye. "It sounds like that the environment at the school is not productive for either of you."

"I may deserve that crap. But our students shouldn't see us yelling at each other." I sighed. "I wish I didn't have to work with people like Kong."

"I feel the same way. In my life, interacting with people has become a burden. It has pushed me away from group work. Japanese tend to love 'teamwork spirit' too much, and they make too big a deal out of it."

"I couldn't agree with you more," I said, laughing. I saw some fish jumping out of the water and diving back in.

"That's why I wanted to become an independent fisherman. I wanted to be my own boss, so I chose to work at this fishery."

"I know what you mean. My grandpa hasn't worked for anybody since he was twenty years old."

"The ocean has been my best friend. But . . ." Ichiro sighed, and his normally cheerful face crumpled in on itself. "The Toyama prefecture will work with Itokawa to implement the Individual Transferable Quota for each fishing boat from next April. So it's in our best interest to either change jobs or work with other independent fisherman."

"Why do you have to work with other fishermen?"

"If you merge with another fisherman, you'll get double the quota. Two revenues, one boat. Or, one person uses one boat for six months to reach the quota, then the other person uses the same boat for the rest of the year for his quota. As such, we have to work together in some way until the stock is revived and ITQ is ended."

"I'm sorry you're losing some of your independence. I understand why it's so hard, I wish I could work in a job where I'm my own boss. I have to work for somebody here and get some experience before I return to the States. I thought living in a foreign country like Japan may open the new door for me, but it's not that easy. Things haven't exactly gone smoothly here."

"This tiny fishing town seems unwelcoming to you. I understand that. I felt the same way when I moved here over ten years ago. It wasn't until I met my wife and she introduced me to her friends that I really got involved in the community here."

"You're married?" I said, and to my surprise, my stomach twisted.

"I was, but just for a year. We got divorced four years ago." He glanced out at the ocean and shrugged. "Some people just aren't right for each other."

I wanted to ask him more about his ex-wife, but I also didn't want to make him feel awkward. Before I could say anything else, Ichiro changed the subject. "My point is, fishermen just don't know how to interact with people they don't know. But the situation is changing. I know because half of the teachers at Hime Junior High are supporting you, not Kong."

He smiled wanly, his voice lowered, as if searching for the phrase or word that would really get through to me. For some reason, I felt Ichiro was trying to persuade me to do something.

"So, what are you suggesting?" I asked.

"It is your life, Lindsey. I can't make you stay. I truly hope that you will find some clue for your future career while you are here, but nothing is guaranteed. I regret what I said to you the other day. I shouldn't have asked you to stay in this town without understanding you well."

We were both quiet for a moment. Ichiro pressed harder on the hose's nozzle to get a stronger spray.

Then, Ichiro continued. "What I'm trying to say is that you are liked here more than you think. Teachers like Erica look up to you like a mentor. Of course, being liked doesn't bring any future to you, though."

"Thank you. I never thought of that. Nobody has ever looked up to me before."

"Let me introduce you to some fishermen here. You have to really get to know people here to make your life joyful."

"That sounds nice."

"I'll think about what I can do. I will call you."

He grinned at me, his teeth bright white against his sun-tanned skin.

◄ ▌▌▌▌▌▌ ►

The Kong situation soon got even worse. The father of one of the students Kong hit worked for a nationwide newspaper. He was an accountant for the paper, not a journalist, but he sent a journalist to the principal and Kong. Despite their courteous explanations, the paper depicted it as a criminality and promised the readers that they would research more about this. Everyone in the prefecture was talking about the article.

The principal called in every teacher for a meeting.

"I strongly believed that today's article in the Fuji Journal was very unfair and biased," the principal said. He always dressed well, with a crisp dress shirt and a beautifully knotted tie. But today, his shirt sleeves were rolled up, his hair messy, and his tie loose around his neck. As he spoke, he pointedly avoided Kong's eyes and mine. "They misquoted our remarks and twisted them. They put too much weight on the parents' interviews. I will make a call to the journalist after this meeting, but we all know that it won't change anything. It will make things even worse if I say something politically incorrect. But I have to oppose it once to show that I have pride in our workplace and in all of you. Then, I will stop talking and leave the rest up to the school board."

Everyone leaned forward, their backs taut with anxiety. Erica whispered into my ear, "The afternoon the article was published, the school board came back to the school again. This time, they brought much higher positioned people, director level."

Kong stood up, his chair squeaking as he pushed it back hard.

"Well, I guess I should say something because I am at the center of this alleged 'education crime.'"

I had never seen his face that red, that full of anger. He had probably never been quoted by a newspaper before. Come to think of it, neither had I. I wasn't sure what to do next, what I should say.

"Unlike you guys, I can't stand the formality. Excuse my French, but banning physical reprimand is some bullshit that the school board came up with. The point is, you care about your students, and you want them to succeed in life. To get them to succeed, you sometimes have to punish them to get them to understand that they're doing something wrong. That's how they learn.

"As you know, my wife and I have not had a kid, so my students are my kids. Boys and girls, smart or dumb, rich or poor, it doesn't matter. All of them are my kids. And I tell you what, I don't discriminate the bad kids from good kids. They are all my kids."

Some teachers nodded along with his statement, which worried me. Perhaps other teachers thought physical reprimand was a convenient tool to have in case nothing else worked.

"I understand that part, Kong san," Erica said. "But I disagree with the way you treat the education policy that our school board has set out. It is not perfect, but it was a good policy, and we all know that every single school district throughout Japan has endorsed this policy. If you put yourself in the shoes of the district director, would you be comfortable operating your district without that policy?"

"I'm not saying anything like that. You outrageously twisted what I said. Listen. I have been in this industry much longer than you, and I know the rules. The school board banned violence of any kind. But physical contact is not prohibited anywhere in the rule book. Have I exercised any violence?"

"That is outrageous. Misinterpretation."

"Not at all."

"Then, where you would draw the line?"

"If it turns out to require medical treatment, sure, that is violence. Or, if it hurts the student's mind, that's violence too. If any students had not shown up to the school because of my healthy open palm tap, I would have resigned immediately. Nothing like that has happened. Never, ever."

"Now it has become a citywide scandal. That means many citizens thought something was wrong."

"It has nothing to do with the quality of education. If I were a director of the district, I would trust the teachers in my district and let them do whatever they believe. It's trust. Mutual trust. Not the rules, Erica."

"With all due respect, that is the same as saying you are the autocratic leader, and as long as you believe what you're doing is okay, it's fine."

"I never said that. I am saying that the most important thing is that the coaches have to be in agreement. Everybody is entitled to their own opinion. But what I wholeheartedly disagreed with was having an ugly argument in front of the students. To me, that is the issue. That shouldn't have happened."

"But you are the one who brought the students into the room—"

I started worrying that Erica was going too far and would say something that would get her into trouble, all to defend me. Before that could happen, I stood up and said, "I know you're still mad at me for disagreeing with you."

"Of course I am still mad. You were the one who stirred the pot."

"Well, then, let's ask all of the teachers here to raise their hands if they believe that we should be allowed to physically reprimand students."

"Nobody would raise their hand for that kind of crap, Lindsey. What you should ask is if the school board should give teachers a little bit more individual discretion when it comes to their students. The fucking blind school board should demand that teachers use their common sense, not the cold hard rule book or curriculum, syllabus."

"It's so unfair for the students to depend purely on each teacher's common sense."

"You had no right to yell at me in front of my students. If you want to say something to me, you could say it anytime we're alone together. But not in front of the students. You broke the harmony of the teachers' room. You broke the team, period."

Kong glared at me, hatred in his eyes. That look was echoed in the eyes of the teachers sitting around Kong. I realized then that this room was divided, the people who were on Kong's side sitting around him, the people on my side sitting near me.

The room felt stiflingly small, so small that I felt claustrophobic.

Kong continued. "You just don't care about the team. You are here only for a year. You don't give a shit about the students at all."

"Stop it! That's enough." the principal shouted. "The reason why I called the all-hands meeting was to find a productive solution for this issue, but both of you refuse to listen to the other side. You guys are just repeating the same thing over and over again, and you're refusing to listen to each other. To me, neither of you care. Both of you failed."

He pounded the table with his fist.

Everyone was silent. I knew I should remain quiet too, but I couldn't stop myself.

"Sir, I understand that I should have talked to him when the students weren't there. But he crossed the line when he slapped those students. He was the one who broke the team."

"Enough is enough, Lindsey!" the principal shouted even louder. For the first time, he forgot to add 'san' after my name. "For the record, I'm not firing Kong. If the school board wants some gesture to the media, I have already asked them to fire me first. Lindsey, I am not judging anybody here. I just wanted all of you to be more attentive to the situation, because you know what, students are always listening to us. This is a small school in a small town. I only have you guys. I cannot easily replace anybody. But I wasn't born yesterday. I know that Kong is carrying his resignation letter in his jersey pocket. I also know that Lindsey is trying to swap positions. But I tell you what: nobody would come to take their places in the middle of the academic year. If you guys want to resign, fine. If you guys want to leave, fine. You guys can put your egos first and the students second. Go ahead and do that. I will be the PE teacher and English teacher, effective tomorrow."

I froze in shock. I had no idea how Mr. Principal found out what I was trying to do. I didn't know that Kong was trying to resign, either.

Kong looked down, not denying what Mr. Principal said. Erica had told me that no teacher had ever quit this job, except on the rare occasion that their spouse got a job in another town.

"Look, everyone." The principal continued with a lower, weaker voice. He took off his glasses and wiped sweat off his face with the sleeve of his white shirt. "Throughout Hime, people are suffering. Most of you have relatives or close friends working for the fishery. We all know that tensions are high with Itokawa, and that's making things tough for these kids at home. Because of that, the kids are having a hard time concentrating on their schoolwork, and they may misbehave more. But we should still correct any wrongdoing that we see, and we shouldn't fight amongst ourselves."

The room was silent again. I still felt angry at the teachers who openly supported Kong, but I also felt a little bad for Kong. I also felt responsible to clear the air, since I was one of the two people who had made things so tense.

It would make sense if Kong and I resigned—it would help release some of the tension from the teachers' lounge. And the resignation would allow me to easily move to Tokyo or Yoko-hama. I had some savings, so I would be okay if it took some time for JET to find me another place to work. Or, I could take time off work entirely. I imagined myself peacefully traveling around Japan, taking pictures of the shores and learning traditional cooking. It didn't seem like a bad life.

A deep voice came back into the back of my head: *Please don't quit Hime Junior High School. The students and teachers like you very much.*

Ichiro was right. If I quit, I was putting students second. I wondered if, subconsciously, I had been hoping by shouting at Kong, the principal would be forced to ask me to resign. That made my stomach twist—I hated to think that was something I would do.

I needed to hear what Ichiro would say about this. I decided to go to the port tomorrow to explain what happened and to finally tell him what happened in Boston.

◀ ▬▬ ◀

"Hello, Ichiro."

"Hey, Lindsey. What is happening?"

I hopped on his boat.

I explained what happened at the all-hands meeting, and then I immediately followed that with my Boston story.

It went like this: I tried to defend a student who had been treated badly by a teacher. In this case, it was the music teacher, a middle-aged woman named Rebecca. Rebecca had told a little girl that she could stay after school to practice her cello, and she could then store her cello in the music room since she had to walk home. But then, Rebecca had left early and locked the classroom, so the girl had nowhere to put her instrument. I was the only teacher staying late at school that day, so the girl found me and told me what happened. When I called Rebecca to see where she was, she got angry and said, "Are you kidding me? I'm on my way to a dentist appointment. I told the kids that they couldn't practice after school today."

Rebecca agreed to come back to the school and unlock the door, but the next day, she shouted at the girl, causing her to cry in front of the entire class. I felt like there was something strange about the whole thing. Rebecca was forgetful, so she could have easily not remembered to tell the girl not to stay late that day. She also hated admitting that she was wrong. I told a few of the kids who took music class to stay after my class, and I asked them if Rebecca had told them about the dentist appointment. They all said no. I was so angry—angry that Rebecca had made a poor girl cry, angry that she refused to admit her mistakes. So I strode over to her classroom, slammed my hands on her desk, and in front of all her students, I shouted, "You should apologize to the cello girl, Rebecca."

While this confrontation seemed small at the time, its effects rippled out as everyone in the teacher's room took sides—should I have said something at all, should I have waited until after school? The arguments continued until, finally, everyone simply stopped speaking to each other.

This was what effectively ended my teaching career in Boston. There were problems before this, where teachers accused me of not being a team player or of taking matters into my own hands too often. But the confrontation with Rebecca was what really did me in—every teacher thought I was too untrustworthy and volatile, that I didn't understand how to behave in front of students. I couldn't recover from that.

"It's amazing that the situation here is almost identical to what happened in Boston," I said to Ichiro after I finished my story. "But this time, only one thing is different. The principal openly scolded me. He cares about the students, and he cares about me."

I leaned against the side of the boat. "I still think I was right, but the way I argued in front of the students was wrong."

"I guess you didn't have much choice after you saw the red marks on the students' cheeks."

"Maybe so, but I still should have had control. I should have been more professional."

"The way I look at it is both you and Kong care about the school and the kids. But the article has hurt both of you and all the other teachers very much."

"I know, and I feel responsible for that."

"You shouldn't feel responsible, you just did what was right. You know . . ." Ichiro hesitated, staring down at the water lapping against the sides of boat.

"What?"

"I don't want to hurt your feelings, but I talked to some of the young fishermen here who went to Hime Junior High School. They all like Kong a lot, and they say he is the one who cares about the students the most. But don't read too much into it. What they said is more about the fishery war than you and Kong."

I silently nodded, my stomach twinging.

Ichiro must have noticed my crestfallen expression, because he said, "I've been thinking about ways for you to get closer with the fishermen here. Why don't you come to the Hime Fishery Association's meeting tomorrow evening? The association is the center of the fishermen's lives here.

"That's because most of the fish we catch are traded through live auctions every day in Japan. Somebody has to operate the auction, and that's the association's role. They work with both local fishermen and wholesalers throughout Japan, including big cities like Tokyo. Plus, since most Japanese fishermen are sole proprietors, the association helps connect us. They're almost like our industry union, or a city hall for fishermen."

"How many people belong to your association?"

"About 2,000 people. Tomorrow morning, the Toyama government officials are visiting the association, and they're going to explain the procedure to implement ITQ on our bay next April. Attending an event like this is the best way for you to get to know people here."

"Thank you. I'll go."

Ichiro smiled. "Despite what I said to you before, I will support you if you feel you need to go to Tokyo or Yokohama for your new career. That's what you came here for."

Tokyo or Yokohama sounded so charmingly irresistible to me. I tried to reject the idea to his face, but I couldn't seem to find the words.

Instead, I said, "Thank you, but I still need to fix the problems for my students before I leave here. Since you heard my Boston story, you understand why this is going to be the last chapter of my teaching profession. It's just not the right field for me—I can't deal with all the politics. I would like to do the right thing before closing the book. For that, I would like to understand more about what's happening with Hime's economy. I'm very serious, Ichiro."

He nodded silently, his eyebrows bunched together, his mouth downturned. That look told me exactly how Ichiro felt about the future of Hime.

◄ ||||||||||| ►

The following day, Ichiro took me to the fish market before the fishery association discussion. It was my first time seeing the inside of the live fish market. The market was as large as a football field, and it faced the unloading pier where the boats dumped their fish. About a thousand people were working there, categorizing the fish, taking the fish to the auctions, carrying ice, and cleaning the place. The atmosphere was lively, and people were constantly moving around and shouting at each other.

"This is awesome. It's totally different from America," I said as a woman ran by holding a huge red fish.

"I know what you mean," Ichiro said. "There, all the fish are sent to gigantic warehouses, and then they're sent to processing factories. Here, it's more similar to a livestock fair. There are 6,300 fishing villages throughout Japan, and about 2,500 fishery associations. Most of the fishermen belong to an association unless they work for a big fishery corporation like Hakodate Marine."

At the mention of Hakodate Marine, I couldn't help but think of Paul. I grimaced, and then quickly tried to hide my discomfort.

"Wow, 6,300 villages," I said, pretending the name Hakodate Marine didn't ring any bells.

"Right, to me, it's too many. But Japanese people just love seafood that much, especially sushi. We feel that the ocean is compassionate—it understands what we need, and it provides for us."

"What an interesting phrase. I wish my grandpa could hear it, he would understand what you mean."

We finished looking around the fish market and walked toward the fishery association office, which was a four-story building just next to the fish market.

We went up to the top floor where they had a big space filled with portable meeting tables, set up classroom style, and hundreds of chairs. We sat at a corner table, close to the entrance.

People quickly filed in, filling up the space. Every time someone walked into the room, they tapped Ichiro's shoulder and said hello. Everyone seemed to like Ichiro.

Ichiro introduced me to all the fishermen. Once they knew that Ichiro liked me, they became very friendly to me and praised my Japanese. It made me realize that in a place like Hime, you needed to get introduced by a local to really get accepted.

Once the room was full, two guys in suits walked in and took their place in the front of the room. They were with the Toyama Prefecture, and they spent about an hour explaining the ITQ procedure to the association. But while they spoke, I couldn't focus on what they said. I could think of nothing but how happy I was to finally feel like I belonged.

◄ IIIIIIIII ►

A week later, Erica called me early in the morning. She asked me to call Ichiro to find out what was going on in the fishery association. She sounded slightly frantic, which didn't surprise me—in the week since the ITQ meeting, the tension had gotten catastrophically worse.

When Ichiro answered his phone, he said, "Hey. Someone from school called you, I suppose."

"Right. I heard that some fishermen from Hime and Nanae City in Itokawa had gotten into a fight. Twenty people got arrested, and that Erica's brother-in-law Hideki was one of them. Is that true?"

"Yes. I just heard from the association that both sides admitted to the violence. The police will release them today, but they were already determined to send the case to the district attorney's office. It probably started off small, but it appears that both sides formed groups to escalate the argument. So, if the DA's office thinks this is a planned event, it is going to be a felony rather than a misdemeanor."

"Oh my god."

"The rest of the association members are furious. The Hime and Nanae Associations have decided to get together and discuss it tomorrow. Would you like to come?"

"Yes. Hana doesn't share much information with Erica. But Erica is worried about her brother-in-law, and the fathers of two of the students in her homeroom class were also arrested. I want to help ease her worries."

"All right. I will get a guest permit from the fishery association for you."

"Why are you guys confronting each other this much? You know, I hope I don't sound like an ignorant Westerner, but from our perspective, Japanese people are a lot more amicable toward each other than we are in the US. You guys don't even boo at a ballgame."

"Well, 400 years of samurai contention has made irreparable differences between our towns. Of course, the samurai war ended 150 years ago. But ITQ is rekindling all the tension between us."

The Nanae and Hime fishery associations held their meeting at a Chinese restaurant on the border of Toyama and Itokawa. When Ichiro and I entered, I saw five directors from each side sitting at a big square table in a banquet room. Dozens of fishermen from each side stood behind them. Nobody spoke, and tension crackled through the air.

When I went to stand on the Hime side, a few fishermen from the Nanae side pointed at me and shouted. One said, "Hey. This is not open to tourists. Get out of here."

Ichiro stepped in front of me like a shield. He said in a thick, low voice, "She is with us. Not a tourist."

The Nanae guy shouted curses at him, and three of the Toyama fishermen fired derogatory words back. Some of the other fishermen pulled the instigators back, stopping the shouting from devolving into violence. The air got even tenser.

For the first time, the bullying incident became firmly connected with the adults' disputes in my mind. The kids at my school were seeing the tension between their parents, and it was feeding into their behavior in the classroom.

Once everyone quieted down, the discussion started. One of the directors immediately began discussing the fight. "It was not just a petty quarrel among a few guys. We have a fundamental problem with the way you abuse Toyama Bay. Unless we solve this abuse issue, many similar confrontations will follow."

"Tell me about it," the biggest guy said. He was in his fifties, and muscles rippled in his arms every time he moved. Ichiro told me that he was the president of the Nanae association and his nickname was Godzilla. It made perfect sense that he was the leader of a rough group of fishermen. Not only was his body big, but I had also heard his fishery wholesale business was hugely successful. He must have had tons of economic power in his region.

On the Hime side, we had five directors, including a president and other administrative people who I heard reluctantly got elected. I heard that most people had really wanted three retired fishermen who had a broader vision for Hime.

Hideki stood and spoke first. He was an average height, but he had wide shoulders and thick biceps, like Popeye. "We found out that Godzilla had other associations issue new special fishermen licenses. Those fishermen are now overfishing in Toyama Bay even more. It is a clear disturbance to our operation. Our catch volume has been declining substantially."

"We do whatever we are permitted to do in our jurisdiction. Nothing illegal. You have no say in our jurisdiction," said Godzilla.

"Fish don't give a shit about the jurisdiction. But you send many fishermen to this area, and you encourage them to overfish more and more. By the end of March, you will have accumulated a higher fish volume than ever before. It will reflect in the new ITQ." Hideki pointed the tip of his ballpoint pen on the map spread out on the table in front of him, indicating the border of Toyama Bay and the Sea of Japan.

"Everything we do is lawful in our jurisdiction," Godzilla repeated, his voice low.

"It's simple economics: if you overfish this much, each boat earns less. You even subsidize your fishermen to continue your overfishing strategy. That is completely unethical."

"That's what you think."

"You also just issued twenty new temporary licenses to trawling vessels. It's insane."

"The prefecture government issues license for trawling vessels, not us."

"I believe you guys are connected behind the scenes."

"You clearly have a very overactive imagination."

Hideki smacked his hands against the table, making the whole table shake. "This is another attempt to deplete our stock using your personal political power in Itokawa. I know your strategy is to make us go bankrupt. Our Hime brand will be revoked and you will rename it as the Nanae brand. The way things are going now, the ITQ will be allocated to you so much more than us."

"Then, perhaps you should do the same thing!"

Hideki dropped his pen, nostrils flaring, and ran toward Godzilla.

A director grabbed Hideki's arm to stop him.

"We can't. You are in the entrance, we are in the back!" Hideki screamed, trying to release his arm.

"Then work with your government and quit participating in ITQ."

"Sure! We will definitely do it!"

After that, the meeting quickly devolved into bickering as both sides screamed at each other, neither actually hearing what the other side said. Ichiro touched my arm and motioned toward the door. We went outside and started walking toward the center of Hime.

"Why is Itokawa getting so much more of the ITQ than Toyoma?" I asked, crossing my arms to keep myself warm.

"Godzilla and the governor are old friends. Because of that, the governor gave Godzilla the license for the entrance to Toyama Bay. So, when ITQ starts, Godzilla will get the largest allotment of fish. It isn't illegal, but it's completely unethical. In return for this, Godzilla endorses the governor, and since he's so respected in Nanae, people listen to him. With the election coming up, the governor will do anything Godzilla wants. He can't lose the votes from Nanae."

"But that's unfair," I said, my voice getting higher, like it always did when I felt something was wrong.

Ichiro shrugged. "It's just the way it is."

We were quiet the rest of the walk, and I tried to think of something, anything, I could do to help Hime before they lost all their fish to Itokawa. Frustratingly, I could think of nothing at all that would help.

◀ ||||||||||| ◀

The fight between the fishermen made the front page of the newspaper for a few days, but soon, people moved on from that, and our teachers' room war became the main focus again. The Toyama paper defended us, but the school board seemed to care more about how the Fuji paper wrote about us since Fuji papers had large nationwide subscriptions. In each article, we were depicted as a bunch of rubes who didn't care about the school, which angered everyone. The Fuji paper also realized that the fishermen's and teachers' room fights had the same root causes, and they started writing more and more articles from that angle.

One day, Erica and I went for sushi at Bamboo Sushi. Of course, we could talk about nothing but what was happening at our school.

"It's no longer Kong versus me. It's no longer if physical reprimand is acceptable or not. It has become if we have control over our own school or if we are simply robots operated by the school board," I said, sipping burning hot green tea from a large cup.

"Since the articles have gained national attention, the school district office can't ignore us anymore," Erica said. "They have to show some action to make the public happy. Focusing on just a mere PE teacher and English teacher is too small for them."

"So, the new target has become the principal for lack of leadership?"

"I think so. I heard that the school board is sending five staff members to monitor our classes. That's never happened before at Hime Junior High."

"I've never heard of such thing in Boston either."

"Many of the veteran teachers are debating if we should accept their surveillance or if we should fight against this treatment. Accepting the surveillance will definitely make us unfocused in our classroom, and that will have a negative effect on our students."

"I agree. Teaching is not a show. In order for you to talk to the students heart to heart, you shouldn't have outsider's eyes in the class."

Erica ate a piece of her sushi, looking thoughtful. "Having said that, if we fight back, I know more reporters will write about how we're refusing to be transparent. They'll wonder what we're hiding. The harder the teachers resist, the more the media will write. At the end of the day, the school district would oust our principal, who we truly respect, and the media would brag about themselves, saying justice was served and the media saved the democracy."

Erica and I didn't speak for the rest of our lunch, each of us lost in our thoughts.

As the media continued focusing on our school, our staff room became more and more emotional. Many teachers refused to talk to each other, simply glaring when someone from the other side walked into the room. There were also often verbal spats—though never in front of the students.

When Kong and I saw each other, we quickly looked away. We weren't shouting at each other anymore, but we also hadn't forgiven each other. Somehow, these nonverbal fights felt even more charged than our shouting matches. With the tension so high, it was clear that things were going to get worse before they finally got better.

◀ ⅼⅼⅼⅼⅼⅼⅼⅼⅼ ◀

In the middle of June, Judy called me and frantically said, "I saw that your name was deleted from the JET teachers' forum. What the hell happened? Were you fired?"

"No. I just decided to stop looking for someone to take my job."

"Oh . . . does that mean you're happier in Hime now?"

"Nothing positive like that. It's just that, with everything happening here, my name has become known, and not in a good way. There's no way I can get someone to take over this contaminated position. If they Google my name, they'll find out everything that happened here. Also, as the principal reminded me, if I leave, the students may lose their newfound passion for English. I would feel a huge sense of guilt if that happened."

"It seems, voluntarily or involuntarily, you are committed to this town."

"I had no choice. And I decided that until the end of March, when my year here is up, I'm going to give teaching my all. If I have any free-time, I'll use it to look for ideas for my future career."

"I'm sorry, Lindsey, but I'm here for you. Anytime you want to talk, just give me a call. And I'm going to visit you soon, I promise."

"Thanks." I smiled, hoping Judy could sense my gratefulness through the phone. I wanted to give her some positive news to off-set everything negative I told her. I could only think of one thing.

the Sea of Japan

"The good news is that Hime has the best sushi in the world. Even far better than Tokyo. As a matter of fact, I moved from my apartment to the second floor of Bamboo Sushi. The second floor was used by Mr. and Mrs. Bamboo's two daughters, but both of them got married and moved out to Yokohama. They were looking for somebody to rent the space. So I took them up on the offer. I feel much more at home here than I did in my old apartment."

"How is the school?"

"The teacher's room war is making things tense outside the classroom, but in the classroom, things are going well. I'm teaching seniors' classes, and I was invited to an English speech club where students learn English as an extracurricular activity. According to them, the former instructor was very mundane and rigid, and they appreciate that I'm letting them talk about literally anything they want."

"Students always love freedom."

As we spoke, I reviewed English papers from my students. It was a joy to see their growth. There were fewer errors, they used more complicated sentence structures, and they varied their vocabulary.

"My students are serious about learning English. They demanded more homework, which is not something I ever thought I'd hear students asking for."

Before Judy could answer, she said she had a call waiting, and she checked and saw it was the Tokyo governor. We hung up after some hasty good-byes. Right after that, my phone buzzed, and a headline from a local newspaper appeared on my home screen.

It said the Itokawa governor criticized the Toyamans for openly considering dropping the ITQ. The sub headline said, "I haven't heard anything more insane than this."

◄ ▯▯▯▯▯ ►

Both fishery associations decided to meet again. Nanae and Hime needed ITQ to survive, so they decided to try and find a compromise. To allevieate Godzilla's tension, we visited them on their soil, at their association office in Nanae. A group of about fifty of us Toyamans went, including Ichiro and Hideki.

Nanae was just another fishermen village, similar in size to Hime. But the big difference was that their fishery process infrastructure was owned by Godzilla and his family. Because of that, things were more orderly than they were in Hime, where most seafood processing was done by small business operators.

"I am a businessman. I am always open to new business. Just bring me a proposal," Godzilla said, and his tone suggested that he felt he was the most reasonable person in this crowd.

"No. This is not a business issue. This is the issue of mutual trust," our president said.

"To me, it doesn't sound too different. If you want a better result, negotiate with us. Give me something that we cannot refuse."

"You are outrageous."

"If you think so, just sue us." Godzilla's humiliating laughter filled the stuffy association office room.

◀ ▇▏▊▎▌ ◀

After that, I attended many internal fishery association meetings. I always stood out, but they still welcomed me and hoped I might bring some fresh ideas to protect the Hime fishery. Before the ITQ was announced, the fishermen didn't get together too often. Afterward, though, they often met up to discuss solutions to their difficult problem. Each time we met, the discussions got more tense.

One day, Ichiro and I went to a discussion that the association president called 'contemplation over a new strategy.' As we entered the room, everyone seemed nervous. I realized everyone knew the news of our failed negotiation with Godzilla.

At a glance, it seemed like almost all of Hime's 350 fishermen were gathered, along with another 300 wholesalers. Most of the fishermen were men, but for the first time, I saw many women wholesalers.

Ichiro noticed me looking at the women. "Those women are married fishing professionals. They don't do fishing. Yet, several husbands and wives actually ride on the boat and do the operation together. From morning until night, the couples are together all the time. We call it a married boat."

The president began the discussion by sharing the disappointing news that the fish market was losing money. The fishermen instantly started grumbling.

"You are not going to raise the membership fee again, right?" one fisherman said. He had a thick gray-black mustache. "You can't do that. The gas for the boat was raised, the membership fee was raised, and the payroll for the associations' employees was raised. And the selling price was lowered. How are we going to survive?"

"We're discussing raising the membership rate, but we haven't made any decisions yet. Right now, we're thinking of merging. I know nobody wants it, but under this severe circumstance with Nanae, it seems like the only option. Take Choshi fishery association in Chiba Prefecture, for example. They have merged with four associations, and they're now the biggest association in Japan. And such volume has created more business opportunities for them. Also, with a merger, we can cut redundancy expenses."

For a moment, the place was silent, but that silence was quickly broken by shouting.

"Merging is only for small associations. We are not a small market," the fisherman with the mustache said.

"As we heard from the Toyama Prefecture bureaucrats in our

last meeting, whether we like it or not, the ITQ system will begin next April. There's no way to stop it, is there?" the president said. A few people nodded, frowning. "In that case, we have to do something like a merger to tackle ITQ."

A young fisherman raised his hand.

"I am leaning more toward the cancellation of ITQ. If we didn't have to do ITQ, we wouldn't have had this many fights and this much animosity toward Nanae. ITQ has made us suffer, and it's going to make us suffer more."

"Wait a minute." Another fisherman stood up. He was short and had a scar across his cheek that was shaped like an exclamation mark. "ITQ is the solution, not the problem. Adult fish are tastier and sell at higher prices than young fish. ITQ will logically stop fishermen from catching small fish."

The fisherman with the mustache started speaking over him. "I was one of the few who opposed ITQ from the beginning. We don't need to have ITQ. There are other, less disruptive solutions. In other prefectures, crab fishermen use large mesh nets so that young crabs can escape from the net. ITQ will make us do more of these conservation efforts, and that is a good thing. However, from an income perspective, ITQ will make us lose money for three to five long years."

"After five years, the good old days will come back," the fisherman with the scar said.

"I disagree," the young fisherman said. "Let's make no mistake about it. Nanae fishermen will gain a huge quota in the next year if Godzilla continues operating the same way, and our portion will be very small even if the stock recovers in five years. Also, we have people working for this market—distributors, process manufacturers, you name it. Once we shrink, these people will leave the city. The combination of ITQ and Godzilla means the end of our fishery."

the Sea of Japan

Another fisherman stood—a man in his twenties with his hair slicked back. "Guys, our population is decreasing. Even if we can survive the three years of profit loss because of ITQ, the city will not survive. At the end of the day, Hime will be dead. So, we have no choice but to merge with another fish market to retain a certain size. That's what banks have done, that's what car manufacturers have done. A merger is the only solution."

A wholesaler in the far opposite corner stood and said, "If we can merge with a special third license port, we will raise our volume and get even with Nanae. But I don't know where the merit is in merging with another third license port like Shinminato."

Ichiro had explained the different types of ports to me. He said there were four levels of fish markets: first license, second license, third license, and special third license ports. The first and second license ports were smaller and just fed local markets. Third license ports, like Hime, were too big to only sell to local markets, so they usually sold to other places in Japan. Still, third license ports were too small to attract large distributors. The big manufacturers typically went for special third license ports. These ports were the ones that distributed seafood all over Japan. There were only thirteen special third licensed ports in Japan, but they supplied one-third of all the food eaten in Japan.

The fisherman with the scar shook his head. "The closest special third license is more than 300 miles away."

A wholesaler in a blue cap stood and shouted, "Guys, you are always looking for reasons not to do it. You should look for how we can do it. If we merge, we can provide a larger volume. With the volume, we will get the upper-hand when we approach corporate buyers. They need volume."

"Slow down, people. I'm not sure if merging with Shinminato will make us substantially large," said the fisherman with the scar.

The president shook his head. "We can't merge with them

because there are two big rivers between us and them. If our 300 boats have to make trips to their river estuaries to unload fish, it will create environmental damage there. It may also further reduce the stock."

"But Shinminato port is the only port that's close to us. That means this is the end of the conversation, isn't it?" said the fisherman with the scar.

"Not really," the president said softly.

"How so?"

"The other option we have is merging with Nanae."

"Nanae? Are you kidding me? That's our enemy," Hideki shouted, standing up. Everyone stared at him. He had two black eyes and bruises on his face and arms. "I just got released from jail for defending Hime from Nanae. Soon, we may be prosecuted with felony charges. Which side are you on?"

"Look, Hideki. Fights or business," the president said, his voice level. "Which one is more important to you?"

Hideki glared at the president and didn't answer.

"We understand how you feel, and we thank you for showing loyalty to our port. But we need business, and animosity and business do not mix. Merging with Nanae is the only effective way to solve the animosity, and move toward ITQ together in the smoothest way."

"That is Itokawa prefecture. Interstate merger is out of question, since fishing ports and associations are controlled by prefectural governments, not by the central government. It's technically impossible to merge with Nanae," Hideki said.

"Just because it is unprecedented doesn't mean we should rule it out in this emergency."

The young fisherman stood up again. "I agree. Mergers at all levels are inevitable in Japanese fisheries. We have 2,500 fishery associations throughout Japan, but the central government strongly encourages people to shrink it down to 250. As an independent prefectural government, Toyama Prefecture may not like the interstate merger, but the central government will love the idea, and they'll issue the merged license."

"That's right," the president said, smiling, clearly pleased that someone liked his idea.

"Wait a minute. Are you guys serious?" Hideki said, his face turning red. "We've been enemies for so long. We can't just become friends with them."

"For survival, I am okay with a merger with anybody, even Nanae," said the young fisherman.

"I agree. The only request I have is I want them to propose the idea to us, instead of us approaching them. Then, we'll get to keep our dignity," said the fisherman with the mustache.

"The only way to keep our dignity is to not merge with Nanae!" Hideki shouted.

Many people nodded in agreement. Other people began shouting, until all their words blurred together into a giant mass of anger and fear.

"Let's get out of here," Ichiro whispered in my ear.

We went out to a big, empty room near the conference room where we had been meeting. We opened a large window, and I started down at the crisp blue ocean spread endlessly in front of me. A breeze blew by, spraying me with salty water. Beyond the protected port wall, the Sea of Japan's waves were high and rough.

Ichiro said, "The fishermen here have so much pride in what they do. I think that's why they're so angry at each other. They need to merge, but it injures their pride."

"I get what you mean. I think pride correlates to independence here."

"You're right." Ichiro gave me a shy smile. "Hey, want to get something to eat?"

"Sure, what do you want?"

"I have the perfect place to go."

We walked out of the building and into a small, old ramen noodle shop next door. The noodle shop was tiny and almost full. There were no tables, just two long counters that were attached to the wall. It was odd to see customers lined up in two rows, with many young students and fishery warehouse workers facing walls and eating ramen noodles quietly.

I thought about how interesting it was that this was the first place Ichiro was taking me out to eat. Most men would take their female friends to an elegant, sophisticated place that was designed to impress them. When Paul and I first started going out, he took me to some gorgeous restaurant that was famous for being a favorite of the Kennedy family. There, small plates of food cost more than some cars. Ichiro knew me better than that, though. He knew this was exactly what I liked—simple places where the focus was on the food, not how trendy the place was.

The place didn't have menus, and instead, the hostess asked us to take a look at a handwritten poster placed on the wall. There weren't many choices listed.

We turned our bodies sideways and moved along carefully between people's backs. We squeezed ourselves into two vacant chairs at the end of the counter. There wasn't much space, so our elbows were almost touching.

"The air conditioning is on a little high," I said, shivering.

"You will know why later," he replied, eyes twinkling.

Ichiro explained that they served 'Toyama Black,' a famous ramen soup that was such a dark brown it was almost black. This was due to the condensed soy sauce they used. Fishermen loved this soup, and to make it more filling, they usually ordered a cup of rice to eat along with the ramen. That way, they could eat a hearty meal while saving money.

Ichiro ordered a large bowl and I got a regular. In just five minutes, the waiter brought out our two Toyama Blacks. Ichiro's face lit up as he stared down at the steaming broth. When he realized I was looking at him, he gave me an embarrassed grin. "This is my favorite food in Toyama."

We both dug into our soups. Soon, Ichiro nodded to himself and then flagged the waiter over and ordered two additional raw eggs. "It will make the soup even better, with today's broth," he explained.

When the waiter brought them, he broke an egg with one hand and poured it onto my soup.

"Do you like it?" Ichiro asked, a piece of noodle stuck between his front teeth.

"I like it a lot. There's no ramen like this in the United States."

I was fine with the high level of spice, but it was hot enough that it made sweat appear on my forehead. I laughed as I wiped my forehead with the back of my hand, remembering what I said about the air conditioning.

Even after he finished his noodles, Ichiro sipped the soup and kept saying how good Toyamans were at making ramen. He was clearly proud of Toyama even though he wasn't a Toyama-born fisherman.

When we finished eating, we walked back into the association office. With a full stomach, I felt ready to face more heated discussion.

The conversation continued on for hours. At times, I felt myself dozing off in the warm room. I was just drifting off again when Ichiro gently touched my shoulder and said, "Lindsey, they have a question for you."

I opened my eyes and saw all the men and women staring back at me. "We were wondering, Lindsey san, what the fishing industry is like in the United States," the president said.

I inhaled deeply, trying to think of the right thing to say. "I have never been in a commercial fishery before, but my grandfather is a fisherman in Massachusetts," I said slowly, speaking Japanese with a little hesitation. "I still remember Grandpa's joyous face when he was on the boat. When the boat was docked, I loved hopping into his skipper seat and turning the wheel, pretending to steer my own boat. More than anything else, I loved seeing how happy Grandpa was when he was fishing."

I looked up and saw that everyone was still staring at me, completely invested in what I was saying. They probably wanted a break from all the yelling, and they wanted to hear from someone with a completely different set of experiences. I cleared my throat twice and continued.

"I don't know any statistics about fisheries in the US, but I do know that American fishermen were suffering from the same declining volume of fisheries until recent years. Their fisheries have recovered well because of the regulations and control, including TAC and ITQ. My grandfather suffered too when the quota was low. In fact, he sailed farther out to catch non-restricted fish. Even though New Bedford is the biggest commercial fishery port in the entire United States, they still suffered."

"New Bedford is bigger than Alaska's fishery?" the fisherman with the scar asked.

"Good question," I said, the words coming out in a high, uncertain tone. I tried my best to smile. I was good at talking to kids, not adults. "Yes, Alaskans do large operations with salmon, pollock, and menhaden. We are proud of New Bedford, and we do about 400 million dollars in volume."

"That's huge. Our volume is about 50 million dollars," the president said.

"Just like we Toyamans want to be better than Itokawa Prefecture, Massachusetts people also love being number one," Ichiro said.

the Sea of Japan

People laughed. It was the first laughter I heard in this room today. I smiled—Ichiro may not have talked much in public, but he knew what to say when he did.

"Today, America's fishery volume is as large as Japan's because of the massive consumption of crab, oyster, and lobster. Believe it or not, America is now the largest fish exporting country, and the volume is 5 billion dollars," I said.

The fishermen with the mustache stood. "Lindsey san, when did America start ITQ?"

"They started ITQ in 2008, rather late."

The young fisherman said, "New Bedford is where *Moby Dick* took place, right?"

"Yes, good memory! Although, we don't do whale fishing anymore because Japanese people get mad if we do."

Everyone laughed hard. I felt very good. I had never felt this comfortable speaking in front of adults before.

"American fishermen are stubborn, too," I said, smiling. "But they change the target fish and fishery methods as the economic environment changes."

"I see. Lindsey san, how do you feel about our situation personally? By now, you know that we are even more stubborn than Massachusetts fishermen," said Hideki.

Everyone laughed again. I looked at Ichiro. He mouthed, 'Go ahead.'

"Well, how about bringing in something new?" I said, keeping my voice upbeat. "Try some new ideas and some new fishing methods before we merge with somebody else. That's what you guys have not discussed yet."

Everyone nodded and started murmuring. Soon, they were discussing my idea amongst themselves. I sat down, pleased with myself. But then, I started thinking about my school, about all the nasty articles the Fuji paper wrote about us. Before I helped these gentlemen save their workplace, I had to save mine. Not for me, but for the students.

And then, I realized one thing I could do to save my school.

I would resign and make my resignation look positive for everyone involved.

◀ ▏▎▍▌▎▏ ◀

On the night of the last new moon in June, Ichiro called me and told me he wanted to take me somewhere special. Ichiro picked me up in his dented red car, and we drove an hour along Toyama Bay, toward Iwasehama Beach. Along the way, he explained that we were going to see the firefly squid dive. He didn't explain what that was, and I didn't ask—some things were better left a mystery.

We got to the beach at midnight. Nobody was there. Growing up in a big city like Boston, I had completely forgotten that the night could be so dark, that so many stars could fill the sky.

"Nobody has been able to figure out why and when the dive happens, even top scientists," said Ichiro as we walked on the soft sand towards the water. "But it has been said that if you go to the beach after midnight on windless nights from March through June when there's no moon, you have a better chance of seeing the firefly squid dive. After the female firefly squids finish laying eggs, millions congregate and swim up to the beach shore to die. Firefly squids literally light up on their legs. One squid has more than 1,000 bioluminescent organs. We may get to see billions of beautiful blue lights in the dark ocean."

We waited for a long time, the air completely still. An hour passed, but they didn't come.

I pulled out my phone and looked up photos of the squid dive. In the photos, the ocean was illuminated with dots of blue lights, like stars. The more pictures I saw, the more I wanted to see that mysterious sight in person. But my wish wasn't granted.

the Sea of Japan

We continued sitting on the sand. Two hours passed. Three hours.

"Are you all right, Lindsey?" Ichiro asked as I shivered.

"Yes, I'm fine. Thank you for taking me here, it's so calming. You know, this reminds me of my trip to Alaska with my mom when I was twelve. My biological mom, I mean. We went there with full cold weather gear and waited all night for the aurora. There have been more scientific studies about auroras than the firefly squid dive, but still, nobody knows when the aurora is going to come. We waited and waited, jumping up and down to fight against our coldness and sleepiness."

"Were you able to see the aurora?"

"No. The aurora never came on that night. But I enjoyed the pure and sacred silence. I had never experienced silence like that before."

"Even in Hime, you cannot find anyplace quieter than this."

I nodded, shivering slightly.

"Are you chilly? This will warm us up." Ichiro pulled a small green bottle from his pocket.

"What is it?"

"It's local Toyaman sake, would you like some?"

"No, thanks." In the back of my mind, I heard the nurse's voice, telling me not to drink alcohol near the ocean.

Ichiro unscrewed the cap and started sipping. The smell of sake got on the slight breeze and blew toward me. The smell was tantalizing, and I remembered how joyously customers at Bamboo Sushi drank sake while eating sushi. I decided that I would be okay drinking near the ocean now, since Ichiro and I could keep an eye on each other. I wasn't alone anymore.

"I changed my mind. Let me try some, Ichiro."

"I already put my mouth on it."

"I don't mind."

I roughly extended my arm to him, dramatically flexing my fingers. He laughed. I sipped the sake. It was a bit bitter, and it had a profound, deep flavor.

"This is now my favorite place to drink sake," I said.

"It is great. But just don't climb up on any rock to take photographs, please."

I laughed. "I won't."

I took another sip of the sake. "This is so good. What's the name of the brand?"

"It's Masuizumi. Meaning, a well full of happiness."

I smiled. "That's beautiful." I imagined the winter snow melting on the Tateyama Mountains. After a while, it sank into the mountains, and then it eventually formed a deep well. If the water came from such beautiful white mountains, it must be full of happiness.

Ichiro and I waited for more than four hours, until the edges of the horizon turned pink and orange with the first light of dawn.

"Sorry, Lindsey, the firefly squids are not coming today," Ichiro said.

"That's all right. Thanks for taking me, anyway."

"Let's try it on another new moon night."

I nodded, but I couldn't help but feel disappointed. It was the end of June—the end of firefly squid season. The squids wouldn't be back until March of the next year.

Ichiro and I walked back toward the car silently. As we walked, all the thoughts I had been avoiding for the past few hours came back to me. All the serious confrontations at my school and the fishery association. The way the city was shrinking rapidly, putting the school and the fishing industry at risk.

"I want to do something for the people in this city, no matter how small it is," I said.

Ichiro nodded, like he had known I was going to say that all along.

I thought of something Mr. Principal often said at the end of our staff meetings.

One Hime, One Heart.

It was time to take action.

It was time to make peace with Kong.

When I got home, I called Kong.

◄ ▌▌▐▐▌▐ ►

On the phone, Kong and I agreed that we needed to change the way the papers covered the school. We needed to do something to stop them.

We decided to have a private meeting at my favorite Starbucks in Toyama City, far away from the prying eyes of the people in Hime.

The coffee shop sat by Toyoma City's river, providing a stunning view of the churning water. When I arrived, I saw Kong sitting at a small table in the back corner of the crowded shop, holding two lattes. He said, "I saw you coming. And I remembered you are a latte drinker."

"Thank you. Did I drink a latte at school?"

"Only once. But I could tell you liked it a lot more than our usual cheap, weak coffee."

We smiled, avoiding each other's eyes. It was clear that we were both trying to be on our best behavior.

He said, "Well, the school district's surveillance has stressed everyone out. Nobody can tolerate it anymore, and because of that, I know it's time for me to resign. I've decided I'll hand in my resignation letter tomorrow. With that, the school and Mr. Principal will be able to save face. The school goes back into harmony."

"I knew you would say that."

"Oh, yeah?" he said flatly.

"Because I have thought the same thing, and I was going to

ask you to review my Japanese resignation letter and correct some grammatical mistakes."

I pulled a white envelope out of my hand bag.

"You don't have to do this," Kong said, and to my surprise, he looked stricken. I thought he would be happy to get rid of me.

"This is the only way to get the school board off our backs. This is the only way to save Mr. Principal's job, and we both know that he deserves his job more than we deserve ours."

"I gave up, Lindsey. You don't have to do the same."

"I quit my teaching job in Boston before I came here, but quitting here is much more meaningful. You and I will save the school, our beloved leader, and our students."

"But you came here to build a new career. Quitting in the middle of the program may hurt your chances of finding a new profession. And won't the school have trouble getting another JET teacher?"

"You're right, and it is going to be hard. But resigning is the right thing to do." A memory came to me then, one that I knew would help convince Kong that I was serious about quitting. "In Boston, I was sued two times by parents over my actions at school."

"Oh, yeah?"

"The school and school district were the co-defendants, and we won at both litigations. But, the two entities both told me I should stay away from trouble, even if my supervisors had to take the fall for me. Now I know that's not the right thing to do. I'm ready to resign, Kong. I talked to JET, and I made sure that they would work with the Toyama prefectural government to save our principal. I made sure to let them understand I am quitting because I love our school."

"I'm impressed, Lindsey. I'm honored to resign alongside you." Kong extended his hand, and I shook it.

The next morning, Kong and I set up a meeting with the

principal. As soon as we sat down, we both took out our letters. "We have both decided to resign," I said.

The principal didn't look surprised. "I appreciate what you're trying to do, but this is ultimately my responsibility."

"No," I said. "It's ours. We started this, and we have to end this. You need to stay here and provide your students with a leader they can look up to. Kong and I want to save the school, and this is the best way we can think of."

The principal shook his head. "There has to be some compromise, some way that we can all save our jobs . . ."

"There isn't," Kong said firmly.

"And you know it," I added.

Mr. Principal pinched his forehead with his thumb and index finger. "You're right. I just wish you weren't." He finally looked up at us. "You'll leave the school next month, when we start summer vacation."

The principal shook our hands, and then we left the office, knowing there was no going back now. Now that my teaching career was officially at its end, I knew I had to figure out what I was doing next as soon as I could.

Even though I felt different, life still went on in Hime after I resigned. The fishermen started getting nervous as more and more of their peers began giving up and leaving Toyama. Hideki brought some brochures from the Nanae fishery association. The brochures showed Nanae's massive marketing efforts, and the fact that they were promising more, better quality seafood to sell to their neighboring regions. They seemed to believe that they would dominate the Toyama Bay after ITQ came in. It also seemed like were planning on misleading people, telling them that the fish belonged to Nanae, not Hime.

The brochures also suggested that with their momentum, there was no realistic way to convince them that a merger with

Hime would help them. The fishermen also couldn't think of any way to get Nanae to approach Hime.

Every week, at least two or three middle-aged fishermen declared that they would leave Hime for a new job. The Toyamans took it personally if a friend decided to leave Toyama.

One day, I told Ichiro that I might be able to introduce Hakodate Marine to Hime. Even though my feelings toward Paul were complicated, to say the least, I thought I could still utilize my connection to help Hime. Ichiro thanked me and told me we would tell this to the people here when the timing became right. Several days later, Ichiro carefully brought up the Hakodate Marine opportunity with a small group of fishermen, but the reaction turned out to be all negative.

Soon, June turned into July. At the end of the month, summer vacation would start, and I would leave Japan. My feelings toward this fact changed every day. Some days I would dread leaving the place I had started to call home, while other days I was excited about the prospects that lied ahead.

The one good part about resigning was that Kong and I started getting along. We often hung out in the teachers' room and talked about baseball. He was a walking encyclopedia of MLB. Ever since he was assigned to be a baseball manager when he came to Hime Junior High School, he had passionately studied baseball. I imagined if he had been assigned to be a basketball manager, he would have taken the same approach to basketball.

I was glad that I was resigning with him. Letting him resign by himself would have haunted me.

I held off on telling Ichiro about my resignation for a couple weeks, but soon, I knew I couldn't keep it from him anymore. When I told him what had happened, he listened and quietly nodded. When I finished, his eyes darted around, and he opened his mouth to say something, but he closed it before any words came out.

For some reason, that made me nervous, and I started talking quickly, "Don't get me wrong, I wanted to stay in Hime. I asked the JET people if there was a way to stay in Toyama, or at least in the neighboring prefectures. But it's the middle of the academic year, so they couldn't get me any job in Japan."

"There should be some," said Ichiro hastily.

"Maybe. But if I were a principal, I would not hire a lady who stirred the pot and resigned after only four months. So, unless something changes, I'll go back to the US."

"What will you do in America?"

"I want to do something challenging, but if I'm being honest, I really just want to be appreciated, just like I am by the students at Hime Junior High. The way they look up to me and ask me for advice is priceless."

Ichiro rested a warm hand on my shoulder. "I hate to see you leave, but I will respect your decision no matter what."

I smiled at him. "Thank you."

◀ ▐▌▐▐▌ ◀

Right after we met, Ichiro and I had decided to have sushi together on his boat every Sunday. On my last Sunday in Hime, I went down to his boat, expecting to see him hosing down the deck or hauling his latest catch onto his boat. But to my surprise, his boat was there, but he wasn't on it. Ichiro never took a day off. He stayed in his apartment only when the sea was too rough for even the most experienced fisherman.

As I stared at his boat, my phone started ringing. It was Ichiro. "Hey, Ichiro. Where are you?"

"Sorry, Lindsey. I'm at home," he said in a low, rough voice.

"That's strange, the weather outside is gorgeous. You played hooky?"

"No, I broke my leg. Can you come to my place? I'm all alone here."

I paused before answering. We had hung around for quite some time, but I still wasn't exactly sure about how I felt about him. From the beginning, I had planned to go back to Boston after twelve months. Sure, Paul had ditched me right before I came to Japan, but that didn't mean that I needed a substitute so soon. The objective of my time in Japan had been to find seeds for my new career, not a boyfriend.

I still couldn't say a word. Ichiro must have guessed what I was thinking, because he said, "Sorry, I just realized what that sounded like. I didn't mean to imply anything. I just can't get around too easily right now, and I need some help."

Help is such a magical word.

It was powerful enough to override all the excuses and reasons I could come up with not to go there. I hopped on my bike while I was holding my cell phone and told him I was on my way. It made sense–he had saved my life, and now it was my chance to repay him.

When I arrived at his building, I knocked on the door.

"It's open. Sorry, I can't come to the door."

I walked into the studio apartment. The place was small and just had a few pieces of furniture–a scratched kitchen table, a tattered couch, and a bed. Ichiro lay on the bed, not moving. He looked truly awful. His left leg was wrapped by a thick white bandage. His arms were bruised and his face was swollen like a knocked-out boxer. His face was pale and drawn, and he looked very ill.

"Did you have a fight?" I almost yelled. Hideki's black eyes came into my mind.

"No," he replied, grimacing with his eyes closed.

When I moved closer to Ichiro, I saw his face was big and round like a Toyama watermelon, the largest kind in Japan. The image made me laugh, which immediately made me feel guilty.

"I'm sorry," I said. "What happened?"

"Yesterday, during that bad rainstorm, I decided to sail out. When I was grabbing my fishing poles, a strong wave knocked the boat and tossed me into the air. Thankfully, I didn't fall out of the boat, but my leg smashed into the raised corner on the side of the cockpit. After that, while I was trying to go home, I used my arms to avoid further damage, but I still got more bumps here and there. Since I lost stability in my leg, the damage went onto my arms, stomach, and even face."

I offered to change the bandage since I saw some blood spots. He hesitated, but I insisted.

As I gently unwrapped the bandage, his face was still full of pain. It made me think of my grandfather falling out of his boat. Even the best fisherman may die on the ocean.

My grandfather was the one who taught me about the dangers of fishing, and they were lessons I would never forget. When I was a kid, I was always Grandpa's favorite, and he spoiled me whenever I visited him. There was just one thing he wouldn't allow: leaving a piece of fish on my plate. More than once, I left the table crying, forcing my mom to yell at her father-in-law.

But no matter how much I cried and how much Mom shouted, Grandpa didn't back down. "A fisherman risks his life catching fish for you people. It is a sin to leave fish meat. You should finish it. That Alaskan king crab you're refusing to eat was caught by a fisherman who probably loses five of his friends each year to the sea."

For the first time, I pictured the pain my grandpa had gone through. I finally understood why he had not tolerated my tantrums.

As I unwrapped the bandages on Ichiro's arm, I noticed that his skin was burning hot. "Have you checked your temperature? I think you have a fever."

"Really? I feel cold."

Keita Nagano

I looked at him again closely. He was thinner than he had been when I first met him. He had also been coughing frequently, and once he started, the coughing went on for long periods of time. "Are you okay? Are you taking antibiotics?"

"Yes, I am."

"Maybe you should try a different antibiotic, this one doesn't seem to be working well. Besides, have you seen a doctor recently for a check-up?"

"No. I'm thirty years old. Unless I have severe symptoms, who would go and see a doctor?"

I didn't agree with him, but he held his jaw firmly, which I had learned meant that there would be no arguing with him. I sighed and decided to get back to that argument later. "Are you hungry?"

He shook his head.

"When was the last time you ate?"

He shrugged. "Yesterday afternoon, maybe."

"You should eat. If you can't cook, maybe you should go the hospital. Or you could stay in your parents' house."

"I have to work."

"I don't think you'll be able to for a while. By the way, where is Satoshi? I thought he was staying with you."

"He moved back to our parents' house."

"In Tokamachi?" Ichiro nodded. "Why?"

"He realized it was time to go back home."

"He moved because of the bullying, didn't he?"

Ichiro grimaced, which told me everything I needed to know. "Did it continue after I stopped those boys?"

"Those particular kids stopped. But some others continued bullying him by emails or texting. For some reason, all the kids at his school believed that Satoshi was from Itokawa, not Niigata."

I winced—cyberbullying was something I was all too familiar with. In Boston, I'd learned it's very difficult to identify, unless the

- 76 -

victim reports it to the school. But most of the victims wouldn't tell their parents until it got very nasty. In my first year at my Boston school, a girl in my class killed herself after being cyberbullied. That was the darkest day of my life, and for months after, I escaped to the casino almost every day, trying to forget my troubles with the simple pleasures of the Blackjack table.

"I'm sorry. I truly am."

"No. Don't be. Satoshi isn't afraid to say what's on his mind, and he stood out too much. The bullying ended before he left, but he didn't feel comfortable in Hime anymore, so he chose to go home."

"When did the cyberbullying end?"

"When Kong found out. You know his style. Once he found out what was happening, he grabbed the bullies' iPhones and made them show him the evidence. Then, he smashed their phones to the ground. He crushed ten iPhones in all. There were more kids who were cyberbullying other kids, but as soon as they heard about what Kong did, they stopped immediately. Word of mouth, you know. When the students threatened to complain about the force he was using, Kong said, 'I am not even touching you, am I?' That was hilarious."

He laughed for the first time that day.

"No parent has come to the school and complained about what Kong did?"

"Nobody wants to be in the Fuji paper, they don't want to look like they're supporting their kids' cyberbullying." He paused and looked up at me. "People really wish that you and Kong would stay in the school."

"I wish that, too," I said, sighing. "But this is the only way to block the prefectural government from firing our principal. And our strategy is working. Today, I heard that the school board decided to withdraw the ridiculous supervision in our classes at

Hime Junior High School at the end of this month. Kong and I feel great about that. Sayonara to the school board."

Ichiro laughed, but then he closed his eyes. "I feel sort of light-headed."

"You need to eat. Do you have any food here?"

He shook his head.

"I'm going to the grocery store, then. Be back soon. Don't move."

"I couldn't if I tried."

I went to the grocery store next to Ichiro's apartment. I decided to cook Ichiro a classic apple cider BBQ chicken breast. Since we had eaten nothing but fresh fish on the boat, I thought it would be a nice change for him. The grocery store was surprisingly well-stocked, and I found good smoky American southern spices and BBQ sauce.

While I searched for ingredients, I decided to call Kong and tell him what had happened to Satoshi. He swallowed his words, held his breath for a long time. I assumed he knew the bullying stopped with his efforts, but he didn't know that Satoshi left Toyama because of it.

"Oh," he said, his voice smaller than I had ever heard it before.

I truly sensed his disappointment. Without thinking, I said, "I'm sorry."

"No, I'm sorry. It was truly my fault."

"I don't have as much teaching experience as you do, but there is nothing that hurts me as much as hearing that a kid fled his school because of bullying. It makes me feel like I've failed as a teacher."

"Me too."

Kong was quiet for a moment. I decided to change the direction of the conversation. "What are you going to do after this month?"

"I am thinking of becoming a coach for an independent professional baseball team. But before that, I am planning to fly to Miami to receive further training on how to become a professional baseball coach."

"That sounds wonderful. At least, it makes me feel less guilty."

"Don't even say that after you ruined your career for me."

"That's ridiculous, you had nothing to do with this."

Kong laughed. "We just can't stop fighting, can we?"

I laughed. "I guess not. At least our fight is friendlier now. Hey, why don't we get together somewhere before we leave?"

"Great idea. We are not talking about your favorite riverside Starbucks coffee, right?"

"Of course not. We're talking about drinking sake until one or both of us pass out."

"That's what I like to hear!"

We picked a date and time and then I hung up the phone, smiling to myself. I finished getting the ingredients for my Carolina BBQ dish and then headed back to Ichiro's, where I cooked the food while he napped. When he woke up, I served him his portion in bed. We ate quietly, both lost in our thoughts.

"This is great, Lindsey. Thank you," Ichiro said as he scraped his bowl clean.

For dessert, I served fruit cobbler with a cup full of blueberries and vanilla ice cream on top. It was store-bought, but I thought the extra flourishes made it seem homier.

After we finished, I quickly washed the dishes. As I dried the bowls, Ichiro said in a weak, shallow voice, "Can you ride on my boat?"

"What do you mean?"

"I can still operate the boat, but I can't do other fishing operations. If you help me on the boat, I could continue fishing—"

I dropped the towel onto the counter. "What are you talking

about? You know I am going home to Boston. I'm leaving Japan at the end of this month."

"I thought you have wanted to extend your stay. Have you?"

"Yes, I want to. But you know my job is gone. And my job search has been a total failure."

"You didn't understand what I mean. I will pay you. This is a real job offer. I'll pay you as much as Hime Junior High School does. You don't have any work waiting for you in Boston, right?"

"Well—thank you for your offer, but I have to build my real career, Ichiro. Just like you are doing. My friend Judy is pushing me to be more serious about my career. When you're thirty years old, you can't just play around anymore."

"Just three months, Lindsey. Three months, and I will be able to work on my own again. That's what the doctor said."

Ichiro looked at me with wide, pleading eyes, and I wanted so badly to say yes, but I knew that I couldn't. "Ichiro, I can't. I'm sorry."

Ichiro sat up, wincing slightly. "You wouldn't only be helping me. You would also help this entire town. We have to turn around Hime or it will be destroyed. Can't you see what's happening here? You must have realized that people in the northside of Hime have a more intense grudge against Itokawa because they are just next to the border, while the southside people are less concerned about the merger. That fight was all northern Hime people. Now, Hime is divided, and each side is so angry at each other. Not good at all. The young fishermen are asking me to do something. I have said no because I was not born and raised here. But I realize now that the clock is ticking. ITQ will start in April. We only have eight months left. Nanae is doing a massive and effective marketing war against us. The president of the Nanae fishery association, Godzilla, has paid the fishermen on the Itokawa trawling vessels to go to the entrance of Toyama Bay to block the good yellowtail from coming into Hime's territory. They are selling a lot and our volume is shrinking big time."

"I know, but what can I do?"

"I think it is time for me to push people to do something new, and I need you to help me. Everyone listens to you, and everyone respects you. And hey, maybe you can even put this on your resume. Saving an entire town has to look pretty good to an employer."

"All right, all right," I frowned and waved my hand as if I was fanning off mosquitoes. I tried to be annoyed, but I couldn't help but feel excited about getting the chance to spend more time in Japan. It may have taken a while, but Japan had grown on me.

Ichiro grinned, his watermelon face getting even larger. I couldn't help laughing. He seemed to take this as a full agreement. I didn't want to say anything that would ruin his excitement, so I simply smiled.

He grinned back, joy in his eyes, like he had forgotten all his pain.

"I want to celebrate this good news. Can I have another chicken breast?"

"I think you're just looking for an excuse to eat more, but fine."

He shrugged, still smiling.

◀ ▐▌▍▐▌ ◀

When Hime Junior High began its summer vacation, Kong and I were officially relieved from the school. Pursuant to Japanese protocol, the principal wanted to host a farewell party for us, but we politely declined. Since Kong and I were taking the blame for what happened, it didn't seem right to host a party for us. We wanted the school board staff to think everyone was still angry at us.

The day I finished at the school, I started helping Ichiro. I bought a set of bright red, heavy-duty fishermen gear and began riding out with Ichiro every day. Ichiro had to wear a cast on his arm and use a cane, which stopped him from doing the labor necessary of a fisherman. Ichiro sat on the deck and instructed me on what to do. At first, he was nervous and would often try and get up and help me. I would glare at him until he sat back down. Eventually, though, he learned to trust me, and soon, Ichiro didn't even have to tell me what to do. I just knew instinctively.

On my first rough day on the water, seasickness hit me hard, leaving me queasy and dizzy. We ended up returning to port early that day, which made me feel guilty, since I was cheating Ichiro out of a day's pay. Thankfully, I got used to the rough seas quickly, and soon my stomach settled, and I was able to ride the rough waters with ease.

As the weeks went on, I learned that commercial fishing was more fun than it seemed. I hadn't been on the ocean for a long time, but I immediately regained the love for the water that I had developed with Grandpa. Every morning, I woke up itching to pull on my boots and run to the port, and every night, I went to sleep still feeling like I was on those waves, like they were part of me.

The three months passed too quickly, especially since late summer was the best season in Toyama. The Tateyama Mountains were so beautifully situated right on the Sea of Japan. They were tall, and the ridge of the mountains were connected to each other, making them feel like one tall wall that protected us from anything that wished us harm.

Near the end of my three months on Ichiro's boat, Judy finally came to Hime.

Judy arrived late on a Friday night. When I met her at the train station, she was in one of her usual dark suits. Underneath, she wore a heavily starched light pink shirt, and a string of pearls shined on her neck.

After dropping off her luggage at my apartment, we went for a walk along a tiny, quiet river that streamed into the ocean. Judy stared at scenery, mouth wide. "I've been in Tokyo so long, I've forgotten what it's like to not be surrounded by people."

"Are you still enjoying your job?"

"Yeah, it's amazing. I work very closely with the governor of Tokyo, and I've even gotten a promotion of sorts. I've become his interpreter and English speech writer."

"Your program has one more year to go, right?"

"Yes. Isn't that great?"

"It is. I'm happy for you, but jealous at the same time. My days here are numbered."

"Right, so you're enjoying being a fisherwoman?"

"It's awesome!"

"Are you still getting seasick?"

"It only becomes a problem now when the ocean gets really rough. But I eat sushi ginger from Bamboo Sushi to prepare for it."

"You sound like you're a very serious fisherwoman."

Judy stopped and bought a bottle of Japanese iced green tea from a vending machine. I leaned against the machine and said, "I don't know if I'm serious about it, but it helps me relax. When I'm on the ocean, I forget everything terrible that's happened in the past few years. Those angry parents accusing me in Boston, the school district bureaucrats in the Toyama prefecture. It all disappears."

"I'm just happy you're not curing yourself with Blackjack anymore."

We started walking again, and Judy asked, "How is the fishery association dispute going?"

"Well, the debate in the fishery association is in a gridlock because the association is divided by north and south, and everyone refuses to work together to find a compromise. I'm asked to speak up more because of my neutrality. Also, I seem to be the only person that both sides will listen to."

"It's funny, you've never been interested in being a leader. And yet, now you're leading this big group of wild fishermen. I think it's great."

She hugged me, and I smiled but shook my head. "I'm far from a leader. I haven't brought any success so far. I thought bringing in Hakodate Marine would solve Hime's financial problems, but no one was interested. They feel like they can't provide Hakodate Marine with the amount of fish they need."

"I understand."

"The one thing the fisherman all have in common is a love for Ichiro. We've gone out with some of the other young fishermen and the doyens—the leaders of the fishery association—for hot pots and sake a few times. Each time, they ask Ichiro to take on a leadership role, but Ichiro is reluctant because of his injuries, and because he simply doesn't feel like he's leadership material. As his doctor predicted, Ichiro has recovered fully now, and it is time for me to leave."

"You have no desire to continue being a fisherwoman?"

"No, I mean, I've thought about it. Over the last three months, commercial fishing has become more and more interesting to me, but it's not a career. I need to be in a field where there's opportunity for growth."

Judy hesitated, and it seemed like she wanted to argue with me. But she must have thought it wasn't worth it, because she simply said, "I hear you."

"As my stay here comes to an end, Ichiro asked me to write an email to Paul. He said that the idea of working with Hakodate Marine may not be popular among our fishermen now, but you never know if people's feelings will change later."

"I don't want to hear that asshole's name."

"Don't worry. I don't want to start emailing regularly with Paul, either. In my email, I gave him Ichiro's address and told him to talk exclusively with him. That way, Paul can start communicating with Ichiro and the Hime fishery association, and I won't have to be involved."

Judy's cell phone rang.

"Oh, I have to take it. It's the governor."

"The governor of Tokyo calls you at 11:00 pm.?"

"He's a workaholic and impatient."

Judy gave me a wink and answered the phone, speaking in fast, fluent Japanese. Judy, my underage drinking and casino buddy, was now working for the Tokyo governor. More than that, he trusted her, and he knew he could count on her to solve his problems. I was so proud of her, and I tried to convey that feeling with a tight hug. Judy just rolled her eyes and mouthed, 'Weirdo.'

The next morning, Judy joined Ichiro and me on our boat. After I introduced Ichiro and Judy, Judy looked around, eyebrows raised. "How big is this boat?"

"It is twelve tons. And it's eighteen meters long," Ichiro replied.

"I don't know what that means, but it sounds impressive," Judy said.

Ichiro smiled. "Let me translate that into American for you. It's approximately 27,000 pounds and 60 feet."

Before we left the dock, Ichiro, Judy, and I set up four fishing poles. Each pole had a long line with fifty branch lines. For bait, we put pieces of squid meat on each of the hooks. Once our poles were all set up, we set off. I steered, and Judy and Ichiro sat and looked out at the ocean.

As I steered the boat, I stared at the deep blue ocean, trying to spot schools of fish. Ichiro had a GPS and fish finder available, but as my grandfather had taught me, these modern tools often aren't as good as a fisherman's eye. He always said to look at the color of the sea, and to use that to judge where the fish were.

While Judy and Ichiro chatted in Japanese, I read the color of the sea. There were so many other things to remember, so many small things that could determine your haul for the day. I always took into account where the moon was before the dawn, and where the sun was once it rose. I thought about not only the weather forecast, but also the speed of the current. I used all these factors to help me decide where to go, and it worked. Soon, fish were continuously tugging on our lines, and we couldn't get them into our boat fast enough.

When we caught enough fish, we stopped the engine and made lunch.

As I always did, I made sushi with the fish we just caught. I cleaned the fish, removed the scales, took all the guts out, scraped the residuals of the guts, and washed the inside body. Then, I peeled the skin, and sliced the meat into four pieces. I rolled the fish with rice to create makeshift pieces of sushi. My cuts were a bit sloppy, but Judy and Ichiro still complimented me.

As we ate, Judy couldn't stop talking about how fresh the fish was, about how much she'd love to try some new recipes with it. Judy and her mom were both passionate about trying new foods, but her father was a bit more old-school. She always tried to persuade her father to try new dishes and maybe even serve them at his New York delicatessen, but he was set in his ways.

As Judy finished her fish, she said to Ichiro, "If you ever decide to set up a restaurant here, I'll help you. I'm becoming a big fan of this place. What a fresh fish. I'm thinking of establishing a new sushi restaurant in Boston or somewhere in the US. Or, maybe I will stay in Tokyo, and we can open a restaurant together there." Then, she turned to me. "That would be a good new career for you, wouldn't it?"

"Sushi is not as easy to make as it seems," I said remembering the taste of Mr. Bamboo's sushi. "You have to have the right ratio of fish to rice to make the dish taste perfectly balanced. Besides, I thought you're focusing on expanding your parents' deli."

"Of course. But the rent in Manhattan is ridiculous. So, I want to expand the business outside of Manhattan, maybe even to a place like Tokyo or even Hime! Hell, if I do that, maybe I can bring some classic New York flavors to traditional Japanese sushi. What do you think about a pastrami sushi roll?"

I couldn't help but wrinkle my nose at that, which made Ichiro crack up. Judy also grinned. "Just kidding, you know I'm not a big believer in fusion dishes. Why fix what's not broken?"

That evening, I took Judy to the Toyama Station, where she was getting a bullet train back to Tokyo. When we reached a small shop selling bento boxes, she stopped and asked for ten bento boxes.

Outside the shop, Judy stopped to put the bag into her suitcase.

"What are you going to do with that many bento boxes?" I asked.

"Lindsey, bento boxes sold at train stations in Japan are so special. They have a long history, they're hugely popular, and they're cheap while still being high-quality. Nothing in the world can beat the Japanese railway bento box. I'll store them in my fridge and do research. It will be tons of fun," she said, her eyes faraway. Perhaps, she was thinking of how she could apply the bento box concept to her parents' business.

I glanced at our reflections in the glass window of the bento box shop. There was Judy, eyes blazing, full of possibility, and there was me, confused and frazzled. I could see the clear difference between eyes with purpose and eyes that were lost.

At the platform, Judy and I hugged goodbye, and then she hopped onto the train. As the train pulled away from the station,

Judy frantically waved at me. She continued waving until she finally disappeared, back toward her vibrant life in Tokyo.

The next morning, I woke up early, a sinking feeling in my stomach. This was my final day fishing. In three days, I would be flying back to Boston.

I grabbed my plane ticket from my nightstand and stared at it, trying to make myself feel excitement about going back to my hometown, the place I had longed to return to since I came to Japan.

This is what you wanted. This is what you've always wanted, I thought, but it didn't seem true anymore.

When I got to the pier, Ichiro was standing next to his boat. He stared down at the wooden boards below his feet.

"What's up, Ichiro?" I asked, concerned.

Ichiro looked at me but didn't smile, which never happened before.

He still didn't say anything, so I nervously kept talking. "I'm looking forward to going on the boat one last time, although maybe in the future, I'll visit Japan and we can go again. We'll have to stay in touch, I want to know everything that's going on in your life."

"Yes, we will," Ichiro said, and his voice was flat, lifeless.

Ichiro didn't say anything after that. To fill the silence, I said, "Are you ready to go out on the boat?"

Finally, Ichiro looked up at me. "Lindsey, I can't sail this boat anymore."

"What are you talking about?"

He pointed at a white slip attached to the rope connecting the boat and the pier. "This is a court notice. Debt collectors are taking my boat."

"You have to be kidding me."

"No, I am serious. I had to go into some debt when I bought

the boat, but it was a healthy, manageable debt. Even though I was losing some money because of overfishing, I was still able to easily pay back to the bank on my original payment schedule. But then, my parents got hit by bad weather two years in a row. So, their rice farm's earnings dropped dramatically. They had to get an additional loan, and I became the guarantor. The boat was my collateral. But more bad weather hit them this year, and they've now defaulted on their loan. Now, their remaining debt has become my own debt, and I can't afford to pay it. I've asked to reschedule the payment to have more time to get the money, but the bank won't allow that. I'm going to have to file bankruptcy, and my boat will be liquidated."

"But if they take your boat, how can you make a living?"

"I have to find a different job."

"Like what? What can you do?"

"I can't think of anything."

"You have to fish."

"I want to, but I can't." Ichiro took my hand. "Thank you for everything, Lindsey. The last three months were the best months of my entire life."

"Ichiro, is there anything I can do to help?" I said, my voice cracking.

"No, there's nothing left to do. Thank you, though."

An idea formed in my head, and before I had time to rethink it, I quickly said, "If they put my name as a guarantor to your loan, will they agree to reschedule your payment? I have a small income to show."

"You are leaving Japan in three days. You are not an eligible guarantor."

"They don't know that."

"Oh, everyone in this town knows you are leaving."

"How about borrowing money from the fishery association?"

"I already did it a long time ago. That is the first place you go."

"How about asking the doyens to become guarantors?"

"Oh, I can't ask for that. Especially from the doyens. That's not how it's done in our culture."

"If you can't, I can. Asking doesn't hurt me. Especially since they think highly of both of us."

"It's kind of them to think highly of me, but I know I am falling short."

"You're not falling short, but if you don't feel like you can talk to the doyens, I will. If I ask the doyens, they will listen to me and they may help you, right?"

"Lindsey, the doyens and fishermen in Hime like you very much. But you are leaving. So in a nutshell, you can't ask anybody anything."

"Wait a minute. You're saying I've lost respect because I'm leaving?"

"Of course not. They still respect you, but they don't, I guess, see you as part of the team anymore."

"That's not fair. Just because you leave doesn't mean that you don't belong anymore. I've been treated like family by you and the fishermen here, but now, you're making me feel I've always been just an outsider."

Ichiro's cheeks turned red. "I didn't mean anything like that."

"Maybe you didn't mean it, but that's what you said. And if I leave now, I'll be filled with guilt about leaving you when you need help. I can't leave you broke and without the thing in life you love most. Not you, the person who saved my life."

"Forget about that. You don't owe me for that anymore."

"I do, Ichiro, I do," I said. Ichiro looked down, his rich black hair blowing in the breeze. I gripped the thick rope connecting the boat and pier.

I said, "I won't leave Hime when you're in trouble. Not when I can help you get your boat and your life back."

"Lindsey, don't say such things. There are other jobs available. I can work for some trawling vessel."

"But working for someone else will make you miserable."

He didn't deny that, which told me that what I said was true.

"I can help you, Ichiro, if you let me. Don't you want me to stay?" I asked.

"Lindsey—"

"Ichiro. Just tell me. Do you want me to stay?"

"You know I do," he said in a soft voice.

"Good." I took a deep breath. I already felt calmer, more in control.

"How long will you stay?" Ichiro asked.

"I'm not sure," I said, but then I thought about something Ichiro had said to me long ago. "You promised to take me to the sacred firefly squid dive. I will stay here until you meet your promise."

"The firefly squid dive only takes place in spring."

"I'll stay until the spring then."

My shoulders and knees shook, but my head was clear.

This was the right decision.

Chapter Two

A few days after I decided to stay in Hime, I woke to my apartment's buzzer ringing. I stumbled out of bed and hit the speaker button. "Who is it?"

"Your best pal, Judy!" a cheerful voice responded.

Judy? She hadn't told me she was coming. I buzzed her in and opened my door. A moment later, Judy appeared.

"Why are you here?" I said, dumbfounded.

"Did you really think that just sending me an email telling me you're staying in Hime was going to cut it? No way. I need details, and I'm here to get them."

I stared at her for a moment, and then I started crying and hugging her. I felt so lucky to have her, to have a friend who always came to see me when I needed her.

We decided to go to the public bath house together. A bath house was the best place in the world to talk about a huge turning point in your life with your best friend.

It was still early morning, and nobody was there. Olive Bath House wasn't anything fancy–it wasn't a hot spring resort people would come from all over the world to see. It was just a pure community bath house for local people, a simple space with high ceilings and plenty of perfectly hot baths.

Even though it was simple, I loved it, and I had come to enjoy talking to local people as we sat in the warm water. I had found that it was a good way to make friends in this town. I had started coming almost every day.

Judy and I decided to sit in one of the outside bath tubs. As we soaked in the warm water, I explained the situation to her.

"So, in a nutshell, Ichiro will have to file bankruptcy and start his life fresh," I said after telling her the whole long story. "But since he will lose his boat, he can't fish."

"And that's why you decided to stay?"

"Believe me. I was truly prepared to leave. I packed up everything and I canceled my cell phone."

"Are you sure you will stay here?"

"I feel bad for him. I felt like I was abandoning him."

"I know the feeling. But he is a big boy. He has to figure it out by himself. Besides, there is not much you can do."

"That's not completely true. There is one thing I can do for him."

Judy knew me too well–she instantly knew what I was thinking. "No. No way."

"He saved my life."

"Lindsey, you've already paid him back. You helped him while he was injured. That was enough."

"I want to think that was enough. But do you truly think that it was?"

"Oh no, Lindsey. Hold on. I don't like this. I can't allow this to happen."

"If you come with me, perhaps you can stop me when I lose control. Grab me before I fall off the cliff."

"Lindsey–do you love him?"

"I don't know. Honestly, I don't know."

"If you don't know, why do you have to make such a big sacrifice for him?"

I didn't know how to answer her.

◄ ▐▌▌▌▌▐◄

Godzilla often went on local TV to promote Nanae's fishery. Their recent sales numbers told us that the consumers had definitely been influenced by Nanae's aggressive marketing campaign.

The Hime fishery association issued a state of emergency. The daily catch number regularly dropped to half of what it had been on the same day in the previous year. One day, it dropped even further—to 20 percent of the level from the year before.

The animosity against Nanae continued rising, but the division inside Hime became more critical.

One day, the Hime Junior High School principal visited me at the port. He said he saw me from a distance the other day, and he realized I had not left at the end of October as planned.

"I'm glad you're still here," he said warmly.

"Me too," I replied in the same tone.

"There are lots of rumors going around about you, Lindsey. I heard that you made yourself a guarantor for Ichiro's loan, and you even asked three doyens from the fishery association to also become guarantors. Is that true?"

"Yes, Ichiro was able to reschedule his payment, and he can still fish."

"People truly respect you, Lindsey. Toyaman people are very emotional. It hits our soft spot when we hear about something like this."

My cheeks got hot from embarrassment. "Who told you about all that, Mr. Principal?"

"Kong did. I'm glad that you two have become friends."

"We just love baseball."

"I think fishermen in Hime will look at you as a true leader moving forward. You should be prepared for that."

"Me? A leader? No way."

"You're too modest," he said, smiling. "Well, I should tell you, I'm not just here to catch up. I was wondering if you could come back to Hime Junior High School and teach our kids."

"What happened to my successor?"

After Kong and I jointly submitted our notice, the school board hired two nice, energetic male teachers from Toyama City to take our places.

"They are good hires. They work hard. But our demand for a native speaker like you has increased. Your popularity among students is just enormous, and you truly made it fun for them to learn English. Our average English grades have reached number one in all of Toyama. Even the kids who once disliked English have raised their grades dramatically."

"Oh, that's great to hear! But what about the school board? They're still angry at me, aren't they?"

"You're not their favorite person, no, but student success is more important to them than squabbles with teachers. Now that you've brought such prestige to our school, they're willing to take you back on a probationary basis. If there are no more incidents, then we can reinstate you fully."

"Mr. Principal, I'm honored that you're willing to take me back after everything that happened, but I've already committed to be on Ichiro's boat at least four days a week. In addition to that, I decided to work in my landlords' restaurant four nights a week."

"I understand. Maybe you could teach part-time. After all, fishing takes place early in the morning, and the sushi restaurant job is at night. With your youth and energy, teaching part-time in the afternoon wouldn't hurt you."

"I don't know—"

"Please, Lindsey. We need you." He looked at me with big, pleading eyes, and I realized how much he truly wanted me back. After all I had been through teaching, it was nice to be wanted, instead of fighting for my place. It was enough to convince me to give Hime Junior High one more chance.

"I'll do it," I said.

"Excellent," Mr. Principal said, shaking my hand. "I'll call you in the next couple days and we'll work out all the details."

I led him toward the end of the pier. As I saw him off, I thought about how glad I was that he didn't know the entire story of how I saved Ichiro.

Yes, I put my name down as a guarantor. I also humbly visited the doyens and asked them to help Ichiro. They became guarantors as well.

But still, we needed to put fifty thousand dollars down to lower the interest rate to one we could afford.

Nobody had that kind of money.

So, I went to the casino with Judy. It took a whole day in the Olive Bath House to persuade her to break my pledge just one time for Ichiro.

Japan had just opened their first casino in a suburban area outside of Tokyo. It was built to attract more foreign tourists to Tokyo, so most employees spoke at least some English.

I sat at a Blackjack table and started counting cards—with my photographic memory, it was easy. Card counting is not illegal, but a casino has a right to refuse players who do it.

Judy distracted the dealer by speaking to him in fast English with an outrageously thick Brooklyn accent. The dealer needed to ask Judy to repeat what she said many times. Judy never yelled at him, but her voice was tense and irritated, which drew the pit boss's attention. I was sure that surveillance cameras focused on her. Then, she pretended she was intoxicated and continued stumbling around until she was forced to move away from the table. She intentionally lost ten thousand dollars, and I won sixty thousand dollars.

On the bullet train back to Hime, I gave her back the ten thousand dollars she lost. The fifty thousand I kept for Ichiro.

Judy said, "You looked so professional. It was amazing. Have you thought about trying to use your photographic memory in your new career?"

"I've found uses for it in my new job at Bamboo Sushi. My sushi is not so great, but I remember everything my customers eat. I try to serve them before they place an order. It surprises them, and it shows them that I care about them."

"That's great, Lindsey. I'm glad you're so happy there. But getting back to the Ichiro issue, to be honest, I still don't know if you did the right thing going to the casino. Even it was for Ichiro, you invited your compulsiveness back into your life."

"Maybe so. But at least the casino is in Tokyo, too far for me to go too often. If you had seen Ichiro, you would have understood why I had to do it. He was crying, Judy. I've never seen him cry before."

"Still, why did you feel like you had to do so much for him? You are not his wife, or even his girlfriend."

"I know."

"Is that what you want? To become his girlfriend or even wife?"

"Oh, um, no," I said.

Judy raised her eyebrows skeptically. I just looked down again.

Judy shook her head. "Well, anyway, you have to promise me that you're not going back to the casino. Japan being loose on card counters is even worse news for you because it makes it easier for you to fall back into your old ways. And then if you somehow lose your photographic memory, you'll really be stuck. I've heard that happens to people sometimes—it goes away, just like that. If that happens to you, you'll still have your gambling problem, but you won't be able to easily win money anymore. You could lose everything."

"Don't worry, Judy. I will never go back to a casino anywhere in the world."

"Can you promise?"

"I promise."

◀ ▮▯▮▯▮ ◀

After I started fishing with Ichiro, Hime's fishermen began treating me as one of their own. I was still the only *gaijin* in the crowd, but these days, the fishermen didn't treat me differently at all. Further, as Mr. Principal predicted, they saw me as a candidate for the future leader of Hime. I had never been looked at as a leader in my life, so I was confused but flattered too.

I was proud to be the first American fisherwoman in Japan. The fact that there was no word, fisherwoman, in the English dictionary made me even prouder.

The Sea of Japan became my ocean.

One day, the three doyens who were acting as benefactors on Ichiro's loan came to me while I was unloading golden eyes snappers onto the auction scale machine.

"Hello, Mr. Doyen. How are you?" I said to the three of them. This was how we all addressed them—nobody used their individual names. When they wore fishermen gears, they looked like triplets with their tanned faces, deep crow's feet, husky voices, and sharp eyes.

"Very good, Lindsey," one said with a slight smile. They were serious most of the time, so a slight smile from them was like a deep, braying laugh from anyone else. "Now, do you remember how we asked you to push Ichiro to take leadership at the fishery association? And do you remember how we asked you to help Ichiro do that?"

"Yes, sir."

Their eyes were filled with gentleness, as if they were looking at their own granddaughter.

"Well, Lindsey. The time has come. It is the time for you to take leadership with Ichiro."

"What do you mean?" I asked.

"It means that you and Ichiro shall come up with a strategy to get us through this confusing time. We know you'll do a great job leading the entire association, no matter how young or inexperienced you think you are."

"Gentlemen, I was a full-time school teacher until last July. I don't think I can do this."

I instantly felt like I wanted to shirk such responsibility, that I couldn't handle it. And besides, it was so out of the blue. But at the same time, I was the one who asked the doyens to save Ichiro. I have owed them since then.

"Well, your grandfather is a long-time fisherman in the largest fishing port in the United States. So, you were qualified for the position even before you were born," one doyen said with a small chuckle.

There was no way that I could say no to these benefactors, and besides, it felt good to be treated like I was special.

"Do we have time to think about it? How soon do you want us take on this role?"

For the first time, the doyens' faces hardened. I even thought that I said something wrong. But before I could ask what was wrong, one doyen said, "We wish we had time, Lindsey. But the updated fishery association financial statement will come out tonight. It will state the probable bankruptcy of the association if this situation doesn't change within two months. We have no time, Lindsey."

The news of probable bankruptcy came later that same afternoon.

◀ ▥▥▥ ◀

The next day, the younger generation of fishermen got together in a small tatami room at the association to discuss the news. Ichiro got there before me, and he texted me that the discussion had quickly devolved into a harshly worded debate.

When I got to the room, Ichiro created a space for me to sit next to him. He whispered, "The news made everyone's ears stand up."

"I understand. Now they know that they don't have much time left."

Hideki finished his sake in one gulp, and then he stood and said, "The biggest merit of being a member of the association is I get cash three days after the fishery auction. Now, the association asked us if we're okay with not getting the cash until fifteen days after bringing in our fish. That would kill us. I have to pay for gas, baits, and tools by cash. I don't know if many of us can survive with these terms."

Ichiro said, "Our fishery volume has been descending, and the association hasn't been able to collect as much from the auctions as they did before. The association is going to go bankrupt if we don't accept the term change."

Ichiro already appeared different since accepting the leadership role. The quiet man had suddenly become persuasive and determined.

Ichiro continued. "We should stop procrastinating and having these never ending discussions. For that, we have to be united, north and south. Otherwise, the Hime fishery will come to its true end."

"How is the ITQ negotiation going with Toyama prefecture? Will they put the ITQ on hold like we asked?" Hideki asked.

"They won't. All of Japan is excited about the ITQ implementation. The governor clings onto the ITQ. That is the ticket for winning his next term."

I thought about my fishing, which I had been taking more and more seriously lately. Also, I had to help Ichiro survive since his whole life was bet on his small boat. I wanted him to be successful with his current boat, and then upgrade it to a bigger boat and hire a couple of staff members. Then, he should own multiple boats and manage the boats. That's what he had been dreaming of. That's how young fishermen in New Bedford grew their business and their income.

"Can the central government give us some kind of remedy? Can we make some sort of the deal with them?" Hideki asked.

"No. Hime is too small to have any real say in the Japan seafood industry. And people throughout Japan are worried about the stock conservation, and they now see hope in ITQ," I said. I still felt nervous speaking at these meetings, but I thought about what the doyens said, and that helped me push through my hesitation.

"Let me tell you a sushi chef's point of view," I said. "Toyama Bay is a special bay for sushi chefs. The warm sea current from the south collides with the cold current from the north. The bay also deepens not too far from the shore, and the bottom of the bay is very cold. The mixture of the two currents and the deep, cold well spring makes this bay unique. There's no port like it in the world. This means Hime provides the best sushi on Earth. Sushi chefs need this bay, and we'll keep this port alive no matter what!"

People began whispering to each other—they had never heard

me sound so passionate before. Everyone looked at me with a new respect.

A young fisherman from the southside of Hime stood and said, "Right. I'm tired of repeating the same discussion over and over again without taking any action. If northern people don't like the merger with Nanae, that's fine. But they should provide an alternative solution. There has to be another way to turn around our port and our city."

Hideki and the other northerners looked upset about the accusation. Hideki was about to say something back, but Ichiro cut him off.

"Hideki, you and your northern people need to listen to the people from southern Hime more seriously. Not everything has to be confrontational."

"I'll do my best," Hideki said. "But let me tell you, you southern people don't understand how painful it is to be under Itokawa prefecture's thumb. Living on the borderline with Itokawa prefecture means we bear the brunt of their long-held grudge against us."

The young fisherman from the southern side started to respond, but I was distracted by my iPhone buzzing. I glanced down, and saw I had a new email from Paul.

I forgot that I had written an email to Paul. It had been so long ago, and he had never responded. I thought I would never hear from him.

For some reason, my fingers shook with nerves as I opened Paul's email and I read it through once, then twice.

Hey, Lindsey, sorry it took me so long to get back to you, but I had to do my own research to respond to you accurately. I now understand the situation in Hime, and I see that it's one of the best fish ports in Japan. Why don't you come to Hakodate? We should talk. My fishery operation with Hakodate Marine may be able to help Hime.

"Lindsey?" Ichiro said, startling me. I looked up and he said, "The meeting is over. Do you want me to walk you back to your apartment?"

"No, thanks," I said, standing up, still feeling shaky. "I'm going to stop by the Olive Bath House."

I didn't have anything with me except a wallet, so when I got to the bath house, I rented a bath towel and bought shampoo and soap. It was late at night, and nobody was there. I had become friends with the manager, a short woman in her fifties. She always urged me to marry. She was very open and direct, but still warm. She also had decided that Ichiro and I were meant to be together. Her parents were a former fisherman-woman couple, and she knew that to really explore our feelings for each other, we had to go on a real date.

That night was no different. As she got my towel and shampoo, she said, "Lindsey, you get off that boat some time, and ask him out for a movie or something."

"Oh, no, like I always say, he and I are nothing. Just working together."

"I hear you. You pretend that you don't care about Ichiro, but your face tells me a different story. But don't date in Hime. Everyone will spread rumors. You should go to Toyama City."

"I'll keep that in mind."

"Enjoy the bath."

I sank into the big inside bathtub, and all thoughts of Ichiro quickly left my mind. Instead, Paul filled my thoughts. I thought about his email, the first contact I'd had with him since our disastrous break-up. I lightly tapped the surface of the water with my palm, trying to calm myself.

the Sea of Japan

I couldn't stop thinking about what to write back to Paul, and once I had exhausted those thoughts, I started wondering why I cared so much about what I wrote to him. Why did a simple email from Paul occupy my thoughts so deeply? Frustrated, I swung my arm hard against the surface of the hot water. The water splashed, the noise and rush of water distracting me from my thoughts.

It was my perfect temperature, 107 degrees. It was just like snuggling into a warm comforter on a snowy Sunday morning in Boston. I never wanted to leave. I loosened my body, determined to stop thinking about Paul. I was there for about an hour, and by the end of my time there, all thoughts of Paul finally left my mind.

I went back to my apartment above Bamboo Sushi, stopping in the small kitchen to make a quick snack before bed. Every time I entered my kitchen, I couldn't help but think about when I asked Mr. and Mrs. Bamboo if I could be their assistant. We had stood in my kitchen, the three of us barely fitting into the tiny space.

Mr. Bamboo immediately looked stricken. "Are you asking to be our assistant because of what I told you about our last helpers? Just because we lost them doesn't mean that we need you to work here. Don't feel like you need to do that in order to keep renting this space. We like you. We want you to stay there as long as you want. You are the best renter. You don't play music, you never party upstairs, and you don't even do hanky-panky."

His wife immediately said, "Hey! Watch your mouth."

I laughed. "I don't feel obligated to help, I *want* to help. I want to take advantage of living in the best fish tank in Japan, and I want to learn how to cook sushi for my family in Massachusetts. That's the main reason, Mr. Bamboo."

Mr. Bamboo looked at me with a furrowed brow. "How long do you think it takes to master sushi skills?"

I thought about it for a moment. "A year, maybe. I know some sushi chef schools in America where people get trained for a half year, and then they graduate and are ready to work as a full-time sushi chef."

"Well, with all due respect, sushi is deeply entrenched in our culture. It's almost an art form. In Japan, normally you have to train for ten years before you're allowed to stand in front of customers as a sushi chef. In my own training, in my first year, I did nothing but clean the restaurant, wash dishes, and deliver food. Then, the next three years, I did nothing but steam sushi rice."

"Wow, I didn't know so much training went into it."

"I know it sounds awful to you, and perhaps you feel that this much training is somewhat ridiculous. Everyone, including me, feels that way when they start. But you know what, as I'm looking back on my training days, I am so glad that I did a traditional course. In my first four years, I learned the most important skill in a sushi operation, even though it sounded too boring to me back then to be taken seriously."

"What's that?"

"Sushi is prepared using bare hands by someone you don't know. You want to feel that the restaurant is clean and sanitized. Because of that, a sushi restaurant should be ten times cleaner than general restaurants. Also, you will eat raw meat. In my first year, I had to deeply understand that cleanliness is the ultimate qualification to be a sushi chef."

"That makes sense."

"The other important thing we learned about in my first years of training was sushi rice. Sushi rice is a special type of rice that you will never eat anywhere else. It is the combination of rice, vinegar, and sugar. But how you mix them with rice is something you cannot research. You just have to master it by making too many mistakes at first. Because every day the temperature and humidity changes. Every bag of rice in a grocery store is different."

"I see."

"But since you are interested, I will give you an abbreviated training since you won't be here for long enough to get the full experience. I'll let you decide when you have reached the mastery level you want to achieve. At the end of the day, it's your sushi."

Mr. Bamboo smiled.

"I'll be right back," Mrs. Bamboo said, and she headed toward the stairs.

I wondered if Mr. and Mrs. Bamboo were being so accommodating because they knew about Ichiro's financial difficulties and me being a guarantor. I had already lowered the wage I got from Ichiro so that he could support his parents. In order to do that, I needed to have another income on top of my part-time teaching income.

Mrs. Bamboo reappeared, holding a brand-new sushi chef coat. She handed it to me and I held it tightly and gently as a newborn baby. Mr. Bamboo clapped me on the back, and I grinned.

Until that moment, I hadn't realized how excited I was to begin making my own sushi.

◀ ⅢⅢⅢ ◀

One by one, the other fisherman decided to quit their jobs and move out of Hime.

The mood at the fishery association got darker each time I visited.

On the radio, an economist said that our city's economy was going to tank since so many people were leaving. After hearing that forecast, many companies stopped investing in Hime.

It became clearer and clearer that Hime needed Hakodate Marine's business to survive. But going into business with them would mean that Paul would truly be back in my life, and I didn't know if I was ready for that.

I needed to talk to someone about everything that was

happening, but I felt awkward talking to Ichiro about Paul. So I decided to get advice from an unlikely source: Kong.

Kong was stuck in Hime for the time-being—he was still waiting to get his visa to go to Miami. He needed a job while he was in Hime, and he had asked me to help him get a job as an assistant coach for Hime Junior High School's baseball team. Since he wasn't actually going to be teaching, Mr. Principal got the school board to approve it. The school board was also upset that our famous baseball team had missed the cut for the nationwide tournament, so they were more lenient than they might have been otherwise.

Kong was very grateful, and he invited me to go out to a restaurant that was famous for their white shrimp dinner.

As we added more savory sauce on our tempura white shrimps, I asked him what he thought about Hakodate Marine.

Kong said, "Hakodate Marine made a killing by going around the world and fishing massive volumes of fish or super expensive types of fish. The founder has been called 'Shark with a GPS' since he was hunting everything he can catch. But now, his son is in charge. The son is a national leisure fishing champion, and his love for fish made his company much more reasonable."

"I think our fishermen would still be very nervous. I'm not sure if this would benefit Hime."

"I know they would hate Hakodate Marine as much as Nanae, but I would suggest that you guys should at least listen to their proposal. Lindsey, this city is in a state of emergency."

After we left the restaurant, we went to a local bar and drank more sake until I felt pleasantly warm. After saying sayonara, instead of going home, I went to the fish market alone.

It was almost midnight.

Even at this hour, there were still a few young men working, cleaning the market by spraying a great deal of water. Some other young men rode forklifts and carried big boxes of ice from ice machine factories. When the junior workers were careless when they held a fish, a senior threw ice cubes at them and yelled, "Hey! The price will get lower if you touch fish that way."

I smiled while I watched this scene. This was their lives. People poured their love and heart into this business. All of us want to save this market.

When I was listening to Kong, I seriously thought about moving forward with Paul. As I stared at the hard-working young men, I knew I would make a deal with him.

Paul was the kind of guy who would do what he had promised, and he would do it quickly. The day after I met with Kong, I asked Paul to send me a business plan. The next day, one arrived in my mailbox. It arrived in a big packet, and there was a note attached to the front of it. It said:

> *The most expensive albacore in the US is a small dish served in Bellagio Hotel in Las Vegas. One serving costs you $500! Just two bites for $500, awesome, isn't it? It comes from Kobe by Hakodate Marine. That's an example of how we like to focus on more high-quality fish rather than shoveling a massive volume of fish from ocean.*

As I read Paul's note, I imagined his cheerful face. He was somewhat nerdy and hated all physical activity, and he had acne scars across his cheeks. But he was very smart, and when he talked, he became much more attractive—he was always logical and strategic, no matter what the topic was, and his eyes glimmered and sparkled. He was also simply fun to be around. On two occasions, he and I got drunk and got into nasty cursing matches with Yankees fans outside Fenway Park. He shouted at them, spewing curses like a machine gun, and overwhelmed them. They lost the appetite for the fight.

When Paul said something, people listened, and they were persuaded to join his side. It took a few dates for me to warm up to him, but once I did, I didn't want to ever stop listening to him. He gave me the feeling that he could truly make things happen.

Right after reading through the business plan, I sent a thank-you email to Paul. Less than a minute later, my iPhone buzzed. Paul wanted to Skype with me. I answered, and his familiar, sunny face filled the screen.

"Hello, Lindsey!"

"Hi, Paul. Thanks for all the information. What's happening in Hakodate?"

"Not much, my friend. So, I heard through the grapevine that you're the de facto leader at Hime. That is awesome! How did that happen?"

"To make a long story short, with so much tension, they needed a non-partisan person in charge. And they asked me to take the role. I wasn't sure if I wanted it at first, but I have asked a few top people there for favors before, so I couldn't turn it down."

"I know they made the right judgement. You always want to be low key, but when you put your heart into it, your passion and your loud voice will move people. They know what they are doing, Lindsey."

"Thank you. I will do my best."

"You think Hakodate Marine can help your people?"

"I think so, and I hope so. My . . . employer has been saying the same thing." I was going to say 'partner' when referring to Ichiro, but changed it to employer because I didn't want Paul to think I was saying 'partner' in the romantic sense. Then, I wondered why I cared what Paul thought. "I won't know for sure if Hakodate Marine is right for us until we start the official discussion," I said quickly, hoping Paul didn't sense my uneasiness.

"Hakodate Marine would love to get a piece of your fish

tank—your fish will be prized around the world, and we'll be able to get you way more money. If you sell a fish for $50 in your region, we can probably sell it for $200 in Manhattan or San Francisco."

"Most people here have never worked for a company before. The culture is very different from Hakodate Marine. That may be difficult for you."

"Lindsey. I want you to remember what I am going to say next." His eyes grew wider, just like they always did before he made one of his persuasive speeches. "If I can do something to make you happy, promise me that you'll tell me. I am a schemer. With my business skill, I'm sure we can find a way to satisfy both Hakodate and Hime."

The way he said it was enchanting to me. I just loved listening to him, loved the way his voice made me feel. Then I thought about what he did to me in the past, the way he dumped me, and some of the enchantment faded away.

"We should have this conversation in person. Why don't you come to Hakodate city? You have never been to Hokkaido in the Big Northern Island, right? I will have Hakodate Marine pay for your trip and anything you would eat here."

"I don't know."

He raised his eyebrows. "Hakodate is the best gourmet city in Japan."

Mr. Manipulative was alive and kicking. He still remembered my soft spot.

"I'll think about it," I said, and then after a quick goodbye, we hung up.

My phone buzzed again right after we hung up. A headline from the local newspaper appeared on my home screen:

"Hime Fish Market is on the verge of bankruptcy."

The association president resigned the following morning.

◀ ▐▌▌▐▌▌▐ ▶

People asked the vice president to take the president's position, but he firmly declined. It seemed that no one would take the job. Moving forward, we would have to depend more on the doyens, who had been directors of the association years ago.

I was frustrated with the way things were going in Hime, but I also felt a responsibility to help. Before, I sometimes spent time daydreaming about my future career in the US, but after the president stepped down, I focused all my energy on Hime.

I knew we had to do something now, otherwise, time would run out.

My daily schedule was packed. I went to the port early in the morning and fished with Ichiro, I taught English in the early afternoon, and I fixed sushi in the evening until the shop closed. After work, I often hosted meetings at the fishery association, where we researched more inter-state mergers and debated about collaborating with Hakodate Marine. I slept three hours at my apartment and three hours on the boat while Ichiro sailed.

Every day I learned new things from each job. The feeling that I was being fully utilized for the community made me feel good. It felt like I was in the right place.

When Ichiro and I were fishing, I was now able to quickly prepare baits, find the fish streets, and lower the lines to our targeted depth. I often competed against Ichiro to see who could catch the most fish, and I sometimes won. Ichiro also loved that I made sushi on the boat for every lunch. The fresh meat made every meal delicious.

At school, the students' average English literacy score continued to rise. We were the number one school in Toyama, and we also entered the top twentieth percentile for the entire country.

At Bamboo Sushi, I got more and more fans. I started making

sake recommendations for my customers. Satisfied customers commonly buy a small cup of sake for their chef. Soon, I started getting multiple cups of sake each day.

My sushi rice got better every day. The taste was still far below Mr. Bamboo, but I trained every day on the boat, too. I also practiced gripping rice. I gripped it hard and soft, increasing the speed and smoothness.

Our meetings at the fishery association were also going well. As a teacher, I was trained in how to properly manage time and how to visualize and find solutions to problems quickly. These skills helped cement our roles as the leaders of the Hime turn-around project. Plus, as the doyens had hoped, people enjoyed our leadership style, and they started asking us to coordinate more meetings.

A few weeks after sending his initial business plan, Paul sent over Hakodate Marine's formal proposal. I called him on Skype right after I received it.

"You're very fast, Paul. My assumption is you have worked super hard behind the curtain."

"I may have greased a few palms, pulled a few strings."

"If the Hime fishery association will not take this proposal, will it affect your credit or promotion? I'd feel guilty if that happened."

"No, don't worry your pretty little head about that. Even getting a foot in the door like this is a huge deal. The fishermen business is the human network business. Even though Hakodate Marine has a great brand name, they have not been able to get a meeting with the fishermen from Hime, since coast fishermen are automatically suspicious of outsiders. So a company like us cannot access coast fisheries like you guys. If it wasn't for you, we wouldn't have even gotten this far." Paul laughed to himself. "Who would have guessed it? The best seafood company in Japan finally gets in at one of the best fish tanks in the world because of two American friends who truly love Japanese fisheries. It's funny how these things work out."

The word 'friends' stuck out to me. It told me that Paul thought this was more than a business deal. I decided to feel happy about that.

I still didn't understand the true depths of Hakodate Marine's proposal, but I imagined that such a big company could easily change the town. I thought about my favorite idyllic Massachusetts fishing towns: New Bedford, Gloucester, and Rock Port. Those places wouldn't remain the same if gigantic Norwegian fishery ships came in. Would Hime lose its heart if I brought in Hakodate Marine?

But then, Kong's voice echoed in my head. This was an emergency, and any options to save Hime needed to at least be discussed. I had to introduce Paul's proposal to the fishery association. I was the only one who could do this.

That night, I invited Hideki, Hana, and a few other fishermen who were looked at as leaders to discuss the issue with me at Bamboo Sushi. Once everyone was there, I explained Paul's proposal. When I finished, there was silence for a moment.

Then, Hideki spoke, "Regardless of whether everyone likes this proposal or not, it is wonderful that we now have a second option. Thank you, Lindsey san."

"Nanae's getting a tighter grip on our neck, and now, we're about to suffocate," I said.

"A seafood company like Hakodate Marine does huge trade with America, China, and the Scandinavian countries," Hana said. "I never imagined that we would work with the big guys, but if they are interested in our fish, it may work out."

I nodded in agreement, realizing that the anti-merger people were now very much interested in the Hakodate Marine deal. The sense of urgency about Hime's impending bankruptcy had caused everyone to think of the deal seriously.

"There's too much on our plates. We have to deal with the war against Godzilla, and we have to really think about how to deal with ITQ. No matter what, the ITQ is coming," a young northern fisherman said. "But managing ITQ is hard work. See, take America for example. Even though they're one of the world leaders in resource conservation, it took thirty-six years for them to implement ITQ after they adopted Magnuson-Stern Fishery Conservative and Management Act in 1975."

"How do you know that?" Hideki asked.

"I've been studying everything I can about ITQ. I have a lot of time since I can't afford to take my boat out to sea these days. Everyone in Japan is excited about ITQ, but we are still not sure if it's truly manageable. For that, some kind of collaboration with Hakodate Marine may benefit us because they can provide guidance on how to manage the ITQ."

It made sense that the northern fishermen were excited about the Hakodate Marine deal—they would do everything they could to avoid merging with Nanae.

Hideki said, "If we hook up with Hakodate Marine, we can have them invest in our infrastructure and buy new ice machines and sanitation water sprinkler systems. We could even get an HACCP license and begin directly shipping our fish to the rest of the world. That will help us grow quickly."

I remembered my grandpa talking about HACCP, short for Hazard Analysis and Critical Control Point. It's an America-led food safety compliance procedure. Since 1997, all seafood coming to the US have to be exported by HACCP-licensed factories or processors. After placing the regulation, America started importing more seafood. But if the fishery's infrastructure is not certified by HACCP, the products need to go through a HACCP factory like ones in Tokyo. That's why there were no direct exports from Hime to the US. Hime only exported fish to a handful of Asian countries where HACCP was not mandatory.

"I disagree," a southern fisherman said. "We can learn from the Alaskan fishery. They have ITQ there, but many people decided to sell or lease their quota to bigger licensors who do more efficient operations. That suggests that a lot of us will also sell the quota to Hakodate Marine."

Everyone looked at me to see if this was true. I nodded, amazed by how much these fishermen were studying to find ways to save Hime. But it also meant that a lot of people had increased their days off due to the stock depletion of the bay.

Another southern fisherman said, "Working with corporations is a good strategy for bringing back our economy. But it also means that fishermen's operations will be absorbed into Hakodate Marine. That's what the Japanese local and central governments want you to do. Fewer boats, more efficiency. I'm not sure if that's something we want to do. When my father started fishing in 1961, there were 700,000 fishermen in Japan. Today, there are only 220,000 working fishermen. See, the government has successfully reduced the number of fishermen working, and they let the corporations who give big donations to their political party retain the fishery volume in Japan. At the end of the day, we all will work for Hakodate Marine."

"You know what, nobody can save the association without Hakodate Marine's investment or loan," a northern fisherman argued. "Further, this almost-dying association will need to hire more accountants to do ITQ for us. It's a no brainer that we have to depend on corporations."

The southern fisherman slapped his hands against the table. "How can you say that? ITQ is our right. Are we just going to give our hard-earned fish to Hakodate Marine?"

the Sea of Japan

In the back of my mind, I heard Mr. Principal say, 'One Hime, One Heart.' This community was so divided, it was hard to imagine them having one heart again.

As the night went on, the discussion got more and more tense. But I continued to stand tall. I still believed that we all needed to have another option, something new. This was something new, something that could save us.

The following day, one of the doyens approached me at the port and said he had heard about the discussion. He told me not to worry about nothing being decided yet. "You should be proud that you were able to move the discussion forward—that's always tough to do with these stubborn fishermen."

"Thank you for saying that, doyen. You know, when I came here about six months ago, I remember looking down at this port from my school and seeing people that worked hard and seemed to always know what they were doing. It looked like rough work, but I could tell there was a strong brotherhood in this market. But now, the possible shutdown of the Hime fishery is destroying the brotherhood."

"This hardship is a mountain we have to overcome. Thank you, Lindsey, for everything you're doing to help us."

Over the next week, we had more heated discussions that would often end with northern and southern fishermen yelling at each other. Sometimes, I would insist that we took breaks where no one was allowed to mention the words "ITQ" or "merger." During that time, we told stories. I talked about my grandpa or New Bedford, which everyone loved. I would also make everyone green tea in the small fishery association kitchen using my own blend of tea leaves.

I would often take a few minutes to look out the discussion room window. Downstairs, I could see the market. It was hard to admit, but it was clearly not as lively as it was before. There were now just 300 fishermen, 200 wholesalers and retailers, and 20 association employees. Every week, we lost about five to ten fishermen.

They were still working hard so that consumers could eat the freshest fish. They seemed to be truly proud of what they did. The only difference between now and last April was that there were no longer hundreds of big pallets filled with fish. Now, there were only ten.

◄▌▐▐▐▐▐▐►

Time went quickly.

I fished, I taught, and I cooked sushi day after day after day, until I couldn't tell one day from another. All three jobs had become almost full-time jobs, on top of my leading fishery association meetings. I wasn't complaining. In fact, I loved everything I was doing, and the days flew by because of it.

Judy started coming to Hime more and more, and she started making friends and building connections in the community. One day, she went out on the boat with me and Ichiro. We had our typical sushi lunch, which Judy loved.

"This is so good, Linds," she said, her mouth full of rice. "We seriously need to think about opening a sushi restaurant in Boston or somewhere when we get back. People would kill for authentic sushi like this."

I smiled. "Thanks, but I'm not that good yet."

"You're too modest." She ate another piece of sushi and then said, "How's the stupid ITQ going?"

"Not great. We tried asking the governor's office to either stop Godzilla or postpone the ITQ implementation. But they wouldn't listen to us. And we're all still debating if we should merge with Nanae or work with Hakodate Marine."

"What's your preference?"

the Sea of Japan

"I personally think the merger with Nanae is the most peaceful and effective solution, but the more I participate in the meetings, the more I realized how much animosity northern Hime residents have against Itokawa. It's crazy, their rivalry goes back to the samurai time. I'm not sure how I can fix a problem that goes back that far."

"I'm sorry things aren't moving as quickly as you'd like. I was thinking, maybe you guys should come with me to Tokyo to see if Hime can learn from their marketing. Your fish is definitely fresher than Tokyo's fish. But marketing wise, to be honest, I think you could do better. You'll know what I mean when you see what they do in Tokyo."

Ichiro and I nodded. Judy continued. "Then, after Tokyo, you should fly to Massachusetts and see their operation. Instead of totally depending on Lindsey's memory, you guys should visit the largest American fishery port once. Learn something from them, too."

"That's a great idea. It would be nice to see my family, too," I said.

"If you do go, I have one request. I want Ichiro to visit my beautiful city of New York and try the pastrami at my parents' deli. I want you to honestly tell me if the Japanese people will like it, and if you think I should try to make pastrami here in Hime with Hime beef."

"We can do that," I said brightly, not wanting to discourage Judy. There were no delis in Japan. While a great deal of American food had been brought to this country, some foods failed to gain popularity. Still, if anyone could make the people of Japan love pastrami, it was Judy.

We headed back to shore, and Judy and I said goodbye to Ichiro and walked over to Olive Bath House. As usual, we sank our bodies into the bath until the tips of our jaws touched the hot water.

Judy, in her usual way, continued on with the conversation like we had never stopped talking. "Americans have sushi fever, and their love for sushi just seems to keep growing. So after Tokyo, Hime should definitely keep an eye on America because New Yorkers or Bostonians may pay more for brand name fish than Tokyo residents, right?"

"I guess so—"

"Right. Also, this will give you a chance to introduce your new boyfriend to your parents."

"Judy, I told you, Ichiro is not my boyfriend. He's my fishing partner."

"Sure, keep telling yourself that." She rolled her eyes and sank completely underneath the water, causing a wave to splash me.

I smiled to myself, thoughts of Ichiro filling my head. But then, before I ever knew what was happening, Ichiro's face was replaced with Paul's. I groaned—what was happening to me? Was I really falling for Paul again?

I didn't want to think about Ichiro or Paul for one second more, so I sank my entire body into the warm water too, until the water washed away all my thoughts.

◀ ▯▯▯▯▯▯ ✖

The next weekend, Ichiro and I went to stay with Judy in Tokyo. Our first morning there, we woke up bright and early and went straight to the world's largest fish market, Tokyo Central Market, where 20 million dollars in deals were made every single day. The place was huge, and Judy explained that 40,000 people worked there, and 20,000 trucks brought in fish from all over Japan.

The size was amazing, but I was more surprised by the hundreds of observers there. The most crowded section was the famous tuna auction. People had to enter a lottery to get a tour of the tuna auction area. The people who were lucky enough to be chosen would get to watch licensed buyers bid for some of the freshest tuna around. Today, I saw many Canadians and Russians waiting to enter the lottery.

"I don't understand why foreign tourists wake up this early and come to the market at 5:00 a.m. There are a lot more things they can see and enjoy in Tokyo," Ichiro said.

"I understand their feeling," I said. "The lively ambience of the market is something special. Especially for Americans and Europeans who don't have a fish auction market in their countries."

After seeing the inside of the market, we were shocked again by the size of the surrounding sushi shops corridor. People came here not only to see the market, but also to enjoy some of the freshest sushi in the world. They were also probably some of the only sushi restaurants in the world to open at six in the morning. Thousands of tourists also shopped in the specialty seafood shops surrounding the market. For seafood lovers, this area was the perfect place to hit on their trip to Tokyo.

"You know what," Judy said as we walked out of one of these specialty shops, "you should copy what they do here on a smaller scale. You could attract tourists to Hime not only with the fish market, but by also putting in restaurants and shops. You just saw the long line for the food, and your food would even be fresher because you catch 500 kinds of fish right in Toyama Bay."

Her voice got louder like it always did when she was passionate about something, and people passing by looked at us.

"I was thinking the same way. Fishery tourism. Seeing and dining. Perhaps we can add something for the tourists to experience," I said, my voice also getting louder as I got more excited.

Judy threw her arms over my and Ichiro's shoulders. "See, folks, that's marketing. Don't narrowly focus on the minutia of the fishery. Let's do a variety of things to attract tourists. Working for the Tokyo Metropolitan Government, I have figured out how Tokyo became Tokyo. It's because they know what tourists want. And now, we'll bring that concept to Hime."

After our fish market tour, Judy took us to some of the more classic tourist sites in Japan. She took us to the Tokyo Tower, the Emperor's Palace, the historical downtown area, and so many old shrines and temples that they all blurred together. Judy seemed to enjoy getting to show us around for a change.

Late in the afternoon, we came across a traditional festival in the business district of Tokyo. People wore old clothes and pulled shrine cars by hand. Musicians and people wearing traditional clothes followed.

"Wow, I've heard about this festival, but I've never seen it in person. It's been around for almost 400 years," Ichiro said, looking entranced.

"See, a festival is another way to attract tourists," Judy said. "Do you have any of those in Hime?"

"Toyoma has a traditional dance from a seventeenth century festival called the Owara Wind Holiday Dance," I said. "It's usually held during the first three days of September, but this year we're also holding it in December because the mayor of Durham, North Carolina—Toyoma City's sister city—is coming to visit. Would you like to see it?"

"Yes, I'd love to. And I bet other American tourists would too. Tell me more about it."

"One of the main events is the Owara dance. Men and women dance together, but they do different moves that still flow well together, creating a unique harmony. The formal dance goes until midnight, and during those hours, only people who are twenty-five or younger can participate. But after midnight, anybody can participate it.

"During the dance, everyone wears a large straw hat so that spectators and their partner can't see the upper half of their face.

Not being able to see the dancers' eyes actually made them look even more beautiful. It's like an exchange of hidden love."

"Hidden love! You've got my attention now," Judy said.

I smiled. "They use a Chinese fiddle for the music, and it creates a slow, sorrowful feeling. Five to fifty young ladies wear beautiful kimonos and dance silently and almost reverently. Male dancers discreetly follow behind the female dancers. Sometimes they dance parallel to each other, and male and female dancers switch positions. As they dance, they move along the street very slowly, and fiddle players and singers follow them. They never touch each other except in one scene."

"What happens then?"

"On this one occasion, a women dancer moves forward, a step ahead of her male partner. He stands behind her, and he places his left hand above her shoulder. Both face forward, not seeing each other. Then, the man extended his palms in front of her, facing up. The woman hesitantly puts the tip of her index finger on his left palm. That's the only time they touch each other in this entire dance. Yet, people always look for that moment, and they seem to understand how much love there is underneath this small move."

"Holy shit!" Judy shouted. "This is it, Lindsey. Hidden love, traditional dances, this festival has everything. All you have to do is make a marketing plan, and then you'll have tons of visitors."

"You're right! I would love to share this festival with other people, it's so beautiful."

"Lindsey and I both love this dance just as much as the native Toyamans," Ichiro said. "Mr. and Mrs. Bamboo have been helping Lindsey learn the Owara dance. She's great at it."

I grinned sheepishly. "I'm not that good yet."

Judy shook her head. "I can't believe how much fascinating cultural stuff there is in Hime. It's like the world's best marketing secret, and I want to share that secret with the world. That's how we can save Hime."

I smiled, happy that she was excited, but my gut twisted too. I hoped that she was right, that this was the key to saving Hime's economy.

After a full day walking around Tokyo, all our stomachs were grumbling, so I suggested that we go to a sushi restaurant. We ended up going to two of them. At both places, I noticed that the fish wasn't as fresh as what we got in Hime. Even the sake tasted less flavorful.

There were also other issues with the sushi, issues I would have never noticed before I started making my own sushi. In the first sushi restaurant, the fish was great, but I didn't like the sushi-rice. It was rather dry. Since they were busy, they didn't lay a cloth over the rice pot, which Mr. Bamboo and I always did. Also, I thought they should have used a bit more vinegar.

In the second shop, the sushi tasted good, but the chef didn't pay attention to the way Judy ate it. She kept her sushi in the soy sauce for a little bit too long. Her sushi rice sucked in too much soy sauce and as a result, the sushi broke into two or three pieces on the soy sauce plate.

"Why are you staring at her sushi?" Ichiro whispered into my ear. We were sitting at the sushi counter, with Judy to my left and Ichiro to my right.

"This isn't good. In Bamboo Sushi, when American customers come in, I serve my regular grip. Then, I watch how they eat it. If they eat it like Judy does, I start gripping my sushi very hard so that the sushi doesn't break up. I don't care if they use a ton of soy sauce or just a drop. Customers should enjoy their sushi in their own way. But a sushi chef should always think about how they can better serve their customer."

Ichiro looked impressed. "You're becoming a real sushi expert."

I blushed, unsure how to respond, so I just simply ate another piece of sushi.

After we finished eating, Judy took us to a small American bar for a nightcap. The place was filled with young Navy seamen from the nearby US base.

As soon as they saw American women, a few of the seamen came over to chat us up. I wasn't in the mood for flirting—I was too busy thinking about what I would have done differently if I made the sushi we ate that night. I responded flatly to the men's comments, and soon, they sensed my disinterest and stopped bothering me.

As the night went on, the bar got even more crowded. Ichiro and I sat at a small table, quietly drinking our whiskeys. But Judy was more outgoing, and she let the men buy her a few whiskeys and gins. Soon, she had a crowd of American soldiers around her, and they talked so loudly I could hear her voice over the din of the crowd.

But then, late into the night, when Judy had had enough drinks to lose her filter, she started ranting about her unfavorable views on war. The soldiers immediately grew hostile, shouting at her, telling her that she was a civilian, she didn't know what she was talking about.

"Let's go help her," I told Ichiro.

Ichiro and I pushed through the thick, sweaty crowd, trying to reach Judy. We got to her just in time to see a soldier spit into her beer mug. "Oops," he said with a cheeky grin.

"You asshole!" Judy shouted, lunging toward him. But Ichiro pulled her back before she could get hurt.

"Judy, let's go," Ichiro said.

Two of the Navy seamen approached Ichiro, eyes red and feet stumbling. It reminded me of my old drunken confrontations between Yankees and Red Socks fans.

"You should keep better control over your woman," one of them said to Ichiro, grabbing his jacket. Ichiro twisted the seaman's hand, and the seaman pulled his hand off Ichiro's jacket.

"We are cool, right? Peace, please," Ichiro said in a low voice.

He seemed so different than the Ichiro I had always known. He was tall. He was solemn. He was as sharp as my master's sushi knife.

The seaman looked like he wanted to say something else to Ichiro, something even more confrontational, but he was distracted by one of his buddies saying, "Who wants shots?"

While he was distracted, the three of us hurried out of the building. Judy stumbled and weaved, too drunk to walk on her own. I held onto her as we emerged into the cool night. I was surprised that Judy was this drunk from just a few drinks, because she used to not get drunk until she was at least five or six rounds in. It made me realize that her tolerance was down because she had seriously cut down on how much she drank. I was proud of her—since college, she had been trying to drink less alcohol, and it seemed like in Japan, she had finally achieved her goal.

We turned the corner onto a small side street that led to the main street. But before we could get to the more populated area, someone behind us shouted, "Hey asshole, you chickened out."

I turned around and saw the seaman who had grabbed Ichiro's jacket. He also had two friends with him. All three of them laughed at Ichiro, who ignored them. This made the soldiers even angrier, and they started cursing and shouting slurs at Ichiro. Ichiro stiffened and seemed to make himself taller. If he wanted to, he could have defended himself. He told me once that he used to practice Judo when he was in high school and at the fishery college. He even got a full scholarship at a PE university to study Judo, but he declined it and went to the fishery college to pursue his dream of becoming an independent fisherman. Still, he had his Judo skills if he needed them. I hoped he wouldn't have to use them now, though, and that this all would end peacefully.

We reached the main road and tried to grab a cab, but Friday night in this district was the worst place to find a taxi. The Ubers were all occupied too.

We started walking east, where we would have a better chance of getting a taxi. Soon, we were in another quiet area, with just a few drunk people wandering around. Still, there were no taxis. The seamen kept following us, and one said something rude about Judy. We kept walking, trying to ignore them.

Then, for the first time, they turned their attention to me.

"Yo, blonde. What's so good about the stinking fisherman?" One of the seaman shouted–Judy must have told them what Ichiro and I did when she was still on friendly terms with them.

Ichiro still ignored them. But I couldn't take it lying down– after all, Bostonians were the undisputed insult champions. "Go away, jerk! You think you look so hot in your uniform, but guess what, you're not impressing anyone. Go back to the base and drink some chocolate milk from your mama's care package."

The seaman leered at me. "Hey, bitch. Is that a Boston accent, whore? How much did the fisherman pay for you?"

Ichiro jumped back and grabbed the guy's jacket, his face contorted with rage.

"Take it back and apologize to her."

"Get your fucking hands off me!"

"I refuse until you apologize to her."

The guy's nostrils flared, and he tried to punch Ichiro in the face. Ichiro ducked quickly, and he threw the guy into the air. The seaman landed on the ground with a hard thump.

The other two seamen rushed toward Ichiro, but Ichiro swayed to the side. He grabbed the seaman closest to him and threw him to the ground. He held the guy's collar with his right hand and his sleeve with his left hand. Then he punched the guy once, twice, three times, his hands blurs. The other seamen tried to ambush Ichiro from behind while he punched the guy on the ground, but Ichiro was too fast for him. He kicked him in the chest without even turning around. Then, he turned around and choked him. Within five seconds, the guy lost consciousness.

"Did he die?" Judy asked, voice quivering.

I put my arm around her shoulder. "No, he's just sleeping for a while."

The two conscious seamen stood and rushed towards Ichiro again. Ichiro threw one of them to the ground and kicked him once. He groaned and clutched his chest. Then, Ichiro grabbed the last standing seaman's shoulder and twisted his arm behind his back. The guy screamed in the pain. Ichiro twisted one more time and released him, and the man cowardly ran away.

Ichiro was furious. I had never seen such deep wrinkles on his forehead or such hatred in his eyes. Ichiro walked toward the seaman who was holding his chest—he was the one who had insulted me. He tried to back away from Ichiro, but Ichiro put a foot on his leg, holding him still.

"How old are you, kid?" Ichiro said.

"Nineteen—" Ichiro grabbed his jaw and pulled it hard. "Nineteen, sir."

"What is the drinking age in Japan, kid?"

"Twenty, sir."

"Show me your ID." The soldier handed Ichiro his ID with a shaking hand.

"I can't read English," Ichiro said, and handed me the ID. It took me a second to realize why Ichiro was lying about not knowing English. But a moment later, I figured out what he meant, and I quickly studied the ID before handing it back to him.

the Sea of Japan

"Okay. Are we good, son?" Ichiro said.

"Yes, sir."

A taxi drove by, and Ichiro flagged it down. As we jumped into the car, I yelled at the soldier, "Good night, Sergeant Anthony Jackson, Department 26, Unit 7th. Navy ID number 6584-58463-49871."

The man's face went incredibly pale. Ichiro and I burst into laughter, and Judy smiled vaguely, clearly too drunk to really understand what had happened.

"That will teach him not to mess with Toyamans or Bostonians," I said.

◀ ▯▯▯▯▯▯ ◀

The rest of our trip to Tokyo was thankfully much more uneventful—we went to tourist sites, ate tons of sushi, and avoided all the bars that the American soldiers loved. After three days in Tokyo, Ichiro and I said goodbye to Judy and flew to America. We planned to go to my parents' house in Boston, then New Bedford to see my grandfather, and finally New York to check out Judy's parents' deli.

After countless hours of plane travel and a long ride in our rental car through Boston's endless traffic, we finally made it to my parents' neat, one-story clapboard house on the outskirts of the city. When my parents saw the car pull up, they ran out of the house and hugged both me and Ichiro tightly.

"It's so nice to meet you, Ichiro, we have the guest room all set up for you," my mom said as we walked into the house.

"Oh no, thank you, but I have a reservation at a hotel. I wouldn't want to impose," Ichiro said.

"Nonsense, you don't need to pay for a hotel when we have a nice room for you here. And it will give us more time to get to know you," Mom said, raising her eyebrows at me.

Keita Nagano

I rolled my eyes. Clearly, Mom thought that Ichiro and I were more than just business partners.

My parents always made a decision about how to treat my guests right after they met them. They believed that the first minutes that you spend with a person can tell you everything about them. Judy did great at this conversation, and my parents instantly loved her. Paul failed miserably.

Ichiro did just as well as Judy at this five-minute test. After my parents met Ichiro, they immediately went to Costco and bought a bottle of Coppola wine and USDA Prime beef on a blue plate. They only cooked USDA Choice beef for their favorite guests. Every time Paul came to our house, the dinner was always chicken.

Dad said he would cook BBQ for Ichiro, and mom would bake a New England apple pie. They liked that Ichiro was a good listener, not a talker, and that he was polite and courteous.

When Mom was slicing apples for her pie, I decided to set the record straight. I sat at the kitchen table and said, "Mom, he is not my boyfriend. I told you. You don't have to do this. He is just a research partner and the employer for my fishery job."

Mom just smiled and said, "Do you know that Ichiro sits straight up in his chair without leaning back? It was hard for me not to laugh when I saw that. Did he come from nineteenth century?"

I knew for sure then that Mom liked Ichiro—she only teased people she was fond of.

As Mom continued cutting apples, I looked at the ingredients for the steak, which were sitting on the counter. Among the usual spices, I noticed a bottle of black sauce. "What is this, Mom?"

"Obviously soy sauce, Lindsey."

"I know, but you've never used soy sauce for steak. I have never seen soy sauce in this house, ever."

"I decided to blend in soy sauce to the steak's marinade a bit. So that Ichiro would feel at home."

I was speechless. They liked him this much already, and I hadn't even told them yet about the time he saved my life.

The early steak dinner was perfect. Dad was as meticulous with his grilling as he was in his day-to-day work as an engineer, and because of that, each steak was perfectly cooked. Mom's new steak sauce also worked out wonderfully.

As usual, Ichiro was exceedingly polite, and he thanked my parents for the dinner three times. He also praised the delicate taste of Mom's sauce and the quality of Dad's steak.

After dinner, Ichiro and I sat on the rocking chairs on the backyard porch, drinking iced tea that I had made.

It was a beautiful sunny midafternoon at the end of autumn.

"I wish I could take you here in mid-autumn. The autumn leaves are beautiful in Massachusetts," I said, looking at the already bare branches in our backyard.

"I would like that," Ichiro said, smiling. "I've only been to one state before, Hawaii, on my honeymoon." He got quiet after that, like he always did when he mentioned his ex-wife. I was still curious about their relationship, but I found it difficult to ask about it.

I looked at Ichiro. He wore a crisp blue jacket and light brown pants with a sharp crease. Under the jacket, he wore a plain white oxford button-down shirt with no wrinkles. He looked warm and gentle. I tried to remember his serious face, the face of a man fighting in the sea. Or, his furiousness when he faced the soldiers who insulted me. Now, his face was simply peaceful.

"Is there something on my face?" Ichiro asked, touching his cheek.

"Oh, no, no, I was just thinking of something else. Would you like more iced tea?"

"That would be great."

He wiped off his lip marks from the glass with a paper napkin before he gave me his glass. I inwardly laughed. That was truly Ichiro.

◀ ▮▮▮▮▮▮ ◀

The next day, we said goodbye to my parents. We were planning to go to New Bedford that evening to see my grandfather, but before we left, I gave Ichiro a quick tour of Boston. We bought a Charlie Ticket Day Pass, which could be used on all the public transportation in Boston, and we went to the Old State House, Boston Massacre Site, Old South Meeting House, and the Boston Common.

I saved the best for last: a one hour tour at Fenway Park. The tour guide took us through the public parts of the ballpark and the parts that were usually only open to the players. We went to the players' lounge, the locker room, and the dugout.

"I've never seen you smile so wide before," Ichiro said as we stood on the dugout.

"I would be even happier if tonight was a game day." I looked out at the sea of empty green seats. When I closed my eyes, I could clearly hear the crowd chanting. *Let's go Red Sox, chan-chan-cha-cha-chan.*

"Wow. It sounds like if I buy opening game tickets for us, you would do anything I ask."

"Of course I would!" I said, my voice rising.

"What would you do if I said I was taking you to a World Series game of the Red Sox?"

"I'd do anything, I'd even marry you!" I screamed.

"That sounds great!" He thrust his right fist into the air, laughing. As the moment passed, I realized what I had said.

Ichiro seemed to realize it too, because he was quiet for a moment. Then, clearly making small-talk, he said, "How are the

the Sea of Japan

Red Sox doing so far? Is there a good chance they'll go to the World Series?"

"Oh, gosh. You are pathetic, Ichiro. The entire baseball season is over. The Giants won again. You know nothing about baseball. I thought you are a Royals' fan."

"That was a gift from my English teacher at Tokamachi."

I sighed loudly. Then, we laughed, and the awkward moment was over, and we were just two friends again. As we walked out of Fenway Park, we discussed what to eat for the late lunch.

Ichiro wanted to go to a place Judy and I usually went, so I took him to Sonsie, at Back Bay. I asked for the table in the far back corner on the left side.

"Now, you will have real Bostonian seafood, Ichiro."

"Is this table special for you?"

"This is the table that Drew Barrymore and her friends dined at in the film *Fever Pitch*."

"Is that right?"

"Well, the movie just used the restaurant's façade, and the inside was a studio set. But while they were filming, Drew Barrymore and Jimmy Fallon came to this restaurant multiple times and ate at this table!"

"You are so loyal to the Red Sox."

"It's not just about the Red Sox—to me, they represent Boston. I'm as loyal to my city and my team as you are to Toyama."

"I hope I am at that level. Your loyalty is so pure and it shines beautifully."

"Oh, you have to see me lining up for cannolis at Mike's Pastry. There are almost always about ten to thirty people in line. It also has more than 7,000 reviews on Yelp, and most of them are positive. We should go there for dessert! There, yes I will shine like a dazzling summer sun!"

"I'm glad that I came to Boston. Seeing you in Boston is like seeing a freshwater fish coming back to the river after venturing into saltwater."

I smiled, glad I could share this part of myself with Ichiro.

We shared two plates: grilled flounder with apple sauce and finely chopped French cabbage, and seared halibut with smoky seasoning, topped with a zesty corn relish with a side of fresh steamed broccoli. The seafood was delicious, so delicious that Ichiro couldn't stop talking about it.

He was still talking about it later that afternoon, when we drove to New Bedford to see my grandfather in our rental car.

"There has to be a way we can recreate that flounder dish using fish from Hime," he said as I merged lanes.

"Give it a rest," I said, pushing his shoulder.

My phone buzzed—Mom was calling. I answered, and she said, "Tell me the truth, Lindsey. Did Ichiro really stay in the guest room?"

"I think so, I mean, he was at breakfast this morning. Why?"

"I went in this afternoon to tidy up but the room was perfectly clean and I couldn't see any evidence that he stayed. The shower floor is clean and dry. The bed seemed to be almost untouched. There is nothing in the trash box."

I looked over at Ichiro, wanting to tell him about the bizarre conversation. But he had closed his eyes. So I quietly said, "Fishermen in Japan never leave trash in their boats. They carry plastic bags, and they put all their trash in the bag and bring it home. That's how they treat their boats. I guess Ichiro felt like he should treat your guest room the same way."

"Your grandfather is going to love that."

"I'll make sure to tell him."

We hung up, and I quickly glanced at Ichiro, asleep in the passenger seat. This guy saved my life. Sometimes, it felt like no matter what I did, I could never repay him for that.

the Sea of Japan

We reached New Bedford, and I drove over the bridge that connected the downtown to nearby Fish Island. The bridge had a pedestrian path, and at the top, there was a spot where you could see the whole town. I wanted to show it to Ichiro, so I parked the car and gently woke him up. Ichiro was still half-asleep as we walked up the bridge.

At the top of the arc of the bridge, we stopped and looked out at the town spread before us. My eyes were immediately drawn to the port. It was the largest commercial fishery port in the US, and many big ships were stationed there. What made New Bedford different from other ports in the US and Hime was their multiple freezing warehouses. The warehouses were built on the edge of the pier along the river, and each warehouse was the size of NASA's garage for space shuttles. Thousands of tons of fish were stored here, frozen and ready to be shipped to all fifty states and international markets. I regretted that I had never paid attention to those warehouses before. I instantly felt that they were going to give us a hint to how we could turn Hime around.

Even this high up, I could smell the fresh sea air and hear the sounds of fishermen refurbishing their boats. All these sensations reminded me of my happy memories here.

When we got back to car, it was 4:00. By this time, Grandpa was usually done fishing and at home. I went straight to his house on Centre Street, which has a slight slope and faced the New Bedford Harbor. Grandpa lived just down the street from the world's largest whaling museum. The ten blocks around New Bedford Harbor were registered as a Whaling National Historical Park by the National Park Service. When I told Ichiro that, he got excited. He said he had read *Moby-Dick* by Herman Melville and watched the movie, too.

Carrying our suitcases, Ichiro and I walked up to Grandpa's house. He answered after one knock. "Hello, Lindsey! My darling!"

"Hi, Grandpa!"

We exchanged a strong hug. The smell of the sea coming off his dark gray cable knit fishermen sweater immediately brought me back to my childhood.

Grandpa was a big guy, and he was also fond of exaggerating his movements, so he always took up the most space in any room he was in. He also claimed that the smile he wore when he saw me was the biggest in all of human-kind. Every time he smiled, his thick white and silver mustache spread over his lips.

I bought his favorite chocolate mousse cannoli at Mike's Pastry. When he saw it, he gave me another strong hug. Ichiro whispered into my ear in Japanese, "You were shining as much a summer dazzling sun when you ate your cannoli, and now, so is your grandfather."

I winked at him and introduced Ichiro to Grandpa.

"I've been looking forward to meeting you," Grandpa said. "I've heard a lot about your operation in Hime from my son and daughter-in-law. Would you two be interested in going out with me on my boat tomorrow?"

"I would be honored. I've been looking forward to seeing your boat since I first heard about it from Lindsey," Ichiro said.

Grandpa clapped Ichiro on the back. "You certainly know how to get on an old fisherman's good side. Alright, it's settled. Tomorrow, we work hard out on the sea, but tonight, we're drinking whiskey. Come on, hurry inside, I'm not getting any younger."

Ichiro and I grinned at each other and followed Grandpa inside.

◄ ||||||||||◄

The next morning, we went out on Grandpa's boat right after sunrise. His current boat was just slightly larger than Ichiro's, and he had one employee who helped with his fishing. He always threw

the Sea of Japan

a huge net into the ocean and trawled it while sailing for one hour or two. Then, he pulled the whole net out. It was called the drum seiners method, and it was good for catching ground fish.

As soon as Ichiro got on Grandpa's boat, he put on his serious fishing face, the one I hadn't seen since we left Hime. He checked out the sailing system, GPS, fish radar, temperature gage, and the trawling equipment.

When Grandpa completed his first trawl, Ichiro asked for permission to help him. Or, more accurately, he begged him to help. If Ichiro didn't look so nervous, I would have laughed at that.

Grandpa nodded, his expression just as serious as Ichiro's. They both seemed to view this as some sort of test. Ichiro rolled up his sleeves and started working, and Grandpa watched over him. Grandpa looked impressed as he watched Ichiro prepare ice from the ice storage and handle the ropes and the net. After two trawlings, Grandpa started breaking up ice for all the fish they caught.

"I like you, kid," Grandpa said to Ichiro. Grandpa was a very straightforward man. "You seem to truly love the ocean and fishing."

"Yes, sir. I'm not a natural born fisherman. I had to work twice as hard to keep up with peers. And when I did that, I found myself loving the ocean and fishing much more than the others do."

Grandpa nodded deeply, contemplating that for a while. Then, for the first time, he offered to shake hands. Ichiro's eyes filled with joy.

After the fourth trawling, we decided to go back to the harbor. On the way, Grandpa asked Ichiro to explain the purpose of our trip to New Bedford. I was a bit offended because I had explained it to him already, but then Grandpa explained that he wanted Ichiro to talk more about the fishery. Ichiro explained the sense of urgency in Hime because of the historical production decline,

— 137 —

the population decline, ITQ, and the attacks from Nanae port. He also said that, for reasons we still didn't completely understand, we had become the leaders of this project.

Grandpa carefully listened to Ichiro.

"Okay, son. I think what you will see later may help you out," he said.

Soon, the boat reached the shore. After tying up his boat, Grandpa immediately took his fish to the auction house, which was just 100 feet away from the sea. Every fisherman understands how important it is to quickly bring fish to a freezer warehouse.

While Grandpa took care of his fish, Ichiro and I wandered around the auction site. It was a totally different system from Hime's market auction. There were many Spanish-speaking employees in the big freezing warehouse, waiting to receive the incoming fish. They moved our fish containers to the ground, then drove them into the warehouse.

After all of our fish were carried inside, Grandpa met back up with us, and we went into the office where the fish auction was happening. As we climbed the stairs, I got an email from Hideki. I read it to Ichiro.

"Hideki says that the central government of Japan rejected our request to postpone ITQ."

"We had anticipated that. No surprise."

"He also says Hime lost ten fishermen yesterday."

"No surprise there either," Ichiro said, sighing. "But I have hope. We'll learn more here, and we'll bring all our knowledge back to Hime."

In the auction office, there were about twenty people sitting behind a long table, and there were two big screens showing data, like airline departure and arrival screens.

"What are they doing, Grandpa? I don't see any auction happening."

"This is the auction."

"But the fish aren't here."

"These people are buyers. They deal with a significant volume of fish. They don't have to see the fish. They just make a bid over the electronic data."

Ichiro and I glanced at each other, matching looks of confusion on our faces.

"Sir. How can you buy fish without seeing them?" Ichiro asked.

"Good question, Ichiro." It was the first time he called Ichiro by his name instead of 'son' or 'kid.' "I understand you people eat a lot of raw fish, so it makes sense that you need to see the fish. You want to make sure you're getting the freshest fish for your sushi or sashimi. But in this country, the majority of fish bought will be cooked. Most fish here are bought by seafood processing and distribution companies. Then, the fish go to companies like Jason Foods or Ocean Beauty, where it's fried or grilled and then frozen before it's sold to consumers. So, to better cater to these types of consumers, you want to give them more information. Just like anything else in the world, the data will determine the value at the end of the day."

Ichiro stood behind the table and stared at the buyers' backs, studying how they reacted to the information. They were all very patient. When there was no new information, everyone was quiet, and they simply sipped their coffee and waited. But once there was a new entry on the screen, they started calling their bosses.

Ichiro seemed like he wanted to spend some time studying this totally different auction system, so I told Ichiro that I would drive Grandpa home and come back to get him.

After dropping Grandpa off at home, I drove to a small beach where I played when I was a toddler. I always tried to find shells. Grandpa told me to find a shell that would fit nicely against my ear, and then, I could talk to anybody I wanted.

"Lindsey, if you talk into the shell, Grandma will say something back to you," he used to say.

I missed Grandma so much back then—she had passed away when I was a baby. I talked with her for hours, sitting on the sand and staring at the waves.

Now, I walked along the familiar beach until I found a beautiful round pink shell. I sat down in the sand and talked to Grandma and my parents. I asked them if they were still arguing. They said they still did, but they were much better off.

I asked them how long I should stay in Hime. They just said I should do the right thing for me. I tried to think of a response, something that conveyed how much I missed them. But I couldn't think of what to say. Finally, they said to me, "This is your life, Lindsey."

I thought about this conversation on the drive back to the auction house. I wished that I could have a real conversation with them, rather than just one through a shell.

When I reached the auction house, Ichiro was still watching the bidding process. When he saw me, he said, "I love how they bring modern technology into the auction process. I do like Hime's more old-school way of doing things, but I have to admit, this is more efficient."

I nodded, thinking about how the Hime auction worked. Starting every day at 5:00 a.m., 200 blue cap wholesalers went to one corner of the market and looked at a big blackboard that listed the day's fish intake. All the workers carried cell phones, and as they looked at the board, they called their bosses and told them what was available. When the auction started, there was no time for them to consult with their bosses.

There were also ten market employees in red caps standing near the blackboard. Once they had a large amount fish, they started the auction. Their voices had a unique rhythm. It was like they were singing high-pitch karaoke, and they moved their body with the beat. The people in blue caps raised their hands or used their fingers to tell the red caps their bidding prices. The blue caps didn't want the other blue caps to see how much they were bidding, so they made sure that their hands could only be seen by the red caps. The only rule was you just wore a blue cap when you were bidding. If a buyer wasn't interested in a particular fish, they're expected to remove their cap. The auction system in Hime was a unique blend of orderliness and chaos, but it somehow worked.

Ichiro and I ended up staying until the auction closed, studying the nuances of it. We also took a quick trip through the big freezing rooms where the fish were stored. Then, we went back to Grandpa's house. We decided to go out to dinner at Grandpa's favorite place, Seafront Grille. It was in an area called Homers' Wharf, which was where Grandpa's boat and many fishing boats were stationed. In daytime, there were always men and women on the docks, working on their boats.

The restaurant sat in front of the wharf. It was an exceptionally warm day, so we sat on the terrace and relaxed in the gentle late autumn breeze.

"So, how did you like the auction house, Ichiro?" Grandpa said, and I couldn't help but notice that, yet again, he had asked Ichiro an important question, not me.

"Yes, it was very interesting for me, sir. Thank you for taking me there," he said. I noticed that he said 'me' instead of 'us,' which also bothered me.

As if he read my mind, Ichiro quickly added, "We felt like it gave us a big hint, sir. When we were driving back to your house, Lindsey and I talked about what we learned there. We agreed that we still need the visual live auction to sell the best quality fish to Hime's local consumers. But, we should also find ways to sell larger quantities of fish to buyers who don't need to examine the fish in person. The sushi chefs we sell to need to look at the fish, but they only make up half of our buyers. The other half will cook the fish, so freshness isn't as big an issue. Many consumers will be just okay with buying previously frozen fish at a much lower price."

"That's what I thought."

"After that, Lindsey and I walked through the big freezing rooms, and we saw how well-controlled they were. People who bought the fish at the upstairs auction could always go downstairs and check the actual freshness of the fish if they needed to. I thought this was very effective."

"Good. So, what are you going to propose to the people of Hime?"

"I would like to propose a hybrid fish market," Ichiro said. "Combining what we saw today with what Hime already does. That way, we can still manually handle brand fish, and at the same time, we could bring the operation expenses down by deploying this type of digital auction. Once our auction is digitized, we can create an online system where buyers from all over Japan can participate."

Ichiro's eyes were filled with hope and excitement, and I felt like I had the same look in my eyes. This could truly be the key for saving Hime.

Grandpa leaned toward Ichiro, completely forgetting about the existence of both his beloved lobster sandwich and his granddaughter. "That would boost the demand volume, and perhaps more fishermen would come to Hime. It's a win-win situation for everyone."

"Right," Ichiro said, grinning. Both men lifted their beers and clinked them together.

Ichiro left to use the restroom, and Grandpa said, "You found a good boyfriend. He is much better than the self-claimed bigshot what's-his-name."

"Oh my god, Grandpa, that's Paul. Ichiro is nothing like that. He is just a fisherman I work for."

"Oops, sorry," Grandpa said, but his mischievous expression told me he wasn't sorry at all.

"I'm doing three jobs: fishing with him, teaching English, and working at a sushi restaurant."

"You make sushi? That can't be too hard. You're just cutting fish, right? You don't have to bake it, steam it, or even add sauce."

"Grandpa, it takes real skill to make sushi, and it's easier than you'd think to tell the difference between well-made and poorly-made sushi. You have to cut the fish just once, quickly, right before you serve it. This prevents too much oxygen from getting into the fish meat and changing the taste. And it's not that easy to make good sushi rice either. You have to have a good recipe, and you have to know the right way to mix it. It takes anywhere from three to ten years to master the technique."

"Wow—I can't believe I am receiving a lecture about fish from my own granddaughter."

I realized then why Grandpa kept talking exclusively to Ichiro about fishery-related issues—he didn't understand how seriously I was now taking fishing. The best way to show Grandpa that I was a serious fisherwoman was to make him sushi. "How about tomorrow I'll make you sushi on your boat? Okay?"

Grandpa grinned. "I would love that. I can't believe my granddaughter is going to cook sushi for me."

I smiled too and was about to respond, but then, my eye was caught by two fish swimming in a fish tank. They were about two feet long, and their upper body was a beautiful red silver and the lower silver.

"Those are red seabream, right?" I asked Grandpa.

"Right."

"Red seabream is wonderful sushi fish. Very expensive. I can tell that those fish were raised naturally, not at a fish farm."

Grandpa raised his eyebrows. "You're right. How did you know that?"

"The tail fin is a beautiful shape. Farm-raised red seabreams' fins are normally damaged by the nets used at the farms."

"I am impressed. The owner received the fish as an anniversary gift from his friend. We call them husband fish and wife. It is rare that fish couples stay together, but red seabream are the exception. Giving a pair of red seabreams is a way of saying that you hope you stay together forever."

I watched the couple swim around for a while, and then I noticed that Grandpa was also watching them. I also realized that Grandpa always took the same chair, the one that faced straight toward this fish tank. I wondered if he was thinking about his wife as he saw these two fishes. It almost sounded too sentimental to be real.

As I watched the fish swim around and around, I thought of my adopted parents and my biological parents. Both couples always stayed together, even though they argued frequently. They never even thought about getting divorced—even when they were having troubles, they couldn't imagine a life without their partner.

◄ ||||||||||| ◄

After spending the morning out on Grandpa's boat, Ichiro and I said goodbye to him and headed down to New York to see Judy's parents. On the way there, Ichiro and I couldn't stop talking about our plans to reform Hime's auction system. I had never seen Ichiro this excited before, and he said the same thing about me. We talked about the best ways to propose the digital-physical hybrid auction to the fishery association, and we also discussed how we could attract new buyers.

"In order to cultivate new big buyers, you need to have a certain volume of fish available every day. That's what people in Hime always say, and that's why they don't think we can attract the big companies," I said. "But with the digital system, I think the new big buyers in Tokyo will have no problem with the fact that we won't always have the same volume of our rare brand fish because they will be informed far in advance through the website."

"Right. We should call it expectation control," he said.

"And you know what, Ichiro, with this new platform, we will have the upper hand against both Nanae and Hakodate Marine. I think with this distribution change and the fishery tourism that we learned in Tokyo, we will be able to develop Hime itself into a new brand. It's going to be a new resort town. We will be the source of the marketing, and we will be much closer to the consumers than Nanae and Hakodate Marine. Then, after three years of building ourselves up, we will partner with Nanae and Hakodate Marine. Our fishery association will get doubled, and Hakodate Marine will place a big investment into our port. New technology and new infrastructure."

"That's it, Lindsey!" Ichiro almost shouted. "That is a happy medium for both northern and southern Hime fishermen. This idea is great because it belongs to no side. Both the northern and southern fisherman can claim a victory."

We were still grinning and our adrenaline was still running high as we reached the outskirts of New York City. We drove through the traffic slowly, until we finally reached the exit closest to Judy's parents' deli shop in the Upper West Side. Once there, we parked in a parking garage and then walked over to their shop.

Judy's mother shook Ichiro's hand and gave me a big, warm hug. "Thank you, Lindsey, for taking care of our daughter in Japan."

"Oh, no, Judy, is taking good care of me," I said.

"Take a seat, I'll fix you something to eat," Judy's mom said, motioning towards the sitting area in the back of the shop. The deli had fifty seats—about the average size of the classic New York delis. Judy's mom noticed that I was looking around the shop, and she said, "New York has always been the home of Jewish delicatessens. But since many Jewish people are now moving out to the suburbs, we are having a tough time surviving."

"But your deli is always full and always has a long line to buy food."

"Yes, but the rent in Manhattan just keeps going up and up. Many great deli owners closed down their shops and left Manhattan not because they were losing business, but because of the rent."

We ate both corned beef and pastrami on rye bread. Ichiro loved them both very much.

"I can see why Judy wants to make pastrami out of Hime cows, it would probably be incredibly fresh," I said to Ichiro.

"Hime has its own type of cow? I never heard about that," Ichiro said.

"I heard about it from Judy. The production is not huge, but people in neighboring cities come to Hime to buy beef from this particular type of cow. The last time she was in town, Judy visited the farm and learned that the farmer uses pure well water from the Tateyama Mountains, which helps make their meat tasty. She also learned that Hime beef is ranked as top quality, just like USDA Prime. And Judy learned that they feed the Hime cows Niigata brand rice."

I stressed the Niigata part, and sure enough, Ichiro's smile grew. "Then, I am sold on this beef."

We should do this in Hime as a part of our tourism fishery plan, I thought. People would come to Hime to eat fish. But in order for us to have them stay one more day, we needed beef. So we could provide our guests with corned beef and pastrami made locally. Tourists would love it—where else in Japan would they find classic New York deli food?

I tapped on the table, my heart and head both racing as I made plans on how to get all these new tourists to Hime. I had never felt this much energy in my life.

We were headed back to Japan that night, and I couldn't have been more excited to get back. We had work to do.

◄ ||||||||||| ►

When we returned to Hime, Ichiro and I called for a special meeting at the fishery association.

Before the meeting, we met with just the doyens at the dining shop above the auction market.

"Last night, the prefecture government of Toyama officially refused to put the ITQ on hold," one doyen told us, confirming our worst fears.

"How many fishermen are coming to today's meeting?" I asked.

"All of them. All 290 fishermen have received the invitation, along with all 200 blue caps and 20 red caps. And since this meeting is hosted by you two, not the association, I know they will all come. They are excited to hear your new proposal, and we're excited too. We hope this third option will break through the gridlock."

Soon, it was time to start the meeting. The doyens, Ichiro, and I all moved to the large dining room we had booked in the association building. When we got there, there were more than 500 people already seated. When Ichiro and I entered the dining room, we received a big round of applause.

"Thank you," I said as I bowed to the crowd. I felt like I had been gone for a long time, but I had now returned home.

I explained what we saw in America. Then, I moved onto our proposal. "Now, let us humbly explain what we have put together. It's not the northern plan or the southern plan, but something entirely different."

Everybody leaned forward, and some people whispered to each other.

"Let's call it the Operation Tripod," I said, changing my serious tone to a more positive one. I tried to make my smile big enough that the people sitting in the last rows could see it. Ichiro grinned too.

I showed them my fifty page PowerPoint presentation, which took an hour to get through. When I looked around, everybody was concentrating, nobody zoning out or whispering to their neighbors. The issue had become literally life or death. No industry in the world had ever survived its revenue dropping to 20 percent of the previous year.

"In a nutshell, we will start by implementing the online auction and using marketing to attract tourists to Hime," I said at the end of the presentation. "After three years, we will merge with Nanae and embrace Hakodate Marine. The beauty of it is all three are related to each other, and when these three get united, it will give us a significant advantage over even the special third license ports."

"So three entities will be united as one? One supports the other?" someone from the crowd asked.

"That's right. However, I understand that many people are worried that Nanae and Hakodate Marine will not provide us with our fair share. So, we've decided that we want to sit in the drivers' seat. That's why we need to gain the upper hand against the other two in phase one. Then, we will make a fair collaboration."

Many people nodded. One fisherman asked me to summarize each phase of the plan one more time.

"Sure. We have to earn our initial investment money to get an advantage over Nanae and Hakodate Marine. If we create a good enough business plan, I am sure some financial institution will lend us money even in this catastrophic situation. Then, with money collected from tourism and shipping more to Tokyo or Osaka, we will set up the online auction. We'll also use the money to do more marketing. Even if we don't catch any more fish than usual, the value still goes up and the sales go up.

"That is phase one. In phase two, we'll implement HACCP. When we're certified with HACCP, we will be able to export processed seafood directly to America. Throughout Japan, there are 252 seafood companies who are already certified with HACCP, but there are none in Toyama and Itokawa. Because of that, our products have mainly been exported to Thailand and China. Having an HAACP certification will allow us to grow our international market.

"By the time we hit phase three, our tourism industry should be booming, and we should have an international export account with the US. Then, we'll invite Nanae and Hakodate Marine to join us on this Operation Tripod. By that point, we won't need them anymore, and that's the key to getting a good deal. We don't need to merge with Nanae, and we don't have to work with Hakodate Marine. We'll be on equal footing, and we'll have leverage.

"At that stage, we'll also be able to start growing even more. We'll ask Hakodate Marine and other seafood corporations to make an investment or loan us money, and we'll build the gigantic freezing warehouse I showed you in my pictures from New Bedford. By phase three, we'll be able to grow from 33 million pounds of fish to possibly 330 million pounds fishery volume. We'll hopefully be able to attract about 400 new fishermen, so we can go back to the level of 700 as we were in late 1980s. Our declining population of Hime can grow from 50,000 back to 80,000. My

Hime Junior High School will not have to merge with the other school. Our kids won't have to make a ridiculous two-hour bicycle trip to school each way. We can even have more students, more schools, and we will win the national high school baseball tournament again!"

All the fishermen laughed—fishermen in Japan love baseball.

"Is it going to be an exclusive agreement with Hakodate Marine?" someone asked, sounding enthusiastic.

"Very good question. The answer is no. We're going to try to get other big seafood process companies from America or Europe to bid for the license to operate a big process factory. That's phase four or five. We'll also invite them to invest in additional corporate fisheries. My hope is that, by this phase, Hime will be the largest fishery base for all of the Sea of Japan, including Chinese ports."

The fisherman and the doyens clapped and cheered. For the first time, everyone seemed to have hope. We could really do this—we could save Hime.

After the meeting, the doyens came up to me and asked me to work as the sole leader for this project. They suggested that Ichiro and Judy assist me in deepening our business plan.

"We'd also like to pay you for this work," one doyen said, and then he named the price he wanted to pay. It was a big fee, more than our expected travel expenses.

"I'm honored, but I don't need money. I just want to help Hime."

"There's no use arguing, we're giving it to you. This has to do with Hakodate Marine, it has to do with America, and it has to do with Hime. Only you can do this," the doyens said.

"Doyens. I didn't mean to earn money for this," I said, knowing my face was turning red. Did everyone think I was just doing this to get more money for myself?

One doyen put a hand on my shoulder. "We knew you would

say that. Don't worry. You are our proud fisherwoman who cares for our community."

I smiled, my panic quickly receding. The doyens unanimously approved the motion to pay me. I told the doyens I would use the money for my trips to negotiate with potential partners who would help us with our fishery tourism and online auction. I also mentioned our future Hime beef pastrami business.

As the fishermen exited the room, I felt good, so good that I grabbed Ichiro's hand tightly. Ichiro looked at me with surprise, but I stared straight ahead, my heart pounding.

When most of the fishermen had left, Ichiro and I sat down to talk about what had happened. An association clerk kindly brought us strong coffee.

"We had anticipated a big resistance for losing independence, hadn't we?" Ichiro said, sipping his coffee. "But having the upper hand against both Nanae and Hakodate Marine changed their mindset."

"It makes sense, I guessed that this was the only way to change their minds. I realized that getting the upper-hand before making friends is an effective strategy."

"That's how America makes peace with others," Ichiro said, smirking, and I hit his shoulder.

Ichiro and I sipped coffee and looked around at the remaining fishermen. They were all so different—some young and new to fishing, some grizzled with skin like leather from years on the sea. Some were from the north, and some from the south, but now, they were all joyous. I now understood Mr. Principal's remarks: "Harmony is the power. One Hime, One Heart."

I named Operation Tripod from the hint I got from his remarks.

After finishing my coffee, I headed over to the restaurant for my shift there. When I walked in, I found Mr. and Mrs. Bamboo waiting for me. They told me they had heard about the meeting, and they were excited about the idea.

Before we started preparing the restaurant for dinner, Mrs. Bamboo brought out her homemade chocolate tuxedo cheesecake. It was a huge, round dessert with layers of fudge cake, chocolate cheesecake, vanilla mascarpone mousse, and thick dark chocolate.

"Let's celebrate, Lindsey," Mrs. Bamboo said, cutting out three large pieces.

"A blue cap vendor told me that you think Americans will travel all the way to here to try our sushi! They're all going to go crazy for Toyoma Bay Sushi, I'm sure they've never tasted any sushi that's so fresh before," Mr. Bamboo said, swinging around his fork, flinging pieces of cheesecake into the air.

I agreed with him—there was no sushi in the world that was as fresh as our sushi. Toyama Bay Sushi was an official registered name by the Toyama prefecture. It was a ten-piece sushi, and to qualify, all the fish meat and the water had to come from Toyoma, and the sushi rice also had to be produced in Toyama. There was no other place in the world where the entire sushi was prepared with local fish, local rice, and local water.

Once we were finished with our cheesecake, we opened up the restaurant, and the night took on a familiar rhythm. After we closed up the shop, I called Judy and formally asked for her help on behalf of the Hime fishery association. I also told her that we wanted her to bring her American deli food to Hime. She loved the idea of Operation Tripod, and she said she would come to Hime next Saturday morning.

I met her at the train station, and we walked over to one of the tea shops near the train station, Tomato Café, to talk. "Thanks for making the trip down here."

"No problem. Anytime you need me, I'm here. You've inspired me, Lindsey. I've decided to follow my dream and bring my parents' deli to Japan, exclusively using Hime beef. My parents have been talking about opening a Japanese branch of their deli nonstop since you and Ichiro visited them. I sent them some Hime beef the other day. They just fell in love with it–they said it's soft and scrumptious and just perfect for their pastrami.

"And that's not all my news. If all goes well, I'm going to move to Hime! I've been talking to the owner of the biggest cattle ranch in Hime, and he's all for me using his beef in my pastrami. I've already started working on a new recipe, and I'm going to check out a space that's for rent today."

"Judy, that's amazing," I said. "What about your job at the governor's office?"

"I gave him my resignation, and he asked me if I would come in one day a week to do his personal assistant duties–all expenses paid, of course. I accepted that offer."

"Wow," I said. "I can't believe we're going to live in the same town again."

"I know, it will be just like college, but with less debauchery." Judy laughed, but then her expression quickly turned serious. "Lindsey, you have to establish a formal business plan. Without that, you cannot proceed with any collaboration discussion, and you can't negotiate finances, or design your online auction and fishery tourism campaign."

"We want you to help us with that, if you're willing. I can't think of anyone better for the job," I said. "Now, with the Operation Tripod, the Hime fishery association formally plans to visit Nanae fishery association to discuss our future merger. Even though we still have three years until we reach that point, we want to start the negotiations and preparations now, because getting a peace treaty with Nanae will stop them from depleting our fishery stock. It will also reduce the negative impact on us for ITQ. We could even make Godzilla remove all the Itokawa vessels from

Toyama Bay with his political power. That will help us bring the quota calculation back to the normal range."

"You have to make Hakodate Marine excited about the future collaboration with Hime, too. But again, I want you to try to find someone else besides Paul to negotiate with."

"I will try," I said, but I was lying. I knew there was nobody in that company who could make it happen but him.

"You have to make them invest in us even though the joint operation won't start until the third phase. It's a very tough sell."

I noticed Judy used 'us,' which made me grin. She was officially on our team.

"We'll pretend that we can take or leave Hakodate Marine as a negotiating tactic, but in reality, we need them more than they need us." As I said that, I realized I had to sit down and talk with Paul sometime soon. "I don't really want to discuss much about our phase one and two plans with Nanae or Hakodate Marine, but I'm worried that they'll hear rumors about it soon. So I'm thinking it would be better if I just went and talked to them so they can hear everything from the source."

"You should talk to the leaders in Nanae, but I don't know if you should handle Hakodate Marine. You're walking a very fine line between personal and professional there."

"I have to do it, no one else can."

Judy sighed. "Fine, but you need to be careful. Don't let yourself get hurt."

"I understand."

"No, you don't understand. Because I'm afraid of what will happen when you see Paul again. And I'm even more afraid that you're lying to me when you say that you're trying to find someone else to work with."

Three jobs kept me busy, but my hope that Operation Tripod would save Hime gave me energy and kept me moving forward. I felt more excited than before, and I was especially thrilled about how quickly our plans were coming together. Judy and I hammered out a business plan the weekend she visited, and by the time she went back to Tokyo, we were ready to put it into action. Our fishery tourism officially started and made its first sales on the next day of the meeting. The online auction system development kicked off on the same day, too, and we learned that the prototype would be available within three weeks.

Every time I went into town, men and women thanked me. They gave me homemade pies, cookies, fruits from their backyard, and invited me to dinner at their home.

Bamboo Sushi had more customers than ever before because fishermen sent their friends and guests to us. At Hime Junior High School, students started talking about Operation Tripod in their English classes. They thought speaking about the most pressing issues for their town was a great way to learn English. But, one student told me that their favorite thing was still sending letters to the Hollywood celebrities.

Everything was going well in Hime, but the hardest parts were yet to come: negotiating with Nanae and Hakodate Marine. A week after the meeting where we put Operation Tripod into action, I called Paul and set up an appointment.

The night before I was supposed to leave for Hakodate, Judy came over for tea. She was still living in Tokyo, but she had come into Hime for a few days to sign the rental papers for her shop. As we drank our green tea, she told me that she had been in contact with someone from Hakodate Marine—a friend of a friend—and she had learned more about Paul's role in the company. He had started as an outside advisor there, but since he had connected Hakodate Marine with Hime, he became more valued. The CEO of Hakodate Marine openly started praising Paul in their newsletters, and he started hanging out with him outside of work.

"Paul has become almost a shadow cabinet chief," Judy said. "And a big part of that is this deal with Hime. I'm not sure if he's going to like the idea of waiting three years to start the partnership with Hime. He's probably going to try and get you to accept his original proposal."

"I know what you mean. But I haven't made any promises to him. I'm leaving for Hakodate tomorrow."

"Do you want me to go with you?"

"No, I think it's best if I go alone. Even if things haven't always been so great with him in the past, I should at least thank him for his proposal. Without it, I wouldn't have gotten this far. And we still need Hakodate Marine to join us in three years, so I don't want to burn a bridge."

I didn't say that the real reason I hadn't asked Judy to join me was that I knew she would get angry at Paul and possibly even shout at him. Judy could be very emotional, especially when confronting someone who had hurt someone she loved.

"I thought you said that if Hakodate Marine doesn't ride with you, you can invite other big fishery corporations?"

"Not quite yet. In three years, once we're more established, then we can shop around. But at this point, we still need Hakodate Marine to make a statement saying that Hime and Hakodate Marine will enter a strategic alliance, the first kind in Japanese fishery history. That agreement will make Godzilla stop what he's doing now. If we lose Hakodate Marine now, we won't be able to put pressure on Nanae. Godzilla would have the upper-hand again."

"Got it. You know, you call this Operation Tripod, but it doesn't feel like all three legs are equal."

"Maybe so. The true shape of tripod will come later when

everybody becomes comfortable and starts trusting each other. Every tripod in the world is wobbly at first. You need to adjust the legs before you can use it, and that always takes some work."

"I see."

"So that's why I need to see Paul in person. I need to make sure everything is good between Hime and Hakodate Marine so I can get Nanae on our side."

"Be careful. I don't trust Paul at all."

"Well, he ditched me once, but he can't ditch me twice," I said, smiling, but Judy didn't laugh.

"That's not true and you know it," Judy said. "I still regret introducing you to him in my first month at Harvard. I didn't know what he was really like then."

"Judy, I had a great time with him when we were together, and sure, those weeks after we first broke up were tough. But now, I'm fine, and I'm strong enough to face him. Maybe now we can simply become friends."

"Lindsey. I don't think you should become Paul's friend. I'm also not sure if there is such thing as a true friendship between men and women."

"I disagree."

Judy shook her head. "Just promise me you'll be careful, Lindsey."

"I promise."

When I looked up ways to get to Hakodate, I learned I could ride a plane or take a bullet train. I chose the latter. I wanted to see more of Japan.

For six hours, the train passed by pristine, snowy winter scenes, the late November air cool and crisp. I stared out the window the entire ride, grinning. But as the train pulled into Hakodate

Station, my smile vanished and tension filled my body. This was it. I was really seeing Paul again.

When I got off the train, I saw Paul standing on the platform, waving at me. "Welcome to Hakodate, Lindsey."

"It's been a while, Paul," I replied, trying to sound casual.

Paul went to hug me, and at the same, I raised my hand and tried to reach for his to shake. For an awkward moment, we both froze. Then, smiling sheepishly, Paul lowered his arms and shook my hand. We walked through the station, and Paul explained the demographics of Hakodate, followed by their fishery volume and trends. As he talked, my tension disappeared. What was I so nervous about? It was just the same old Paul, with his quick speech, constantly moving hands, and lopsided smile.

Judy's warnings had been echoing at the back of my head, but they softened more and more as Paul kept talking.

"You haven't changed, Paul," I said.

"And you're even more beautiful than the last time I saw you. Amazing."

I batted at his shoulder. "Knock it off."

"I'm serious."

"You look good too. Healthy. You truly like this place, don't you?"

"Oh, this is the best gourmet city in Japan. As an avid foodie, you should have chosen here, instead of Hime."

He continued to talk about the Hakodate fishery, famous for a certain kind of long squid. Before he escorted me to the home office of Hakodate Marine, he took me to a fishery market that was open to public.

As always, he never let silence slip between him and me. I wondered how I could explain our business plan to him.

After a quick walk through the market, we went to Hakodate Marine's headquarters. The building was large and pristine, with not a plant out of place. A receptionist greeted me with a large smile as Paul and I walked past her. As we walked through the open-plan office, Paul introduced me to every executive we passed, and he also took me into CEO Doigaki's office for a quick meet-and-greet. Everybody handed me their business card, and I wished I had my own to give back.

After all the greetings, Paul escorted me to a lavish conference room with a marble table and a shimmering chandelier.

"I booked the room just for the two of us. I figured we could discuss the plan ourselves."

I nodded, grateful. The office and all the executives were intimidating. It was good Paul and I could just talk intimately about my business plan.

"Anything to drink?" Paul asked, opened the door of a refrigerator in the corner of the room.

"You are trying to impress me, Paul."

"Of course. Is it working?"

"It sure is."

I took a Diet Coke and started explaining our business plan. Despite my anxiety, Paul didn't oppose the 'three years preparation clause.' He didn't even ask any questions during my hour-long presentation.

"I understand why you want to wait, and I'm okay with that," Paul said.

I waited for him to say more, to argue or to ask for more conditions. But all he said was, "Let's get some bento boxes. You are hungry, aren't you?"

I ignored the question. "You don't need to ask your boss for authorization?"

"Yes, when you guys bring a specific agreement to us, I will need to explain it to my boss and ask for his signature. But no, I don't have to have his authorization for making things move forward because I have already received his buy-in. Like I said in my email, Hime is an amazing port. It's the best port out of all the ports facing the Sea of Japan. At Hakodate Marine, we feel like getting into business with Hime is an absolutely wonderful thing, and historically, nobody has been able to do that. If I didn't have this connection with you, I don't think anything would have happened. What you do doesn't matter. Who you know matters."

I nodded in agreement. I could never imagine the fishermen I knew in Hime accepting business from a faceless corporation.

Paul continued. "I've been excited about partnering with Hime from the first moment you emailed me."

"Why did it take you so long to respond then?" I asked.

"I wanted to respond right away, but I needed to do research first so I could have supporting evidence when I explained to my boss why I thought partnering with Hime was a good idea. It's one of the things they stressed in my MBA program."

I laughed–of course Paul would use tactics from Harvard. Paul believed in Harvard with a religious fervor. He loved everything about it. He especially loved the MBA campus, which was secluded from the main campus by the big Charles River. We used to hang out in the posh lounge area, studying together on the leather sofas. Or, we went to the courtyard next to the faculty residential building, McArthur Hall. This was the quietest outdoor place in Harvard, and there were always one or two professors giving private lessons to their favorite students. That little place was protective, open, and full of hope, just like the rest of Harvard. Everyone there believed that they would make something of themselves, that they would have the career they wanted.

"Sure, I would like to make it happen sooner than three years from now, but now Hime is my territory in my company and nobody would invade here," Paul said. "So don't worry about the three-year wait. I kind of anticipated that. Hakodate Marine is a dynamic company. While we wait, we can do many things. For example, I will research the possibility of bluefin tuna farming in Toyama Bay."

I was impressed with Paul's knowledge. Nobody in Hime knew about the bluefin tuna farming. Paul hadn't changed with success. He was still positive, forward thinking, and proactive. He still talked too much, still had a great sense of humor, and still was just nerdy and awkward enough that I never felt intimidated by his intelligence.

Paul had a different business approach than Judy. Judy was passionate in all aspects of her life, and she used that passion to fuel her business ideas. Paul, on the other hand, tried not to carry emotion into the business. He just liked to use the strategies he was taught at Harvard, and he felt like he had no time to waste on his own emotions.

Both made sense to me.

The bento boxes came in and we started eating.

"By the way, I like your online auction and fishery tourism idea. I think Hime has a ton of potential as a tourist destination, and distributors will love getting their hands on some fresh Hime fish," Paul said as he dipped his sushi in soy sauce.

"You think so?" I hadn't explained phase one and two of Operation Tripod to him, but I guessed he found out through his own connections. Fishermen are not good at keeping secrets. In Massachusetts, Toyama, and everywhere between, they love talking about all the gossip over a stiff drink.

"Sure. And I'm sure, once we get involved, we'll be able to make use of your newfound popularity. We can probably tie our brand into it somehow."

"Right, like, if we create an aquarium, maybe you could sponsor it and we could name it after your company."

"There you go! Now you're thinking like a Harvard MBA.

Also, during the three years, I know you guys will have to deal with the massive administrative work required for ITQ, but we will assist you. We are experienced with foreign countries. Count on us."

"That sounds great."

"So, please go ahead and continue making your full-blown business plan, and don't worry if there are parts you can't share with us or Nanae. Over the next three years, we'll build mutual trust, and then we will proceed with dating, engagement, and marriage on our third anniversary."

"Wonderful. What's the next step for you?"

"I need to visit Hime as soon as possible. How about next week? Are you available?"

I nodded, and Paul and I both quickly checked our phone calendars and picked a day.

"Great, now that we've hashed out all the boring business details, we can have some fun. I'm going to show you around Hakodate."

Paul drove me all around Hakodate, and he pointed out his favorite spots to eat, drink, and work. At the end of the day, just before the sun set, he took me to the top of the Hakodate Mountain, which had a sweeping view of the surrounding valley. It was freezing, but there were still many couples there, arms wrapped around each other as they gazed down at the sparkling town. I had never seen such a beautiful view. Paul and I stood silently for a while, taking it all in.

Sadly, though, the time came where we had to leave so I could catch the last train back to Hime. I turned around, and ran right into Paul's chest.

Before I could say I was sorry, Paul grabbed my arms. Then, he wrapped my body in his long arms.

"Paul, we shouldn't—" I started saying, but he cut me off by kissing me. After a second, I kissed him back.

After a couple minutes, we broke apart, and he said, "Lindsey, would you ever want to get back together?"

A few months ago, I would have said 'no' immediately. But now, I wasn't as sure. "I don't know, Paul. I'm not sure if that would be a good idea."

"You don't have to give me an answer now. But think about it, okay?"

After a moment of hesitation, I nodded.

◀ ▮▯▮▯▮ ▶

I floated all the way to Hime, my thoughts back in Hakodate with Paul, a smile etched onto my lips. But as soon as I got back to Hime, I crashed back down to Earth. The morning after my trip, I went down to the auction market, where I saw piles of empty fish buckets. Godzilla was still abusing his power, and our catch stayed at historically low levels.

I called for another all-hands meeting that night, and I reported my discussion with Hakodate Marine to the fishermen. Everyone was excited that Hakodate Marine fully embraced our direction and were willing to move forward with the mutual agreement.

Knowing that we had Hakodate Marine's support motivated us to finish creating the details of our business plan. Judy and Ichiro helped me, but in the end, it was my responsibility. But I didn't mind. I felt good, and things in Hime were good. The air was no longer thick with tension, and for the first time in a long time, the fishermen were able to focus on what they truly loved to do: fishing.

One night, Kong and I met for sake and sushi. He told me that his application to the Florida school was denied, but he was not giving up. He asked me to review his English application package, which I did while we waited for the sushi to arrive.

When I finished, I said, "I can correct your English, but if you'd like, I can also give you some more advice."

"Of course I want that! That would be great."

"American teachers would probably want to see a bit more visual material, like graphs or charts. Also, I would like to see more supporting evidence for your specific coaching accomplishments."

"I see."

"Bring me all the data of your coaching accomplishments. Let me put it together."

Kong thanked me, and I nodded, wondering why I was taking on another project. I was already busier than I had ever been before, but I was happy. For the first time in my life, I felt like I was truly contributing to my community. It was also the first time I had the sense that I was doing a job nobody else could do.

I found that I loved helping people, and I wanted to help even one more person if I could. That's why I took on Kong's project.

When I wasn't working on one of my jobs, I usually found myself in Olive Bath House. A group of female friends, including Hana, had invited me to join them there as often as I wanted. I often asked them how they felt about Operation Tripod while we soaked in a huge bath tub.

After talking business, we would move on to lighter topics, and then, usually went to the cool down room. There, we often ended up practicing Owara on the cool down room's tatami mat. The women were passionate about Owara, and they loved teaching me everything they knew about it. I still was a bit clumsy, but I was slowly getting better.

After that, we usually went to Judy's deli and ate her sample pastrami. Judy appreciated our feedback, and she laughed and chatted with us as we ate slice after slice of pastrami.

But on the day before Paul was supposed to come to Hime, Judy's attitude changed. She was quiet and solemn, and she eyed me warily as she handed out her pieces of pastrami. I was even more boisterous than usual—laughing louder, joking more—as thoughts of the kiss Paul and I shared on the mountain echoed in my mind. At the end of the night, when we were all saying our goodbyes, Judy clasped my shoulder and quietly said, "Be careful, Lindsey."

"I know," I said, smiling at her. "I always am."

◄‖‖‖‖►

The next morning, I got to the Hime Train Station thirty minutes before Paul was due to arrive. I wanted to be sure I was there right when Paul's train arrived because I had asked him for a big favor, and it was important that I made a good impression. Also, I was just eager to see him.

I had bought a new dress in Toyama City, a camel and navy colored piece, and I wore that along with black stockings and shoes with low heels. I also wore a chic, fitted coat. When I looked at myself in the mirror, it felt like a real businesswoman was looking back at me.

When I saw Paul getting off the train, I waved at him. It felt like the moment he ditched me by a text message was long ago, so long ago it was almost like it never happened.

"Hi, Paul," I said. He hugged me tightly, and I hugged him back. I wasn't sure how a hug with someone of the opposite sex would look to the people in Hime, but I found myself not caring much.

I glanced down and saw he had two big suitcases.

"I'm planning on staying in Hime for a while to make sure everything is in place for our agreement," Paul explained.

"Paul, I know I've asked you this before, but are you truly sure Hakodate Marine is okay with waiting for three years?"

"The answer is yes, just like it was every other time you asked me," Paul said, giving me a reassuring grin. "Japanese fishermen have been fishing for more than two thousand years. Three years is nothing. For a long time, Hakodate Marine has been saying they need to find a new market, but they're all talk, no action. I have actually acted and found Hime. Our CEO likes a person who takes action, and my educational credentials are pretty helpful too." Paul pointed to his crimson jersey, which said, 'Harvard' in big letters.

We walked into town, and Paul looked around, taking it all in. "I want to know much more about this town," he said. "I want to know everything there is to know about Hime."

I took him all over Hime, stopping in the fish market and the port, and even going to my school and Bamboo Sushi.

As we walked, I kept thinking about what he said to me after our kiss on Hakodate Mountain. Even though I had enjoyed the kiss, I hadn't really thought I wanted to get back together with him.

But when we stopped in my favorite traditional Hime gingko nut rice cake shop, I happened to see my reflection in a mirror. As I looked at my reflection, I wondered why I bought a new dress for a 'friend'.

◄ ▌▌▌▌▌ ►

A tour of Hime should have only taken half a day at the most. But Paul had a lot of questions about Hime and Toyama Prefecture, and even by his third day, he was still asking questions nonstop. His questions weren't only about the fishery, but also about the city itself and the people who lived here.

"What's Toyoma famous for?" Paul asked as we sat in his hotel room, drinking coffee.

"Well, they produce the most tulips in all of Japan. Also, the home ownership rate is the highest in Japan. They also have the highest female employment rate."

Then, I bragged about the Hime Udon noodle being one of the most recognizable noodles in Japan and Hime's unique black

the Sea of Japan

ramen noodle. I also quickly listed some of our other accomplishments: the highest household spending on education, one of the three biggest Buddha statues in Japan, an old Buddhist temple and a garden that were called national treasures, and ski lessons in the winter time at the school.

"Wow, I'm impressed. I think you even said that all in one breath."

I laughed. In front of Paul, my memory skill seemed to work even better than usual.

"I have more stats, like the number of public bath houses per capita is the highest in Japan, and Hime is the only place in Japan that serves real crab in their school lunch, and—" Before I could list any more, Paul stopped me by kissing me again. I kissed him back, and then we both stood up and slowly walked back toward the bed.

"Is this all right?" Paul asked.

I nodded and turned off the lights.

Bad weather came to Hime and stayed for a while, but when the thunder groaned and the lightning flashed, all the fishermen got excited because December thunder was believed to lure in yellowtail. Everyone in town seemed happier, more energetic.

I felt that excitement on one of my trips to the Olive Bath House. More than twenty women joined me that day—mostly the wives and girlfriends of the fishermen.

"I heard that the divided fishery association has become truly united again. Perhaps even more united than before," one woman said.

"That's true," I said. "I'll give you an example. Most fish here chase sardines. So, even the boats that don't fish for sardines now let other fishermen know where the sardines are when they find them. This had never happened in the history of the Hime fishery."

– 167 –

I ran my hands through the warm water. "I wish I could tell you that everything is perfect, but there is a little bad news. Despite our collaborative efforts, the catch volume has only risen a little bit, far below the association's estimate. Our catch volume has become double, which means it's still only at 40 percent of last year. We will probably see more fishermen who quit soon."

The women nodded solemnly. "Thank you for being honest with us," one woman said.

After that, we moved onto lighter topics. We shared a lot of mutual interests, like cooking, movies, and men. When we had first started spending time together, the other women weren't sure what to make of Ichiro and my relationship. I explained that our relationship was strictly professional, but the older women, the ones who had the most life experience, straightforwardly recommended Ichiro as a serious boyfriend. Even as a husband. I had dismissed that idea, saying Ichiro was my business partner, nothing more.

Now, the conversation moved back toward my love life. "I heard that Paul is your ex-boyfriend," one older woman.

"You get your information so quickly. Yes, he was."

"Well, we had to find out about him. A cute *gaijin* boy stands out," an older housewife said.

"He's not in his twenties anymore. I'm not sure if cute is a right word."

"Since I'm in my forties, he still looks like a cute boy to me."

"I guess I'm classified as a cute girl then," I said with a laugh.

"Of course. If Ichiro procrastinates any longer, some brave fisherman will knock on your door with a bunch of tulips."

"Tulips?"

"Of course. Why should we make Itokawa richer by buying their roses?"

We got out of the bathtub, put clothes on, and went to the cool down room. Afterwards, the housewife and I bought ice cream and ate together.

The housewife said, "You know the language of flowers, right?"

"I've heard of it, but I only know what a few flowers mean."

"Do you know what red tulips mean?"

"No."

"It's declaration of love."

"Big words."

The older woman looked at me sternly. "Seriously, if my eyes are not mistaken, you're not completely over Paul."

"I'm not sure—"

"I just wanted to tell you, if there is anything I can do to help, don't hesitate. Okay? I don't care either way, but I will make things easier for you."

"Either way? What do you mean?"

"I know you know what I mean."

"Right."

We shook hands and went our separate ways.

Only three days later, Paul established a subsidiary office of Hakodate Marine in Hime. It was a clear sign that Hakodate Marine was serious about establishing a relationship with Hime.

In the days after Paul set up his office, I connected him to the fishery association executives and employees. I also had him meet the three doyens. He bowed just like he was supposed to, and the doyens were clearly impressed. His Japanese was also outstandingly smooth, and he pronounced the words beautifully. He even made some jokes in Japanese and made people laugh.

After that, I took him to the Hime City Hall and the Prefectural Government of Toyama, which oversaw all the fishery associations and non-coastal fisheries. They were going to be ultimately responsible for managing ITQ when it started in April in just four months. Paul made sure to study up on Toyoma Bay fisheries before the meeting, and he impressed the government official with the statistics he remembered.

Exactly three weeks after Paul's first day in Hime, I finally took him to Judy's delicatessen. Her shop had formally opened a week before.

The restaurant was packed from the first moment it opened. Her pastrami had become exceptionally popular, and she gave away samples outside the shop for pedestrians. The long lines for samples were reported about on the local TV news, and after that, there was always a line in front of the shop.

Judy personally delivered our pastrami sandwiches. "Hey, Linds," Judy said, giving me a hug. Then, she gave Paul a cold look. "Paul."

Without another word, she went back into the kitchen.

"I'm sorry," I said.

"No, that's okay. In business, the person who falls into the emotional trap is the loser." He smiled, but his words still had a bite to them.

I looked away, heat rising to my face. I wanted to shout at him for calling my best friend a 'loser,' but I couldn't talk back to him and risk losing what we had built in Hime. Besides, it seemed like he was joking. Or, at least, I told myself that so I felt less guilty about saying nothing.

Judy went behind the counter to talk to her partner, Nakata san. Nakata san was a mellow man in his late sixties, and he owned Hime's biggest stock farm.

After his first bite, Paul said, "This is delicious."

"I'm glad you like it. The pastrami shop is owned half and half by Judy and Nakata san, and they seem to be getting along extremely well. When they start talking about beef, they never stop. They named this place 'Judy & Peter's New York Deli' since

Nakata san's first name is too long and his favorite actor is Peter Fonda."

"I saw a big Harley Davidson in the parking lot. He must be a big fan of *Easy Rider.*"

"Good catch. He flies to Milwaukee every other year and spends a full day at the Harley museum."

Paul quietly ate his sandwich, and I thought more about his statement about Judy. I thought about the word he used, "trap," and I wondered what he meant. Had Paul anticipated Judy's cold look? Was he worried Judy would turn me against him and threaten his business in Hime? Did he think that, if he showed me that he was the bigger person, I would stay on his side? All these questions made my head ache.

After we finished eating, we separated for the day. As soon as Paul disappeared, Judy and Nakata san came out. I shook hands with Nakata san.

"Good to see you again, Nakata san."

"Same here, Lindsey san. You're still number one in Hime Junior High School's popularity contest."

"Is there a popularity contest?"

"Only amongst students. My grandson secretly told me."

We laughed.

"Everybody seems to love this shop, Nakata san."

"Of course," Judy interrupted. "We're the best, and only, pastrami sandwich shop in all of Japan. If you google pastrami and Japan, you'll see a whole bunch of hamburger shops. Not an authentic New York Deli. But now, that will all change."

When Nakata san went back to the kitchen, Judy brought two coffees and sat next to me.

"Lindsey, I'm sorry I couldn't be nice to Paul," she said in a monotone.

"That's okay." I shifted in my seat, wishing I could avoid this conversation. It wasn't going to lead to anything good. To change the subject, I said, "Are your new business cards finished?"

Judy nodded and pulled one out of her apron. It had a cartoon of Judy wearing a big blue apron, holding a pastrami sandwich in her right hand and a chicken leg in her left hand.

"Judy Cantor, MD," I read it. "MD? This should be MBA, shouldn't it?"

"Look at the fine print beneath. MD stands for Maven of Delicatessen."

"Nice," I said, smiling.

"Thanks. I got the business card idea from Ziggy Gruber, one of the most respected deli men in New York. Flip it over, Lindsey."

I flipped it over and read the quote on the back: *Anytime a person goes into a delicatessen and orders a pastrami on white bread with mayo, somewhere a deli man dies.* —Milton Berle

"Oh," I said, sighing.

"See, Paul ordered pastrami on white bread, and he poured over mayo as much as French dip. That was an insult to me."

"Come on, Judy, that's just the way he likes his sandwiches."

"You think?"

I thought of the word 'trap' that Paul used.

"You don't seriously think he was mocking you with his order, do you?" I asked.

"I wouldn't put it past him. After all, that's the Paul I know."

"I don't think that's a fair statement."

"Have you introduced him to Ichiro?"

"Not yet."

"Why?"

"I don't know . . . we've been busy, I guess."

"That's not true, and you know it. Have you told Paul that every place you took him was a place that Ichiro showed you? I'm sure you haven't. You seem to have forgotten that Ichiro turned your mundane and boring Hime life into a great one. In the beginning, you thought about nothing but escaping from this town. Now, every one of the 50,000 people in this city knows you."

"I'm not that famous."

"Ichiro isn't stupid. He wasn't born yesterday. Since Paul came to the town, you've been more joyous than ever before."

"Joyous? No. I'm not."

"Yes, you are. You're spending all your time with him, and you're making excuses to see him when you don't really have to."

"As you know, he is the bridge from our fishermen to Hakodate Marine."

"How close have you become with Paul?"

"What do you mean? We're just colleagues and friends."

"You say that, but that's not what it looks like."

"I don't know what I look like."

"And you don't even protest."

"What can I say?"

"Do you love him?"

"I did once. I'm not sure if I do now, but it's fun to be with him."

"Did you ask if he has a girlfriend now?"

"I did. He said no."

"He said 'no,' but that might not be the truth."

"That's not fair."

"Anybody eating my pastrami with mayo on white bread deserves negative treatment. And you told me once that he's a jerk."

"Nice try, Judy, but I never said that to you."

"I'm sure you did."

"No, I didn't."

"Yeah, right. You remember everything."

"Only things I'm paying attention to."

"Did you sleep with him here?"

"Judy!"

"I deserve to know. I can't even count all the hours I spent listening to you talk about him back in Boston."

"The answer is yes, but only once. But I have to be honest. I can see it happening a second time, followed by a third time and many more. I still want to draw a line between us so that I won't get burnt again."

"Lindsey . . ." For the first time in our long friendship, Judy looked disappointed. That look made me bristle with anger.

"Why did you bring this up?"

"I just saw Ichiro the other day."

"And?"

"He looked fine, but I can tell that he's lonely, even though you guys are working together five days a week."

"I haven't sensed that."

"You know that's a lie, Lindsey. I know you know what I am trying to say. He loves you, don't you see? And he feels jealous of Paul, but since he's so reserved, he can't just say that to your face."

"Judy—"

"You now are happy to be in this town, right?"

"Absolutely."

"And you are happy that you didn't move somewhere else, correct?"

"Right."

"And who turned around your gloomy days in Hime?"

I sealed my lips tight.

"And who saved your life?"

Tighter. What else could I do?

"But Ichiro never says such things to you or me. I don't know why I'm saying this to you. I really don't. I just, I've experienced too many of your dark days, back when you felt purposeless and joyless in Boston. I just want you to be happy. I think Ichiro is right for you. Through Ichiro, you'll finally get the happiness you've always been looking for. Mayo guy can't give you that."

"I can't say that I've never noticed his feelings before. But once we hop on the boat, we have no time to think about it. We think about nothing but the fish. And besides, fishermen gear is basically the least sexy outfit in the world."

We both laughed weakly at that. I realized that we hadn't even touched our coffees.

"Let's go to the bath house tonight, and let's discuss anything but men," Judy said.

"Agreed," I replied, smiling, knowing that no matter what else happened, our friendship was still solid.

◄ ▊▊▊▊▊ ►

Several weeks passed.

Ichiro, Judy, and I spent most of our time putting together the final version of our business plan. We were so busy, we didn't even have time to enjoy Christmas. The same situation applied to Paul.

It was all worth it, though, when we presented our business plan at an all-hands fishery association meeting. The fishermen only had one issue: they were worried about the safety of the public.

"There's a ton of dangerous equipment at the fishery. How can we keep the public from getting hurt?" Hideki asked.

Ichiro thought for a moment and then said, "How about we ask fishermen with empty boats to carry tourists around the fishing area—for a fee, of course. That way, the fishermen can escort the tourists to the sites where other fishermen are working, and they can keep an eye on them."

The fishermen agreed, and some volunteered their boats.

Once we agreed to make that change, all 290 fishermen unanimously voted to approve the plan.

A few days after that, Judy, Ichiro, and I met up at Bamboo Sushi to discuss everything that had happened since the plan was approved.

"Every major newspaper and TV network is now broadcasting our Hime fishery tourism commercials," Judy said to Ichiro and me. These days, I felt a lot more comfortable talking to Ichiro with Judy by my side.

"I saw one the other day, it's strange seeing a place you know so well on TV," Ichiro said.

"I know, right?" Judy replied. "It's such a weird feeling."

Judy and Ichiro continued chatting, seeming to almost forget that I existed. I was happy that two of my best friends were now also becoming friends. Yet, at the same time, I knew that Judy had another motive: she was analyzing my relationship with Ichiro.

Since Paul came to town, Ichiro had still been friendly toward me, but I felt a distance between us. He seemed to understand that the two of us needed to work together, so he just put his feelings aside.

"I was thinking, for an extra fee, we can invite tourists to become fishermen for a day, and they can even sell any fish they catch at the auction," Ichiro said. "Plus, for the first time, the Hime fishery association is allowing recreational fishermen's boats to dock at our pier for a fee. Those fishermen can now unload their fish at the port and ask the association employees to sell them."

I finally found the area that I could contribute. I said, "As a result, people keep bringing more friends to Hime, and they're all staying in local hotels."

"How is the online auction system developing?" Ichiro directed the question to me, but he looked at the space between me and Judy rather than looking me in the eye. Guilt filled my stomach.

the Sea of Japan

"It's going well. Judy and I hooked up with one of the fishery IT companies in New Bedford through my grandpa's connection. They created a prototype of the online auction system for our fishery association at a discounted price," I said.

Judy said, "Now, Tokyonians have started monitoring how many brand fish we catch, and they're sending their auction offers remotely. By the way, have you met with Godzilla yet, Ichiro?"

"The doyens met him a few days ago. They tried putting together a plan for our future merger, but Godzilla didn't listen, and he just kept attacking Hime. Since we haven't made any progress, our fishery volume is still stuck at 50 percent of last's year level. We're all happy that we're valued so highly in the Tokyo market, but in order to retain the value, we need to increase our volume."

Ichiro took a sip of his green tea.

"Some fishermen have said that you should do the negotiation with Godzilla instead of the doyens because the doyens are too Toyaman." Ichiro directed that to me, but he still wouldn't look me in the eye.

"I'm ready," I said.

"I will tell them so," he said coldly.

My face flushed, and my guilt turned into anger. Before I could convince myself not to, I decided to get back at him. "As we expected, Michelin 3-Star restaurants in San Francisco and resorts in Las Vegas have started asking for initial orders of Hime brand fish. We shipped them to the United States through a Tokyo seafood handling company today, but *Paul* is helping us get our fishery ready for the HAACP inspection so that we can directly ship our fish to the United States."

I smiled broadly as I said Paul's name, and I stared directly at Ichiro. Ichiro immediately started looking at his iPhone.

"That was childish," Judy whispered into my ear. I shrugged.

After a short silence, Ichiro asked how Judy & Peter's Deli was doing.

Judy's face lit up like it always did when someone asked about her deli. "We're doing extremely well. People have come from all over Japan to try us out. And we've also gotten visitors from Korea, China, and Taiwan."

"Great to hear!" Ichiro smiled, but it was clearly artificial. "I've heard that your pastrami customers are also going to the sushi restaurants, especially Bamboo Sushi. It seems like sushi lovers and pastrami lovers are meeting in Hime."

Their conversation continued, but I tuned them out. I started thinking about Paul, sitting alone in his hotel room. I took out my phone and texted him.

"How's it going? Can I see you tonight?"

◀ ||||||||||◀

The fish market grew more and more lively as the economy in Hime improved. Every time I saw the doyens, they loudly praised me. It was a little bit embarrassing, but I was happy that they were happy.

We had a lot of obstacles ahead, the biggest of which was finding a way to make Godzilla come to the peace treaty discussion table. But overall, everything was going right in Hime.

The students at my school also seemed to be more cheerful, and they were doing better in the classroom. The English literacy score at school had entered into the top five percentile for all of Japan. The school now received admission inquiries from all over Japan.

Everyone seemed to be very happy. The only exception was Ichiro.

Ichiro and I still sailed five days a week, and he was still treating me well. He didn't say anything was wrong, but his smile was tainted by concern and disappointment. It wasn't hard to figure out why.

Paul called me every night, and sometimes I went to his hotel and stayed there. Occasionally, I even called in sick to Ichiro, and the two of us relaxed in the hotel room, eating omelets Paul fixed in his room while we cuddled up in bed.

One day, when he was serving breakfast to me, he kissed my forehead and said, "You know, I was born and raised in a very poor family and all the education I got was on full scholarship. I was happy when I found a full-time job. It was the end of the tunnel. But now, I know I didn't know true happiness until I met you. Oh god, I love you, Lindsey."

He got back into bed, pulled me hard, and we made love again.

Later that day, I made sushi for Ichiro and me on his boat, both of us quiet. Ichiro stared down at the water, frowning. His gloominess annoyed me. What right did he have to be upset that I was in a relationship? He had never said he loved me. He hadn't even officially asked me out on a date. We had had many date-like events, like the firefly squid dive at Iwasehama Beach and the many things we did in Massachusetts and New York. Our conversation on the boat was always full of laughter, and we had tons in common.

Ichiro had had a million chances to ask me out, or even to just tell me that I was an important person in his life. He had never tried to kiss me—he hadn't tried to hold my hand. There were no indications he had romantic feelings for me.

I told Judy that later that night while we sat in a peaceful bath-tub at Olive Bath House. It was around one in the morning, and we were the only ones there.

"You know that's not true, Lindsey. You know Ichiro well enough by now to know that he shows his affection in other, more subtle ways. I think you're lying to yourself so you feel better about spending so much time with Paul."

"I'm not lying to anyone."

"Do you know where Ichiro goes at night now?"

"No, what do you mean?"

"Didn't he used to go to Bamboo Sushi all the time? But now, he doesn't go there anymore, right?"

"Right."

"To be honest, it's sad that you didn't even notice it."

I turned away from Judy—the disappointment in her eyes made guilt curdle in my stomach. "Where does he eat?"

"He comes to my deli every night. He eats my pastrami or matzo ball soup. I'm normally busy in the kitchen or serving customers, so I don't speak to him much. But it's clear that he's hurting, mentally and I think physically too. Is he alright? I mean health-wise?"

"I don't think he's ill. Does he look sick?"

"I don't know, that's why I'm asking. He orders our food every night. But he always leaves a lot and he doesn't ask for a doggie bag. Before, he was one of the biggest eaters I had ever seen in my life. Nobody eats two bowls of Toyama Black Ramen at once. But he doesn't finish my food these days. And I know it's not because my food isn't good."

"He told me once that he had leukemia when he was younger, but he recovered from that a long time ago."

"Some types of leukemia can suddenly come back. But you don't suspect that, right?"

"Right," I said, trying to sound confident. He couldn't be sick, could he? "He works hard and is just fine on the sea."

"If that's true, I think I know what's wrong." Judy looked pointedly at me.

I dunked my head under the water to avoid answering her. When I emerged, Judy continued talking.

"I know he wants to talk to me. He wants to know how serious your relationship with Paul is. And I'm sure he's wondering how he can show you how he feels."

I laughed. "If that's true, he sounds like a teenager with his first crush. Ichiro is such a smart person, but he really is lost."

"Ichiro and I did talk once, a few days ago, after I closed the deli for the night. He told me about how his wife cheated on him, and how that made him lose his confidence." Judy looked at me. "You did know that, right?"

I shook my head. "Why didn't he tell me that?"

"I think he was too embarrassed to tell you. But he was okay telling me, since he doesn't feel the same way about me as he does about you."

I didn't say a word. For so long, I had been curious about his ex-wife, but now I found I wasn't as interested. I couldn't say that to Judy, though. It would sound too cold.

"Ichiro's worried, Lindsey. He's worried that he's going to say the wrong thing, and then, you'll leave the boat, the fishery association, and maybe even Hime. He can afford that, but the association can't afford to lose their leader now."

"Perhaps you can be the leader of the association instead of me."

"Don't be ridiculous. I haven't gained that much trust from the fishermen, and I don't have a fisherman grandpa."

That made me think about how Grandpa liked Ichiro so much more than Paul. But that wasn't relevant—what mattered was what I felt.

Judy continued. "Look, Lindsey. When Ichiro came to my deli, I pretended that I was preoccupied with work. Because I didn't want to talk with him about your relationship with Paul. I didn't want to lie. If I were asked, I would have to tell him, 'Yeah, Lindsey fucks Paul every other night. Didn't you know that?'"

"Judy! Stop it."

"On the one night we talked, I think he hoped if he told me about his wife, I would tell him about you and Paul. But I just vaguely smiled and pretended that I had to leave because I was meeting a friend. The way I avoided his questions told him every-thing he needed to know. That's why he doesn't ask you about anything. I understand where he's coming from. I wouldn't ask a question if I knew the answer beforehand. Especially if the question might hurt 290 of my friends if I got the wrong answer. Would you, Lindsey?"

"Probably not."

"He just sits there each night and quietly eats my pastrami. I want to see a customer smile when they bite into my pastrami. My soul food. The recipe that my grandparents and parents have poured their heart into, generation after generation. But Ichiro doesn't taste it. His face doesn't change. He just chews it like cardboard."

I understood what Judy was saying. Yet, at the same time, I couldn't help how Ichiro felt toward me, and I couldn't help how I felt toward Paul.

"Let's get out here. We're turning into boiled octopuses," I said, turning my back to Judy.

◀ ▌▍▎▏▕ ◀

Ichiro accepted one young fisherman onto his boat.

The boat's license allowed for two rods for each fisherman on the boat. With this new guy, Yoshi, we now had six rods out.

Yoshi brought a lively atmosphere back to the boat. He was a talkative person, and with him acting as a buffer, it was easier to talk to Ichiro as a friend again. With Yoshi around, Ichiro and I chatted like nothing had changed.

Every day, I fixed sushi for the three of us, showing off my hard-earned skills. My sushi had been praised by many people now. Memorizing how Mr. Bamboo made his cuts had helped a lot.

I was glad that it had become my official task to spend more time with Paul. Judy seemed to accept that he wasn't going away, and she was courteous toward him, although it was clear they were never going to be friends. But most other people in Hime liked Paul, and he even started making friends with Itokawans.

One morning, I Skyped Grandpa to tell him about Hime. We had been speaking more regularly—he finally saw me as a professional fisherman, rather than just his granddaughter.

"Hey, fisherwoman! How are you?" Grandpa said. It was evening there, and he sat by his fireplace and held a glass of his favorite whiskey.

"Good to see you're still alive and kicking, Grandpa!" I said.

"Of course, I'm not going anywhere," he said with a wink. "And I'm still kicking all the younger fishermen's asses. Yesterday, I set a record for the most fish caught at our port this winter."

"That's amazing! What's your secret?"

"Nothing. Just listen to the craving of the fish."

"C'mon, Grandpa. I'm still a rookie. You have to spoon-feed me your professional advice."

"First of all, you're not a rookie. Once you sail out, the ocean treats all fishermen equally. It doesn't go easy on you just because you are new. Second, you have a great mentor. If Ichiro comes to New Bedford and fishes in the same place I fish, I'm sure he will reach to my level in three years or less."

"I've never heard you praise another fisherman before."

"That's because this is not just a job. We bet our lives on it."

"I truly understand what you mean by that, and I get why you used to yell at Dad when he said anything negative about fishermen. Also, I understand that fishing is really the art of the gut feeling."

"You got that right. I can hear the sound of halibut swimming under the sea. I can smell the sea bass traveling. I can see the color of the fish street. And I know Ichiro can, too. He also does a unique technique that's only taught in a fishery university. Remember how he took the black snappers out of the net and immediately poked their nervous system?"

"Yes, I do."

"I have never seen that. But I realized recently that he did that to make sure the fish didn't feel pain. It also slowed down the rigor mortis and preserved the fish. Yesterday, I was catching fish for this expensive French restaurant in New Bedford, and I tried his technique. When I brought the fish to the restaurant, the chef gave me three times the market price. For the first time, I truly respected the Japanese fishing style."

He laughed at that, but I didn't. I couldn't stop thinking about what Grandpa would say if he knew that I was back with Paul, that Ichiro and I couldn't even speak to each other alone anymore.

◄ ⅲⅲⅲⅲⅲ ◄

Tourism to Hime's fishery continued to grow, and because of that, the restaurants and shops in town also got new customers. Bamboo Sushi was especially popular, and I had even gained my own fans who loved trying my original sushi. But I still had a long ways to go before I reached mastery. Mr. Bamboo often laughed about the inconsistences in the sizes of my sushi nigiris.

At Bamboo Sushi, we served one-piece sushi nigiris that weighed exactly 0.63 ounces for lunch and 0.56 ounces for dinner. Every time I had a break between customers, I stood in the kitchen and practiced gripping rice. I made twenty nigiris at a time and placed each on the scale. Over time, I got closer to my target weight, but I still wasn't as precise as Mr. Bamboo.

Mr. Bamboo made the job more difficult by not allowing me to use the 'throwback rice' technique.

Throwback rice is a very common practice where a chef grabs rice out of a rice wooden bucket and weighs the rice with his fingers until he feels like he has precisely the right amount. Then, he throws the extra back into the bucket. Mr. Bamboo didn't like this technique because the rice sucks the moisture from your hand when you handle it. That changes the taste of rice slightly, and Mr. Bamboo also felt like it looked unprofessional. He told me that once I grabbed the rice and lifted my hand up, that was the end of it. I had to discard the rice that I didn't use.

I ate many failure rice pieces, which helped me develop my palate even further, and I started noticing how different the rice tasted. Sushi rice always tastes different depending on the season, temperature, humidity, or even my emotional status. Every day, I thought about how I could make better sushi rice.

Paul came almost every night for dinner, and after work, I went back with him to his hotel.

Mr. Bamboo was always polite to Paul, but I got the feeling that he disapproved of him. Since he was a service professional, he had never showed that expression on his face. When he saw me looking at him, he would smile, his eyes light.

I simply replied with a smile of my own, showing my gratitude for everything he had done for me.

◄ ▖▗▘▙▚ ◄

The day came for me to finally visit Godzilla's office in Nanae. I wore my best dress and walked in with my head high, trying to project confidence to hide my nerves.

"I can't believe you came by yourself," Godzilla said.

"You suggested I should come alone, since you didn't want to talk to Toyamans."

"I know I said that, but I didn't think you would be that brave."

"It's not a big deal, sir. You're not going to eat me, are you?"

Godzilla leaned back in his chair and stared at me. "When I was a little kid riding on my dad's fishing boat, no women were ever allowed to board a boat in Nanae."

"That's why you guys didn't grow as much as you possibly could have." I crossed my arms. We didn't even shake hands or say hello, and I was still standing.

Godzilla seemed to realize that at the same time as me. "Be seated."

"Not necessary. If you think men are superior, shouldn't I be cleaning your office while we talk, or fixing you lunch?"

"Come on."

"I thought that I was here to have a conversation with a respected businessman, but the person sitting in front me is just another sexist redneck."

"Okay, okay. Calm down. This all came out wrong. I didn't mean to say that I think men are better than women. My grandparents and their generation simply believed that the goddess of the sea gets jealous if a woman goes on board a boat."

I paused, surprised—that was actually kind of cute, and I couldn't help laughing. He smiled back.

"I apologize for my rudeness. Please, have a seat."

I'd never heard him apologize or say please before. I sat down, and for the first time, I had hope that we would actually be able to strike a deal with Nanae.

◄ ‖‖‖‖‖ ►

A few days after the meeting with Nanae, Judy called me to give me an update on how many tourists were visiting Hime. I sat on the bed in Paul hotel's room while she quickly listed off the numbers.

"I can't believe how well our tourism campaign is working," Judy said. "And I also got a call from a representative at Marriott—they're thinking about building a hotel here."

"That's amazing. All our restaurants are doing well, from the small seafood spots to the three-star places. I also heard that a lot of houses have joined Airbnb. Hime residents no longer feel that we live in a shrinking city. We are a city of growth."

"I know, we're doing very well, and we're still getting tons of media coverage. It's been positive so far, but you always want to be careful when dealing with the media. When things go south, they will write more."

I nodded, thinking about how I was depicted by the Fuji Paper when the bullying incident happened. I was about to respond to Judy, but my phone buzzed, telling me I had another call. It was from Godzilla. I quickly said my goodbyes to Judy and took his call.

"Hello, Lindsey, I'll make this quick," Godzilla said. "I want to get together one more time. I feel like we made some progress last time we talked, but we really need to hash out all the details on how we're going to do this merger and what we're going to do about this stock depletion. How's tomorrow?"

"Tomorrow's fine, can you come after school ends at about three? I'll book a classroom for us to use."

"I'll be there."

The following afternoon, he showed up at three on the dot. We sat down in an empty classroom, sitting on opposite sides of the desk.

"Thank you for coming . . ." I paused, unsure what name to use. I'd always just called him Godzilla, but now that we were on friendlier terms, it didn't seem right. "What should I call you?"

"You can just use my nickname. I like it."

"But you yelled at Hideki when he used your nickname at a meeting."

"Like I said, I hate Toyamans. But you are not Toyaman."

"I've lived here almost ten months."

"You have to live here for more than ten years to call yourself a Toyaman."

"I see," I said, smiling. Bostonians had a similar mindset.

Godzilla smiled too, but it felt like there was something a bit predatory behind that grin.

"So, are you moving forward with our proposal, Godzilla san?" I asked.

"It depends on how you play your cards, Lindsey san."

"We're not hiding any cards. We showed you our whole hand."

"You know, the Nanae fishery association is going to have ITQ as well. We have the same sense of urgency. But we don't have tourism or an online auction system. Hime clearly has the advantage in that, but at the same time, you are experiencing a significant decrease in catches because of our activity. It is time to negotiate."

I inwardly groaned—I thought both sides were finally loosening up. But I did have one more trick up my sleeve. I grabbed my bag from the desk and pulled out a box.

"What's in there, Lindsey san?"

"I'm from New England. This is our recipe, New England apple pie. I heard you originally came from Aomori, the largest apple production region in Japan."

I opened the box to reveal a double-crusted twelve-inch apple pie. "This recipe is passed down through my family. It's a caramel apple pie. We use three kinds of apples, bake it very slowly, and finish with condensed caramel sauce."

"This looks great. Are you trying to bribe me into stopping our overfishing, Lindsey san?"

"No bribery here. It's just a friendly gesture, to show that we're on the same side now."

I pushed the pie toward Godzilla so that he could see it well.

His eyes grew bigger, and he moved his face even closer, like he was counting the number of knife holes I made on the pie.

"Go ahead," I said, handing him a fork and knife.

He stuck the tip of the knife into the center and carefully pulled out a slice of pie. He ate three bites, savoring each one. Afterwards, there was a long silence. Finally, he inhaled deeply and said, "Maybe this is a bribe, but it's the best bribe I've ever had. I would like the recipe, if you don't mind."

"Certainly. I will email it to you."

Godzilla ate quickly. It almost seemed like he forgot the purpose of the meeting. I poured English tea from a thermos into a cup, and Godzilla nodded thanks and took it.

"May I be frank, open, and honest?" I said finally.

Godzilla finally put down his fork. "That's why I didn't bring anybody else with me. Go ahead."

"Our fishery tourism is doing extremely well. Nobody expected it to grow this much this quickly, but here we are. And I realized recently that you can't even start a tourism campaign to compete with ours because you have to work with the tourism industry in Itokawa prefecture in general. If you tried to promote tourism in Nanae, your existing supporters who are living in other areas in Itokawa, not Nanae, would think you're trying to compete with them, and they would pull out their support."

"I admit that you're right. For centuries, City of Kanazawa, which people call Little Kyoto, has been the most profitable city facing the Sea of Japan, with super tourism power. Their tourism benefits all cities in Itokawa including Nanae. For the first time, it is working against Nanae."

"Exactly. So it's time to negotiate."

"Right. But I have to warn you that if you try to ask for something outrageous based on Toyama's current success, you will regret it. Because I don't have to close a deal with you. This suicidal fishery stock depletion is meaningless for both sides, but if we both die, who you think will get resurrected? That would be the city with more financial power, and that's still Nanae."

"I understand. I want to avoid offending you Itokawans. I know that Itokawa is still more powerful than us."

"See, I was right. You are the one who understands logic, unlike the stubborn Toyamans."

I wanted to defend the Toyamans, but I knew that would be a mistake. To give myself something to do, I added English tea to his cup.

"When we enter the agreement, will you promise to cease the trawling vessel attack on Toyama Bay?" I said.

"Certainly."

I paused for a moment, thinking about all the variables in this situation. If I pushed beyond what Godzilla felt was reasonable, not only would it become a deal breaker, but it also would create a significant backlash from Itokawa.

Godzilla sat back in his chair, a smug smile on his face. He knew he had the advantage. But at the same time, I told myself that Godzilla visited me. This was significant because in their whole long history, Toyamans had always visited Itokawans, not the other way around. Itokawans didn't realize the importance of this, but Toyamans did. Toyamans have also felt always underestimated, less respected, and mistreated by the Itokawans. An Itokawan visiting Toyoma meant that, for once, we had the advantage. Godzilla's visit had made every fisherman in Toyoma feel good.

"So, Godzilla san, would you like to draft the merger agreement, or should we?"

"You can do that, but we need to talk about the timing. It's necessary for us to marry you in April instead of in three years."

"I don't know if the fishermen will agree to that. Marriage shouldn't happen without preparation."

"I know you guys need to take time to adapt the changes. But you have pushed us to the cliff, and your collaboration with Hakodate Marine adds even more pressure. It's tough for us to accept waiting three more years under all this pressure. If we wait, many fishermen will be forced to leave Nanae."

"With all due respect, you pushed us very hard from the beginning, Godzilla san. Our fishery tourism and online auction ideas came from the hardship you gave us. You're the mother of these inventions."

Godzilla ignored me and continued on, "In addition to that, your Hime beef has become a threat. Judy's pastrami has become famous throughout Japan, and a lot of tourists are skipping meals in Itokawa and going for her pastrami instead."

"I can't do anything about that. But you and I both know that the merger has to be successful. For that, both sides need to be careful. Compared to all the previous contention between Itokawa and Toyama, three years is literally nothing. Let's not make this issue a deal breaker."

"I theoretically agree with you. But I'm not sure if we can persuade people in Nanae to wait for three years."

"We both need to get the go-ahead from our fishermen before we can implement the merger. There are still many issues to discuss, but I think we need to put something together to show that we're moving forward. Let's prepare a non-binding memorandum for now."

"Good idea."

"Do you still promise to cease the trawling vessel attack on Toyama Bay? That would be a deal breaker for Hime, I know that for sure."

"Understood. You have my word. We will bring down the licensed vessels to the exact level of the last year."

"Very good, sir. Then, we are open to any suggestion."

That night, Ichiro, Judy, and I put everything Godzilla and I discussed into writing. Once it was typed up, Erica and Hana edited everything into a nonbinding memorandum that discussed our merger and Operation Tripod. We were all excited.

The next morning, I called Godzilla and said, "The pro-tem president of the Hime fishery association put his John Hancock on the memorandum five minutes ago."

"Good," Godzilla said. "I'll come to Hime tomorrow to see it for myself."

The doyens and I arranged to meet with Godzilla in the evening at Bamboo Sushi. When he arrived, we shook hands tightly, our faces relaxed.

"Our non-binding memorandum is not a formal agreement, but it is designed to confirm that we're heading toward a merger, and it lays out the terms we discussed," I said to Godzilla and the doyens.

Godzilla said, "I promise to end the trawling vessel attack on Toyama Bay. We're going to have the first inter-prefecture fishery association merger in Japan. The only remaining issue is the timing."

I was grateful that we were moving forward. I knew Godzilla had carefully weighed the pros and cons of the merger, and he had decided to ride along with us. He could have chosen to stick with the status quo, which would have given the advantage to Itokawa when we started ITQ. He knew that even if it was called Tripod, the steering wheel would only be given to Hime. But he chose to trust me.

The next morning, the trawling vessel attack stopped.

Everything in Itokawa's part of the Sea of Japan went back to normal. Still, I knew that moving to the real agreement was not going to be easy.

the Sea of Japan

We decided to celebrate the memorandum working with a party at Judy & Peter. But soon after the party began, Hideki ran in, face flushed. He had snuck into Nanae's fishery association meeting, blending into the large crowd. Godzilla announced the upcoming merger with Hime, and the room quickly erupted into chaos.

"For the first time, people are questioning Godzilla's decision," Hideki said. "One of the parts they're most angry about is waiting three years. They feel like in this time, Hime will grow much larger than Nanae, and they won't be able to do anything about it. Still, Godzilla stuck with his guns, and he said he decided to trust us and move forward. He said that he thinks this will ultimately be the best arrangement for Nanae. But not all Nanae people agree."

It was hard to believe people were actually questioning Godzilla. Before, he had been the undisputed leader of Nanae, and his word was law.

"The Itokawan fishermen's distrust of Toyamans probably went deeper than even Godzilla had assumed," Ichiro said. "Godzilla is a businessman, but fishermen are fishermen. It is sometimes more than money. I understand their pride and disposition."

I said, "Also, I think that the fishermen realized Godzilla's conflict of interest between Itokawa tourism and the Nanae fishery. Godzilla's position never allows him to approve fishery tourism in Nanae. He's hoping to grow other tourist destinations in Itokawa, especially Little Kyoto, since Godzilla is the vice chairman of the traditional tea house association there."

"How is the negotiation with Hakodate Marine going, Lindsey?" Judy asked. "If we get a formal agreement with Hakodate Marine, it could help Godzilla to persuade the Nanae fishermen to also move forward on a formal agreement."

I stared down at my feet—I had hoped nobody would ask that question.

"I thought everything was going smoothly, but now, Hakodate Marine is hesitating in approving the formal agreement." Everyone immediately got quiet, and I quickly said, "I will follow up with Paul."

Nobody spoke. I felt like I needed to say something encouraging, so I said, "I don't think they're backing out or anything, they still seem very on-board. It's just that they're too big. Perhaps their in-house counsel is in the middle of reviewing our agreement. I'll meet with Paul tomorrow to discuss it."

Everyone started talking again, but the atmosphere was much less joyous than before.

The following day, after I called him and insisted on a meeting, Paul met me at Bamboo Sushi and gave me the signed agreement.

Paul was quiet as he handed me the agreement, which was strange. His mouth was a thin line, and his eyes kept darting around the restaurant. I quickly read through the document, looking for whatever was making Paul so nervous. I didn't have to look far: right in the title, I saw the words 'non-binding,' which made no sense.

"I think there's a mistake here," I said, even though I knew it wasn't true.

"It's not," Paul said quietly. "But, um, don't worry, we're going to delete the non-binding part very soon. You know how these companies are, they need to argue about the little minutia. Once we finish that internal discussion, we'll cut that part right out."

"Okay," I said, and I smiled, wanting more than anything to believe him.

◄ IIIIIIII ►

Several days went by, and my routine continued. I fed Paul my sushi at night, we spent the night together, and then I headed to the port at 4 a.m. As always, I slept in Ichiro's boat to recoup my lost sleeping time. While I was awake, I had to work twice as hard to keep up with Ichiro and Yoshi.

The ambiance in the port had become lively as all the fishermen talked about the exciting changes coming soon to Hime. Everyone was more cheerful, even the usually solemn fishermen like Hideki. I tried to be as happy as everyone else, but I couldn't stop thinking about Paul's non-binding memorandum.

Paul explained that Hakodate Marine believed that a non-binding memorandum was no different than a formal agreement. It was just a corporate formality. Paul also said that the CEO of Hakodate Marine, Doigaki, had told him to go ahead with everything we had agreed on.

I recalled the way Paul explained this to me, the words he used. He acted like a salesman trying to sell a pyramid scheme or an expensive timeshare. It wasn't his usual way of explaining things, and it made me think he was hiding something from me. Since then, he had changed the subject whenever I brought up the agreement. I was frustrated, but I knew I had to keep working with Hakodate Marine and Nanae to get our business plan in order.

The only other fisherman who wasn't cheerful was Ichiro. He stared down at his hands, bags under his eyes.

As much as I liked working on Ichiro's boat, I started wondering if it would be better for both of us if I left. Even without fishing, I would still be plenty busy with Bamboo Sushi and Hime Junior High School. I was proud of the work I did at the school—their English proficiency score had now reached the second percentile for all Japanese schools.

I laid down on the bottom of the boat and thought about permanently separating from Ichiro. This, inevitably, led to me thinking about my biological parents.

Every time I faced a potential separation with somebody close to me, I thought of my parents' funeral. They had died when I was a teenager, and in the months before their death, I had been stereotypically surly and rebellious toward them. At the funeral, my relatives asked if I remembered my last conversation with them, but I couldn't. Any conversation on that busy morning of the car accident? Or, anything that month? I couldn't remember at all. At that point, I realized that I never knew what would be going to happen to me in the next second. All I had was my past, and if I didn't have that, I had nothing.

For a week after, or maybe even a whole month, I tried to remember what my parents and I talked about in those last moments I had with them. I wanted to remember every detail of what they looked like, what they sounded like. I meditated constantly, like one of those monks in India who wore yellow dharma robes. I felt if I couldn't remember them, I would lose my parents forever. My memory grew stronger, until I naturally gained my unusual photographic memory.

I quickly found more uses for my new skill. I realized that if you remember details, people think you are smart. People tend to believe a person with memory, and they may even give them a job over someone else. Out of my strong desire, unbelievable fear, and sense of loneliness, I further developed my photographic memory skill. My uncle and his wife tried to integrate me into their family, but I drew more into myself. I believed that memory was the only protection I needed. My photographic memory helped distract me at school when the loss became too much, it helped me impress my teachers and made them think I was listening to them even when I was lost in my thoughts. It gave me the lifeline I needed. Without it, I'm not sure how I would have survived the worst period of my life.

Sometimes, though, I disliked being able to remember things so vividly. Because if I left Ichiro's boat, it was going to be incredibly painful to think back on this time. I didn't want to remember

Ichiro's smiling face as the wind blew back his hair or the joy of a cooler full of fish. But I had no choice but to remember it all, good and bad.

◄ ▯▯▯▯ ◄

One day, when we got back to the port after our morning fishing, I saw that I had a voicemail on my phone. It was from the pro-tem president of the association, inviting Ichiro, Judy, and me to join him and the three doyens for a discussion with the governor of Toyama that night at Judy & Peter.

"The governor said he had a conference call with the governor of Itokawa today. He wants to share the conversation with us and get our opinions," the pro-tem president said.

As requested, we went to Judy & Peter that night. The shop was closed, and Judy's employees had already gone home. When I walked in, everyone else was already there, sitting around a long table. Nakata san welcomed everyone and started serving pastrami, potato pancakes, and matzo ball soup. He also handed out beers to everyone. Due to his loyalty to Harley Davidson and Milwaukee, it was Miller Light instead of Kirin or Asahi.

Before anyone could take a bite of the food, the governor said, in his usual blunt way, "Nanae is a threat to Toyoma."

"What do you mean, Governor?" I asked.

"The Nanae people have become fearful."

"That's a good thing, Governor," one doyen said with a grin. Everyone laughed except the governor.

The governor sighed. He took his glasses off and wiped them on his shirt. "Look, I am a Toyaman too, so I have no love for the Itokawans. But this morning, the Governor of Itokawa phoned me and said that the Nanae association is not in good shape. Once Godzilla started asking the fishermen to accept Hime's proposal, people stopped respecting him, especially when he told them to stop trying to occupy Toyama Bay. Many people wanted to continue with the planned hijacking of ITQ. After all, stopping in the middle means that all their efforts were meaningless. The fishermen are questioning Godzilla's leadership.

"To make things worse, Godzilla is using his veto power in votes about Nanae's fishery tourism instead of recusing himself. He has a conflict of interest between Little Kyoto and Nanae. That angered many fishermen in Nanae. In normal circumstances, it has not been that way. But everyone is tense. And now, Nanae is divided."

"What do those Nanae fishermen want?" one doyen asked.

"They want us to amend our business plan and drop the three-year wait time for the merger."

"How can you marry a person who's so hostile toward you?" another doyen said. "The more I hear about their attitude, the more I'm convinced that the three-year wait was the right idea. In three years, they'll see our tremendous growth, and for the first time they'll be humble and ready for our merger."

"That's right," the third doyen said. "This has been our plan, and we've done everything. We've put the scheme together, researched the probability, explained everything to the association members, made an online auction, and attracted tourists. This has all happened because of our efforts. Nanae does not have a right to amend our plan. I know Nanae tried to copy what we are doing now, but without proper human resources and preparation, I heard that they have miserably failed."

The governor said, "I know, and I understand your feelings. Just like you, I only care about Toyamans. But I don't think it is a good idea to push them to the edge of the cliff."

That last statement clearly angered the pro-tem president. He leaned forward and said, "With all due respect, Governor, when we all were on the real edge of the cliff three months ago when Godzilla was attacking us, what did you do for us?"

The governor said nothing.

"We asked you to put a moratorium on ITQ implementation three times, but you refused it three times."

"It's out of my control. The central government has already decided to implement ITQ, and there's nothing I can do about it."

"No, there were things you could do. You could delay or even stop the ITQ process. And now, you are asking us to amend our business plan because Nanae people are suffering? Who do you work for, Governor?"

"That's not necessary," the governor said loudly.

"I think it is necessary," one doyen said, also raising his voice. "When your own people suffered and one of your cities was shrinking, you didn't do anything. Now, your neighbors asked you a favor, and you are trying to change our plan. Seriously?"

"You got me wrong, doyen. Putting a moratorium on our ITQ will make all Toyamans look self-centered, and it will make people think we hate the environment. What if Tokyonians boycott buying our fish? They're the ones who are buying most of our fish, so if you lose Tokyo now, you will have to change jobs. Not only that, Tokyonians could decide they're not even going to buy manufacturing products made in Toyama. I couldn't allow that to happen."

"You can say whatever you want now. We were dead, once. These three young people saved us," the same doyen said, pointing his finger at me, Ichiro, and Judy.

The governor shook his head. "You're not thinking this through. If we make the people of Nanae desperate, they could decide they're okay with taking rash actions that harm themselves, so long as it also hurts Toyamans."

"What do you mean by that?" the pro-tem president asked.

"My hunch is they're going to turn to Hakodate Marine. What if Nanae makes a deal with them that lets Hakodate Marine work with Nanae fishermen before we merge with them?"

"No way. That's suicide to all fishermen in Nanae," the pro-tem president replied.

One doyen said, "That is correct. Without preparation, letting Hakodate Marine into their territory is like letting a tiger into your house without a leash. Most of them will have to abandon their fishing boats."

The governor said, "But all of them will be employed by Hakodate Marine. They don't have to leave Nanae for jobs." The governor finished his beer, and Nakata san quickly brought out another one.

"If Nanae does marry Hakodate Marine, all the fish they catch will only belong to Nanae. Our catch volume will fall even lower," the governor said, sipping his beer. "It's clear that if this happens, Hime won't be able to survive."

"No, we won't," a doyen said.

"What do you three think?" the governor asked, looking at Judy, Ichiro, and me.

Judy cleared her throat. "Hime is a small city. At this point, the population is descending. But we have many people coming to Hime for tourism these days. We have created more new business in the last three months than the last four years combined, and most people who visit love Hime. Because of that, I know more people will move here. The population in Hime, and maybe even all of Toyoma, will expand. But people who move here are going to be looking for jobs. In order for us to create more jobs, we definitely need those three phases. That's the only way we will be able to expand enough to ship products to super high-end consumers like Manhattan or Las Vegas. That is the dream we are selling to people moving here, and people will move here because they like our dream. Having said that, I'm not sure if Hakodate Marine will make this dream come true. I don't think they will care about our city and the fishery association."

Ichiro added, "We need time to gain the upper hand, and getting the upper hand is the only way to make this Operation Tripod happen peacefully."

Now, the governor pointed his fingertip at me—it was greasy from the pastrami he had been sampling. "What do you think, Lindsey?"

Every time I heard Hakodate Marine's name from someone's mouth here, my heart plummeted. But I pushed past that and said in a firm voice, "As everyone here has said, it's impossible for us to fight against Nanae if they collaborate with Hakodate Marine. But I don't think that will happen. I'm a fisherwoman too, and I know fishermen are very reluctant to join with corporations. Fishermen have a culture of independence. They don't work for companies. That's what my grandfather always taught me, and fishermen in Nanae are as independent as anyone."

"Okay, okay. What about Hakodate Marine?" the governor said.

"As you know, my friend is leading the Hakodate Marine deal." I didn't want to say 'boyfriend' in front of Ichiro. "And I trust him."

Then, one doyen said, "Mr. Governor. You should remember that Hakodate Marine will be the biggest investor in the Hime-Nanae fishery association. If we can't trust them, we shouldn't consider collaborating with them at all. Since we have come this far, it means we have decided to trust Hakodate Marine."

The governor shook his head reluctantly, looking like he couldn't think of anymore arguments. "All right, ladies and gentlemen. If you all firmly believe what you said tonight, I will say to the governor of Itokawa that we won't change our plan. I still sense the risk, but I will take the risk with you people."

The tension immediately dissipated, and we all exchanged firm handshakes with the governor. We spent the rest of the evening eating and talking. I tried to join in, but I was still anxious. I couldn't stop thinking about Hakodate Marine.

Paul must have been hiding something from me.

That was the scariest thing I could possibly think.

I had been there before.

◀ ⅢⅢⅢ ◀

Rumor reached us that Nanae's internal argument had intensified. Even after our governor told the Itokawa governor that we wouldn't amend our business plan, the Nanae fishery association still didn't back down. As a matter of fact, every time I called Nanae, Godzilla was not in the association building. He later called me back from his cell phone. He said it was the first time so many fishermen had defied what he said. He also apologized for the delay.

I told him not to worry and sent another apple pie, hoping that would keep him on my good side. This time, I used four apples produced in his home prefecture. He was thrilled and told me it was the greatest alleviation for his stress.

The next morning, Judy texted me a link to an article in Itokawa's local newspaper. Before I even had time to read it, she called me and quickly said, "For the first time, they're saying that Nanae fishermen should take the Hime merger deal. They said they need it to survive."

"They're definitely starting to feel the pressure," I said. "We've never felt an actual sense of urgency from the Nanae fishermen. It's interesting too that the Itokawa tourism industry finally seems to care about what's happening in Nanae."

"That's because they're seeing a drop in sales because tourists from Tokyo are stopping in Hime and not continuing onto Itokawa."

"Right," I said, almost feeling guilty.

"How's the fishing going?"

"Unfortunately, these days, the ocean is running wild. Some days we catch a ton, some days there's nothing. But Ichiro is making good use of these off-days. He's using them to coach young fishermen about how to do his nerve breakdown method for yellowtail. Fishermen normally keep their techniques to themselves, but Ichiro feels like we need to have everyone share their unique skill with each other."

"Good strategy. That sounds like Ichiro, he likes speaking with action over words."

Judy regularly made statements like this, statements that were designed to push me toward Ichiro and away from Paul. I always pretended not to notice.

"Right, we need to be united, that will help us put more pressure on Nanae," I said.

In my head, I heard Mr. Principal say, "One Hime, One Heart." Right now, more than anything, I wanted my one heart to be with Paul. But it was difficult to get closer to him with things so up in the air with Hakodate Marine. I sighed and sat down on my bed.

"I heard Hime Junior High School's senior students are studying like crazy for the high school entrance exams," Judy said. "I also heard that teachers have been working long hours, providing whatever help they can for the students. Is that true?"

"Yeah. The entrance exam is a huge deal, and they're all stressing out. I've basically become a mother-like figure for them and I'm making myself available 24/7. But it's fine—it will be over soon. Speaking of mothers, how is your parents' deli doing?"

"Not great, the New York deli industry is experiencing more difficulties. The other day, one of our competitors, Andrew, had to close shop. His shop has been around for eighty years, and it was loved by many New York celebrities, but it still wasn't enough. It's making my parents nervous. The deli industry needs to survive. And a need for survival is the mother of invention."

"Right," I said, trying to think of something that would comfort her. "You're the most inventive person I know, I'm sure you'll think of something."

I hung up and went down to the sushi shop, where I met up with Mr. Bamboo. We walked to the port together, me to go fishing and Mr. Bamboo to do prep work at his new restaurant.

Even though things with Nanae were tense, Hime had still made great progress on its tourism campaign. A couple of weeks before everything started with Nanae, we began working on one of our biggest projects yet. We refurbished an old building by the port and turned into the Hime Gourmet Center. On the first floor, we had a casual food court. On the second floor, there were full blown, expensive restaurants where we hoped famous chefs would come and open restaurants. We had already gotten a few chefs from around Japan to sign leases, but we decided that we also needed to show off our local *Toyoma Bay Sushi*. Mr. Bamboo decided to open a restaurant on the second floor, and he asked me to take charge of a few night shifts in the original location. Flattered, I accepted his offer.

Mr. Bamboo began spending most of his time at the new shop, training a newly hired assistant chef. I took over at least three night shifts a week, and sometimes more if the new space was very busy.

A couple days after the Itokawa article came out, I was working at one of these shifts. Bamboo Sushi was packed—the counter was full and about ten people were waiting in line. I was busy making my sushi, completely focused on what I was doing. But then, I heard someone shout, "Hey!"

I looked up just in time see Ichiro push through the line and come up to the counter.

"Lindsey, can we talk now?" he said, his voice quavering with anger.

"No, I'm working."

Ichiro ignored me and said, "When did you last see Paul?"

"I don't know, a few days ago."

I stared down at the fish meat I was cutting, avoiding Ichiro's eyes. If he saw my eyes, he would know that I was lying. Paul hadn't called me or emailed for the last five days, and he ignored my texts. I guessed—or hoped—that he was extremely busy putting together our deal.

"Did you call him today or last night?" Ichiro said, his voice angrier than I ever heard it before.

"Why are you asking that, it's none of your business."

"I'm your partner, I deserve to know."

"That doesn't justify your prying into my private life with my boyfriend."

That was the first time I called Paul my boyfriend in front Ichiro. To my surprise, Ichiro's face didn't change at all.

"I don't care about that. I only care about our Hakodate Marine deal."

All the customers at the counter stared at us, frowning. Anger rose in my chest—they shouldn't be watching this unprofessional scene.

"Can we talk about this later, Ichiro?"

"No, we can't," he said, and I sensed that he was getting to the point of his visit. "Hakodate Marine is playing politics with the Itokawa governor."

"What?"

"The worst possible scenario may be coming. Hakodate Marine and Nanae will cancel the memorandum with Hime."

I dropped the dish I was holding. It shattered, the sound echoing through the restaurant.

"Call me when you are done tonight," Ichiro said, and he walked out without turning back.

◀ ▦▦▦ ▶

Bamboo Sushi closed at 10:00 p.m. Then, I washed dishes and cleaned the shop. Tenaciously. Mrs. Bamboo said she would do that for me tonight, but I refused her help. Cleanliness is the spirit of sushi. If I neglected that, I knew Mr. Bamboo would be disappointed in me. He had been extremely friendly and understanding to me, but he was still my master. Treating masters with the highest respect was something I had to do, and I wanted to do it in the Japanese way. And besides, scrubbing the dishes hard helped me relieve my tension.

When I finished work, it was already midnight. Normally, I got up at three, went to the port, got on the boat, and slept until we reached the fishing area. As I cleaned the shop, I called Paul more than ten times and sent ten texts, but he never answered me.

I also called the pro-tem president, who told me what Ichiro said was true. The information was given to Ichiro from a local newspaper journalist who had high credibility. The news would spread through the whole Hime fishery in the next day or two.

Ichiro and I needed to talk right away, but at midnight, there were no restaurants or coffee shops open. So, for the first time, I invited somebody besides Judy into my room. I hadn't let anybody in because I considered it an extension of my sacred workplace. I had never even let Paul come to my room.

Ichiro arrived soon after I finished cleaning. I let him in, and he stood on the doormat, refusing to come farther in. He didn't even look around my room, which I guessed was his way to show he was considerate of my privacy. But still, in this small room, he must have seen Paul's picture on my writing desk. I had thought about hiding it before letting Ichiro in, but I decided not to.

"Nanae is miserably divided, more than we could have possibly imagined," Ichiro said.

"We were divided too until a few months ago."

"Yes, but it's very different—they're completely broken. Even when we were at our most divided, we still discussed our situation with each other. In Nanae, nobody talks anymore. As far as I'm concerned, Godzilla is the only person who understands why this deal is best for both of us, and that's why he entered discussions with you. But unfortunately, most of the Itokawa fishermen don't trust Toyamans. They think three years will turn out to be ten years."

"Why do they think that? We're going to have a contract."

"They are well-experienced merchants. They understand that contracts don't always mean that much."

"What do you mean?"

"Well, if both associations agree on the three-year term, and if the Hime fishery association breaches the contract and decides not to merge with Nanae three years later, what do you think is going to happen?"

"The contract will be binding. We can't breach it and we won't breach it."

"See, that is how naïve people think."

I wanted to glare at Ichiro, but I couldn't show him how much that insult angered me, so I just took a deep breath.

Ichiro continued. "In reality, there are many people in business who don't honor contracts for various reasons."

"Okay, fine. Let's say, hypothetically, that we breach the contract? Then what?"

"The only remedy for them is to file a suit to the court. But the court cannot make us merge. The court can make Hime pay damages to Nanae. But the association does not possess any assets. It's like your home owners' associations in the US. You can get a verdict of tens of millions of dollars at court, but you won't get that money because the Hime fishery association doesn't have the money. That's it. Fishermen including you and me will not be affected by any of it."

"But we're honorable people. We wouldn't do that."

"So what? That's your perception, not theirs. The Nanae fishery association isn't functioning. The group who opposes Godzilla have now filed a motion to impeach Godzilla from the presidency. That's the only way they can survive because they have created a new enemy."

"Who's that?"

"The residents of Itokawa prefecture. Their tourism industry is in danger because of our fishery tourism. The Itokawa governor also has a vested interest in keeping the tourism industry afloat. The majority of his constituents work in tourism or are directly influenced by the tourism industry. Itokawans want to convert Hime fishery tourism to Hime-Nanae tourism. Or, they will destroy Hime by bringing Hakodate Marine to the Toyama Bay tomorrow."

"Wow."

"I know. The Itokawa governor will issue an executive order and give a license to Hakodate Marine next week, so that Hakodate Marine doesn't have to wait for three years. Hakodate Marine can come into Toyama Bay in the next month or so."

"What?"

"I know, I couldn't believe it either. Hakodate Marine will employ existing Nanae fishermen, and they'll only sail in Itokawa's jurisdiction. But Itokawa is situated in the west entrance of our Toyama Bay fish tank. They can easily deplete our fish because most of our fish travel from the west into the bay. They'll get all the fish before they can reach us."

"This is all so crazy. But someone must have connected the Itokawa governor with Hakodate Marine. I wonder who did it."

"Nobody in Itokawa for sure."

"Then, who?"

Ichiro stared at me, a look almost like sympathy on his face, and I knew why. "It's Paul, isn't it?"

After a long pause, Ichiro mumbled, "Who else could it be?"

I looked away, swallowing hard, refusing to cry in front of Ichiro. I thought of all the days I spent crying after Paul ditched me back in Massachusetts. I cursed my memory, which made all these memories too vivid.

But it was different this time—Paul had said he loved me, that he wanted to be with me. Paul couldn't have done this. It had to be someone else, because I couldn't imagine someone doing this to someone that they said they loved.

I called Judy the next morning and told her about Hakodate Marine. She was furious, and she demanded that I skip fishing and meet with her and Paul in her shop.

I walked into Judy's shop about an hour later, tired and nervous. Paul came in right after me, looking just as exhausted.

"Hey," he said, kissing me on the cheek. "I'm so sorry I haven't been able to return your calls, work has been crazy. Hi, Judy." He smiled at her, and she glared back.

"We know you've been going behind our backs. Tell us what your plan is."

"What on earth are you talking about?" he said, eyes wide and innocent.

Judy didn't buy his act for a second. "Hakodate Marine must not have liked the idea of waiting three years. And instead of saying no to us, you decided to do a secret deal with the Itokawa governor."

"What?"

Judy explained what we had learned. When she finished, Paul shook his head. "I didn't know that they canceled the memorandum."

"You're the only Hakodate Marine employee in Hime. And you're the only one who's gotten an inside look at the Hime fishery association. Only you can pull the strings."

"I can't believe this. I didn't do this, I wouldn't do this. I know you don't like me after what happened last time Lindsey and I dated, but now you are just being so unfair."

I had to agree with him—she was being unfair. I sometimes thought she put extra pressure on him to make sure that he didn't hurt me again. But today, it didn't feel like her feelings were personal. It was pure anger about him endangering the future of Hime.

"Who cares if I'm being unfair? It's the truth," Judy said.

"Look. Ask Lindsey. I've been good to her, and I've been good to Hime."

"Cut the crap, Paul. You are such an asshole, using Lindsey and me and Hime for your benefit. All you care about is your career. If it will benefit you, you will ruin people's hard work and lives with zero hesitation."

Even though Judy was clearly certain that Paul was to blame, I wasn't so sure. I hated going against Judy, but I couldn't stand by while she accused Paul of something he may not have done.

"Look, Judy, we don't have proof that Paul did this yet," I said.

"I didn't do it," Paul added. "But believe me, I'm going to find out who did."

"I can't believe this," Judy said, and to my surprise, her eyes filled with tears. "My best friend is choosing to believe her scumbag ex over me. This is some bullshit."

Judy tried to walk toward Paul, but she swayed and stumbled into a table. I walked closer to her and smelled alcoholic fumes wafting off of her.

"Judy, are you drunk? It's eight in the morning," I said, holding her arm to steady her.

"What do you care? You don't care about me," Judy said, stumbling backward.

"Of course I care about you. Don't be silly," I said.

"You have a real funny way of showing it." Judy glanced at the clock. "I need to finish preparing my pastrami. You two can hang out here if you want, I don't care anymore."

"Judy," I said, following her behind the counter. "Are you okay? Are *we* okay?"

"I'm fine, it was just a bad night. And we're fine too, Lindsey. I'm not mad at you. I just don't want you to get hurt again."

"I won't," I said, and we hugged. Judy headed into the kitchen, and I went back to Paul.

"Lindsey, again, I'm so sorry for not responding to your messages," Paul said. "I was crazy busy, and I didn't even have time to check them. Can you forgive me?"

"I was upset, but I'm feeling better now, after hearing you apologize. I missed you."

"I missed you too." Paul hugged me, and I hesitated for a moment before hugging him back. He whispered into my ear, "I didn't want to say this in front of Judy, but I also sensed that something was going on in Itokawa. I have been scared and running around to collect the real information from Itokawa and Hakodate."

I nodded. He squeezed my cheeks with his hands, our faces so close I could see the stubble dotting his face, which was surprising. He hated having facial hair. He must have been truly busy.

He kissed me. It was the kiss I had been waiting to have for the last seven days. As we broke apart, I decided to trust Paul and believe what he said.

After that, Paul headed to work, and I went to the port to wait for Ichiro. I had to let him know about our conversation.

When his boat came back, I hopped onboard and helped Ichiro and Yoshi unload the fish. As we did that, I explained what Paul and I discussed. While I talked, his face was in total denial, and he said nothing. He didn't even nod. For the first time, I saw hatred in his eyes. He tossed our anchoring ropes into the water wildly. I glanced at Yoshi and saw he was staring at Ichiro helplessly and almost fearfully.

I knew then at no matter what happened, he was always going to have an irrational hatred toward Paul. Ichiro's hatred made me feel closer to Paul, made me want to spend more time with him. I decided to see Paul again after I unloaded all the fish from off the boat.

The next morning, Mr. Bamboo handed me two papers, the Toyama paper and the Itokawa paper. Both headlines were the same:

"The Itokawa Governor will issue a special license to Hakodate Marine."

The Itokawa paper praised the governor's actions to save Nanae and its fishery. But the Toyama paper pointed out the real political motivation was saving the tourism industry in Itokawa. They also condemned the Toyama governor's office for its clumsy handling of the situation, and it warned about the negative impact this would have on the newly reviving Hime port.

I put the paper down after reading the first paragraph of the article, too horrified to read more. After seeing my surprised face, Mr. Bamboo said, "The Toyama paper explained that the Hime-Nanae merger might not happen because Hakodate Marine is now the most influential financial contributor to the Nanae association. Since the Itokawa governor is allowing them to go into Toyoma Bay, there's no reason for them to collaborate with Hime. The paper also says that the Itokawa governor is allowing Hakodate Marine to catch all coast fish, including yellow tail, white shrimp, and firefly squid."

"But those are Hime brand fish, Mr. Bamboo."

"Yes, but fish swim, Lindsey. And if the Hime fish are in Itokawa's jurisdiction, there's nothing we can do to stop them. Hakodate Marine is giving Itokawa a significant cash investment, and they're using it to build a state-of-the-art frozen warehouse and an HACCP-compliant process center in Nanae port. The Toyama paper even revealed that Hakodate Marine may invest in the non-fishery industries in Kanazawa city. It's open bribery, but what can we do?"

Mrs. Bamboo came in silently, carrying two cups of green tea. I said good morning to her in a weak voice.

"At the end of the article, the paper predicts that the only way Toyama will be able to survive is if the Hime fishermen leave their fishery and work for Hakodate Marine. Or, Toyama needs to back out of the ITQ deal."

"Quitting ITQ at the last minute may harm the credibility of Toyamans in general. The nation's first ITQ implementation has drawn a lot of attention," I said.

Mr. Bamboo sat in a chair and read the paper over and over again. His hot green tea sat next to him, untouched. It was one of the first times I ever saw him sitting—he usually stood and worked on two things simultaneously. The worrying made the lines on his face more pronounced, making him look much older than sixty-four.

I tried to alleviate his pain by saying, "But our brand will stay. People will still pay respect to the brand, right?"

"No. This means the end of Toyama Bay Sushi. If we go to the Hime market a year from today, our market will not carry any brand fish, or any real fish at all. Just cheap, small, thin baby fish."

He looked up at the ceiling for a while. "There's a stain," he muttered. He got a stepladder, climbed up it, and polished the ceiling.

I went to the market.

The fishermen in Hime had all heard what had happened, and they understood how devastating this would be. When I walked into the market, the fishermen closest to me stopped talking and walked over to me.

"Lindsey san, we were wondering if you would go with us to Paul's office," one fisherman said.

I nodded. They needed to hear about all this from the source.

Paul was in his office, and he came out when I knocked on the door. He usually dressed business casual, but today he wore a suit and tie. He must have expected this.

Paul greeted the large crowd—by the time we left the market, we had about fifty people with us, including the doyens.

"Can you tell us more about this?" one doyen asked, pointing to the front-page article.

"I wish I could, but I don't know anything about it. Like the article says, this all came from the top of the food chain. It was a deal made between the Hakodate Marine CEO and the Itokawa governor. They didn't even tell me it was happening. Doigaki didn't even come here to see me. The whole deal was made over the phone while he was still in Hakodate."

For a moment, I felt doubt—would the CEO really make a deal that big over the phone? But I had to trust Paul; there was nothing else to do.

"Can you meet with your CEO and find out more about this deal?" another doyen asked.

"I'll try, but I can't promise anything," Paul said.

A few people in the crowd muttered to each other, looking at Paul in disbelief. Paul seemed to sense that he lost the crowd, and he grabbed me and pulled me next to him. He put on a large smile and turned straight to me, like a presidential candidate welcoming the vice-presidential candidate to the podium.

"Lindsey, you trust me, don't you?" he said it like a question, but it sounded almost declaration.

I saw Judy in the crowd. And Ichiro. I hadn't realized either of them were here, but seeing them made me feel even more pressure.

As all the fishermen stared at me, the fact that I was their leader truly sunk in. I hadn't sought out this enormous responsibility, but I didn't shirk it. I couldn't just make a vague response. I had to be firm in my answer.

In front of all the people watching me, I said, "Yes, I trust you."

"Good," Paul said, his relief clear.

"Please continue to help us do the right thing. All we want is win-win solutions for all three entities," I said as I looked toward the crowd.

Many people in the crowd smiled or sighed with relief. They thought if I trusted Paul, then things were okay. I shifted uncomfortably—I didn't like my own comment, it sounded almost fake. But that was all I could come up with.

Paul turned to the crowd again and said with his arms spread, "Ladies and gentlemen, I am a mere employee, a mere expatriate that came to Hakodate from very far away. I only know a little about the company's executive decisions. However, Hakodate Marine is a fair company. I'm willing to listen to you and do what's best for Toyama and Itokawa. I'm doing this because I respect both prefectures, I love this bay, and I'm happy to be part of this wonderful collaboration, despite what certain newspapers may say."

Then, Paul straightened his back and donned what I knew was his "serious" look. "But, ladies and gentlemen, I feel like you did mislead us about something very important. You said that we could collaborate with both you and Nanae, but I don't see how that was ever possible. There's just too much animosity between your towns. Isn't that true? With all due respect, I think you had a duty to explain this deep war to me and Hakodate Marine. After all, it was you, not Nanae, who approached us. It was your obligation to give us a fair and honest assessment of how you thought Nanae would take the wait-three-years strategy."

The fishermen were quiet, but I nodded, because he was right. We neglected to share how deep the animosity with Nanae went—we had underestimated it.

"Don't get me wrong, I'm not criticizing you," Paul said. "At the end of the day, it was your call. But you guys seemed to blame everything on your historical disagreement. And I mean no offense, but I think you need to let it go."

Everyone looked at me, trying to decide how they should take this. I wasn't sure how I felt about it—there were many reasons for Hime to have problems with Nanae. But I didn't want to tell Paul off. We needed Paul, and we needed Hakodate Marine. So I decided to simply ignore that last statement.

I said, "I don't know anything about what they're discussing behind the curtain in Hakodate Marine. But I know this person, Paul, very well. I trusted him before, and I trust him now. I will talk to the CEO of Hakodate Marine as soon as Paul arranges it."

Ichiro silently walked away, shaking his head, hunched over in disappointment. Nobody seemed to notice him leave except me.

◀ ‖‖‖‖‖▸

The week after that was dark and silent. Membership at the Hime fishery association started dropping again. In just a week, twenty people quit, leaving only 270 members.

I started fishing again every morning with the still-friendly Yoshi and a mostly silent Ichiro. We focused on golden eye snappers. I was in charge of guessing where the fish were. I smelled the sea breeze, looked at the slight color change of the water, and listened to the wind. I also made use of our modern technology and used the GPS, fish radar, and water temperature gage.

I was getting better, but we were catching fewer and fewer fish, and the fish we caught were smaller than usual. The larger fish were being overfished, leaving just the tiny ones for us.

One morning, I went to work with Mr. Bamboo after I finished fishing. Together, we prepared sushi rice for that night. As we made the rice, Mr. Bamboo said, "I know you need to fight like someone is punching us. But for our true survival, harmony is needed. The fish are in a war zone, and because of that they don't taste as good. The sea is contaminated by human anger."

I stopped fixing rice, focusing on what he said. I was sure he said that to alleviate my frustration—all the sushi I had made recently had tasted terrible. I tried my best, but the taste kept getting worse. It was clearly because of my muddy heart and my confused head—like Mr. Bamboo always told me, my emotions affected the taste of my sushi.

Mr. Bamboo said, "Don't feel bad. Even my sushi is not at the level it should be these days."

I looked at Mrs. Bamboo for confirmation, and she nodded.

"Even though the fish meat is as fresh as ever, it now tastes different. When we lose the appreciation to the sea, the sea will not provide us with tender fish," Mr. Bamboo said.

I sighed, knowing what he was getting at. We needed harmony if we were going to survive. It was ironic—I had never cared about workplace harmony before, but now, I had to be the one who restored our relationships.

Throughout the long, disappointing week, I kept trying to call Paul, but for seven days I couldn't get through to him. I started worrying that Paul had been used by Hakodate Marine to get into Toyoma Bay. He thought he had climbed up the long corporate ladder and almost reached the top, but the reality was he was just the bait. When Hakodate reeled in the catch they wanted, they simply discarded what was left of Paul.

Once people started realizing that Paul wasn't doing what he promised, people in Hime started to treat me differently. Men especially didn't seem to know what to say to me, and they couldn't hide the concern on their faces.

The women tried to comfort me. I needed that comfort more than ever about a week after Paul's speech, when we lost a historic thirty members of the Hime fishery association in one morning. After the news broke, Hana called me and asked me to meet her and a few of the other fishermen's wives at a local tea shop, Tomato Café.

Over green tea, Hana said, "No matter what the consequences are, women in Hime will be on your side."

"That's right," a rosy-cheeked woman said. "Don't feel like this is your responsibility. We all underestimated the risk Ito-kawans felt waiting three years. And even though the Itokawans attacked us first, we can't justify attacking them back. I have to admit, I'm happy we're looking past Itokawa for solutions now."

After we finished our tea, we went for lunch at Judy's pastrami shop, and then we headed over to Olive Bath House. While we were in the bath, my favorite female manager calmly came by and gave us each a wrapped ice cream.

"Thank you," I said, my voice almost inaudible.

"Don't tell the health district, okay," she said with a chuckle. Her chubby, short arms swung back and forth as she walked away.

I ate my ice cream, grateful that I was still loved, even with all the mistakes I had made.

The following night, Judy asked me and Ichiro to join her for a short meeting at her shop. When we arrived, Judy immediately said, "I've arranged for you guys to meet with a big seafood company called Jason Foods. They're based in Arkansas. I know that there's just a small chance that they'll partner with us, but you guys should give it a shot at least."

"Thank you, Judy, but I'm not sure if that's realistic," Ichiro said.

"I know, but what choice do we have left? Now many Toyamans are saying that we should drop the ITQ and fight as much as we can. I can't see that ending well."

I sighed and looked out the window. It was snowing, the scene peaceful and lovely, but I could feel nothing but sadness and guilt.

If I hadn't brought Hakodate Marine to Hime, we would have just been fighting Itokawa. Now the war was against Itokawa and Hakodate Marine combined, and Toyoma had no chance against them.

"I'm going to head home. I'm pretty tired," I said.

"Are you all right, Lindsey?" Judy asked. Even Ichiro, who barely glanced at me these days, looked concerned.

"I'm fine," I lied.

It started snowing harder as I walked, the flakes turning my hands and face into ice. When I got home, I didn't go upstairs. I didn't even bother to shake the snow off my shoulders. I unlocked Bamboo Sushi's door, turned on just one light, and sat down at the counter where I served my customers. I was freezing, but I didn't even have the energy to go turn on the heat.

I cried. I had come to Hime with good intentions, but in the end, I destroyed this small fishermen town. Everybody said it was not my fault, but it was clear that they were just trying to make me feel better, since there was no point in saying the truth: I had ruined everything. It was too much pressure. It was all too much.

I put my head down on the counter, crying into my arms.

After a while, someone patted my back gently. It was Mrs. Bamboo.

She didn't say a word. After we locked eyes, she just nodded once deeply and walked back toward her residential annex. I heard her humming a slow song that sounded almost like a lullaby. After a moment, I realized that it was an Owara dance song, a beautiful but melancholic song about someone whose true love died when they were young. After that, the person always waited for the cherry blossoms to bloom, but they were then disappointed by how quickly they died.

Mrs. Bamboo's soft voice faded away and then got louder as she walked back into the restaurant, holding a big mug full of a hot, sweet-smelling drink. At first, I thought it was coffee, but that didn't make sense because at Bamboo Sushi, we never served coffee. The smell of the drink simply didn't match the food. After a moment, I finally realized what the drink was, and it took me right back to my childhood.

It was ginger butter cocoa, something my mother always made for me when I felt low as a child. As a rebellious teenager, I told my mom that I hated the drink, and she quietly stopped making it for me. I hadn't had it since she died. I had talked about it with Mrs. Bamboo a long time ago, and I was touched that she remembered.

"Thank you, *Okamisan*," I said, sipping slowly.

"You are welcome, Lindsey. Make yourself warm and sleep tight." Mrs. Bamboo touched me gently on the shoulder and then walked back to her residential annex.

Cocoa and ginger keeps you warm, and butter makes the taste more profound and relaxes you. I inhaled the scent of the heavenly drink, and then I put the cup to my lips. My sorrow and disappointment in myself got mixed with my nostalgic memories of my parents. I could perfectly picture my old house and my toys.

Ginger butter cocoa warmed me up from the inside. I realized that this was what I wanted. I didn't need any kind words from anybody because I wouldn't believe them anyway. I just wanted warmth.

I cried more that night, but I also felt like I was healing.

◀ ▥▥ ✕

Ichiro and I began preparing for the trip to Arkansas to meet with Jason Foods, which would take place in the middle of February. I checked my phone constantly, but Paul never returned my emails and calls. I was sure he was in the middle of turmoil, running around without sleep trying to help me and Hime. He lost face in Hime. We had all overestimated his presence at Hakodate Marine. He was just being used.

Judy didn't believe that Paul was off trying to help us. She didn't say anything out loud, but every time I went to the pastrami shop, she gave me her I-told-you-so look. And she also gave me pitying looks that told me she thought he had ditched me again.

I opposed her firmly. "Out of all the bad news, the only piece of good news is that Paul and I are proud of each other, working harder than anybody for the sake of our community. When everything is over, perhaps I will follow him to wherever he will relocate. I will help him to build his career from scratch."

"What about your own career path?" Judy asked.

"Obviously, I am done. No more career building. I deserve this."

Judy gave me another pitying look, and I quickly turned away.

A few days later, Ichiro and I left for Arkansas. We had a three-hour layover at Haneda Tokyo Airport, and while we were waiting, Ichiro checked the news on his phone. He breathed sharply and handed me his phone. He was looking at an article from the Toyoma paper that said one-third of the Hime fishermen decided to leave the association today. Now, there would be only 200 fishermen left in Hime. With so few men and women working, there was a good chance that we would be forced to close the Hime port soon.

Ichiro and I stared at each other for a moment, both our faces darkening.

We said at the same time, "We have to get to Jason Foods to come to Hime."

Chapter Three

*O*ur three days in Arkansas were a blur of meetings in non-descript conference rooms with nondescript executives. We shook tons of hands, showed our PowerPoint numerous times, and answered hundreds of questions. Then, in what felt like no time at all, we were on a plane back to Tokyo. As soon as we hit the ground in Japan, I turned on my iPhone. One notification jumped out at me immediately.

"Ichiro, I already received an email from Jason Foods," I said, my heart pounding hard.

"What did they say?"

It was a short email. It said that the Jason Foods respectfully declined our proposal.

The disappointment hit me in waves of shock, anger, and sadness. "I thought the meetings went well. Didn't you?" I said, not bothering to hide my frustration.

"Of course I did," he said, his voice filled with anger.

"In that last meeting, the Jason Foods executives mentioned that they would give us an answer after they did their own market research. They must have found out about all the contention between Hakodate Marine, Nanae, and us."

"We tried not to make a big deal out of it, but I had a feeling they guessed something was wrong when they asked why we came to Jason Foods while Hakodate Marine is coming to Toyama Bay."

"I know, I was worried we lost them then too, but I hoped they could look past it." A few tears leaked out and ran down my cheeks. I quickly wiped them away.

"We did our best, but I think we lost," said Ichiro, not hiding his sorrow either. "In April, Hakodate Marine's ships will come to Toyama Bay, and they'll catch all the fish before they swim into our jurisdiction."

"There is no such thing as fishery tourism when there are no fish. No fish, no tourism."

Ichiro and I were silent as we got off the plane and went through customs, both of us lost in our thoughts. We also didn't talk during our ride on the bullet train from Tokyo to Toyoma. I pretended I was asleep. Ichiro bought two bento boxes for us. I didn't touch mine. Neither did he.

When we arrived at Hime, it was early afternoon. There were a lot of tourists watching over the auction, riding on the tourism boats, and eating fresh Hime brand fish at the newly created restaurant complex. Everything looked normal, but I knew pretty soon, this area would be abandoned.

"Fishery tourism will stop very soon," Ichiro said, echoing my thoughts.

"With Hakodate Marine's finances, Nanae will copy everything we have," I said as I watched the blue cap people working at the auction. I heard the sound of a hose spraying water, ice mounting, and an auctioneer shouting. Outside, it started snowing again. Pure snowflakes landed on the surface of the ocean and melted there. It was all peaceful and so fragile.

This was all my fault—I was the one who had invited a bull into our China shop. Paul still had not responded to me. I had emailed the CEO of Hakodate Marine, Mr. Doigaki, before we left for Arkansas, but I had gotten no response.

What if Paul had played us, just like Judy said?

My chest tightened and my head spun, and I finally admitted what I had subconsciously known for a while: I was wrong and Judy was right. Paul was gone.

Still, I wasn't ready to admit that to Ichiro yet, so I faintly said, "I'm sure Paul will make things right in Hakodate."

Ichiro didn't answer, and we silently walked away from the port.

As we walked, we passed Asahi Kaizuka, an ancient house that had exhibits tracing Hime's long history, all the way back to 5000 years ago. Normally, this was a very quiet historical site, but now, tourists had started visiting it.

This town with 5000 years of history would die soon.

A week passed. I finally told Judy that she was right. Paul had used me, and he ditched me and Hime. I should never have trusted him again.

Emotions swirled in my head, but I never let myself show what I was feeling. I couldn't break down now. The destiny of the fishermen was on my shoulders. I became firm, stood tall, fighting as hard as when I was frivolously sued by parents in Boston.

Ichiro and I decided to visit the governor's office in Toyoma again to see if he had any more information. But when we got there, the secretary said he was not in his office. "Next time, please call and make an appointment before coming over," she said curtly.

"We have tried to get a hold of him by telephone, email, and even by fax," Ichiro said, his voice quavering. "But you have not responded to us at all. Physically visiting this office was the only way for us to see him."

"I'm sorry that I made you upset, but the governor is serving all of Toyama's people. And I'm only here eight hours—I can't meet everyone's demands."

"Why don't you do overtime, just like a whole bunch of Toyamans do?"

"Overtime is not allowed here. We are supported by taxpayers' money."

"You don't have to charge your overtime."

"Funny. Anything else?"

"I thought he truly understood we were helping him, even though he hasn't helped us at all," Ichiro shouted, and the secretary stared at him with flared nostrils.

I gently grabbed his arm and pulled a little bit. "Ichiro, let's go. There's nothing for us to do here."

We backed off and left the prefecture building. Because we had nothing better to do, we wandered around Toyama City.

We bought Toyama's famous trout sushi and went to the Toyama Castle Park. We sat next to the samurai castle with its pure white facade and black roof tiles sitting on the tall stone wall foundation, and we shared the sushi. Once we finished, I said, "Since we are done talking with the governor, we probably won't come back to Toyama City for a while. So, before we go, I want to ride on a river boat."

He nodded with a sad smile.

The river boat took us down the Matsukawa River, passing by Toyama Castle. Along the way, we went under seven beautiful small bridges. I took pictures of all seven bridges for my mom.

From the boat, I saw the Tateyama Mountains beyond the City Hall Tower. I still had a hard time believing how beautiful this country was.

By the time we finished the boat ride, it was already dark. The straight, wide street in front of Toyama Station was illuminated with blue lights. The blue lights together formed an image of rough waves in the Sea of Japan.

We went to my favorite Starbucks and bought two lattes. We sat on the outside terrace, looking down on a slope of green grass that led to a wide creek.

It was a chilly night, and no one sat outside besides us.

We were supposed to talk about our next steps. But the conversation did not continue for long. We were in a complete silence. Because there was no next step.

Then, Ichiro said, "I want to marry you."

"What?" I said, raising my voice.

"I want to marry you," Ichiro said again, but the words still sounded unreal.

My brain seemed to short circuit, and I couldn't think of what to say, what to do. Finally, I simply said, "Why are you saying that now?"

"Because you are going back home to Boston."

I stared at him, his face half-illuminated in the dim patio lights. "How did you know?"

"I know everything about you."

"That's not true."

"Oh? So you're staying here, then?"

"Ichiro . . ."

"I can say a hundred great things about you anytime, at a breath. I know that doesn't mean much to you, though."

"You still didn't answer my question. You have nothing to prove that I'm leaving Hime."

"You went to Tokamachi to see the snow country, that is evidence that you are nearing the end of your stay in Japan."

Judy was the only person who knew about my quick overnight trip to Tokamachi, Ichiro's hometown, for the snow festival. She guessed right away why I was going: I wanted to see Japan's oldest snow festival before I went back to the States. Clearly, Ichiro understood what this meant too. Maybe he did know more about me than I thought.

"I should yell at Judy for breaking her promise to keep my trip secret," I said, shaking my head.

"Even if Judy didn't tell me, I could have guessed. It's all so predictable. Hime will die. Toyama Bay Sushi will die. You will move back to Boston. But I had to ask you to stay before you left. I had to give it a shot before I surrender."

"Surrender?"

"You're probably going to re-establish your relationship with Paul, right? I should congratulate you. But I won't. I can't."

"By now you have to know that Paul has simply used me and ditched me again."

"Yes, but you're still leaving, even if it's not with Paul. You will leave Hime and find a fine man and marry him. I am a narrow-minded person. I can't congratulate the lady I love for marrying another guy."

"Why—why are you saying you love me now? You have never said that before."

"Because I am a fisherman. Fishermen don't waste words."

"Oh, that's bullshit. Fishermen are talkative. You're just trying to come up with excuses for why you waited so long to tell me this."

"No, fishermen are not talkative. They only talk about fisheries, fish, boats, and their earnings. Other than that, they don't talk much."

"I don't believe you really want to marry me. You're just coming up with a convenient reason to have me stay in this town." I said. I was angry, although I wasn't completely sure why.

"No, that's not it, Lindsey. I know you don't really think that."

"See, that's more bullshit. You don't know anything about

me. We just work together. That's it. I bet Kong even understands me better."

My voice quivered. I grabbed my latte and stomped down the slope toward the riverside trail.

Ichiro followed me and grabbed my shoulder. "What do I have to do to make you believe what I'm saying is true?"

"I don't know," I said, practically shouting the words.

"Don't lie to me, Lindsey," he said, his voice as loud as mine. "Just say what you want. You can leave me if you don't like me. That's fine with me. Just say it."

"I knew you would say that. That's not fair." I walked farther down the slope, closer to the river. He followed me and I sped up.

"What's not fair?"

I ignored him. I walked on the paved path, just beside the river. I could hear Ichiro behind me, but I didn't stop.

"Wait, Lindsey!" Ichiro shouted so loudly that people walking on the other side of the river looked at us.

I didn't turn around. I walked faster.

"Lindsey!" Ichiro grabbed my arm. But I was prepared. I swung my shoulder to pull up my arm. I started walking fast again. Same speed. An angry speed. But this time, I didn't hear his footsteps behind me.

"So you want to end things between us, just like that?"

I still didn't turn around, I was still so angry, and underneath it, strangely sad. I couldn't handle another relationship yet, not right after Paul. Not even with Ichiro.

"Goodbye, Lindsey," Ichiro said, his voice calm and light.

After three more steps, my anger seemed to fade away as quickly as it came. I stopped and turned around.

Ichiro smiled at me. And I knew then that he may have had feelings for me, but that's not what this proposal was about. He was just checking things off his list, finishing things as neatly as he cleaned up his fishing boat at the end of every day. That's why this proposal was so informal, so uninspired. He just wanted to say he had done it.

He turned around and started walking back to the Starbucks. "Ichiro."

He turned back, smiled more. Saying nothing, he resumed his walk toward the Starbucks again.

"You've treated our relationship as strictly professional and now you've brought something very different into it. To me, that's wrong," I said.

"Nothing wrong. I am human. I sometimes love people," he said, not bothering to turn around. For the first time, I realized I was losing him completely.

"But you've never even said that to me before. And now, you're asking for my hand in marriage. Can't you see why that's not right?"

He just kept walking.

"Why aren't you even turning around? Why won't you look at me?"

I ran toward Ichiro. He stopped when he heard me. When I reached him, he held me tightly in his long arms. It was too much to take in, and I hit him. As I tried to separate our bodies, I hit his chest and arms very hard. He let me go, but he held my hands and said, for the last time, "I love you, Lindsey."

There were so many reasons to be with Ichiro. He saved my life. He was my Japanese best friend. He looked energetic and attractive while he was fishing on the ocean. But it wasn't right. At least, not now.

He smiled with unsounded laughter and said, "Don't worry."

"What do you mean, don't worry?"

"I know you know what I mean."

I wasn't sure what he meant, but I didn't say anything. He smiled again beautifully. I smiled, too.

We decided to walk to the station, along the slow river. He asked for my hand. I let him hold it, telling myself this was going to be the first and last time I let him hold my hand. I felt a callus on his palm. It reminded me of my grandpa's hands. Fishermen's hands are never soft and gentle.

"I think we're at the end of our time together," he quietly said.

I nodded. He didn't say a word. He tightened his grip on my hand, looking far ahead, as if he could see our destiny.

"When the fish port is gone, you will file bankruptcy and let the creditor have your boat. When the fish port is gone, I will go back to the United States," I said, bitterness entering my voice. This wasn't how it was supposed to end, but it was how it was going to end.

I couldn't think about this anymore, so I tried to change the subject. I started talking about how wonderful the Tokamachi Snow Festival was. There were many gigantic snow sculptures, the detail incredible.

"They made small holes every twenty feet in the wall of snow on the road, and they stored candles inside and lit them up at night."

"I remember, I always liked that very much."

"When the sky grew darker, the white snow became the same navy blue as the sky. It made me feel strangely lonely. It snows a lot in Boston, but it somehow looks more beautiful in your hometown."

"Thank you."

"For what?"

"Thank you for visiting my hometown before leaving for Boston."

He stopped walking. He tucked his chin in a little bit and looked at me. His black eyes reflected the lights over the creek.

"I did know how you feel about me, and I'm so sorry if I have hurt you," I said. "And, I know it may be crazy, but I still trust Paul. I feel like I have to trust him, or I'll completely fall apart. If he is proven guilty, I don't know what I'll do. Maybe I'll go to the Tokyo Casino." I laughed to show that I was joking.

"It's been wonderful working with you, Lindsey. Thank you for sailing out to sea with me."

"Are you going to end our relationship now? I will continue to fight for Hime until the final moment comes, and I know you will do the same."

"I am making it easier for you. You don't have to stay here."

"I want to stay until the final moment comes."

"Come on, Lindsey, just ditch me and move on." Ichiro pulled my hand in and kissed it. He released it, smiled, and started walking toward the station by himself.

He didn't turn around, but I couldn't let him leave just like that. So I shouted, "Ichiro, wait!" He finally turned back around. "I want you to take me somewhere."

◄ ▐▌▐▌▐▌ ◄

Nanae got its big payout from Hakodate Marine, and they started construction planning for the new larger market facility and distribution center facing Toyama Bay. Judy somehow got her hands on the confidential blueprint of the construction—she wouldn't tell me how she did it, but she did say that it involved some expert flirting. Hakodate Marine also bought a huge property in Nanae and announced they would build the largest freezing warehouse in Japan as soon as the central government's fishery agency issued a license for it. Judy also got the planning booklet for this project.

We met up at Tomato Café, where Judy shared the blueprint and booklet with me. "I also learned that, along with these two projects, Hakodate Marine is also expanding their offices. They're going to make Nanae their headquarters for the Sea of Japan side of the country."

She took a sip of her coffee. "Their warehouse will comply with HACCP and other major international regulations, so they can export their fish to basically anywhere in the world. They also decided to bring modern electrolyzed water in, which proves that they're dedicated to making sure their facilities are completely sanitized."

I flipped through the booklet and saw that they were also planning to set up the Nanae Gourmet Complex near their port. I threw the booklet onto the table. "They're completely copying us!"

"I know, when I saw the blueprint of the construction plan, I couldn't breathe. Hakodate Marine must have just copied what we prepared and given it to Nanae."

"Which means, I'm to blame for this. I'm the person who shared the business plan with someone outside of our team: Paul."

"Speaking of Paul, his office is empty, and I saw some Japanese men's names on the paper adhered to his door. I Googled the names and saw that they're all Hakodate Marine executives, so they must be transferring here. I didn't see Paul's name anywhere."

"That's even more proof that Paul was just used by them. And we were too."

I put my head down on the table, and Judy gently touched my back. There was nothing else to say—this was all my fault.

◄ |||||||||||| ◄

One morning, as usual, Ichiro, Yoshi, and I were out fishing. But then, the association called Ichiro and asked him to return to the port. Shocked by the news about Nanae's new building projects, a lot of people had come to the port and asked the association staff for an explanation. The staff simply could not answer them and asked for Ichiro's help. We scheduled an all-hands meeting of the Hime fishery for the next evening. There, I was going to explain my total failure to get a hold of Hakodate Marine. There, people would probably vote for a desperate renegotiation with the Toyama governor to drop the ITQ one last time.

After we set the meeting, we headed back out to sea. Things were back to normal between Ichiro and me after our emotional night in Toyama City. That was because of what happened after his proposal.

After Ichiro tried to walk away from me, I asked him to take me to the Iwasehama Beach, the place where we had tried to see the firefly dive last spring. We hopped on a train and rode it the short distance to the beach.

It was a cold night, and Ichiro put his arm over my shoulder to warm me up. Without conversation, we decided to walk on the beach, then, after a while, we sat down in the sand. The dark ocean was illuminated by a full moon. Ichiro was close to me, warm and familiar, and if he had kissed me then I probably would have kissed him back. But nothing happened. We sat there for a long while, and then went home to Hime. Spending those few quiet hours together seemed to restore our balance. It made it easier to get on the boat the next morning and let things get back to normal.

After setting up the all-hands meetings, we spent the rest of the morning quietly fishing. When we pulled up our fishing lines, I found a number of golden eye snappers and a Japanese red seabream. I looked at the fish's body and realized it was a female fish.

"Ichiro. Can I release this seabream?"

"If you want to. But why?"

"It's just . . . I feel bad for the husband seabream."

Ichiro nodded. I grabbed the seabream's jaw, and with my

index finger and thumb, I quickly pulled out the fishhook. I confirmed the damage on her jaw was very minimum. I released it to the sea, and I looked down deep to see if I could find the husband seabream. I couldn't see it.

"Your handling of the hook, line, and rod has become very professional now, Lindsey. You could probably fish by yourself in New Bedford if you wanted."

"Thank you, Ichiro. But I still don't feel like I'm built for a one-person operation."

We steered toward the port, the boat flying through the water.

I inhaled the sea breeze. I felt like my days were truly numbered in this port.

When our boat arrived at the port, I saw about 100 people in non-fishery clothing congregated there. When they saw us, they ran to me.

"Lindsey san, what are you going to do with this? Fish swim. When big ships take all the fish in Itokawa territory, nothing will be left for Hime," said a man in a crisp suit.

I blinked at the person talking, trying to figure out who they all were—none of them were fishermen. A moment later, I got it. They were the business owners who had been asked by the Hime fishery association to invest around the Hime port. They owned restaurants, gift shops, and other tourism-related businesses.

"We are doing our best to bring tourists to the town," the person in front of me said. "We advertised and marketed to those fishery tourism customers. But now you guys are losing your association members, and many people have stopped fishing. It's also embarrassing that you're trying to plead with the Toyama prefecture to cancel the ITQ. Seriously? You are now shifting us from a national hero to a national villain. When the news spreads to the rest of Japan, we will lose customers. The customers even started lowering their reviews on Yelp."

"And now I heard that we may be even shutting down our port. Is that true?" a woman who owned a souvenir shop said.

I stared at my feet, trying to decide what to say. The fishermen weren't mad at me, even though everything had gone so wrong. They said they knew the risk they took, and there was no alternative since the association had been torn apart between north and south. But the retail and tourism people didn't feel the same. They didn't know the heated discussions that had led to our decision to make a deal with Nanae and Hakodate Marine, and they didn't care anyways. For them, my efforts didn't count. They just valued everything by the numbers.

I knew it was time to accept responsibility for everything that had happened.

"I'm sorry that things aren't going as smoothly as we promised. We'll have an all-hands meeting tomorrow, and we'll discuss all options," I said, standing up taller, strengthening my back. If I didn't do that, I might have broken down.

"Discuss? How many options do we have?" someone in the back yelled.

"We don't have much choice."

People began shouting. One voice rose above the rest, "If you close the port, what should we do? We will become just like gift shops inside a foreclosed zoo."

More people shouted, even louder than before. The people who had just established their restaurants or gift shops at Hime Gourmet Center were especially furious.

I wondered if the real aim of Ichiro's marriage proposal was to push me away from Hime as soon as possible so that I didn't have to face this.

A guy in a blue suit said, "I didn't want to say this, but your fiancé set us up, right? All of us saw you and the traitor walking in the city hand-in-hand, or even kissing in public."

Ichiro tried to cut through the crowd and get to me, but I shook my head. I had to face this by myself.

"He's not my fiancé, and we have no evidence that he pulled the strings," I said.

"Use your common sense, Lindsey san. He came here, got very close to you, and he took all our information to Nanae. And now, Hakodate Marine is in Nanae, and he is gone. What else do you need to hear to think of him as a traitor?"

"Nobody should be accused without evidence."

I vividly remembered that I said the same phrase at the witness stand when I was at the court in Boston. Everyone looked at me as the source of trouble, even the school district, who were supposed to be on my side. This was why I had to defend Paul: I knew what it was like to be accused of something without any real proof.

"But don't you feel you are the source of the information leak?" the guy in the blue suit asked.

"During my negotiation with Paul and the Hakodate Marine executives, I admit that I told them more than we had planned to say. I needed to get them excited about Operation Tripod. It was one of my negotiation tools to get the best possible deal for Hime. But at the end of the day, I am responsible."

A man who had been planning on building a big resort hotel said, "Someone in Itokawa showed me an article in their local paper. It says you are receiving money from the Hime fishery association for leading the Operation Tripod, and you used that money to travel to America with Paul for a vacation."

"That's not true, sir." I wasn't surprised to hear this. I knew there were false rumors floating around. "It's true that I recently flew to the US for some negotiations for this project. It's true that my airfare was covered by our association. But I didn't fly with Paul, and I didn't have a vacation over there. It was strictly business."

"We don't know what you did in America. You could say anything," the man in the blue suit said.

"That's not fair to her," Ichiro said, pushing people aside to get to the front of the crowd. He was furious, his face as dark red as a boiled octopus.

Ichiro looked over the crowd. "Hey, guys, I am responsible for all of this. She was just an advisor for us." Despite his friendly tone, Ichiro's face was full of anger. I knew immediately that this would make people even madder. "We were divided by our own reasons. It was so ugly, uglier than you could possibly imagine. So we asked her to take leadership to come up with a third idea and bring the fishermen together again. And she did wonderfully."

I touched his shoulder, trying to signal that he should stop, but he kept going. "Don't accuse an advisor, accuse me. I'm the true leader for this deal."

People started shouting even louder, and harsh language erupted. This time, I could feel true anger in their criticism about the way the association handled the information. It hurt me much more than what they were saying before.

"You and your association asked us to come out here," said the man in the blue suit. "We all borrowed money from the banks to participate and start new businesses. How are you planning on assuming responsibility for all this shit?"

"I wish I had money to buy you out, but I don't have money. But I'm here for you, and I'll do anything you need. Tell me what you want me to do for you," Ichiro said, and his voice was belligerent. I had never seen Ichiro like that.

"What's up with the attitude?"

"I don't have any attitude. You are the one with an attitude problem."

Ichiro was very confrontational. It was the total opposite of when we had a fight against drunk Navy soldiers in Tokyo. He was doing his best to find peace then. Now, Ichiro almost seemed to be looking for a fight.

"You asked us to come here, and now you are giving us attitude. I thought you were businessmen, too."

"Fishing is beyond business. We bet our lives. One hundred Japanese fishermen die in the sea every year. You are eating our lives."

I tried to say something else, but Ichiro talked over me. I could have yelled to be heard, but I didn't want to make tensions even higher by showing my own frustration.

"We bet our lives, too. Nobody earns money in Toyama without betting his life."

"Good to know," Ichiro said.

"So you recognize how critical it is to fix this disaster, this freaking comedy show. How will you make yourself accountable?"

"You haven't had any tangible damage yet. And besides, maybe it's not our fault. Maybe you just don't possess any common sense when it comes to business."

"What did you just say?"

Two businessmen got closer to Ichiro, and they were clearly just moments away from moving from a verbal fight to a physical one. I realized that Ichiro was making them angry at him to protect me. That was not fair to him. I decided to shout to get everyone's attention.

I inhaled air to my lungs until they felt like they were about to burst, but before I could let my scream out, Hideki and about twenty young fishermen ran toward us from the auction area. They pushed people aside and stood next to me.

Hideki's face was red in anger. "Hey guys, it was not him, it was us. All the fishermen unanimously agreed to present this business plan to you. If you have something to say, don't accuse Ichiro, talk to us. We are collectively responsible."

I felt warmed by his words. Hideki smiled at me. I looked in the group and saw Hana, Erica, and many of the fishermen looking back at me. Many of them nodded, showing they were with me.

More fishermen, young and old, ran to our side. Finally, three doyens came to the argument and told everyone to calm down. That did the trick. The doyens were well-connected in the city hall, chamber of commerce, and other industry networks, so the retailers wanted to avoid fighting with them. Their harsh words were extinguished. The doyens suggested that the retailers request a formal meeting with the fishery association. They could ask their questions there, rather than shouting at us without any preparation.

They reluctantly agreed.

After the retailors had gone, Ichiro and I shook hands with fishermen there. The doyens said they would scold the association staff members who sought Ichiro's help. Ichiro and I asked the doyens not to.

Ichiro and I went to Judy & Peter. Erica came along with us, too.

As we waited for our pastrami sandwiches, Erica said, "I'm not sure if you've noticed this in your classroom, Lindsey, but I've seen a lot of anger against the children from Itokawa, from both the children of fishermen and children who have no connection to the fishery. The sense of losing the city has clouded the parents' minds, and their children are noticing the tension."

"I've lost my spot as the winner of the popularity contest," I said jokingly, but Erica looked down and did not deny it. The three of us grew quiet.

Judy brought out the sandwiches and sat down next to me. "All business has risks. The retailers took a risk. They can't complain when things go south."

"I understand, Judy," I said. "But things are little more

complicated than that, because I brought Paul to Hime, and Hakodate Marine ran wild."

"Don't ever mention that jerk's name in front of me. I still think that Paul is pulling the strings."

I just shrugged. Judy glared at me, wanting more of an answer. Ichiro cleared his throat. "Your shop seems to be doing very well. That is the only good news for us."

It was obvious he was changing the subject, and everyone went along with it. We were all tired.

"I'm trying to advertise as much as possible. The bottom line is bringing more tourists to Hime. While the fishery stumbles, I hope my shop will draw more tourists to Hime," Judy said.

Recently, she had leased the adjacent building and doubled the size of her shop. The shop still had a long line of customers.

However, we also knew that pastrami could draw in only so many customers. Hime was truly a fishery town.

Nakata san pulled up in front of the shop on his motorcycle. As always, his leather jacket, pants, scarf, and cap all had big Harley Davidson logos. When he walked in, he took off his rather intimidating dark sunglasses and gave me his usual warm smile.

"Hello, Lindsey san."

"How are you, Nakata san?"

I stared at the gas tank of his motorcycle—the one area where Harley fans put their own decorations. Nakata san had attached a sticker featuring the flags of the US and Japan, crossed tightly over other. As I stared at the Star-Spangled Banner, I felt that my departure date for Boston was coming closer.

We went to court—it was the only thing we could do. During our first hearing at the court, the judge granted an injunction, stopping Hakodate Marine from using the license the Itokawa governor gave them to fish. Hakodate Marine had already been doing a test run trawling with one of their big ships, but they stopped upon the injunction.

The only reason why the judge granted the injunction was because Hakodate Marine's earnings would lower each Hime fishermen's quota significantly when ITQ started within two weeks. And the judge hinted that the ITQ management would be a prefectural issue, but the authorization of ITQ was under the control of the central government. The judge meant that he needed both parties to have the jurisdictional argument on the trial and he wanted to keep the status quo until then.

The judge was absolutely right on this. But at the same time, the fishermen in Hime knew Itokawa would retaliate.

The next morning, Itokawa prefecture announced that they would hold a special congress session to discuss this matter further. In other words, as a prefecture, Itokawa would show full support for Hakodate Marine, and together, they would try to be optimistic about the court's decision.

Judy, Ichiro, and I decided to go to the Itokawa congress session. The observers' seats were located on the second floor, looking down on the congress. We saw a group of Hakodate Marine executives in the corner of the room in a guest speaker's area. I guessed that the Itokawa government had invited them to keep Hakodate Marine on their side. The legal procedure would take some time, and the worst-case scenario was that Hakodate Marine would find a third port and do the same business plan in the Sea of Japan. If Itokawa didn't keep them happy, Hakodate Marine could withdraw from the whole thing, including their invested money.

"Look, Lindsey!" Judy almost shouted.

A security guard came to us and sternly said, "We are in the middle of the session."

Judy ignored him. With her face red, she said my name again and pointed down, into the guest speakers' area.

I followed her finger and found what was she was looking at. "Oh my god," I muttered.

Paul had just walked in. He sat in the front row, in the center of the cluster. He had on a sharp suit and a flashy yellow tie. His smile was confident—the face of someone who had won.

◄ ||||||||||► ◄

Judy was right. Paul had been pulling the strings all along. He had betrayed me.

I owed so many people so many apologies. Paul had slowly gotten me to tell him Hime's strategy, at the coffee shop, hiking, or in bed. Then, he leaked the information to Hakodate Marine to prepare for their Plan B. This seemed like criminal conduct, but I knew Paul would say that there was no non-disclosure agreement.

Now, I could admit that a part of me had known all along, but I hadn't wanted to believe it was true. I hadn't wanted to believe that I could fall for Paul's tricks again. It had to be different this time, I thought, because what kind of monster would hurt someone so badly twice?

I looked at Ichiro. He just stared straight ahead.

Before the congress began discussions, a number of stakeholders were given the chance to speak. They stood in a long line in front of the podium, facing the governor.

"I recognize many faces from the fishery industry in Nanae," I said.

"I do, too," Ichiro said. "They still support the corporate license to Hakodate Marine because they know they will die otherwise."

"I don't see Godzilla."

"He's probably not here. None of the executives or middle management people who participated in the first discussion at the

Chinese restaurant on the border are here either. The swing of the pendulum seems to have pushed Godzilla and his fellows away from Nanae."

"Even with his strong network and power, the Itokawans' allergic reaction to Toyama was too overwhelming to control. It's sad that the only way they would have accepted Godzilla's plan was if we moved forward with the Tripod immediately instead of waiting three years," Judy said.

I looked back down at the floor and saw many journalists were invited. As the session went on, they wrote notes while everyone spoke. Soon, I realized that this session was scripted. It was a political gesture against the court, reminding them that there was no such thing as a jurisdictional issue in this battle in the first place.

"This is also a demonstration for the Hakodate Marine executives. The ones who are sitting next to Paul," Judy said angrily.

After a long pause, I said, "I feel guilty."

Ichiro looked at me for the first time that day. Nobody said a word.

"I thought Paul was too busy negotiating with CEO Doigaki to fix things for Hime, but in reality, he had been working with the Itokawa governor's office to arrange this political session. I thought he had been in Hakodate while I was trying to reach him, but he must have been in Itokawa all along. For him, there was no difference between Toyama and Itokawa, nor Godzilla's side and the other side. All he cared about was getting fame and credit and advancing his career. He didn't care about Hime. And he didn't care about me."

Judy patted my hand gently.

Soon, it was Hakodate Marine's turn to speak. Paul stood up. Judy curled her hands into fists. Ichiro continued to look straight toward the governor of Itokawa. I looked down. I wished I was angry, but I wasn't. I just felt so damn helpless.

When Paul approached the podium, everyone applauded him, all the political parties cheering regardless of if they were conservative or liberal. Paul waved like an American congressman, and then he bowed to the governor and politicians and the auditorium. For a second, he caught my eye. But his expression didn't change at all. He simply didn't care. The applause continued. It was the ultimate evidence that Paul had made more friends in Nanae than we possibly could have imagined.

"I have to give Paul tons of credit for this, Lindsey," Judy said, her jaw clenched. "Godzilla tried to walk a fine line and he failed. He tried to honor your intentions and find a happy medium. But Paul succeeded because he let Godzilla go first. And when Godzilla fell off the fine line, Paul decided not to follow him. He decided to ignite more anger within Itokawans toward Toyamans, and he then created his own fat line between Nanae and Hakodate Marine. He could do that once he disregarded the merits of Hime."

"I understand it all now. It just proves that I am helplessly stupid."

When the applause slowed down, Paul began speaking. "Thank you, members of congress, for this opportunity. Hakodate Marine's comments have already been distributed to the congressmen here. We're excited to work with you Itokawans, and we plan to make Nanae the biggest fishery port in the Sea of Japan within five years. Once that happens, we will become the center of exporting to the US market and beyond. As soon as the court lifts the injunction, Hakodate Marine will resume our investment, and we'll build a HACCP warehouse and food processing center here. At the end of the day, our estimate is we will triple the employment in Nanae."

That got Paul another big round of applause. He now looked like an American president giving the State of the Union address to Congress.

Judy shook her head continuously and said, "Bullshit, bull-shit, bullshit!"

The security rushed over to her once again. "Final warning. If you shout again, you'll be thrown out."

Judy glared at him, but she also quieted down.

As we anticipated, the Itokawa congress said that they would fully support Hakodate Marine's entry into Nanae. They tied the knot. Then, surprisingly, one congressman stood up and submitted an emergency proposal that was to decide if Itokawa prefecture would postpone their ITQ indefinitely. Then, they would be able to fish as much as they wanted in Toyoma Bay without consequence. And Hime would be devastated.

The three of us held our breathes.

"I now remember his face," I said. "I'm sure I met him once at the Hime fishery association with Paul. He was introduced to me by Paul as his friend. He asked me many questions about New Bedford and made me feel good about my grandpa's community. Then, we talked about ITQ in Massachusetts, then our strategy about ITQ, including our attempts to ask the Toyama governor to postpone the ITQ."

Judy nodded powerlessly.

I closed my eyes as the weight of everything I did wrong sunk in. I still didn't even feel a bit of anger towards Paul. And, unlike last time he ditched me, I didn't even feel sadness or any pain. I was just upset with myself for causing this unfixable damage to my friends.

A congressman in the opposing party asked how the rest of the country would react to them postponing ITQ. The congressman had an answer ready for him. "I understand your concern, sir. But the Hime fishery association has submitted the same message to the Toyama governor's office multiple times. We can tell the rest of Japan that we are not the only ones to postpone ITQ, and Toyama did it first."

It would make a good headline for the Toyama paper. The papers in Toyama had been reporting that most people in Toyama wanted to drop ITQ, but they said that the governor's office had never received any formal request. The fact that we had sent in a request was supposed to be top-secret, but I had hinted about what Hime did to this congressman.

The Toyama governor would be surprised by the headline, and they would know someone had leaked a private conversation they had with him. He might even be able to find out I was the one who talked about that with this congressman. I hadn't told the congressman everything, but he had guessed most of the truth.

"I can't believe Itokawa wants to drop the ITQ too," Judy said, clearly trying to distract me from my thoughts. "This will put more political pressure onto the court. Now, Itokawa prefecture is fighting the injunction ruling by postponing the ITQ. No ITQ, no jurisdictional issue, which means no injunction."

Ichiro nodded and said, "It also paves the way for Hakodate Marine to come to Itokawa and invest. It will open the door fully for Hakodate Marine and let them deplete Toyama Bay. When it becomes truly empty, Hakodate Marine can still go out into the Sea of Japan and use Nanae port as its distribution station."

It was ironic that the Toyama governor had denied multiple requests to suspend the ITQ from the Hime fishery association, but now, he would have to inevitably cancel ITQ because of Itokawa's action.

The Itokawa congress unanimously approved the move to put a moratorium on their ITQ.

"Everything had been prepared and shared with all parties," Judy said, almost talking to herself. "Everyone in Itokawa saw the merit in the plan. But they had to get fully united before they declared war against the central government. And to do that, they had to kick Godzilla out. Once he was gone, it was easy for Ito-kawa to get a united front."

I shook my head, frustrated and disappointed in myself. I wished Judy and Ichiro would criticize me for my mistakes—it was like they thought I was too fragile to handle it. "Paul must have not slept more than two hours every day. I'm sure he was the one who visited every corner of Itokawa before this congress started. He made them unite. This is his victory."

The following day, the news spread across Toyama. For the next few days, it was all anyone talked about. A week after that, Toyama prefecture held a special session of congress and paused their entrance to ITQ too.

Local Toyama papers support the opting out, but the nation-wide papers condemned both Toyama and Itokawa.

One local paper openly criticized Hakodate Marine's move and mentioned Paul's name. But that wasn't the worst part. The paper also suggested that every move we made in Hime was secretly monitored by Paul with the help of his girlfriend, and she was the one who was totally in charge. At first, the paper didn't use my name, but a few days after the ITQ decision, it appeared in an article. They even used my middle name.

"Our hands were secretly read by the opposing poker player," they wrote. They also quoted one of the hotel executives who almost got into a fight with Ichiro. He said, "We're not that angry that we got hit by our opponent. That's understandable. But we are angry that we had an internal spy leak our strategy to Itokawa. We're also upset that confidential information from the gover-nor's office was leaked to Itokawa prefecture. It makes us crazy to think Itokawans knew about every move Toyama was planning to make. Crazy."

The businessman in the blue suit who also confronted Ichiro was also quoted: "And guess what, nobody in the Hime fishery association was careful about hiding the obscene love affair between this female spy, Lindsey, and the representative from Hakodate Marine. It is not a laughing matter. As soon as we find out if she received financial incentives from this Paul guy, we're more than ready to press charges for her fraudulence. We will sue her and the doyens in civil lawsuits."

I couldn't handle it, and there was nothing that could make me feel better. Not fishing, not making sushi, and not seeing Judy. There was no remedy.

Except for going to the casino.

I felt guilty about breaking my promise to Judy. But I had no choice.

I was going down, deep.

◀ ▥▥▥▥ ◀

I started going to the casino in Tokyo every weekend.

I took a bullet train, hopped in a taxi at Tokyo Station, and gambled all night long.

My memory was getting weaker. I didn't remember well, or I remembered wrong. I still earned a little bit of money, but not much. I didn't care, though. I felt numb in the casino, and I could block out the world. This was where I escaped when I had my bad days in Boston, when I was sued by parents, condemned by teachers, and bullied by the school district.

I drank a lot of alcohol and stayed awake until the early hours of the morning, just drifting through the casino. I exchanged a few meaningless words with a dealer or neighboring players, but beyond that, I didn't speak. The combination of fatigue, numbness, and the flashes of joy of winning created the perfect atmosphere for me to escape in.

One night in April, I found myself sleeping on a couch in the casino hotel aisle with no money. I didn't even remember if I lost all the money at the casino or if someone had snatched my casino chips. I just didn't care. It was not a lot anyways. Earlier that night, I read an article from the Toyama paper that said another group of fishermen left Hime. Now there were only 170 fishermen left, compared to the 350 when I became a fisherwoman.

I looked and felt exhausted all the time. The Toyama papers continued to report how many fishermen were leaving. My name showed up every day. The way they depicted me was no different from a felony suspect. They showed picture of me frowning, wearing no makeup, worse than a mug shot.

The journalists came to the port, Hime Junior High School, and Bamboo Sushi. I didn't want to make trouble, especially for the kids in the school and customers at the shop, so I walked outside and answered the journalists' questions instead of hiding like I really wanted to. Mr. Principal and Mr. Bamboo both came and stood beside me and asked the journalists to make the interview as short as possible and take it easy on me. Their faces were harder than I'd ever seen them before.

I started suffering insomnia. I also had trouble eating. I couldn't eat fish or meat. I started eating Toyama's traditional "medicine dish," which consisted of vegetables with eastern therapy. Hana and Erica fixed it for me. It was far from delicious, but it was the only thing I could eat that didn't upset my stomach. Yet, as the local paper's campaign to depict me as a villain to Hime continued to escalate, my health became worse.

At my sickest, I couldn't get out of my bed for two days in a row. Hana and Erica brought medicinal food to my apartment.

"How is the bay?" I asked Hana. "I haven't been keeping up on the news at all. It's been hard to look at the newspaper knowing that my name will be there."

"A lot has been happening, Lindsey. Hakodate Marine still has their big ships in Itokawa's water jurisdiction. With the injunction, they can't fish, but they've started doing thorough marine research. They're collecting data on the types of fish in the bay, their value, and the volume of fish. They're also fishing just outside of Toyama Bay. We saw a further decline of fishery tourists in Hime."

"So we truly dropped ITQ?"

"Yes. All fishermen are back at independent status. Nobody helps the association with fishery tourism boats anymore. Fishery tourism suddenly stopped, and customers became furious and bad mouthed us on social media. The unity between retailers and fishermen is totally broken. The retailers came to the association to beg them to bring back the tourist boats, but fishermen simply ignored them. There's disharmony everywhere in Hime."

"Regular citizens are starting to leave Hime," Erica said. "And many non-fishery citizens are relocating to Nanae for jobs since the local economy is now getting a big financial boost from Hakodate Marine. A few parents have come into the school to talk to Mr. Principal about relocating. People must have realized that the financial influence by Hakodate Marine is ten times larger than the influence of Godzilla."

"It hurts me when I think of students who sacrifice their schooling because of this," I said.

"Lindsey, I have more bad news. We are not comfortable discussing it with you, but we know you want to know everything."

"Thank you. Please tell me, Erica."

"Since Toyama and Itokawa Government dropped the ITQ, the central government has stepped in. The degree of the central government's involvement is a hundred times worse than people expected. After an unrelated bribery scandal, the senate demanded the impeachment of the prime minister. Then, the prime minister dismissed the senate in return. All of a sudden, the national election came near, and one political party pointed out the ITQ in Toyama Bay as a sample of the lack of management skills in the current cabinet. The prime minister promised other countries that he would implement ITQ, and now it wasn't happening."

"I haven't paid any attention to national politics. So, in a nutshell, Toyama has become the center of the Japanese political hurricane because of the ITQ."

"Correct. Japan is still one of the biggest fishery nations, and the cancelation of ITQ has caused significant opposition around the world. The opposition party used this issue in their political campaign and the ruling party sent many fishery agency bureaucrats to Toyama and Itokawa to try and get them to put ITQ back in."

"And when the pressure from the bureaucrats didn't work, the Ministry of Agriculture and Fishery exercised their power and imposed new TAC, Total Allowable Catch, onto Toyama Bay. TAC was meant to control the endangered species throughout Japan, but now the government issued an unprecedented 'regional TAC.' They've imposed this regional TAC on all kinds of fish in both Itokawa and Toyama prefectures' water jurisdictions. This is pure retaliation from the central government to the prefectural governments."

I shook my head. "This is a death sentence to both the Toyama and Itokawa fisheries."

"I agree," Hana said. "We started depleting our fish stock to a suicidal level after ITQ was put off, but this is the real death sentence."

"An expert on CNN said this would put 80 percent of our fishermen out of business," Erica said, showing me the article on her smartphone.

"If that's true, it means that 140 fishermen will quit out of our current 170 members. There will only be thirty fishermen left. It's truly going to be the end of the Hime fishery, even before we shut down the port." I wanted to scream, but I held it in for Erica and Hana's sake.

Erica nodded. "Both governors issued protesting speeches, but the national papers and TV supported the central government, since they're self-claimed eco-protectors. People in Japan are becoming so sensitive to the fishery stock. Nobody agrees with overfishing. The rest of the nation has zero sympathy toward Toyama and Itokawa."

◄ ▐▌▌▌▌ ►

Darker and thicker clouds covered the association every day. The central government's fishery sent many administrative clerks to Hime port, and they calculated the daily catch. We all knew that we would reach the maximum of TAC very soon. Desperate fishermen caught as many fish as they could, came back to the port, chose mid-sized and large fish, and then dumped the small fish into the sea in front of the bureaucrats. Trashing fish was illegal, but there was no penalty. This was the only way they could keep the volume of fish under the severe TAC limit. TV camera crews taped the fishermen trashing fish and broadcasted it the following day. The YouTube video received thousands of views every day. Fish lovers around the world were angry to see professional fishermen trashing fish.

Judy said, "We are hurting our brand."

Ichiro said, "This is a survival game for everyone. People overfish to survive and trash fish to survive. The video killed fishery tourism completely. A perfect vicious circle."

Since tourists didn't come to Hime anymore, the total consumption of the fish declined, and the premium value vanished. Big consumers in Tokyo lost interest in the Toyama Bay brand.

Bamboo Sushi's new shop at the Hime Gourmet Center had to close.

As we prepared for dinner one night, I said to Master Bamboo that I now knew how temperamental customers were.

Mr. Bamboo said, "No, Lindsey. They know exactly what they are tasting. They can taste the disharmony in the bay and port. Too many people are mad, and their anger contaminates the ocean." He made a quick piece of sushi for me as he was talking. "Remember this taste, Lindsey. This is the worst sushi I have ever made."

When I threw the piece into my mouth, I could immediately tell the difference. And I knew my sushi would be a lot worse. Mr. Bamboo spit his own sushi into a trash can.

"I am ashamed of myself. My sushi knife has gotten dull. It has gotten contaminated by my own anger. Tonight, you run the dinner shift. I will stay home and repent."

"Mr. Bamboo—" I started, but he walked away. I knew what he was trying to do. He sensed that I was just about to give up on my sushi. The fish was contaminated with the fishermen's anger. My knife was dull with my desperation. This, then, was my final training: how to pour my heart into my sushi regardless of my mindset.

Someone silently tapped my back. I turned and saw Mrs. Bamboo. "Do you understand what my husband was trying to say?"

"Yes, *Okamisan*. I do."

"Good. We have good days and bad days. But professionals have to keep the shop open every day, no matter what."

"Would you mind tasting this sushi?"

With hesitation, I handed her a piece of my snapper sushi.

Mrs. Bamboo chewed it a couple of times, and then she spit it into the trash can. She didn't say anything as she stared into my wide, surprised eyes.

After a moment, I nodded. "I will fix the sushi rice from scratch, and I will clean up the whole shop one more time."

"Good idea, Lindsey."

Mrs. Bamboo turned and went back into her home.

the Sea of Japan

Soon, many fishermen lost the will to sail out, and they just hung around the port with their friends, drinking sake. Nobody had ever seen fishermen drink sake at the port, and seeing that made more people lose hope. Ichiro's assistant, Yoshi, decided to leave Hime. I fixed a farewell sushi bento box for him. Ichiro and I liked him and wanted him to stay, but with the new TAC imposed, Ichiro had no reason to keep employing him. Yoshi knew it, so he resigned instead of making Ichiro fire him.

Godzilla sent me a letter and told me that Nanae was also taking a big hit. The letter started with his sincere apology to me that he could not keep promise he and I agreed upon. To make up for everything, he sent me his favorite apples, Big Dippers, which were only grown by a few farmers in Japan. He also said if I used Big Dippers in my apple pie, it would be the best pie in the world.

Then, his letter explained the current situation in Nanae:

With the central government's TAC retaliation, Hakodate Marine must have changed their strategy. Hakodate Marine cannot afford the regional TAC either. They can operate outside of Toyama Bay and do their fishing in the Sea of Japan, but if they stay in Itokawa's marine jurisdiction, they are controlled by this TAC. They are still in love with Toyama Bay fish and the Sea of Japan, but they cannot stick to Itokawa or Toyama.

The last line of the Godzilla's letter surprised me the most: *I was totally kicked out of Nanae. I now live in Kanazawa, aka Little Kyoto. But I shall return. Until, then, so long, Lindsey san.*

Soon after I received Godzilla's letter, the new president of the Nanae fishery association and Hime's pro-tem president met several times, but they found no middle ground. They had multiple harsh debates, but there was no positive outcome.

Paul and the CEO of Hakodate Marine showed up on TV and in the papers. They openly criticized the central government's TAC ruling as unfair. But at the same time, they were trying to get the Itokawa government to let them out of their agreement so they could create a similar business plan with another good fishing port. Panicked about losing his best financial source, the governor intensified his fight against the central government. Due to the national election, the fight became super politicized.

"It's going to be very bad," one of the doyens explained to me and Ichiro late one night at Bamboo Sushi. "Japan may be a small country, but we have a lot of ocean to work with. The Japanese exclusive territory, called the Exclusive Economic Zone, is the sixth largest in the world, right behind Canada. There are up to 34,000 fish in this region, and we have 14 percent of all maritime creatures in the world. Thus, the control of the fishery is too big a burden for the central government to oversee itself. They truly need to depend on the prefectural governments' management."

The doyen sipped his tea. "The central government can issue TAC because the stock revitalization laws are subject to the Fishery Act, which is overseen by the central government. However, the central government also gave the governors the ability to manage their own resources under another national law, the Fishery Cooperative Union Law. That has been controversial."

"I see," I said. "The central government wants to have control of the big picture, but they admit that they depend on local government for the day-to-day management. So the prefectures understandably get mad if the central government tries to overturn the decisions they make."

"You got that right," said another doyen. "The central government technically has the power to overturn a prefecture's decision, but then, all the minute jobs that make up the seventh-largest fishery industry in the world goes back to the central government, which is insane for them to take on. It's like the FBI becoming responsible for all 911 calls in the United States. It's just unrealistic. That's why the central government still hasn't come up with a penalty clause for fish trashing. Each side has a gun pointed at them, but both sides are deadlocked. They're at a draw."

"They're not at a draw. They're both losing. Toyama and Itokawa are both losing. The prefectures and the central government are both losing. Hime and Nanae are both losing."

I nodded, sighing. "I've seen many central government employees wandering around the port, but soon, they won't be able to handle the backlog."

Ichiro had been silently drinking hot green tea, and he hadn't even touched the sushi I made for him. Now, he said, "They are bureaucrats. They can't even tell the difference between halibuts and snappers."

"Only Hakodate Marine isn't getting hurt since they can choose a different port," I said, running a hand through my hair in frustration.

Ichiro and the doyens continued talking about politics, but I couldn't focus on what they said. I thought about the CEO of Hakodate Marine, Doigaki. He was a well-known leisure fisherman. He personally went to many fishing games in Japan, and won many championships. He knew the Japanese fishing industry professionally and privately.

I thought about how I could talk directly to the CEO, bypassing Paul.

I knew Paul would try to block all possible access points.

The following day, I drifted through the casino in Tokyo. As I wandered around, I heard a couple of regulars saying some famous Japanese casino whales were going to Las Vegas. I remembered that Paul once said that Doigaki was a whale, too. I gave all my chips to the dealer, and said, "Is Doigaki going with the group to Las Vegas?"

The dealer nodded.

On the way home from Tokyo, I swung by Judy & Peter. I wanted to talk to Judy about my new plan, a plan that involved CEO Doigaki. But for some reason, the restaurant was closed. I grabbed my phone and Skyped Judy.

"Hi, Lindsey," Judy said in a weak voice. Her face was very pale. Behind her, there was a plain white wall.

"Hey, I came by your restaurant to see you, but it's closed. What happened?"

She didn't answer. Just slowly shook her head multiple times.

"Are you alright? Where are you?"

"I'm in Tokyo, visiting my lawyer's office."

I was about to say that I was also in Tokyo three hours ago, but then I realized that I shouldn't, since Judy would able to guess that I was at the casino. "I don't remember having any court hearings or anything this month."

"No, this doesn't have to do with our fight against the governments. This is about my case."

"Your case?"

"I lost my shop in Hime."

"What do you mean? How did that happen?"

"Paul tricked me. I got stuck in Paul's trap."

And then, Judy began to cry.

◀ ▐▐▐▐▐ ◀

I hopped in a taxi and went to the new Hakodate Marine office in Nanae.

I was so angry I could barely even think. I kept seeing Judy's face crumbling in as she sobbed. I had never seen Judy cry before. I had never seen her so totally defeated.

After Judy stopped crying, she had told me the whole story of how she lost her shop. She said that back before the government implemented the regional TAC, she and Nakata san desperately wanted to do something to save Hime. The only thing they could think to do was sell the franchise rights to Judy & Peter to Paul. In return, he would have Hakodate Marine withdraw from any Itokawa deal. Nakata san and Judy thought Paul, out of his ego and his desire to make money, would agree to the proposal, and he actually did. Nakata san did it for his love for his community, and Judy did it for her best friend.

But Paul didn't ask Doigaki to withdraw from the Hakodate Marine proposal, and his promise wasn't legally binding–they had trusted him to follow through, and he had tricked them. Judy became furious and demanded that he do what he promised, and she screamed at him and hit him. Paul went to the police station and filed a complaint. Judy saw her lawyer, and he said Judy should forget about Paul and his promise. To make things worse, Paul told Judy that she needed to stop operating her original pastrami shop. He said he was now the franchisor and a franchisee should comply with franchisor internal rules. Apparently, there was tricky language in the Paul's draft of the agreement. Judy missed the potential legal trap. Judy's lawyer saw that Paul's demand was legitimate based on the agreement. He advised Judy and Nakata san to close their shop.

When I got to the office, Paul was there alone.

He smiled at me as I stomped into the office, the charming smile I used to love, but now made my stomach turn. "Hey, Lindsey, what a surprise–"

I grabbed his tie and pulled it until his face was close to mine. It has been a long time since my blood boiled this strongly.

"What did you do to Judy and Nakata san?" I screamed, my nose almost touching his.

"Oh, that? We just had a business deal."

"What kind of business deal screws two people out of their

own business?" I was so mad I couldn't breathe. I had to pause between each word.

"You don't understand the whole picture, Lindsey. We made a deal. If there was a fraud in there, she could nullify the agreement. But she didn't because there was no fraud. Instead, she just harassed me and got violent. That's why I went to the police station."

"I do know the whole picture. The entire Japan franchise rights were sold to you at a ridiculously low price because Judy asked you to end the Hakodate Marine and Itokawa deal. But you didn't. You didn't keep up your end of the bargain."

"Lindsey," he said, his voice still infuriatingly calm. "I don't mean to brag about my higher education and experience, but a contract has to comprise of two things: give and take. If not, you can nullify the contract even after both legitimately signed. But she didn't. Because I paid the price, they sold the rights to me."

"It was only $50,000. Their initial investment was much larger than that."

"Yes, but the price you pay is always the market price. They haven't started any franchise operations yet, and there's only one shop in Hime. I thought my evaluation was fair, especially since they will receive the recipe license fee from all franchisees. Further, Mr. Nakata will make a killing by selling more cows to the operation. They agreed to it."

"Bullshit!"

"You want to see the copy of the agreement?"

"Judy emailed it to me, but the real term of agreement was Hakodate Marine's withdrawal. If I had known this in the first place, I would have told them not to make this deal. They shouldn't have made this sacrifice for me."

"There's no such thing as a real term of agreement, Lindsey. In business, all that matters is what's on the contract."

"You are such a jerk!" I shouted. Then, I took a deep breath, steadying myself. "What can I give you so that you'll give back the franchise rights? I'll do anything."

"You've already given me exactly what I want, Lindsey. You have nothing left to give."

I wanted to scream, but I held it in. My mind raced, trying to come up with a plan. Then, I decided: if Paul wouldn't negotiate with me, there was only one thing I could do. I pulled his tie again and then hit his temple with my open palm.

For the first time, Paul looked surprised. "What are you doing?"

I hit him again, using more force. Then I hit him again, and then one more time. The temple is a vital spot to hit during a fight. It gives a significant shock but doesn't leave a trace.

"Stop it, Lindsey."

I held onto his tie as tightly as an unruly dog's leash.

"Bastard."

I hit him again. Paul lifted up his arms to try and block his face, but I easily pushed them away and hit him again and again.

"Stop!"

He extended his arm to block me, eyes closed. I hit him more and more, until finally, he could take it no longer and hit me back. It was like something had been unleashed within him. His eyes were red, and he blindly grabbed my necklace and pulled it down, breaking it.

There was a mirror in the room. I checked my face, but there was still no damage. I hit him again on his temple. When it comes to violence, he was clumsy person whereas I had plenty of experience. That experience worked for me here.

I went to hit him again, but he pushed my hand back and hit me on the nose, hard enough that my nose started bleeding. That's what I was waiting for. I ran down from his office and onto the street, letting my nose bleed freely.

A few pedestrians walking by saw me and stopped, eyes widening.

Eyes wide, voice trembling theatrically, I shouted, "Help! Please call the police!"

◀ ⅢⅢⅢⅢ ◀

I booked a ticket to Las Vegas for the next evening. The day before I left was a normal one. I fished with Ichiro and came home and prepared for the opening Bamboo Sushi.

I wiped all the windows and cleaned the restroom. I wiped down the entire restaurant. I counted the money in the register, and prepared ginger, garlic, and other condiments. Then, I washed the fish refrigerator and sanitized the kitchen until everything sparkled.

As I worked, I thought about what Judy had told me when we talked earlier that day. Paul was still officially the sole franchisor of Judy & Peter. Judy and Nakata san couldn't open the shop again without his consent. Nakata san hired Judy to work as a register clerk in his Japanese BBQ shop. I encouraged them to start serving their pastrami, but Judy didn't feel like it. New York deli was her soul, and the deli girl had lost her soul because of Paul. Because of me.

I had to fix everything I had done wrong.

The following night, I arrived in Las Vegas.

◀ ⅢⅢⅢ ◀

I hadn't been to Las Vegas in a long time, not since Judy and I had gone to celebrate graduating college. I forgot about how much everything sparkled, how many signs flashed on the streets trying to get your attention. I ignored all the signs and went straight to the casino where I knew I would find Doigaki: Casino Florence. The casino I went to in Tokyo was affiliated with Casino Florence, and many of the dealers had connections in the Las Vegas branch. I had asked the dealer I bribed with casino chips if he knew anything about what Doigaki got up to at Casino Florence. He said he heard Doigaki always went to the Italian restaurant there for dinner.

I was not allowed to enter the casino floor because Casino Florence's Atlantic City branch once caught me card counting and kicked me out. But in the restaurant corridor, there were far fewer security cameras on the ceiling.

I found Doigaki sitting in a small booth next to the window, sipping on a glass of red wine.

"Mr. Doigaki," I said.

He frowned. "Yes. Who are you?"

"*Konni chi wa. Watashi wa Hime no ryoushi desu,* (Hello. I am a fisherwoman at Hime,)" I said, thinking that speaking Japanese would make him take me more seriously. "May I sit?"

He nodded, and I slid into the seat across from him. "You're from Hime?"

"If you remember, I met you once in your home office in Hakodate."

"Oh, you are Paul's girlfriend?"

He scowled, clearly connecting the dots between Paul's stay in the detention center and what he had heard from his criminal defense attorney.

"Indeed. As of now, I have to put 'ex' before girlfriend." I gave him my best friendly smile. He didn't return it.

"Why are you in Las Vegas?"

"I think you know why. Can we talk now, Doigaki san?"

After a moment, he nodded. "Let's move to the bar. You're going to buy me another drink."

He only gave me five minutes. Each gambler has his own jinxes and myths. Doigaki believed that having a business conversation before going into the casino would result in him losing money. But he said he wouldn't regard a five minutes chat as a business discussion.

Even though it wasn't much time, I took advantage of it. I explained what had really happened between me and Paul. I emphasized the fact that Paul had used me, in more ways than I could count.

I thought hearing the truth would make Doigaki sympathetic to me, but it had the opposite effect. Doigaki shook his head and said, "Lindsey san, why are you trying to get me to turn against my trusted people? Can you prove what you said?"

"Call me Lindsey. Doigaki san, I have many witnesses."

"You're not saying that all of your witnesses are Hime people, are you?"

"I'm afraid I am."

"Then, you can't prove anything. Why should I trust you more than I trust him?"

I was going to say more about how dirtily Paul had played the game, but I stopped. It would make things worse.

"I'm sorry, but this conversation is over, Lindsey. You and I are on opposite sides of the Itokawa-Toyama feud. There's no reason why I should talk to you."

He got up and entered the dining area. I followed him, saying, "Wait, Doigaki san, please."

He didn't stop. I followed him out of the restaurant, still talking. "What about you and I compete in Blackjack? If I win, you give the Hime fishery association a chance to talk to you officially. The lawsuits are between the two prefectures. We are not suing parties. We could talk."

Doigaki finally turned around.

"Blackjack? Here in Vegas?"

"Yes. But not at this kind of gorgeous resort on the Strip. I'd prefer playing in my favorite kind of smoky, old casinos in Downtown Vegas, if that's okay with you."

"I like old Vegas. But why do you want to talk so badly?"

"Because you are the best fishing gamer in Japan and I am the best fisherwoman in Japan," I said, smiling.

"Okay. I'll only give you one chance. We will do thirty hands, and if you win more money overall, we'll talk."

We met a few hours later in a smoky, old-school casino in Downtown Vegas. I waited for Doigaki at the bar, playing a penny slot machine to kill time.

When he showed up, I stood and shook hands with him.

"Thank you for coming, Doigaki san. Shall we?" I said.

"Let's get a drink first," he said, motioning to the bartender.

I ordered a martini and he ordered a whiskey.

"So why are you doing this?" Doigaki said, sipping whiskey slowly.

"I think you know why."

"I'm acutely aware of the current business complications in Toyama Bay. There are so many conflicts of interests between my company, Hime, and Nanae. And there are so many lawsuits between Itokawa and Toyama. Also, I'm not sure if you heard, but just an hour ago, the Itokawa governor finally sued the fishery agency at the central government. Since you cannot have control over where fish go, a lot of people are going crazy."

"You sound like you're going crazy too."

"You bet I am. My life is full of fish. Commercially and privately. Every fishery business is my baby. Our Toyama Bay business has become my baby already. I don't give a damn who's going to work with us. My focus is the world's best fish tank, Toyama Bay.

But, at the end of the day, I have thousands of employees to take care of. If worst comes to worst, I'll leave Toyama Bay and move onto the next best option."

"If you hadn't used Paul like a bad spy, you could have just stayed with us in Hime and gotten everything you wanted."

"Paul is such a smart guy. He may try to play too many games, but I like him. Do I believe he truly used violence against you? No. I know he had no bruises or cuts, while his fingerprints were on your broken necklace and his shirt had drops of your blood. But I trust him, and I bailed him out before I came here. Do you want to know where he is now?"

"No, I don't. I don't need to know, and thinking about it may mess up my gambling skills and cause me to lose."

"Okay. But you still haven't answered my first question. I know why Hime needs this, but why are you the one advocating for them?"

"Everything was unplanned. I wasn't a big fan of Japan in the first place. I didn't play Nintendo or PlayStation, or even Pokémon-Go. I don't read manga and had no interest in Kuro-sawa movies. My only connection to Hime was that I was raised in a seafood loving family, and my grandpa is an active fisherman in the biggest fishery port in the US. I just happened to be assigned to Hime to teach English. I have been there ever since."

"A mere job opportunity wouldn't make someone like you love the community this much."

"This community has become my second home. My students at my school, my customers at my sushi restaurant, my partner in the ocean. They've all accepted me, and they treat me like family."

"Fair enough." He took a long sip of his drink. "So again, your request is if I lose, I will talk to your representative and try to break through this impasse. Just talk. I don't guarantee anything."

"Understood."

Doigaki stared at me, unblinking. I forced myself to sit still, to not show my discomfort. "Your eyes have changed, Lindsey."

"My eyes? Have I changed since I met you at Hakodate?"

"Yes."

"Maybe I look tired and beaten up."

"That's probably true, but that's not what I mean. You look much more determined, like a samurai on the night before a battle. See, I'm a very peaceful guy and have no interest in martial arts. I don't necessarily agree with the samurai era and I don't value the samurai spirit. I am a businessman. Still and all, I think your determined-samurai aura makes you look beautiful."

"So you're saying I'm beautiful like a samurai? I'm totally lost."

"I'm just saying you are charming."

I rolled my eyes. "Are you kidding me? I'm a fisherwoman and sushi chef, and that's the best compliment you can give me?"

"Can't you say simply say thank you?" Doigaki laughed.

"Fine, thank you," I said. But I didn't want to just leave it there, didn't want to let him get the last word.

I pushed my martini away, and bowed to him. "Thank you, Doigaki san, but beautiful is not the right word for what I am. I feel something changing in me, too. You're the first one who has noticed it."

"Good." He pushed his whiskey away too.

"And thank you for taking this match with me. May I ask why you agreed to this?"

"Lindsey, gamblers gamble. Good ones don't pursue the reasons."

I smiled—that seemed like the perfect note to end on. I stood up. "Shall we?"

"Let's go."

We chose an empty Blackjack table. I paid my respect and gave the chair on the right-side to Doigaki.

The dealer was an old man whose face didn't look sharp when he saw us taking seats. He must have been bored and lost the energy to be nice to customers in exchange for a better tip.

He was the perfect dealer for my card counting—he wouldn't notice anything.

He dealt the first hand, and we began.

◄ ▐▐▐▐▐▐ ►

As soon as Doigaki and I finished, I Skyped Judy and told her the good news. "I won. Doigaki is going to come to Hime as soon as he gets back from Las Vegas."

Judy grinned, but then her face darkened. "Lindsey, this has to truly be the last time you ever visit a casino."

I nodded. This time, I was sure that I was done.

A few days after I got back to Hime, Judy and I met up for brunch at Tomato Café. For most of the meal, we just chatted idly, keeping things light, trying not to dwell on everything going wrong.

But then, as we were about to leave, Judy touched my hand and said, "I think Ichiro should see a doctor. He seems to have lost a lot of weight. I thought it was just because of all the crap happening. But now I'm thinking something else is wrong too."

"Thank you for the heads up. I'll talk to him."

I went back on our boat the next morning, preparing my sushi-rice as we sailed out to sea. That day, we saw amberjack swimming. It looked very similar to yellowtail, but unlike yellow-tail, it swam alone, which made it rarer and more expensive.

Americans and Japanese love to eat fish meat with fat. But on amberjack, the non-fatty, crunchy meat was the tastiest part. I was excited to see the amberjack because I thought eating amberjack sushi would increase Ichiro's appetite.

It took twenty minutes to catch the fish—it was one of the

fastest swimmer, reaching more than thirty miles per hour. When I pulled it onto the boat, I cut the fish open and saw wonderful white meat. My sushi rice was also moist and sweet, the perfect complement to the fish. Ichiro looked joyous as I handed him a piece. He ate it quickly and immediately reached for another piece.

As he ate piece after piece of my amberjack sushi, Ichiro denied any sickness. "I think I should be more worried about you," he said, referring to my recent weight loss when I had been too anxious to eat. I had regained my appetite now and ate just as much sushi as Ichiro.

Still, I felt like Ichiro was hiding something—he looked pale, and he turned his back to me right after denying anything was wrong. But I didn't have the right to further pry into his health.

I continued making more sushi, and Ichiro kept praising it. I also felt like my sushi was back at my old standard. The win against Doigaki had made me more confident, and that shined through in the sushi.

As we ate, Ichiro and I talked about how I should negotiate with Paul. The DA had confirmed that if I asked with a good reason, they would drop the charges altogether, saving Paul from having a criminal record. I would use this as a weapon to make Paul cancel the franchise agreement with Judy and leave Japan. But at the same time, I had to be cautious so that this wouldn't be seen as extortion.

I had to be patient.

I had to make Paul propose the idea to me.

◀ ▮▮▮▮▮ ◀

That night, Doigaki emailed me to tell me that he had returned to Japan. He said he would keep his promise. He was coming to Hime.

To avoid the eyes of journalists, we decided to use Judy & Peter's New York Deli for our meeting. The shop was still closed, so we didn't have to worry about customers overhearing us. Judy made her pastrami for Doigaki and the two associates that accompanied him. Judy, Ichiro, and I represented Hime. I asked the doyens to attend, but they said I was still the leader, and I needed to have confidence in myself.

We all understood that this was our final chance to save Hime.

The meeting started off well. We ate Judy's pastrami while Doigaki and Judy casually chatted about Hime beef pastrami and other Jewish deli foods. He brought the best wine in Japan, and we all passed the bottle around. Doigaki and I also took turns talking about our Blackjack match. I told everyone about how I barely won, but as always, we both had big ups and downs. Needless to say, Judy, Ichiro, and I didn't talk about my memory skill.

By the time we opened up the second bottle of wine, we had pushed our reservations away. We talked about our side of what happened with Paul, and we listened to his side of the story.

Doigaki was a tough business man, one of those lone-wolf types. But he was a gentleman. He said, "So the long and short of it is that Paul unethically used his relationship with you. Then, he offered to make a deal with the Itokawa governor when Operation Tripod went south and the people of Nanae got divided."

"It was more than unethical, sir," Judy said, "but that is correct."

Ichiro said, "That's why we are meeting here. We're not seeking any legal remedies. Bringing this to the court will not solve anything."

We talked for a while, trying to come up with a solution. But no one came up with a good idea to resolve this fairly for everyone.

Doigaki slammed his hands against the table. "Alright. We're at an impasse. Theoretically, there is no such thing as a win-win solution for everyone in this case. Somebody has to win and somebody has to lose. Well, you guys are all gamblers, including myself. Why don't we have a gambling duel to determine who will win?"

"What do you mean? You want to go back to the casino?" Judy asked, glancing at me.

"No. I mean most of you guys are fishermen, including me. You are commercial fishermen and I am a sports fisherman. If anybody has the guts to challenge me, I will accept it. I propose we do a classic competition: we simply fish at the same time, and whoever catches the largest volume of our targeted fish wins."

"What are you going to do if you lose?" I said to Doigaki.

"If I lose, Hakodate Marine will back off from Nanae. You can try to figure out how to move forward with Nanae. Or, you can go back to your original plan and merge with Nanae in three years and invite a good company to invest in Hime-Nanae. I know there will be more companies who will be interested in investing in you."

"What if Hime loses?"

"Then, you will allow us to fish in the parts of the bay that are in the Toyama jurisdiction. You will license us through the governor. We will pay for the license, of course. We will try our best to hire the people from Hime who will become unemployed because of our move. ITQ will be back, and TAC will be lifted. Everyone goes back to the peace."

"What will people from Nanae do?"

"I don't know. Ask them. But as far as I am concerned, the two prefectures are battling it out at the court, the central government is fighting against prefectures, a new crazy TAC was imposed, and Nanae's situation is totally the same as yours. That's what you called an impasse."

"That means the entire ITQ in Toyama Bay would go to Hakodate Marine."

"Pretty much. As ugly as it sounds, Hakodate Marine will dominate the quota. That is the reward if I win. Not bad for us. Not bad at all."

"The Hime population will continue to decline. Some people may be hired by Hakodate Marine, but I know most of them will simply leave Hime."

"That's your problem, not mine, Lindsey. But you know what, when it happens, your fishermen will change their minds and would work for us, just like Nanae's fishermen."

"I am not sure about that."

"Well, it's your call. We don't need to employ your people. Like I said, I don't give a damn about Hime fishermen or Nanae fishermen. But I wanted to be fair to you, Lindsey. We trusted Paul and he did a good job for us businesswise. But I feel a little bad about the way he treated you."

"You talked to him recently?"

"Yes, I did. He said you set him up. But even if that's true, he still used you for his career. It was not a gentleman's deal. Besides, I owe America a bit."

"You owe America?"

"When I was an eighth grader, I was taught English by an American teacher. I grew up in a poor village with only two thousand people, much, much smaller than Hime. Back then, my father was a young fisherman, doing single pole-and-line fishing, just like you, Ichiro. But the English teacher did everything she could to educate us. Without her, I would never have become interested in learning English. Without my English, I would not have done this much global business after inheriting my father's company."

"Why did your small village have the American? Was she married to a Japanese fisherman or something?" Judy asked.

"No. She was sent by JET program as well." Doigaki and his

mostly silent associates stood up. "Think about it. And when you decide to do it, call me."

◄ ▮▮▮▮▮▮ ◄

When the three of us took the conversation to the doyens, they said they liked the idea. There was no choice anyways. With the central government imposing TAC on all fish in Toyama Bay, Toyama's injunction against Itokawa wasn't helping. The only way we could save the Hime fishery association and Hime itself was to have this duel and win.

The doyens called for an all-hands meeting. At these meetings, the doyens usually quietly sat behind the active fishermen, and they helped only when asked. Discreet and low key was their motto. But this time, they led the meeting themselves. They stood around the podium on the association meeting room's stage and held a question and answer session.

"What kind of duel is he proposing?" a young fisherman asked.

"Since Doigaki is a champion leisure fisherman, he wants to see who can catch the most of his favorite fish: golden eyes snappers," one of the doyens said.

"So single pole-and-line fishing?"

"Right, with four rods. Doigaki and our fisherman will both have one assistant, but the assistant can only sail–they can't touch the fishing rod. The two boats will sail at 7:00 a.m., and they'll fish for ten hours. We're judging by the weight of the fish, not the amount caught, so the person with the heaviest load of fish wins."

Everyone was silent for a moment. Finally, Hideki said, "Do you guys like the idea of this duel? You said Lindsey has three more days to answer, and the ball is in our court. This is truly black-and-white gambling. Are you guys willing to take this risk?"

"We are," one of the doyens said. "But since it's a gamble, we won't do this unless we have your unanimous agreement."

People began whispering to each other. They seemed like they couldn't believe what they just heard. Conservative people like the doyens were now endorsing gambling to decide our destiny. That proved to the fishermen that we were really on our last legs.

"Come on, people," the doyen who hadn't spoken yet said. "You guys are always looking down on those gamers. We are professionals, they are amateurs. I have heard you say that every day. So if that's really true, shouldn't it be easy for you to win?"

That was true, these professionals had pride and couldn't help looking down on leisure fishermen. Leisure fishermen went out to the sea when the season was good or the ocean was calm. But we sailed out every day regardless of the weather. We bet our lives.

"It's okay with me," Hideki said, and his words seemed to break the dam. After that, most people in the room chimed in with their own agreement.

Finally, one of the oldest fishermen in the room said, "We will be done anyway if we don't do something. I ain't going to work for Hakodate Marine."

I looked carefully at each of their faces. They all had bags under their eyes or new lines on their foreheads, clear signs of their stress and exhaustion. None of them would willingly leave Toyama.

"Okay. Is there anybody who opposes this idea?" one of the doyens said.

Nobody raised their hand.

"All right. Then, who would you like to represent us in the duel against Doigaki?"

After a short pause, a handful of people pointed to Ichiro. Then, many followed.

"The numbers don't lie. Ichiro is the best fisherman in the traditional pole-and-line fishing," said Hideki.

"Are you willing to take this fight, Ichiro?" a doyen asked.

Ichiro raised his hands, shaking his head. "I—I can't take someone's life on my shoulders."

Many fishermen started talking at once, pleading with Ichiro.

"Ichiro, please. You are our only hope," said one of the young fishermen.

"I wasn't even born in Toyama. I am not qualified."

"Don't be silly, Ichiro. We would look stupid if we don't elect the best fisherman for the duel."

Ichiro crossed his arms and closed his eyes.

I knew what he was thinking. He was good, but he was a hardworking fisherman, not a genius fisherman. If he was stuck working within a limited number of hours, he couldn't be superb.

"Okay. There is one condition," Ichiro said.

"Tell us," one of the doyens said.

"Give me full discretion to choose my fishing partner, who shall be the person I can trust the most."

"Whoever you say. Fire away."

"Let me think about it, and I'll get back to you guys within two days."

That night, Ichiro called me at about midnight, just as I was finishing cleaning up at Bamboo Sushi.

"What's up, Ichiro?"

"Hey, tonight is the new moon, and it's totally windless. The perfect timing for the firefly squid dive, if you are still interested."

"I'm on my way."

"No, I'm on my way to pick you up."

◄ ||||||||||►

When Ichiro parked his car, nobody was on the beach. We sat down and started sipping sake. For some reason, the salty breeze always made me crave good sake. After a long silence where we just sipped sake and listened to the waves crashing, Ichiro said, "You still think that we should fight against Hakodate Marine?"

"Yes. That's a no brainer. There's no other option."

"You think Doigaki is a trustworthy person? This gamble cannot be written out as a legal agreement."

"I know, but I do trust him. No one, including Doigaki, thinks the status quo is acceptable. And you know what, this may be a good adjustment of our own attitude."

"Our attitude?"

"Maybe we've been too self-centered. We were focused on our animosity against the Itokawa people, and we never cared about the consequences for Nanae when we started our business plan."

"You think the three-year term was the wrong strategy?"

"No, I still don't think so. It was necessary tool for us to get united. But how about our heart? Many people wished that Nanae would be totally destroyed. That hurt them and destroyed us too. I now realize what Mr. Bamboo meant about the ocean needing harmony and feeding off our anger."

"I agree," Ichiro finally said. "The Nanae people attacked us first, but that didn't justify our squeezing out Nanae from the bay. We became too greedy and wished Nanae people's misery. Pigs get fat, but hogs get slaughtered."

We were quiet for a moment, the sound of the waves rushing in to fill the spaces where our voices had been. I looked around the beach, wondering where everyone else was. Then, I realized people had given up on seeing the firefly squid dive tonight. But there was still a chance that the squids could show up and give Ichiro and me a private, peaceful show.

"You will do it, right, Ichiro?" I finally asked.

"Right."

"And, who are you going to pick to be your fishing partner? Yoshi? Or Hideki maybe?"

"I have already made up my mind."

"Who are you choosing?"

He pointed at me.

"Me?"

He nodded without smiling. He turned his face to the ocean.

"You're joking, right?"

"I'm dead serious."

As he was saying that, Ichiro still looked out at the ocean, like he was hoping if he stared hard enough, the squid would appear. He even seemed to try to smell the squid.

"Are you crazy, Ichiro? Why me? There are many people who can do single pole-and-line fishing better than me. I know the assistant is not going to fish. But still, they have to do a lot of calculation and assumption to figure out where the fish are. The person needs to be very experienced."

"You know, this is not going to be commercial fishing. This is going to be a duel. To be honest, I'm probably angrier than anybody about this. For me, I don't give a damn about Doigaki or Hakodate Marine. I am just mad at one person in particular."

"You mean Paul?"

"Who else? I met you, I loved you, but that guy basically revived himself from the dead and haunted you. My hatred for that son of a bitch is the size of a 200 pound bluefin tuna." He stood up and stared toward the black, silent ocean, crossing his arms over his chest.

I stood too. "I've never heard you say son of a bitch before."

"When people bring such animosity to the ocean, the ocean will treat them differently. When the duel starts, I have to focus and become connected with ocean. For that, I need to be with the person I trust the most. Otherwise, I would continue to be angry and I would receive a penalty from the sea."

"I don't know if I can handle the responsibility," I said. "It's purely gambling. I used to gamble, but I have never gambled with someone's life."

"You gambled for us once. Very recently."

"But that was an exception."

I won the Blackjack competition by a very small margin. I had trained and gained some of my memory skill back, but I was afraid I was losing it rapidly. Like Judy told me before, the memory power may come to you suddenly and leave you just as quickly.

I had used my memory power to defend myself, to protect myself.

Didn't I still need that power to protect me? Or, had I met someone who would protect me instead?

I laughed at that—that had to be the most unfeminist thought I'd ever had. I was independent. I didn't need to rely on anybody.

"Whatever you say," said Ichiro.

"I have pledged not to gamble anymore."

"Please make an exception for this. Afterwards, you can talk to me if you're having any unhealthy urges to gamble. I'll always be there to listen and help you."

"Ichiro."

"Lindsey, will you marry me?"

It didn't surprise me at all this time, and I didn't respond right away. I silently looked for a perfectly round seashell with my iPhone light. I found a pink one and brought it to my ear.

I sat down for a while. Ichiro sat next to me. He pulled out his sake, Masuizumi. It reminded me of our first try to see the firefly squid dive last year. Finally, Ichiro asked me what I was doing.

"I was asking my mom how she feels about your marriage proposal."

"What did she say?"

"She said she has to see you first in person."

We laughed at the same time.

"I need to think about my answer to the proposal for a little while longer. But I will be your assistant for the duel."

Ichiro grinned. "Good."

We sat quietly for a while longer, waiting for the squid dive. Then, Ichiro asked me if I wanted to dance the Owara.

He said, "Mrs. Bamboo gave me a set of kimono for you to wear at the Owara dance this morning. It's sitting in my trunk."

"Alright. I could use the practice. And there's no one around to watch me."

Ichiro jumped up. "I'll be right back."

A few minutes later, he reappeared with the kimono and a Chinese fiddle. "There are many traditional dances in Japan, and the dance methods and music have a ton of variety. But we only use a Chinese fiddle for the Owara dance."

"I know. I like the sentimental and melancholic tone it makes. It's great match with the dance, isn't it?"

As I said that, I was thinking of how far Ichiro and I had come since we sat on the same beach almost a year ago.

Ichiro handed me the kimono. "Most festivals are meant to be joyous celebrations. But this dance is about the sorrows of life. People need to share their pain before they can let go of it. Then, they can slowly become happy again."

It was almost completely dark, so I felt comfortable changing my clothes under the stars. Ichiro turned around and promised he wouldn't look.

I slipped on the kimono. I put on the kimono sandals. I lowered the Owara straw hat over my eyes.

Ichiro played the Chinese fiddle as I changed. I closed my eyes for a while and listened to it. I imagined many people dancing, looking back on their melancholic memories and silently sharing them with loved ones, including those who already passed away. I loved the concept.

Once I was dressed, I told Ichiro he could turn around. He kept playing the Chinese fiddle, and I started dancing. Since Ichiro played the fiddle, he couldn't dance with me. Yet, I felt like I was spiritually connected with him. With my Owara straw hat on, our eyes never met during the dance. But I knew we were in complete synchronicity.

When the dance was done, Ichiro said, "That was wonderful, Lindsey."

"Thank you."

Ichiro spread his arms. I stepped in toward him. We got closer to each other, and I pulled off my hat.

Ichiro slowly took my hat and dropped it on the sand. I fell in his arms.

"You are absolutely beautiful," he said in a soft voice, perfectly matched with the weak sounds of the gentle waves hitting the shore.

"I love you, Lindsey."

"I love you, Ichiro."

I kissed him.

◀ ▌▌▌▌▌ ◀

I woke up to my iPhone shrilly ringing the next morning. I blearily reached for it, opening my eyes just enough to read the time, 6 a.m., and see the caller ID.

"Hello, Mr. Bamboo," I mumbled, my mouth dry.

"Lindsey, sorry to wake you up on your day off. The doyens asked me to contact you."

"Okay—I can go downstairs really quickly."

"I'm not downstairs."

I sat up, awake enough to notice the panic in Mr. Bamboo's voice. "At 6 a.m.? Where are you, Mr. Bamboo?"

"Ichiro fell into the sea."

"What?"

"He is in the Itokawa Medical University Hospital. I am in his room right now."

I knew where that was. It was ironic that when we were in the middle of the fight against Itokawa prefecture, he got hospitalized in the best medical school in Itokawa prefecture. But that was the nearest hospital to Hime.

I rubbed my eyes, trying to wake up. "Did he hit his leg again? Is it broken?"

"Lindsey . . . He's in a coma."

I dropped my cell phone onto the floor. When I reached for the phone, I had goosebumps all over my body.

"The doctor told me that he should be all right today. He will regain consciousness very soon."

"What do you mean 'today?'"

"The injury was not serious. But he is in serious condition because of . . . another issue."

"What is it?"

He paused for a moment, and when he spoke his voice was softer than I ever heard before. "His leukemia is back, Lindsey."

"What?" I said, my voice quivering.

"It was diagnosed as chronic meningeal leukemia. We called his primary physician in Tokamachi, who has watched his symptoms for a decade. He thought Ichiro was completely in remission, but the leukemia came back suddenly. The leukemia was the reason Ichiro lost consciousness while he was out on his boat, and he fell into the ocean."

"It's not life threatening, right?" I said, desperation creeping into my voice.

Mr. Bamboo breathed in for a long time, stopped, and then breathed out slowly.

"He has a 20 percent chance of surviving for five more years."

I jumped up and quickly changed into the first outfit I found. "I'm out of bed and getting dressed. I'll be there as soon as I can."

As I was moving, I asked him to tell me more about what the doctor said.

"He said that sometimes, symptoms can hit a person all at once, which is what happened to Ichiro. The doyens and I told the association that Ichiro fell, but we decided not to tell them about the leukemia part. We only let them know that he has a terrible unknown medical condition, so he won't be able to do the duel."

I finished getting dressed, said a quick goodbye to Mr. Bamboo, and called for a taxi. As I dove into the taxi, I called Judy hysterically. I asked her to meet me at the hospital. The taxi driver turned off the radio and ran five red lights without saying anything.

Judy and I spent the day sitting by Ichiro's bed, Judy holding my hand. The doyens joined us later in the day, and they silently joined our vigil. Finally, that evening, Ichiro woke up. I cried and kissed his cheek, and Ichiro groggily smiled up at me.

I stayed in his room for three days, barely leaving his side until he got discharged. There was a current of fear running through us, but we still were able to talk lightly and even laugh. I was grateful to have this peaceful time with him.

I took him to my apartment. I insisted that he sleep in the bed, even though he protested. I slept on the couch.

I fed him in morning, went to the school, came back, started preparation for Bamboo Sushi, and fed Ichiro dinner. Mrs. Bamboo fixed traditional Toyama medicinal lunches for him.

He continued to feel weak and nauseous, but he regained some color in his face.

A week later, the doyens held an emergency association meeting.

When I entered, people avoided my eyes. Everyone knew

Ichiro was sick, and they guessed there was more to it than the doyens were telling them.

The air was heavy. I could barely breathe.

"Hello, everyone," one of the doyens said. "Unfortunately, Ichiro won't be able to represent Hime. We want to know what you would like to do now."

"Can we postpone until Ichiro recovers?" Hideki asked.

"No, he probably won't be able to fish for another six months," one doyen said.

"How serious is it?"

"Not serious at all. But it takes time," the doyen lied in a flat tone.

Another doyen said, "We still have to take this gamble, or we are over. Ichiro told me that he wants somebody to take his place in the duel. Even today, seven fishermen decided to leave Hime. We're down to 114 members. Look around, folks. You can see that there are many vacant seats. Now the fishery association membership is at only a third of the last year. We see many citizens leaving town, too."

The doyen looked around the room. "Does anybody wants to take this duel, instead of Ichiro?"

Nobody raised their hand.

A young fisherman stood up. "There's only part-time fishermen left for single pole-and-line fishing. The majority of us do trawling or fixed shore net-fishing."

There was another long pause, and then I stood up.

"I will do it."

"Lindsey san–" Hideki began, his voice hoarse.

"I promised Ichiro that I would fulfill his wish to save Hime. Most of you were born and raised here. But Ichiro was not. Yet, you guys have embraced him. He wanted to pay back this community. It is time to make my husband's wish come true."

Everyone froze, all tiny movements and murmurs ceasing.

I knew they would react like that. But I couldn't find a better time to do this.

After a long silence, one of the doyens stood and said, "Lindsey. Did you say your husband? Ichiro?"

"Yes."

"This sounds like an awfully stupid question, but I have to ask, did you marry?"

"Yes. We had been trying to find a time when his parents could come from Tokamachi and my parents could come from Boston, but we decided that we couldn't wait any longer. It was not a spontaneous decision. You know us. We always plan ahead. He has proposed to me twice, and I just needed the time to think. I needed to decide whether it was realistic for me to live in this town until I die as either a fisherwoman, school teacher, or sushi chef. Or maybe all of them."

Nobody spoke—everyone just looked at me with wide, surprised eyes. I continued on. "We had no wedding, no party. But we trust each other, and we love each other. Most importantly, we have spent so much time together on our ocean. Our Toyama Bay." I looked around and smiled at everyone. If I stopped smiling, I knew I would break down and start crying. "One by one, we will check off the formalities. We have done the easiest one. We went to the Hime City Hall and registered our marriage."

Nobody made a sound. Nobody even moved.

"He is not here. But I am his wife. My husband did not shirk this difficult responsibility. So I wouldn't either. Now, gentlemen, it's your call to endorse or veto my intention."

◀ ▍▎▏▕▏▎▍ ◀

After the meeting was over, Judy grabbed my arm while everyone left the room.

"Where did you come from, Judy?"

"I snuck in. Did you guys really get married?"

I looked around to make sure no one was watching. Once the coast was clear, I shook my head no.

Judy told me that she would wait for me at her deli shop.

After I wrapped up at Bamboo Sushi that night and fed Ichiro, I went over to her deli. We sat in the dim light in her empty restaurant, and she gave me her matzo ball soup. The soup was warm and light and perfect.

"Thank you for the soup, Judy. This is wonderful."

"Why did you say you would compete against Doigaki?"

"Because that's what Ichiro would like to hear. I know he wants me to do it rather than any other fishermen in Hime."

"How confident are you? If you lose, you will lose everything."

"It has to be me. I'm the only professional single pole-and-line fisherman left in Hime. I'm far better than any veteran fishermen who's used to using a different fishing method. They may sound similar, but each fishing method requires completely different skills."

"Okay," Judy said, and for once, her normally expressive face was still. We cleaned up the kitchen together, locked up the shop, and went to Olive Bath House. It was already past midnight. Nobody else was there this late at night.

"What are you going to tell Ichiro when he wakes up tomorrow?" Judy asked as we sunk into the warm water.

"I will bring him a bunch of Toyama red tulips."

"Red tulips?"

"Toyama is known for having the best tulips in Japan, and red tulips are a declaration of love."

"Then, what you are going to say?"

"I will say, marry me."

"Ichiro won't take it. You know that, Lindsey. He doesn't want you to say all this just because he's sick. He wants you to actually mean it, not give him a cheap, clumsy display of love. It's like a soap opera in the '70s where people believe the power of love can solve everything and cure any sickness. Love means never having to say you're sorry—you know that bullshit."

I glared at her. "Don't say he's going to die. He will survive, no matter what."

"Lindsey, face the reality. He will refuse your proposal because he knows that he won't be around to provide for you. Once he learned that he was sick again, he felt like his marriage proposal got nullified due to him not being able to fulfill one of the contractual terms."

"He's not dying, Judy!" I screamed. My voice echoed and bounced off the roof high above our heads. "He's not. And he and I will live happily ever after."

"You know this is a bad idea, Lindsey. You know you're just going to get hurt in the end."

Slowly, I shook my head. I was crying, but the fact that my face was wet shielded me, prevented Judy from seeing. "I love him, Judy. I think I do."

"You think? You can't just think you love him. You have to feel it, wholeheartedly."

"When it comes to men, it's always supposed to be black and white. Simple and clear. You can't *think*, you have to *feel*. But for me and Ichiro, I am not sure. If I said I love him, period, it sounds like a lie to me."

"Then you just proved that you don't love him."

"That sounds like a lie to me, too. I just—I feel so warm when I'm with him. Just like this hot bath. The water is always guaranteed to be this perfect consistent temperature, and it makes me want to stay here forever. That's how I feel with Ichiro."

Judy shook her head, closed her eyes, and sank her head beneath the water.

the Sea of Japan

◀ |||||||||| ◀

As Judy predicted, when Ichiro woke up the next morning, he was furious that I lied about us getting married. I stayed calm because Judy was in my room, too. Even though Judy had her issues with Ichiro and me, she was still on my side, just like she always was. She would defend me no matter what.

So, before I could say anything to Ichiro, Judy stepped in. "Ichiro, you proposed to Lindsey. She finally accepted it. Nothing peculiar."

"It is peculiar. It was not my will. And besides, it was a blatant lie." He laid down in his bed. His pale face was almost porcelain.

"It's not. You're going to get married," Judy said. "You just haven't yet."

"What if I die? What is going to happen to her?" He pointed his long, beautiful finger at me.

"I would direct Lindsey to move back to Boston and find a good-looking man."

Ichiro trembled, the words 'good-looking man' seeming to stay with him. He swallowed and looked away.

I put my red tulips in a crystal vase. These were surely the most beautiful tulips in Toyama. For me, they symbolized more than just my love to Ichiro. They also represented my determination to win this fishing duel and my gratitude to Ichiro. They were everything I felt toward him.

"I'll find a good guy like you, and I'll set him up with Lindsey," Judy continued in a flat, administrative tone, like this was not a big deal for anybody. She put a hand on Ichiro's shoulder. "So, Ichiro, don't worry about Lindsey. Worry about your health, okay? And if you're worried about Lindsey during the duel, you can communicate with her by radio. You both have to fulfill your responsibility to the people of Hime."

I felt like I should say something, but I couldn't think of anything to say. I wrapped Ichiro's head in my arms, laying my head against his. Soon, I felt warm tears sliding down my arms. I raised my head and wiped off his tears with my fingertips. I still didn't say anything.

Then, I kissed him, bending over him like someone doing CPR. I expected him to lift his arms from out of the blanket to make the moment feel more romantic. But he didn't. He froze, seeming not to know what to do with me, especially in front of Judy. So I wrapped my arms around his shoulder and neck. I held him and cried softly. Ichiro stiffened even more, and I decided that I would never cry in front of him again. I wouldn't let him see my fear.

And I kept the promise, even the next day, when Ichiro had a high fever and bled from his mouth nonstop, and an ambulance carried him back to the hospital and even farther away from me.

◄||||||||||►

Both the school principal and Mr. Bamboo kindly offered a long, paid vacation so I could prepare for duel.

I sailed out every day. I only caught golden eyes snappers. These fish lived deep in the sea, normally staying deeper than 1,000 feet. This was the fish that Ichiro and Doigaki both loved the most. The meat was slightly pink, and it could be better sashimi than bluefin tuna if it was super fresh.

Ichiro's condition was volatile. Most of the time, he looked fine. He begged his doctor to discharge him, but he refused because when Ichiro coughed, he coughed hard. And if he bled, he needed an immediate treatment or the bleeding didn't stop.

The doctor didn't say if Ichiro was getting better or worse. They took his blood every other day to test his blood cell count. I believed he would get better. I chose not to worry about his future at all.

We talked often, and we always sat hand in hand. I read some books to him. He told me more clues about how to find and catch fish. I kissed him a lot. He got out of bed every hour to brush his teeth since he thought the illness gave him bad breath, which I found adorable.

I brought him a thermos filled with ginger butter cocoa every time I visited. I talked about my adopted parents and my biological parents. I talked about how rebellious I was when I was a teenager.

"I learned a new Japanese proverb yesterday," I said. "It goes, 'When one becomes grateful to their parents, one realizes they were gone.'"

"Right, I've heard that one."

"I'm thinking I should invite my parents and Grandpa to Hime when this duel is over. How do you feel about that?"

"It's a great idea."

"I'm sure they would love my Toyama Bay Sushi."

"Promise me to cook your sushi once we're back on my boat."

"I will make it for you a million times."

"Promise me you will dance Owara at the real Owara festival among hundreds of Toyama Owara dancers. I want to do the male dance right behind you."

I pictured it in my mind—me wearing the straw hat, Ichiro swaying behind me, looking at me with clear love in his eyes.

"I promise. And promise me that we'll go to a Red Sox game together."

"I promise. Will that be what we do to celebrate my full recovery?"

"No, it will be our honeymoon."

"Lindsey—"

I didn't want to hear what he would say, the practicalities he would bring up. So I gently squeezed his cheeks and kissed him.

The day of the duel finally arrived.

It was a rough, windy Saturday morning. I went to the shore and checked the status of the ocean. The ocean condition was way beyond what an average fisherman could handle, but it wasn't beyond my capabilities.

The doyens called me from the port. "Per the rules we mutually set, we could postpone the duel if you want, Lindsey."

"No, sir. This is actually good for me. Gamers never fish in this kind of horrible weather, but commercial fishermen do. Does Doigaki want to postpone?"

"He said it is totally up to you. I think his manly pride won't allow him to postpone if you say you're okay with going out today."

"Good, then I will do it today. I want to."

I went back to the hospital.

The night before, Ichiro's fever had risen again, and he had coughed for hours. But the fever broke overnight, and his cough passed.

"I'm feeling fine," he said. "I can be your assistant on the boat."

As he talked his nose started bleeding, first a few drops, and then a continuous stream. He put a tissue to it, his face flushed. "I can still do it."

"No, Ichiro. The best thing you can do for me is stay here and rest. Then, we can celebrate when I win."

I kissed him and hugged him tightly, and then I hopped on my bike and went back to port. On the way, I called and asked Judy to sit by his side.

"Of course, I'll head right over," she said. "I'm at the deli, just setting things up. I can't believe it's mine again."

I smiled—I was so happy for Judy. The day before the

competition, I had met with my lawyer. He confirmed that if I asked articulately, the DA would drop the indictment for the benefit of the victim. Paul initially tried to fight at the court all the way, until he realized that because there's no plea deal in Japan for this kind of offense, once he got indicted, he would lose any control over the case, and he might have ended up with jail time.

My lawyer said to me, "Based on my conversation with Paul's counsel, I'm guessing that he told Paul that he has a very small chance of winning at court. After all, Paul's fingerprint was on the necklace, your nosebleed was witnessed by more than ten people, he had your blood on his shirt, and there's more than enough situational evidence to convince the judge beyond reasonable doubt that Paul is guilty."

Paul agreed to pay my medical bill of ten bucks, but more importantly, he canceled the franchise agreement with Judy & Peter. We settled. Paul was freed but had to leave the country within forty-eight hours. Judy and Nakata san were allowed to open their deli back up immediately.

After I hung up with Judy, I turned on the local radio news on my iPhone and listened as I rode my bicycle back to the port. The news said that the relationship between the central government and Itokawa and Toyama prefectures had become even tenser. The fishery volumes at Nanae and Hime were going to reach the new TAC in ten days. The central government said that all fishery associations had to comply with their regulations. If the associations didn't comply and let fishermen go out to the sea after reaching TAC, the government would issue an executive order to force them to stop. According to the news, the coast guard was already ordered to standby. In the history of Japan, the coast guard had never been used against the country's own fishermen.

I was glad that my duel was happening right now. If it was

one month later, or even two weeks later, everything would have been ruined.

I arrived at the port and was shocked to see a huge crowd standing around the dock. As I looked around, I noticed over a hundred fishermen who had left Hime had come back to cheer me on. There were also probably another two hundred Hime citizens. Mr. Principal, Erica, and all the teachers were there. I shook hands with every teacher firmly.

As I talked to Mr. Principal, a big Harley Davidson roared up and parked nearby. It was Nakata san. With his Ray-Bans on, he gave me a thumbs up and a big grin.

Mr. and Mrs. Bamboo were there too. Mr. Bamboo gave me his Toyama Bay Sushi in a bento box.

"I know you don't have time to fix your own lunch today."

"Thank you, Mr. Bamboo. Tonight, I will make sushi for you and Mrs. Bamboo with all the golden eyes snappers I catch today."

"That sounds great. I'm sure Ichiro is waiting for your winning sushi."

I nodded, swallowing hard.

I noticed that Hideki and Hana were washing my boat for me, filling it up with gas, and loading lots of ice. I was about to go thank them, but someone ran up to me, shouting my name. I turned and saw Kong arriving with many of my students. They ran up to me and gave me high-fives.

Kong said, "I just came back from Florida last night. Here."

He gave me a brand new, authentic Red Sox baseball cap.

"Oh, thank you, Kong!"

Then, I saw an autograph by the legendary David Ortiz on the side of the cap. It read, "Fish more, Lindsey!"

I was speechless. I put the cap on my head and gave Kong a tight hug.

the Sea of Japan

The three doyens directed the kids to the designated area inside the market for Hime citizens.

Young fishermen ran up to Hideki and Hana and helped them finish cleaning my boat. I smiled as I looked around, as I realized how large my world here had become.

Finally, Doigaki came. He wore black fishing gear with a sharp yellow line on the side. It made him look like a police officer.

"I heard about your husband's hospitalization. Is he okay?"

"Thank you. He will be just fine."

"Who will you have as your assistant?"

"If I had anybody on my boat, it would have been my husband. So, since he can't be here, I'm not having any assistants. Besides, assistants are not supposed to touch the fishing rod, according to your rule. In that case, I don't need the help."

"Okay. If you change your mind and you want to have an assistant on your boat, radio for anybody in your association. So you won't lose your time."

"Thank you. That's fair."

"The radio is open at all times for safety. You can communicate with anybody by radio. But your conversation over the radio is available for everyone to hear, except me. Also, the judge will operate two drones with cameras. People here will watch the duel, and we'll be able to see what the other person is doing on the monitors in our boats"

"As might be expected for a CEO of such a big company, you have thought everything out well. I'm impressed by your preparation."

"Thank you for your compliment. We don't necessarily always comply with the minutia of the laws crafted by bureaucrats. But for this, I wanted to be completely fair. It is not only the Hakodate Marine's name, but also my name on this duel."

"That's why it's worth it to fight."

I went to the locker room in the association building and changed from my blazer and pants into fisherman gear. I had brand new white gear with a Red Sox logo on the front of my fishery jacket. It was a gift from the doyens and all the fishermen here. They ordered this special gear from the authentic MLB gear shop, and it truly resembled the Red Sox's jersey.

I also wrapped a long-bleached cotton cloth around my waist over and over again until it was super tight. This was a traditional Japanese way to support a fisherman's waist when the weather was wild.

When it was time to start the competition, I ran out to my boat as the crowd cheered. Doigaki was already in his boat. Right when it hit 7:00, a big vessel blew its horn. Doigaki and I started sailing. Immediately, the wind became wilder, as if it was waiting for us.

I chose to go to our usual fishing place, and I punched the latitude and longitude into the autopilot. Doigaki appeared to be going to the same direction.

When I got close to the spot, I stared at the fish finder radar, and I slowed down the boat when the radar showed many red clusters.

"I think I'm ready to start fishing," I said into the radio.

"What do you see, Lindsey?" Ichiro responded, the radio crackling slightly.

"I see many red dots in the area between 1,150 feet to 1,300 feet. I'm lowering the lines."

I quickly stopped the boat and put the rod down, lowering a line deep into the sea. The line had many sub lines and bites. The end of the line was connected to a piece of iron, so it rapidly went down into the deep sea.

"Very good. How is the weather?"

"Getting worse every minute."

"What does the seabed look like?"

"It's pretty flat. I'll lay down the sublines on the bed slowly."

"Very good."

When I guessed that the iron reached the seabed, I slowed down the reeling immediately. I also stopped the engine of the boat and let the boat ride on the current. Fifty sublines were lying down on the seabed, waiting for the golden eye snappers to come and bite.

"I stopped the engine, Ichiro. I already see the tips of my rods are knocking. Fish are biting my bait!"

"Awesome! Be careful though. Even though you stopped the engine, today's current is strong. Your boat is floating faster than usual. If the hooks catch on rocks or sea grass roots, the line gets pulled hard, and it will get cut. At the speed you're going, you won't have time to release the rock. You will lose everything."

In our daily fishing, that happened often. But as long we were watching the rod carefully, we got a gut-feeling of when that would happen. We often reversed the boat a little bit to release the rock or root. But today, that wouldn't work.

"I put the black line double with the regular line just in case that happens."

"That was a good strategy," he said, and I pictured him smiling warmly.

The black line was a thin rubber line that connected the reel with the regular long nylon line. The rubber was flexible, and it absorbed the shock when the line or hook got stuck in the seabed, preventing the line from getting cut. Using double long black lines further helped protect the lines. But the drawback was that with too much flexibility, I wouldn't know for sure whether the baits were getting bitten.

The wind got stronger, and the waves rougher. It started

raining. I put the new baseball cap on, but it didn't protect me much. The temperature dropped too, making it feel like we were back in the middle of winter.

"Hang on, Lindsey. Doigaki's having to deal with the same conditions," Ichiro said.

I watched the reel's gage meter show how deep the line was sinking. I slowed it down a little bit, and gave a thumbs up to the drone flying above my head. I didn't see Ichiro, but he saw me.

It got even colder as the wind and rain got stronger.

It got to the point where I couldn't stand. My fingers almost lost all feeling. I couldn't believe this was May. I had never felt this type of coldness in Toyama, that kind that reached down into your bones.

But I was still able to focus. This was a pure duel. When I pulled up the line, I saw many golden bodies flickering in the dark sea like candles. As the fish came closer to the surface, they became brighter and more golden red.

The ocean got wilder. The waves were higher and I couldn't see more than fifty feet in any direction because of the walls of waves.

I pulled up many golden eyes snappers. Usually, on fifty sub-lines, I got ten to twenty fish. But the bad weather seemed to make the fish congregate closer together, and they took the bait more than usual. I got thirty or even forty fish per rod.

The drone camera flew over my head, capturing every fish I pulled into the boat. Over the radio, I heard people in Hime's joyous screams each time I pulled up a line. I glanced down at my monitor to check on Doigaki. He was catching many golden eyes snappers, too. He caught less, but each fish was larger than mine. I looked at them hard, trying to count them quickly.

We looked to be neck-in-neck, which made my stomach twist with nerves.

"You're doing great, Lindsay!" Ichiro shouted.

"Thanks, but mine are lot smaller than Doigaki's."

"How small are they?"

"Mostly medium, around 1.5 pounds or so. Very few are large or super large."

At the auction market, there was a big assembly line with a 'divider' equipped. It instantly weighed each fish and threw it into one of four fish tanks: small, medium, large, and super large, ranging from 0.9 pounds to 2.2 pounds.

The waves changed direction and started hitting my boat on the sides, making it tilt dangerously. I could hardly stand, but I hung on.

"You might want to move north a little bit," Ichiro said. "The tiny fish the golden eyes snappers are chasing may have moved north to look for a warm current."

"I see. How long do you think I should—"

Before I could finish talking, a wave crashed onto my boat, pushing me all the way to the back of my deck and blinding me. For a moment, everything went dark, and the world got fuzzy. When the world came back into focus, I coughed, salt water running down my chin.

On the radio speaker, the doyens shouted, asking if I was okay.

When I tried to reply, I coughed hard. Pain ran through my entire body, but I didn't seem to be bleeding. Even though my head pounded and my back ached, I was lucky. If I hadn't been knocked onto my back, I might have been tossed out to sea. I was also glad that I had wrapped the long cloth around my waist. Without it, my back would have been broken because it would have been forced to bend more than it could handle.

"I'm all right," I screamed into the radio microphone.

As I sat up, I thought of my grandpa, how he had fallen into the sea several times. I wondered if he was scared, or if he just felt more determined, like the sea had issued him a challenge that he had to meet.

I laid still for another moment, shivering. The coldness reached murderous levels. Many times, I had been splashed by water when I was out with Ichiro or Grandpa. Usually, we laughed it away. When conditions were rougher than usual, Ichiro warned me when a wave was about to hit, and I was able to brace myself. He had been protecting me from day one.

Finally, I felt steady enough to stand. I started the engine and headed north.

The aggressive waves continued to jump over the rim of the boat and attack me. But I started to notice the patterns of their attack—the sea and I understood each other. My new fishing gear saved me from getting totally soaked. But I was still wet and cold, and the heavy rain kept pouring down.

I thought I would hear more from Ichiro, but his channel was quiet.

"Hey, Ichiro. Are you there?"

No answer.

Maybe the weather had caused the radio to disconnect at the hospital.

As soon as I realized I couldn't talk to Ichiro, I felt exhausted. I remembered I hadn't eaten anything this morning because of my anxiety. But I needed some energy now.

When I had put my third rod down and lowered the line, I opened the bento box Mr. Bamboo gave me and ate his sushi. He put his soy sauce on the fish directly so that I didn't have to open a soy sauce pouch. He avoided crunchy meat like squid or octopus, and chose soft meat like tuna or eel, perfect for someone whose teeth were chattering—he always seemed to think of everything. He had clearly gently gripped the rice, and I could tell his sushi-rice included double the usual amount of vinegar and sugar to rejuvenate my beaten-up body.

I tried to say thank you to Mr. Bamboo, but the microphone could not pick up my voice because of the wind.

When I reached a warmer current, I quickly started catching larger fish than before. We didn't normally sail this far out because we couldn't miss the auction, which closed at 3:00 p.m. But today, that was irrelevant. I felt like I was gaining the upper hand against Doigaki. On my monitor, I saw he was still catching some fish, but definitely less than before. As a gamer, he was focusing too much on doing one thing at a time—one rod, one line. But in commercial fishing, you have to focus on the bigger picture, which helped me multitask.

I kept checking on the temperature gauge. It kept dropping. That meant that the golden eyes snappers were sinking deeper to avoid the cold water on the top of the sea.

Then, the fish finder blinked and turned blue. I tried to restart it, but it didn't budge. It was frozen and useless.

"Ichiro! Something happened to my fish finder. What should I do?" I shouted.

No answer from Ichiro. The line at the hospital must still have been disconnected. Hideki chimed in. He gave me a few different suggestions and told me how to reboot the fish finder. But it didn't fix the problem.

"I think the transducer is broken," I said.

"I think you're right. Sometimes, in Toyama Bay, the mahi-mahi bump into the transducer."

The transducer was a sensor device mounted to the bottom of the boat. Mahi-mahi are large fish, reaching thirty pounds when they're adults. They like swimming on the surface of the sea, and they're attracted to floating objects, so they sometimes knock against boats.

"Is there anything I can do?"

"There's nothing you can do once you are in the ocean," Hideki said.

Through the video monitor, I saw Doigaki find another spot and put his rod down for the fourth time.

I didn't even know where I should go now. The GPS still worked fine, but I couldn't see where the fish were.

I thought about going to some of the spots where we fished on a daily basis. With a GPS, I could find my way there. But the freezing temperature must have affected the fish streets. They had probably moved on.

I decided to just do my fourth try where I was, but the result turned out to be miserable. I got only five fish.

I had to try somewhere else out. I needed to get more than five.

But without the fish finder, where could I go?

The radio was quiet, everyone seeming to be at just as much of a loss as me.

The wind blew even stronger, and fog filled the sky. I couldn't see the line dividing the sea and sky. The boat shifted right and left, up and down, and I stumbled around. I strengthened my lower abdomen for stability and threw the five fish into the cooler box.

The clouds were dark and heavy, hanging low in the sky. The wind raged, so strong I worried about water spouts forming. If one hit my boat, I would be powerless. My boat could flip, and I could fly out into the open sea.

Doigaki was pulling up a lot of fish.

His face was pale and his hands trembled. Gamers normally don't play in wild weather. I wished he would give up and go back to shore, but he still seemed to have energy. He paused, leaned over the boat, and vomited. A wave hit him right then, and his boat rolled. I held my breath, fearing he was about to be tossed out to sea. But he had a harness on, and it pulled him back. He slammed onto the floor, hard.

I heard thunder. Lightning, too.

One doyen said, "Lindsey, you have done well. You don't have to continue. We are worried about your safety now. We can give up. I'm sure Doigaki will quit soon."

"No," I yelled back, and the wind was too loud for me to say anything. Every time I said something, the air froze my lungs, reminding me of my waiting for the aurora with my mom on a winter night in Fairbanks.

I thought about Ichiro. Even if we couldn't communicate verbally, he was watching me. I couldn't give up.

I tried to use the color of the water to find fish. But rain and sea water splashed over my face, making my vision fuzzy.

Even the fog had become thicker.

I was at an impasse. I couldn't move, I couldn't fish.

"Lindsey."

It was Judy.

"Yes?" I said, my breath hitching.

"I just wanted to tell you that Ichiro's condition is worse."

"What?" I screamed. "Is he okay?"

At that moment, a wave lifted the tip of the boat more than ten feet in the air. The boat slammed back into the ocean, knocking me off my feet. My right knee slammed onto the boat's floor.

"He's okay," Judy said, her voice seeming to come from faraway. "The doctor said the symptoms aren't as bad as the last time he was unconscious."

I tried to stand, and my knees buckled. I stood up slower, and my knee continued to protest. But I could still walk. I could continue fishing.

"He's all right, Lindsey. I wouldn't have told you anything if it was really bad."

"Good."

"Let me take care of him, and you focus on the duel."

"Thank you. Never leave him, okay?"

"Understood. I will never leave him."

"Please. I will win. I will feed him the best golden eyes snapper sushi tonight."

She paused for just a second. "I know you will."

I took a deep breath, steadying myself. The wind died down for a moment, and in the sudden quiet, I heard the sound of an engine, getting closer to me. In this weather, nobody would be fishing. I wondered if I was hallucinating.

I looked back but I couldn't see anything beyond the fog.

The sound of the engine got louder, the boat getting closer. Apparently, the boat was aiming toward my boat. I had set up the collision alarm radar, and it started beeping.

"Who is it?" I shouted.

I now saw the vague shadow of the boat. The beeping got louder and faster.

"Who is it?" I screamed again.

I saw two men standing on the deck and one man in the captain seat.

"Hey, who is it? Change directions, idiot!" As I shouted, I jumped toward the engine controller and tried to back up.

"Lindsey, I'm here," a voice from the boat shouted, and I stopped moving immediately.

I couldn't believe it.

It was Hideki's boat.

And the guy standing at the front of the boat was my grandpa.

"What are you doing here, Grandpa?" I said, talking into a microphone that was connected to the boat's speaker.

"I was planning on surprising you last night," he said into his boat's speaker. "But my flight was canceled. I just arrived here now."

Hideki waved at me from the captain seat.

The third person on the boat stepped forward. It was Kong. He grabbed the microphone. "I will get your grandfather onto your boat."

"No, it's too wild today. It's too dangerous for Grandpa."

"What are you saying, Lindsey? I still operate boats, see the color of the sea, and smell the fish better than you. I may not be as young as I once was, but I'm still the best fishermen in all of Massachusetts."

"Are you sure?"

"And I am going to finally retire. So, this is going to be my last time fishing."

I nodded.

Kong threw a rope, and I grabbed it, connecting the two boats. Once we were close enough to each other, Grandpa leaped out and landed on my boat.

"So, your fish radar isn't working," Grandpa said.

"Right."

"Okay. You focus on the rods. I will operate the boat."

Grandpa stood by the temperature gauge, checking the temperature of the sea every fifteen seconds. He also checked the direction of the wind and stared at the weather forecast. Then, he said, "This place is no good. Let's move."

He sailed west, speeding through the water, while Doigaki gradually moved to the east.

I used to call commercial fishing another form of gambling. That was probably part of the reason why I was interested in it. But now, it felt more like Russian roulette.

My rod started moving as fish ate the bait. I imagined all the golden eyes snappers biting the bait, more and more until hundreds were there.

I tried talking to Ichiro, but there was no answer. After a delay, Judy came onto the radio and told me not to worry about Ichiro.

"Judy is with him," Grandpa said. "Trust her. Your husband will be all right."

I met his eyes, wondering who he had talked to in Hime, who had told him about Ichiro and me.

"Thank you, Grandpa."

He steered the boat, stared at the temperature gauge, and then got out of the cabin and inhaled deeply, smelling the sea wind. He also looked at the color of the sea. He had brought his usual navy fishing gear that said 'New Bedford' on the back. For the first time in my life, I was grateful that I was born and raised in Massachusetts.

I no longer felt alone, and having someone else there made me more energized. I still couldn't feel my fingers, but the cold didn't affect me as much anymore. I could also forget about my injured right knee for a while.

Our fifth throw turned out to be big. I pulled in seventy-four snappers, the most so far.

For the first time, I actually believed that Grandpa could smell the fish. I told him that while he ate some of Mr. Bamboo's sushi, and he said, "It may just be a gut feeling. But I do believe that the ocean has its intention. I was talking to your sushi master earlier, and we both agree that the ocean doesn't like internal fights. For the ocean, Hime or Nanae are just like siblings, and it doesn't like seeing siblings fighting each other."

I nodded—I was starting to believe Grandpa and Mr. Bamboo's theories more and more. I looked at my watch. It was already 3:30. We had to go back to the port and unload the fish onto a designated spot at the market by 5:00 p.m. That was the rule. If I missed it, I would automatically lose.

"I know what you're thinking, Lindsey. Doigaki is already headed back to the port," Grandpa said.

"I've been watching his progress. I think he's winning now.

We caught a similar amount of fish, but weight-wise, his fish are larger than mine."

"What do you want to do?"

"I'll do one more try."

"I'm not sure about that."

"I have to."

"Just because you think he's winning doesn't mean he actually is. You just made a very vague assumption. I wouldn't risk delaying your return to port."

"No, Grandpa. I was watching every move Doigaki made. Even while I was doing my own fishing, I always paid attention to him."

"Then, what? You just added up all of the fish. How? How you can remember that without using a calculator or even pen and paper to do the math."

"Grandpa. I remember everything." I had never really explained my memory to Grandpa—I didn't think he would understand. "Everything I'm interested in, I remember. I am positive that he is winning now. I have to try one more time."

Grandpa pondered this for a few seconds. He looked at his watch and thought it through.

"Okay. Let's make it quick."

"Thank you, Grandpa!"

He hopped into the captain seat again and blew the engine.

I squatted right behind him, and tried to reach for the bait box. But it was gone.

"Oh no," I muttered. "No, no, no."

"What's wrong, Lindsey?"

"My bait's gone! All my tiny squids, everything!"

I cried out, trying not to panic. I realized that one of the many waves that hit my boat must have thrown out the backup bait box, which I hadn't secured. That was my fault. I should have spent three minutes and squeezed it into the crew bed.

"I didn't think I would need the fucking backup bait box," I groaned, running a hand through my hair.

"You have anymore?"

"No. That was my fault, Grandpa."

"You're positive?"

"Right."

"Okay, let me look around inside the cabin."

"Grandpa. I know this boat well. There may be some lures in the drawer, but probably not more than five."

He searched all over the place. After five minutes, he found some of Ichiro's old T-shirts crumpled up on the floor. He grabbed a pair of scissors and started cutting them.

"Lindsey, help me and cut these into strips. This is going to be our bait."

"How?"

"Just cut them into the size of your squid bait. Believe me, they will bite them."

I had never heard of fish biting simple pieces of cloth. But I had no time.

The weather got even worse. When you fix baits, you have to use both hands. I had been clinging onto a pillar, but I tried to release my right hand. Immediately, I slid to a corner of the deck and banged the shelf where we stored extra ropes. Then, I slid to another sharp corner. I used my left foot to absorb the shock and protect my right knee, and I wedged myself in, my legs trembling from the effort. My whole body ached—I felt like one big bruise.

"Lindsey, how long does it usually take you to fix baits for one line?"

"There are fifty baits for one line. It will take ten minutes. For four lines, I will need forty minutes."

"We can't afford to lose forty minutes."

"Agreed."

"Make it two rods. We don't have time for four. I understand I'm not allowed to touch the lines, so you have to do this all by yourself."

"I know."

"I was thinking of going to a spot about ten miles ahead of us, but I think we should give up on that and go toward the port. We can find a fishing spot on the way."

"Got it."

Grandpa steered toward Hime, and along the way, he looked around, trying to find the best fishing spot. He held the wheel and stuck his neck out of the window to see the sea. Heavy rain and wind kept attacking his face. His gray hair and face were all wet. His mustache dripped with water.

When I was done with the baits, I signaled Grandpa.

He decided the new targeted spot, and I threw two rods to the sea.

"Lindsey, I can slow down only so much. I can't stop the boat, otherwise I can't make it by 5:00 p.m. So don't let the line sink deep. Once the line hooks with the seabed, that's the end of the story. With this speed, the line will be easily cut even with the double rubber black line. Needless to say, I won't have time to reverse the boat before it happens.

"I have to make it sink deep, Grandpa. Golden eyes snappers only swim in the deep sea. And, when the upper sea is affected by the bad weather, they'll go even deeper."

"You are truly betting all your chips on this, aren't you?"

"I have to sink it deeper. We only have one shot, Grandpa."

"Okay. But I want you to remember, you are not controlling the sea. You are a part of the sea. You don't brag about how big the tuna you catch is. You just have gratitude to the sea for giving you fish to feed you and your family. That's what divides true professionals and amateurs. We are not gamers. We live here. We die here. Are you a fisherwoman, or you just Ichiro's assistant?"

I felt a oneness with the ocean. For the first time, I didn't feel like I was just Ichiro's assistant. I could do this on my own.

Grandpa turned back to me and said, "We are all gamblers. Only those who are connected with the ocean can see and smell things others don't. To be connected with the ocean you have to be connected to your true-self."

"If you're aligned with your true-self, you can see and smell the ocean. Is that it?"

"Good girl, Lindsey. That's all I can teach out of my seventy-plus years of professional fishery experience. Now, adjust your lines depending on the speed and the water depth."

The fish finder was still dark. I put two irons instead of one on the tips of the lines to keep the line from floating up if Grandpa went faster. At the same time, there was a higher chance of the two irons sticking in the seabed. This would cut the line easily, too. I used a special extra thin line, called a sacrifice line, to connect the irons with the tip of the regular line. If the irons got stuck, this thin line would be cut quickly, and it would save the regular line from being damaged.

I threw the two lines with fifty white cloths attached to each of them.

I was watching the sonar and read the depth carefully. Just like on land, there is no such thing as a completely flat seabed. There were steeps ups and downs that would act as obstacles. But golden eyes snappers lived in the deep ocean. If I stayed on the safer side all the time, I wouldn't catch them.

"How are you doing, Lindsey?"

"Grandpa, you found a great spot! The two rods are being pulled hard. I see that. The fish are biting!"

"You still don't know if it's a great spot or just a spot."

I nodded. I was starting to understand how to be one with the sea, the Zen-like state it required. I tried to use all five of my senses, along with a mysterious sixth sense, a sense that helped me understand what the sea was and how it worked. I felt wide awake, but also like I was in a daydream, diving into the wide sea below us, deeper and deeper where the golden eyes snappers were swimming. I felt gratitude that they gave their lives so we could keep our lives.

It was 4:10. There were fifty minutes left. On the monitor, I saw that the Doigaki was about to reach the port. A lot of Nanae fishermen greeted him. But he wasn't grinning like usual—he looked rather somber. He didn't allow himself to be treated as a hero or the savior for their community. I now realized that he had brought no one from Hakodate Marine, not even his secretary.

As a champion game fisherman, he was treating this duel as sacred. I truly saw that now.

I turned back to my own rods. They were being pulled, back and forth. There had be tons of golden eyes snappers, heavy ones, grabbing onto the bait deep in the sea.

I was careful as I dropped the line farther, going fast but being cautious. If even one of the fifty hooks got stuck, it would be the end.

I thought of Ichiro. I wondered if he was watching me at the hospital.

I felt him very close.

I was seeing him, touching him, hearing him, and smelling him.

We would become just like Hideki and Hana. A married fisherman and fisherwoman. We would fish together, while I continued to work at Bamboo Sushi.

I carefully pulled the line and dropped it back.

I thought about the days when all I thought about was returning to Boston. When all I cared about was building my career.

All of a sudden, the right rod sharply pulled back.

"Wait a minute! A hook got stuck!"

I immediately fed more line from the reel so that the line wouldn't get cut. But it was too late. I lifted the right rod. It felt so light.

It was like I was fishing air.

"What happened, Lindsey?" Grandpa said.

"The line got cut."

Grandpa didn't say anything. He just inhaled deeply.

"I'm cueing the line up now."

After only two minutes, the line reached the surface. I found the tip of the line miserably hanging in the air. The rest was cut. No fish.

Frustrated, I dropped the line onto the boat's deck. "There's nothing on the right rod. Do you think I should do it again?"

"No, Lindsey. It's 4:30. We really don't have time. The wind is getting harder, and the waves are becoming even higher. This is almost like a hurricane now. There's no way you can fix up another line before our time is up."

"Okay, Grandpa, keep sailing."

"Concentrate on the left one. This is your lifeline now."

Grandpa increased the speed so we wouldn't be late getting back to port, but the problem was at this speed, the time sensor that told me what the seabed looked like was useless. I just had to go by my gut feeling.

Grandpa closed his eyes. He didn't believe in any religion, but it still looked like he was praying now.

Ichiro, hang on with me.

I lowered the left rod's line even farther.

In my mind, I swam with Ichiro in the deep, wide, and warm sea.

I will be your proud wife.

Ichiro nodded with his beautiful smile, with his bright white teeth. Then, he eyed my rod.

Got it. I decided to pull the line in. Three, two, one, go!

I quickly reeled up the line and felt the weight of the fish resisting. There were probably about twenty to thirty on there. I probably needed more to be equal with Doigaki. I kept pulling.

The golden eyes snappers appeared on the surface, more and more coming at each second.

I counted them all.

There were forty-one golden eyes snappers. The best result that I could possibly expect.

◀ ▥▥▥▥ ◀

At 4:53, we finally got close to the port entrance. I was back in the captain seat and driving the boat since there were many regulations inside the port, and all the signs were written in Japanese. We got to the seawall, which stopped the waves from reaching the port. As soon as we passed, the water calmed. But then, I saw a number of boats in front of me, blocking the way into the port. I blew the horn.

Over the microphone, I heard the people from Hime and Nanae arguing because the people from Hime thought they were the Nanae fishery association's boats. But the Nanae fishermen denied the accusation, and said it was the gamers from Itokawa. I wasn't sure if they knew the rules to our competition, but we had just six minutes to park the boat. I blew the horn again, loud and long. I was sailing at the maximum speed allowed inside the port. I couldn't afford to slow down.

The gamers shouted at people on the shore, ignoring my horn. I started zigzagging instead of slowing down. I yelled at them to move.

"Lindsey, you should slow down. It's dangerous," Grandpa said.

"No, I don't have time, Grandpa."

They were coming at me and cutting me off. I didn't slow down. I almost crashed into one of them. I yelled at them. They yelled back.

Then, I looked over at the crowd by the port, and I saw a tall, muscular guy walk out, followed by three guys who looked like clones.

That was Godzilla, marching furiously toward the gamers.

Even though he had resigned from the fishery association of Nanae, he still retained his charismatic aura. His influence over the entire Itokawa tourism industry and politics was still unchallenged.

He grabbed the bullhorn and yelled at the gamers. He threatened to take away their business licenses or chambers of commerce memberships if they didn't move.

One of the gamers noticed Godzilla and motioned toward the others to pull back immediately. They quickly moved out to sea, and the path in front of me was clear.

I made it into the port. I had three minutes left. I couldn't park the boat that fast.

Grandpa tapped my shoulder and silently motioned for the wheel. I jumped toward the cooler boxes and prepared to unload them. Hideki and the others extended their arms. "Throw them down, Lindsey!" Hideki shouted.

"I can't!" I shouted back. "It's against the rules. I have to do it myself."

Grandpa parked the boat beautifully.

Ninety seconds left.

"Grandpa, I don't have time to tie the boat with rope."

"Can you jump off?" he said, eyeing my injured right knee.

I nodded, ignoring the twinge in my knee.

He switched the gear back and forth, wheeling right and left almost crazily.

I held one cooler box and jumped off the edge. When I landed, my right knee ached with pain, but I could endure it.

I had to do it eight times.

Sixty seconds.

"Use this forklift, Lindsey san!" Hideki shouted. The crowd parted, and I saw the forklift behind them, the engine already roaring. I put the cooler boxes on the shovel of the forklift. When all eight boxes were loaded, I hopped on the lift.

Thirty seconds left.

I stepped lightly on the gas pedal, but the forklift didn't move. I tried stepping down harder, and unbelievable pain from my right knee struck me. Grimacing, I twisted my waist and used my left leg to step on the gas pedal. It still didn't move.

I had never used a forklift before, but I thought it would be as simple as a golf cart. I moved the gear into 'Drive' and pressed the accelerator down fully.

It still didn't move.

"You have to release the hand brake!" Hideki yelled.

"Where is the freaking hand brake?" I muttered, glancing around wildly. I finally found it and pushed it down. The forklift moved.

Twenty seconds left.

I rushed to the fish scale. All I had to do was just physically put my body in the designated scale area.

I moved so fast inside the port. There were two intersections where I had to make turns. I barely touched the brakes both times, and the tires squealed.

I got close to the scale, but I knew if I took the time to stop the forklift, I wouldn't make it. Everyone was keeping their distance, and so I decided that I wouldn't stop the forklift—I would deliberately crash.

Five seconds left.

I aimed for a pile of Styrofoam boxes, a pile that was in the scale area. The forklift crashed into the pile, and I flew into the Styrofoam, the force making me lose my breath. I laid still for a second, heart racing, trying to catch my breath. I was in the designated scale area. I had made it.

I literally had one second to spare.

Once I stood up and showed everyone that I was okay, the judges began weighing my fish. I thought I had caught a little more than 500 pounds of golden eyes snappers in total. They had already weighed Doigaki's catch—in total, it was 531 pounds. I felt mine would be almost as heavy as his. I would win or lose by a margin of just a few pounds.

The market workers unloaded my fish onto the belt conveyor. They moved toward the newly equipped scale we had put in for ITQ. It started weighing my result. The number of the weight, accumulating, reaching 50 pounds, 100 pounds, 200 pounds . . .

Many Hime fishermen surrounded the machine.

. . . 300 pounds, 350 pounds . . .

The doyens were situated in the front of the crowd, right next to the number display.

. . . 400 pounds . . .

Hideki and Hana looked worried. The scale reached 450 pounds. Now, all the big fish were done. The smaller fish went onto the scale.

. . . 500 pounds . . .

I saw Nakata san, Mr. Principal, and Kong, Erica, Mrs. Bamboo, and the manager at Olive Bath House—everyone had different expressions. Confident or concerned. Optimistic or worried.

. . . 510 pounds. Just 21 more pounds needed.

Grandpa came up behind me. He placed his calloused hands on my shoulders.

. . . 520 pounds . . .

The scale at stopped 524 pounds. Nobody spoke. All the fish

had gone into the body of the machine, but there were still some fish inside the machine, waiting to be weighed. Slowly, the scale creeped up.

. . . 529 pounds . . .

People started clapping their hands rhythmically, just like Red Sox fans when our pitcher had gotten two outs in the ninth inning.

. . . 530 pounds . . .

More people clapped. When the scaler reached 531, everyone clapped louder, and then stopped.

Then, it seemed like the end of it.

We had a draw.

What would happen, if it was a draw?

The doyens stood up.

Were we done? We couldn't be done.

Wait a minute. I saw another number on the ITQ scaler, which said 306.

I asked Hana, standing next to me, what that meant.

"That's the number of fish you caught."

"Then, wait a minute!" I screamed.

"What is it, Lindsey?" one of the doyens said.

"I caught 307 golden eyes snappers. Not 306."

It must have sounded very odd to everyone. No fisherman counts the fish.

"Are you sure?" another doyen asked.

"I counted, and I remember them."

Just like that, many of the Hime fishermen's eyes lit up. They must have just remembered my memory skill.

The designated judge, the pro-tem president of Hime, and the new president of Nanae ordered the staff to turn off the power on the machine, and they went inside it.

Soon, our pro-tem shouted from inside of the huge machine, "There! One more fish!"

keita Nagano

Everyone moved closer to the scaler, trying to see the mysterious last fish. The three men walked out of the men, the pro-tem president holding a small fish by its tail.

"One fish was derailed," he said.

Our pro-tem put the fish back on the conveyor belt and turned on the power. The conveyor belt carried the one last fish to the scale.

The number indicator blinked.

Then, it showed 532 pounds.

Everyone cheered and applauded, the sound louder than the thunder outside.

We did it!

I won!

I hugged my grandpa. "I did it, Grandpa! I did it!"

"Lindsey, my granddaughter," he said, his eyes gleaming with pride. His mustache was still fully covered by ice.

Doigaki came up to me, a gentle smile on his face.

"Congratulations, Lindsey. You are excellent."

"Thank you, Doigaki san. This is my grandpa. He's the best fisherman in the best fishing port in America."

Doigaki and Grandpa shook hands. "Nice to meet you, sir."

"Terrific work, Mr. Doigaki. And thank you for being fair."

It was the first time I had ever heard Grandpa call someone "mister."

The Nanae fishermen came into our circle and congratulated me and Doigaki. The word 'no side' came to my mind.

Many fishermen came up to me and shook hands.

"Thank you, Lindsey san. You saved our port, our city. We will grow again," a young Hime fisherman said.

"Thank you for taking an outsider, a *gaijin*, into your community."

"We have never thought of you as an outsider. We know that your heart belongs to this town."

— 316 —

"Thank you."

I hugged the fishermen. Then, many fishermen started hugging me even though I smelled fishy. Some of them didn't even bother wiping off their tears. All fishermen in the world are emotional and sentimental deep in their hearts.

I looked for Grandpa again. He was sitting in the corner. Despite his energetic performance on the boat, he now looked as exhausted as an emergency room doctor who had not slept for seventy-two hours. I decided to thank Grandpa again and then fix him some winning sushi. Then, I would go see Ichiro in the hospital and bring him sushi too.

Right before I went over to Grandpa, a familiar voice stopped me. "Good job."

I turned around, "Mr. Bamboo!"

I hugged him.

"Mr. Bamboo, I did it!"

"You were fantastic, Lindsey," he said, but his eyes were filled with tears.

"I have never seen you crying, Mr. Bamboo. Thank you. You are truly my master. Thank you for making me your best Toyama Bay Sushi for dinner. Now, let me grab one of golden eyes snappers I caught and fix the winning sushi for you and Ichiro really quick."

"There's no time for that, Lindsey," he said, tears running down his cheeks.

My hands started shaking. "Mr. Bamboo. What's happening?"

"Lindsey—"

"Are you all right?"

"I just came back from the hospital."

"Is my husband all right?"

"Lindsey. Ichiro's condition worsened about twenty minutes ago. You need to come with me to the hospital now."

◄ ▯▮▯▮▯▮ ◄

During the ride to the hospital, I sat in a complete silence in the passenger seat of Mr. Bamboo's car. He held my hand and told me, "You are almost frozen." He turned the heater to the maximum level.

I was still wearing my wet Red Sox fishing gear and cap, powerless, exhausted. I closed my eyes and was surrounded by memories of the snow festival in Tokamachi. I was buried in a blizzard of snow.

Ichiro's hometown.

I was half-asleep and half-awake. I heard the strong air coming out of the vents, and I felt my cold muscles gradually warmed. But I was still in the snow country.

There was so much snow, more than I'd ever seen before. Houses were fully covered by snow, and the snow shoved off of the roofs created walls between the houses.

I imagined myself as the wife of a man from the snow country. I imagined visiting a house where a husband and wife in their late sixties were waiting for me.

"Lindsey san!"

The husband said in his loud joyous voice. The wife came out from the kitchen and gave me a hug. They were my in-laws. I unloaded my backpack and showed them fish I had caught that morning, ice keeping them fresh.

"Here you are."

"That's wonderful. Looks so fresh."

"Mother, can I start cooking?"

"Oh, you should rest first. I will fix a dark green tea for you."

I washed my hands thoroughly and began preparing my first sushi for my in-laws.

"Lindsey, we're here," Mr. Bamboo said gently.

the Sea of Japan

I opened my eyes, and we both got out of the car. We rushed into the hospital and to Ichiro's room. I had never imagined that Mr. Bamboo could run that fast.

In Ichiro's room, there were three or four doctors and nurses standing around Ichiro. One of the doctors looked down at him, frowning. A young nurse pushed her palms against Ichiro's chest.

In the corner, I saw Judy, pale as an old Chinese vase, arms clasped around herself. She looked at me as I walked in. I had never seen her eyes so sad, so full of grief.

I wanted to shout, *Stop, just wait a minute, guys! Tell me what's going on.* But when the doctor looked at me, I simply said, "Thank you, Doctor. I'm his wife."

He nodded, chin swaying, and the nurses cleared a path to his bed. The one young nurse kept trying to pump his heart.

I serenely sat at Ichiro's side. I slowly took off my cap and took his hand.

"Ichiro, can you hear me?" I squeezed his hand, wishing he would squeeze back. "I won, Ichiro. You know that, right? We won. You and I won. Operation Tripod will resume, Ichiro. All of us will go back to the sea tomorrow. The three organizations will cooperate, save the sea stock, nurture the ocean, and develop the new age of the fishery. Fishery tourism and the online auction will probably resume by next week."

No word. No reaction. The nurse was still pumping his heart, probably knowing this wouldn't save his life, but trying to delay his death for his wife.

"Ichiro. Ichiro—just open your eyes, will you? Just for a little bit. Just talk to me, Ichiro."

My voice was still firm. I didn't break down. I kept my promise not to cry in front of Ichiro anymore.

The doctor pulled a pen light from his pocket. The nurse stopped pounding. The electro cardiogram displayed a flat line. The nurse pounded a couple more times again. Then, the cardiogram fluctuated again. But when the nurse stopped pounding, it went back to the sad, cruel, helpless flat line. The doctor turned on his pen light and opened Ichiro's eyes. He moved the light in front of Ichiro's eyes once, twice, three times. Then, with a sigh, he turned off the light.

He checked his watch.

"I am very sorry for the loss of your husband. It's 6:19 p.m."

"No!" I screamed. "Don't go, Ichiro. Don't leave me alone."

I couldn't breathe, couldn't catch my breath, and everything went dim, the world going black around me. I felt like I was adrift from time, like I was here with Ichiro and still on the boat, like everything was happening at once. I blindly swung my arms and tried to reach for the pillar of our boat.

"Grandpa! Help!" I screamed as I fell to the floor.

Someone grabbed me, and I forced myself to focus, to come back to this moment. I looked up at the person holding me, and saw it was Mr. Bamboo. I looked around the room and saw Judy's pale face. She was shaking.

I stood up. Everyone was watching me. The doctors, nurses, Judy, Mr. Bamboo. Ichiro was the only one who didn't look at me, his face peaceful. Immovable. I ran to his side. I squeezed his cheeks, like I used to do right after we kissed. I was shaking. My hands were shaking terribly.

"Ichiro! I don't accept this. You can't die, alright?" I said, and some small part of me almost believed this would work. If I begged enough, he would come back to life.

By the age of thirty, I had witnessed so many deaths, too many deaths. I thought I had become used to it. I even thought I possessed the strength to easily accept a loved one's death. But I was screaming now. I just couldn't take it. This was all wrong. I wanted to resist. I wanted to scold whoever had control of Ichiro's life. Because the judgment was just wrong. Ichiro was my life.

I realized then why I had been imagining our life together as idyllic scenes in the snow: it was because of a stupid classic movie that my parents liked, *Love Story*. It ended at the snow-covered winter Harvard Campus after the protagonist's bride's death. As he stands in the snow, he says, "Love means never having to say I'm sorry."

Bullshit.

I was sorry for everything.

I was sorry for going out on the ocean today, for not saying yes to Ichiro earlier, for thinking that we had so many years together. I was full of regrets, full of hatred for myself.

I was so empty. I tried to remember some of the things he said to me. I tried to think about the phrases he loved and what he said when the ocean ran wild. But I couldn't remember it. I couldn't remember anything.

I heard Judy calling my name, and I realized she had been saying it for a while. I looked at her and saw concern etched into every line on her face.

"Judy, where is my grandpa? Oh my God, I am losing my memory power."

I felt it. I felt my memories with Ichiro fading away, everything good and bad. Judy gently wrapped me in a hug, squeezing my shoulders.

"Lindsey, I'm sorry."

"Judy, I can't remember how I met him at first. When was his first proposal to me? Why am I here in Japan?"

"Lindsey, stop. You know why you're here."

"I'm dying, Judy. That's why I'm losing my memory. I'm dying. Ichiro is me. He is my husband. I am going to disappear, too."

"Lindsey! Look at me! You're not dying. It's going to be hard, harder than anything you've done before, but you're going to keep on living."

Keita Nagano

I turned away from her. "Oh my god, I don't even remember the last words he said to me. I'm dying!"

Judy didn't say anything else. She just hugged me as I sobbed and sobbed for everything I had lost.

Epilogue

While Judy and I were sitting in the waiting room, hospital employees came in and cleaned Ichiro's body and moved him to the hospital morgue. As we sat there, I realized that I was still in my fisherman's gear. This was the longest day of my life.

Once everything was set up, they invited us to go and see him. The room had the capacity for ten bodies, but at this moment, Ichiro was the only one in the huge room. He was covered by a pure white silk cloth.

Judy and I didn't exchange any words. We just listened to the smooth sound of the air conditioner and the ticking of the clock on the wall.

The chief doctor, assistant doctors, and all the nurses who had taken care of Ichiro came into the room. They bowed to me and bowed to the body. Then, one by one, they stepped forward, put their palms together, and prayed. Then, they bowed again to me. I bowed back to them.

The doctor's assistant handed me a piece of paper. That was the death certificate that I would have to bring to City Hall. This was the official goodbye from Ichiro to the society he loved.

Everyone bowed to me one last time, and they exited the room.

Powerless, I simply handed the death certificate over to Judy.

Judy read it, and then whispered, "Would you like me to explain the situation to doctor and have them redo this certificate? This was written for you, as his wife."

"Why would they have to do that?"

"You can't give this to the city hall. You're not really his wife."

"Ichiro is my husband."

"I understand that you're married to him spiritually, Lindsey, but if you do this, they will figure out you weren't married legally. It's a crime."

I shook my head. I hadn't wanted to tell Judy just yet—I had wanted to keep the secret between just me and Ichiro for a little while longer. But now, it was time to let her know the truth. "Judy, you got it wrong. Ichiro is my husband. We actually submitted the real marriage registration."

"What? How?"

"I asked him. I wanted to be truly connected to him. The man who saved my life. The only man in this world who unconditionally loved me."

"When?"

"Yesterday."

"Oh, my—"

"Judy, he and I have always been on the spousal fishing boat. And we will be on it moving forward as well."

I took off my jacket, finally feeling warm. I realized I could have died today. But I never feared losing my life. Because I was with Ichiro, and I was on the sea, and the sea understood me.

"Lindsey—"

"I will inherit his boat. I will inherit his debt, too. I will continue fishing with him. I will master sushi making. I will become the ultimate sushi chef, as great as Mr. Bamboo."

"Are you saying you will stay in Hime?"

"This is my home, Judy. My husband will live here forever. I'll get a permit from the health district so I can cook on my boat, and I'll have Americans try my sushi. This is the best fish tank in the world. I will make every American who visits fans of Toyoma Bay, one by one."

◀ ▐▐▌▐▌▐▌▐ ◀

After the duel, everything went like it was supposed to.

Hakodate Marine and the Nanae association canceled their collaborating agreement. Then, the two entities and the Hime fishery association reentered the three-way alliance agreement. Hime and Nanae decided to merge within six months, instead of three years. They went to straight to the prefecture governments of both Itokawa and Toyama, and they decided to implement ITQ on the day of the merger. The central government's fishery agency accepted this, and they immediately lifted the new TAC on all Toyama Bay fish.

Over the next few days, everyone thanked me for saving Hime. Even a nurse who had helped Ichiro waved at me when she saw me on the bus. I talked to some of the fishermen at the port and learned that while there were currently only ninety-eight active fishermen, many of the former fishermen were planning on going back to work within the next month. Soon, there would be many more fishermen going out every day.

As planned, we had an Owara dance at my junior high's baseball field to celebrate the revival of Hime fishery. It was Ichiro's wish before he died, and he had done most of the planning for it, so I was asked to pick the date of it. I chose the day of Ichiro's funeral. We would have the dance in the morning and the funeral in the afternoon. The Toyama governor issued a special permit to let us have a funeral at sea.

I put Ichiro's picture, his blue gear, and his Royals baseball cap on a chair in the first row of the stadium.

Owara can be cheerful, but it can also be lamentable. The committee in charge of the dance only chose sad but beautiful songs for the commemoration of the end of our difficult journey. They were very attentive to my grief.

Before the dance began, I sat languidly in the stadium, trying to keep my eyes open. I hadn't slept since the duel. I hadn't eaten. But I decided to join the dance, because Owara was Ichiro's love. I wore Mrs. Bamboo's beautiful Owara kimono.

I put the straw hat on, making sure it covered my eyes. It was the perfect situation for me. I danced, hiding my sorrow and grief, which I didn't want to let others see. The dance was slow, serene, sorrowful. I paid attention to the tips of my fingers, my elbows, the degree I bent my knees. Focusing on the technical aspects helped me forget my grief for a few short moments.

Turn right.

Turn left.

As I was dancing Owara, I felt Ichiro dancing right behind me.

When Ichiro's coffin and I arrived at the fishery association's courtyard in the afternoon, the doyens gave me a small rose-red flag. This meant that my boat was owned and operated by a fisherwoman. It was a special way for the association to pay respect to fisherwomen.

Judy, Kong, Satoshi, Mr. Bamboo, Hideki, and Hana carried the coffin for me. I hugged Satoshi when I saw him and thanked him for bringing me and Ichiro together. Ichiro's parents were too old to go on my boat, and so they decided to see him off from the land. I apologized that we didn't have a wedding while he was alive, since the ceremony was a big deal in their hometown. They silently hugged me.

"Thank you, Mother. Father." It took all my bravery to call them that.

"Thank you, daughter," Ichiro's mother said, and my eyes filled with tears.

Grandpa was going to operate my boat. His last run. I had never seen him cry before, but he did now, and it made me tear up again.

The coffin was loaded onto my boat.

The rose-red flag was raised to the top of the flagpole. I made a short speech in front of the crowd.

"Thank you, everyone, for gathering. Ichiro is so loved by all of you, it makes me a little jealous."

There were small murmurs of laughter throughout the crowd.

"He was always obsessed with the firefly squid dive. Since he came to Toyama, he had been wanting to see the dive. He wasn't able to see it in his life, but he loved the story. The mother squid bores the babies and then ends her life, diving to the shore while she glows bright blue. Ichiro will now dive into the ocean because he thinks he has done everything he was supposed to do in his life. He died, but he left his beauty for the rest of us."

Many people started crying. I wanted to tell more stories, but everything was blurry, my memory still failing me. All those years, surrounded by all the uncomfortable, sad, and harsh memories, I had hated my memory power. But now I wanted the skill back so I could be with Ichiro forever.

I bowed deeply.

They bowed back.

It was a local tradition to give alcohol to all the fishermen to say goodbye. I chose Ichiro's favorites: Masuizumi sake and Miller Light. Everybody filled their glasses and raised them.

"To Ichiro."

They bowed a bit and drank silently.

Hideki, the other fishermen who were carrying the coffin, and the doyens went onto my boat, and Grandpa started sailing out. It was a completely calm ocean. I didn't even hear the sound of the ripples bouncing against the edge of the boat. Then, more than a hundred boats started following me. Today, the entire fish market was closed. All fishing boats were waving black mourning flags. My rose-red flag was now at half-mast.

When I reached our usual fishing point, I saw another hundred or so boats coming toward us. Those were the Nanae fishermen.

I didn't know that they were coming for my sea funeral.

When they got near us, they stopped the engines. All of them took off their caps and placed them on their chests. I saw Godzilla among them in all-black fisherman gear.

The doyens on my boat bowed to them. I did the same thing. They bowed back.

The Toyamans moved slowly to the east so that the Nanae boats could join us. Together, all the boats formed a complete circle. I was in the center of the circle.

One by one, ten previously chosen boats came up to my boat, and they each tossed me a fish they caught while they were sailing up here. When I had all ten fish, I put on my Bamboo Sushi chef coat. It was pure white and brand new, ordered for me by Mrs. Bamboo.

I fixed ten pieces of sushi for Ichiro. As I watched my hands moving, I felt like they were somebody else's hands. They were skilled and precise, so different from when I first started out.

Everyone was watching my hands. Many were using binoculars.

I opened the top of the wooden coffin. There, my Ichiro was still sleeping. He had a slight smile and the big dimple I loved on his right cheek. I couldn't stop myself from crying. My tears poured onto his lips, his eyelids.

the Sea of Japan

I placed the sushi into a bento box and put it by his side. I kissed his forehead firmly and then closed the coffin and read the engraving on top one last time: One world. One ocean. – Ichiro Yamada.

Then, three young fishermen drove wooden nails into the edges of the coffin with hammers.

All 200 boats blew their horns. I was crying hard in the midst of this enormous mourning sound.

I felt something wet and cold hit my cheeks, and I looked up and realized that snow was falling down. It was unusual weather for this time of year. It started falling heavily, as if the sky was trying to make both ends meet. It reminded me of my trip to Ichiro's hometown.

The ocean was very peaceful. There were still almost no waves.

The snow was getting heavier, and I was losing sight of the 200 boats.

The rose-red flag waved in the silent snow.

Then, just like that, my memories started coming back to me, the fog around them lifting. I remembered our first date, when we tried to see the firefly squid dive. It was a new moon night in June. We drank Masuizumi on the dark beach and listened to the calm ripples. That was the night I became a real Toyaman, even if I didn't realize it then.

I had my memory power back.

Ichiro would be with me all the time. He was ever present.

The young fishermen raised the coffin and slid it over the edge of the boat. Then, they released it into the ocean. It must have made a splash, but the snow absorbed the sound of it immediately. People sailed to the point where Ichiro's coffin sank and tossed white tulips.

Judy, who hadn't spoken that day, hugged me. We cried.

I thought of my parents, of their funeral, but also of all the moments before it, all of the memories we shared. For the first time, I had felt truly grateful to them.

The boats blew their horns again. Following my request, three doyens carried a pair of raised male and female Japanese red seabream in a bucket. We released them by the coffin area. For a few seconds, they swam through the hundreds of white tulips. Then, they sank deep.

Judy held me tightly. Very tightly.

"Sayonara, Ichiro," I whispered.

◀ ||||||||||▸ ◀

When everything was over, I went to the Olive Bath House and washed my hair and body. Then I took the night's last light rail train to Iwasehama.

I could feel Ichiro telling me that tonight was the night.

Nobody was there at the beach at 1:00 a.m. on a cold May night.

The snow had stopped falling a while ago, but the shore was still covered in white.

I put a rubber seat, the kind used on ballpark bleachers, down on the snow, and sat on it.

I waited for an hour. I sipped from a thermos full of warm Masuizumi sake. When I felt hungry, I opened a brown bag from Judy & Peter's Deli. There were wonderful latkes made with onion and garlic, Hungarian-style stuffed cabbage, and half of a pastrami sandwich.

An hour later, I saw blue lights coming down to the shore.

It had to be the firefly squids.

The blue lights lit up the ocean, getting closer and closer. It was the perfect conditions for them. New moon, windless night in late spring. I thought about when I danced Owara for Ichiro here. Just he and I.

the Sea of Japan

All the way out toward the horizon, as far as I could see, thousands of firefly squids were swimming, getting closer to the shore. Now, there were millions of blue lights.

The mother squids had done everything they were supposed to do in the ocean, and now, it was time for them to dive to the shore and die.

There was nobody around.

I sat on the beach and watched the squid dive. I was with Ichiro. Through me, he was seeing this phenomenon he had been waiting his whole life to see.

Hey, Lindsey.

Hey, Ichiro. Did you enjoy my sushi?

Fantastic. When was the first time you fixed your sushi for me? Remember?

I closed my eyes. All my memories were vividly coming back to me.

I said aloud, "It was a bright summer day, August 10th. You took me to the Toyama Black Ramen noodle shop and I became a big fan of it. You told me how much you liked my hairstyle, and I said I didn't do anything different than usual. You said it looked different, so I told you that you were weird. You told me that I held my ponytail higher than usual, and I doubted you. We pulled up photos we took together on your iPhone, and sure enough, I realized my ponytail was a little higher than usual. You laughed and you said I had to fix sushi for you since you won. So I made it that day on your boat.

"Ichiro. Ichiro? You're seeing this firefly squid dive, right? Ichiro? I miss how you used to compliment me. I didn't always believe you, but I always liked to hear them. Oh, yes, I do remember your first compliment. You said, 'I have never seen such beautiful cursive in my life.' That was funny. Later, you said, 'It is your life, Lindsey. I can't make you stay,' when you realized I was trying to leave Hime.

– 331 –

Oh, and your Tokyo street fight was awesome. You yelled at them, 'I refuse until you apologize to her.' Remember?

"You're not a talkative person, but you read people's minds well. When I was about to depart Japan because of my failure to negotiate with Paul, you read my intention. You said, 'You went to Tokamachi to see the snow country, that is evidence that you are nearing the end of your stay in Japan.' How did you know? You also yelled at me, 'Don't lie to me, Lindsey. I didn't waste my words, you shouldn't waste yours.' As a matter of fact, that day, you were very handsome. That doesn't mean you're not handsome on other days. But you know what I mean, right? It was the first time we held hands. 'Nothing wrong. I am human. I sometimes love people,' you said. Yes, I sometimes love people, too. And when I do that, I love deeply. Especially when I lose the guy I truly love. Ichiro, do you hear me? I love you, Ichiro. I love you."

The waves splashed onto shore, soaking my legs. I stood up and walked along the beach.

I found a round seashell and slowly picked it up. I wrapped it with both my hands. Then, I saw something bright white on the ocean, gradually coming closer to me. I illuminated it with my iPhone light. It was a white tulip. I reached for it and stared at the petals for a while.

And then, another wave crashed onto shore, soaking my whole body below my shoulders. I gripped the seashell and the tulip tightly, knowing I would never let them go. I would protect them.

The sky was still dark, no light in sight. But when the dawn came, I would go back to the port and sail out to fish.

I am Ichiro's wife.

I am an American fisherwoman.

—End—

Acknowledgments

I am deeply grateful to many individuals who helped me write this fisherwoman story.

Tom, Fran, Joyce, Tim, Sandy, Tracey, Mark, Merrill, and Char, who made me a big fan of the US and embraced me as part of their families even when all the English I could say was hello and goodbye in the '80s.

My mentors, Glen, John, and Brian, who graciously offered me an internship opportunity back in 1997. My pursuit of authentic American life started then.

Kent—who I admire as a true American culture guide—gave me detailed descriptions of every aspect of America and taught me the profoundness of English, movies, and baseball.

Mr. Frank Dulcich, who kindly showed me the American fishery distribution system. Mr. Kousuke Ogura, a great master of single pole snapper fishing, and Mr. Isao Ishi and his family, one of the best bottom trawling fishermen in Japan, both of whom generously accepted my request and had me on their boats on the rough ocean.

Mr. Masatsugu Mizuno, who let me look behind the curtain at one of the largest fishery market operations in the world. Mr. Hajime Oshima, who explained to me the differences between fisheries in the US and Japan.

Keita Nagano

And many active fishermen who answered my questions, in New Bedford, MA, Gloucester, MA, Long Beach, CA, Katsuura, Chiba-Japan, Hota, Chiba-Japan, Kouzushima, Tokyo, Himi, Toyama-Japan.

My sushi master, Mr. Takashi Asai, who taught me everything happening behind the sushi counter. Ms. Masako Taniai and Mr. Kouichi Ito, who arranged my deep interview with the largest fishery association in Japan and the active fisherwomen Ms. Tsuyako Ishii, Ms. Naomi Obata, and Ms. Tokuko Ito.

Sho-Chan explained the deep culture of Toyama, his hometown. Ms. Reiko Nakamura demystified the beautiful Kanazawa Geisha House lifestyle and the profound Ishikawa prefecture culture. Awesome author photo, which is more than I deserve, was taken by Janae Ball.

Marika Flatt, Brittany Graham, and Tatum Sapinoro, superb publicists, who kindly believed in long-term impact of this publication that goes beyond the book.

Rachel Shapiro, as a mightily talented freelance editor who happens to love Japan, helped me to make my original manuscript presentable to the publishing industry.

Brooke Warner and Samantha Strom have graciously taken this never-heard-of-author in America, decided to believe in my story, and polished it further. Having published more than twenty books, I have never come across a publisher like Brooke who pours such life-size passion into her books.

Last but not least, my parents, wife, my daughter, and friends who always support me. I dearly love them.

This is a novel. Any errors of fact, geography or fishery methods, procedure, and distribution are purely the fault of mine.

Many Rivers, One Ocean,
Keita Nagano

About the Author

Keita Nagano is an award-winning Japanese author who has lived almost equally in Nevada and Tokyo—more than twenty years in each place—and reflects the difference of the two cultures in his novels. He has a bachelor's degree in economics from Keio University in Japan, as well as an MBA in global business and PhD in management from Walden University in Minnesota. The pursuit of the authentic American experience is his hobby: he has been to all fifty states, all thirty major league ballparks, and the top sixty big cities in America. He has published seventeen business nonfiction and eight fiction books in Japan. In 2013, he received a Nikkei (Japanese *Wall Street Journal*) Award for Contemporary Novel for his missing-child thriller, *Kamikakushi*. He is also an official weekly columnist for *Forbes Japan*. Nagano lives in Henderson, Nevada, with his wife and Welsh corgi. Their teenage daughter is currently studying in Tennessee.

SELECTED TITLES FROM SPARKPRESS

SparkPress is an independent boutique publisher
delivering high-quality, entertaining, and engaging content
that enhances readers' lives, with a special focus on
female-driven work. www.gosparkpress.com

And Now There's You: A Novel, Susan S. Etkin. $16.95, 978-1-68463-000-4.
Though five years have passed since beautiful design consultant Leila
Brandt's husband passed away, she's still grieving his loss. When she
meets a terribly sexy and talented—if arrogant—architect, however, sparks
fly, and neither of them can deny the chemistry between them.

Sarah's War, Eugenia Lovett West. $16.95, 978-1-943006-92-2. Sarah, a
parson's young daughter and dedicated patriot, is sent to live with a
rich Loyalist aunt in Philadelphia, where she is plunged into a world
of intrigue and spies, her beauty attracts men, and she learns that love
comes in many shapes and sizes.

The Cast: A Novel, Amy Blumenfeld. $16.95, 978-1-943006-72-4. Twen-
ty-five years after a group of ninth graders produces a *Saturday Night
Live*-style videotape to cheer up their cancer-stricken friend, they
reunite to celebrate her good health—but the happy holiday card
facades quickly crumble and give way to an unforgettable three days
filled with moral dilemmas and life-altering choices.

Bedside Manners: A Novel, Heather Frimmer. $16.95, 978-1-943006-68-7.
When Joyce Novak is diagnosed with breast cancer, she and her daughter, Marnie—a medical student who is on the cusp of both beginning
a surgical internship and getting married—are forced to face Joyce's
mortality together, a journey that changes both their lives in surprising
and profound ways.

The Opposite of Never: A Novel, Kathy Mehuron. $16.95, 978-1-943006-
50-2. Devastated by the loss of their spouses, Georgia and Kenny think
that the best times of their lives are long over until they find each
other; meanwhile Kenny's teenage stepdaughter, Zelda, and Georgia's
friend's son, Spencer, fall in love at first sight—only to fall prey to and
suffer opiate addiction together.